HER IRISH TREASURES

JOELY SUE BURKHART

Shamrocked, Leprechauned, Evil Eyed

Her Irish Treasures

PUBLISHED BY:
Joely Sue Burkhart

❀ Created with Vellum

SHAMROCKED

HER IRISH TREASURES

SHAMROCKED

HER IRISH TREASURES

A gargoyle, a leprechaun, and a motorcycle gang walk into a bar...

Scratch that. A human woman (me) accidentally walks into a Faerie bar run by a leprechaun who keeps a cursed gargoyle on a shelf. Somehow, that gargoyle goes home with me, and I start dreaming of a man.

Doran. He's trapped in stone and darkness, and only I can free him.

He says I'm the treasurekeeper, and I need to find his friends, the other treasures, so we can break his curse. He haunts me night and day, driving me to hurry. I can't sleep. I can't think. I have to find them. I have to free him.

Turns out his friends aren't that hard to find, because they're drawn to me, too. But these whiskey-drinking, tattoo-loving, motorcycle-riding badasses are resigned to their fate. Over the centuries, they've lost too many treasurekeepers to risk their hearts and souls again.

I have to find a way to convince them to join me. Before it's too late.

For my Beloved Sis.

Thank you to my beta readers, Sherri Meyer, Laura Walker, Melissa Joy Vailes, Mads Scofield, Shelbi Gehring, Alyssa Muller, Meagan Cannon West, Courtney Brown, Shannon Morgan, Kirsty Bladen, Sheryl Frid, Ivory Streeter, Lydia Simone, Courtney Baxter, Nethsy Anderson

1

In hindsight, partying my way through a string of bars to celebrate my divorce was probably not my smartest decision. In fact, it ranked up there with marrying the asshole in the first place.

Bleary eyed, I rolled over in bed and cracked my head on something. Fuck. My head already pounded. Rubbing the bump, I blinked furiously, trying to make my eyes focus long enough to figure out what, exactly, was lying on the pillow next to me. Sadly, it wasn't the bartender who'd been flirting with me last night. Somehow, I'd ended up in bed with a statue. A very ugly statue.

A two-foot tall gargoyle leered up at me.

He had a huge, crooked nose, elongated arms, and massive hulking shoulders. His features were harsh and mean. Everything was too pronounced and overdrawn, from a heavy brow down to large clawed feet.

I picked him up, wincing at how heavy he was, and set the statue on the nightstand. "Where the fuck did you come from?"

I vaguely remembered seeing the statue behind one of the bars last night. Did I steal the fucking thing? I couldn't even remember the name of the bar to take it back. Something Irish, I thought. *Lucky's.* No, but it did have something to do with a clover.

Shamrocked. Yeah, that was it.

I slid out of bed and made my way to the bathroom, concentrating so I didn't stagger. My back itched as I walked across the floor, imagining the gargoyle's stare. I wasn't naked, but I still think he enjoyed the view of me in my tank-top and undies.

Stop it. I told myself with a firm glare in the mirror. *It's just a statue.*

But I still dressed in the bathroom, dragging on a pair of sweats and a T-shirt out of the dirty clothes hamper.

Without sparing a second glance at the gargoyle, even though that meant not grabbing my glasses on the nightstand, I headed down the hallway to the kitchen. My best friend, Viviana, stood at the coffee pot, immaculate in an expensive berry-colored pencil skirt and knee-high leather boots. I couldn't pull boots off like that. Not with my thick calves. But she was practically a giant at six feet tall and model thin, so she looked drop-dead gorgeous in everything. Her flaming red hair and perfect complexion only added to her appeal.

"Oh, honey." She laughed softly as she handed me a cup of coffee. "You're looking worse for wear today."

I grunted beneath my breath and took a long drink, even though it was scalding hot. "I should have left when you did. Then maybe I wouldn't feel like death warmed over."

"Are you doing okay? With everything?"

Everything—which described what my ex-husband had taken. Without her, I wouldn't have a roof over my head. Hell, who was I kidding? If she hadn't let me move in with her almost a year ago, I'd be dead. I wouldn't have been able to survive another month in that toxic environment. "I might be penniless, but I'm free. As long as you don't mind a moocher for a few more months until I get a nest egg built up, or I sell a nice commission or two."

"You're welcome indefinitely. I love having you here and I hate living alone." Headed toward the door, she paused to give me a quick hug. "I mean it, Riann. Stay as long as you want. You're the sister I never had and I've got plenty of room. I love seeing you stretch your wings, so thank you for letting me watch your art grow and expand with new adventures."

My eyes burned, my throat constricted, and all I could do was bob my head and lean against her. But after nearly twenty years of friendship, she knew exactly how moved I was, even if I couldn't say it. She kissed the top of my head and grabbed a leather portfolio on the counter. "Boss man will be in court all this week on a big trial, so don't wait up for me."

"I'll sneak in a few hours at the diner this evening, but I'll try to have something for dinner around nine or so. Does that work for you?"

"You don't have to cook or clean or do anything." She gave me a firm glare. "You're my guest. I'll eat at work so don't worry about me, and don't work crappy hours at the diner when you could be here, creating something beautiful." Her phone dinged and she sighed. "That's the car. I really need to go."

"Have a great day, and don't let boss man run you around too much."

Shrugging on a long wool coat, she laughed. "Oh, don't worry about me. I've got his balls in a vise and he knows it. He couldn't manage to take a shit without me, let alone get to trial on time."

She breezed outside and I watched from the window as the driver got out of the sleek silver sedan that screamed money, and lots of it, to open her door. She waved, slid inside, and in moments, she was gone. I turned around, propped my butt against the counter, and took a long sip of my coffee. With each swallow, I felt a little more human. In fact, the familiar itch started in the back of my brain that warned a new idea was coming in hard and fast. My favorite kind of inspiration.

If I'd still been married, I would have squashed that feeling and tried to smother it. I didn't have time to indulge in a *hobby*, as my ex called it. I had to work and keep the house in shape and get his dinner on the table by six o'clock. Just remembering pissed me off, and I wasn't mad at him.

I was mad at myself for putting up with that bullshit for so long.

I'd allowed him to clip my wings and slip blinders on so all I saw was the safe little house, the boring corporate job, and the debits and credits on our balance sheet. None of which I cared about in the slightest. I didn't care if we had a nest egg that would let us retire when we were forty. I'd hated my cubicle and the neat green patches of yard framed by invisible picket fences. I'd hated watching my imagination wither and die. I'd always loved painting, and while he'd never explicitly tried to forbid me from indulging in my art, he would make passive-aggressive comments that made me feel guilty.

Yeah, I was obsessive. I got lost in my art sometimes. Hours might pass before I came up for air.

No, I wasn't a *professional* artist, but only because I didn't have the time to work. When I started a new painting, I wanted to finish it. I might work hours and hours on it. I might stay up all night, or burn dinner, or, God forbid, not even start dinner.

Evidently his arms were broken and he couldn't manage to help with dinner even one lousy night.

I slammed the cup down too hard on the counter and stomped back toward the room Viviana had given me. If I wanted to paint all day and all night, then that was exactly what I was going to do.

2

"Riann? Riann!"

I blinked, finally hearing her calling my name. "Hey, you. I thought you were going to work late."

"Um, I did." Viviana came closer. "Have you been painting all day?"

I looked at my phone, shocked to see that it was nearly ten o'clock in the evening. I'd started painting right after she'd left for work, so that must have been seven-thirty or eight this morning. I tried to remember what I'd done all day, but I'd come back into my room, thrown open the curtains, and dragged out my easel. I didn't remember much after that, other than occasionally hurrying to the bathroom, or pouring cold coffee and heating it up in the microwave, drumming my nails impatiently on the counter.

"Did you eat anything?"

My stomach chose that moment to growl like a Tyrannosaurus Rex. "I was too busy to eat. What do you think?"

We both stepped back and looked at the canvas I'd worked on all day. I'd always been drawn to Gothic-style landscapes or fairy-tale settings with an edge. Like I'd paint a quaint cottage in the woods, but the trees themselves would have mouths and hands, or something whacked out like that. This time, my muse had come up with another dark forest with tall, huge trees that looked like they were trying to devour a crumbling ruin and wipe it from memory.

A large, ugly gargoyle was prominently centered on the canvas. The very same gargoyle I'd brought home from that bar, although in the painting he would have been at least seven or eight feet tall, not the miniature statue I'd woken up with this morning.

"Wow. Is that an old church?"

I leaned closer to the ruins, studying them like I'd never seen them before. In a way, I hadn't. I hadn't thought about what I was doing—it just happened. Sometimes it was like dreaming, only with a paint-brush in my hand. "Yeah, I think so. There's a hint of a window here that looks like old, broken stained glass." In the tall weeds, there were more stones. Some broken off from the church, but others looked more like headstones and there was a heavy Celtic cross nearly buried by debris. "I think this might be a graveyard."

She knew my process well enough not to ask how I couldn't know what I'd just painted. "He has a way of sucking you in. It's really creepy. In a good way."

The gargoyle definitely stared back at me with a strange compelling intensity in his stone eyes. At least he wasn't leering in the painting like a lecherous old man. "I guess my muse was really inspired by the statue I brought home last night."

"What statue?"

Without looking away from my painting, I pointed over at the nightstand. "That gargoyle. I remember seeing him at the bar last night. I guess the bartender gave him to me."

"Um. Ri. You mean this one?" Her voice came from the other side of the room near the window.

I dragged my gaze away to find her reaching down to pick up the gargoyle off the floor. "That's weird. I must have grabbed him for reference."

"Well, it's certainly the same ugly fellow." She laughed and set him on the window sill. "Let's go get a bite to eat. I'm starving, so I can imagine how hungry you must be."

I didn't want to stop. The back of my mind still itched and burned.

Inspiration hovered inside me, a hungry beast that had been denied too long.

But it could wait. At least long enough for me to eat.

MY EYES HURT SO BAD, TENDER AND ALMOST SWOLLEN, BURNING WITH exhaustion. I closed my eyes to get some relief for even a moment, but my hand continued to move over the canvas.

I couldn't stop.

A sob broke out of my throat and I dropped the paintbrush. Sinking down to the floor, I braced my head on my knees and cried. At least the tears soothed my aching eyes a little.

"Oh, honey." Viviana sank down beside me and dropped her arm around my shoulders. I hadn't heard the car drop her off, but I was so glad she was home. Though I had no idea what day it was. "Is it all catching up with you?"

"No. It's not the divorce. I'm glad about that."

"Then what's wrong?"

"Look around. What do you see?"

Her arm tightened around me and her voice sharpened. "You've done all of these? This week?"

I nodded and another sob cracked through my throat. "I can't stop. It's his fault."

"Whose?"

"That fucking gargoyle. He won't let me sleep."

"Riann, honey, you're scaring me. You know that gargoyle isn't real. Right?"

I lifted my head and shoved my too-long bangs out of my eyes. "He moves by himself. I think he's haunted or something. When I try to sleep, I have horrible dreams about him and some of his friends."

"I don't believe in ghosts," she said firmly. "Let alone haunted gargoyles."

"I'm telling you, there's something weird about him. It's not my imagination. I mean, look at some of these paintings. It's all things he's making me paint. I can't stop."

She took my hand and helped me up to my feet. I looked at the canvas I'd been working on and flinched. I'd dragged a thick, red brush stroke down the middle of the man's forehead like a barbaric war stripe. Even though the stroke ended abruptly, it looked perfect on him. Like it was meant to be.

"That's Keane."

Viviana gave me her trademarked side-eye. "How do you know?"

"Doran, the gargoyle, told me. He said if I could find Keane, I'd never walk away unsatisfied."

She laughed sheepishly, staring at the man's lush mouth and the sultry heat in his eyes. "Yeah, I can kind of see that, I guess. He's gorgeous in a rough, sexy kind of way."

Propped against the wall were the other canvases I'd blown through like a crazy woman. At one point, I'd had to run to the art store and buy more supplies. On Vivi's credit card, of course, because I didn't have two pennies to rub together until I got paid from the diner. Which, of course, had probably fired me, because I couldn't remember what day it was or when I'd been scheduled to work. Lou didn't have much patience with waitresses who didn't bother to show up or call.

"Who's this?" She'd moved down to the next canvas. This one was mostly a man's back, but he peeked over his shoulder with a mean furrow between his eyes like he was pissed and headed off to kick some serious ass. He wore a black leather jacket with a pirate skull—though the crossbones were replaced with swords—a Celtic cross, and roses painted on his back.

"Aidan. Once he's revealed, there's no escape."

In each hand, he held long, thin, wickedly curved blades.

The next painting was super dark. Thick shadows hung around the man in the center, and the dark color of his skin made him hard to see. But the center of his chest glowed, illuminating a blood-stained white tank top, the hard, broad slope of his shoulders, and the chiseled planes of his face. "Ivarr. No one can stand against his light."

The last man stared out of the canvas with a mean, formidable glare. "Let me guess, that's the man hidden in the gargoyle."

I nodded. He still looked like the statue, down to a rough, bumpy nose that had been broken in one too-many bar fights. He glared out of the canvas, his shoulders and neck corded with strain, his hands fisted at his sides. In the same red paint, I'd written *free me* in thick block letters across the top of the canvas.

When I looked at him, I heard his voice in my head. *"Find me. Find them. Before it's too late."*

The words he repeated in my head whenever I tried to close my eyes.

"These are all fantastic," Viviana whispered softly. "Some of your finest work."

"Yeah, I know. But it's fucking driving me crazy. I can barely sleep."

She took my aching hand, my fingers coated in splatters of paint, and dragged me down the hallway to a barstool at the granite-topped island. "Sit. I'm going to make us some chamomile tea, and we'll decide what to do next. Okay?"

Numbly, I nodded and mustered enough strength to climb up into the high stool. My thighs already ached because the chair was too fucking tall for me, and I couldn't touch my feet on the support bar. It sucked being so short.

"What day is it?" I asked her as she filled a kettle with water and readied our mugs.

She gave me another careful, slow look. "Friday."

Fuck. I'd lost the entire week. "I remember you leaving for work in that raspberry suit that looks so good on you. We grabbed a bite of dinner that night. Then nothing but painting and painting and painting."

Grimly, she shook her head. "That's not good, honey."

"I know."

"So what can I do to help you break out of this obsession? Was it triggered by the divorce?"

"No. Not at all. I haven't spared a single thought on that dickhead.

It's the gargoyle, I'm telling you. I felt the inspiration burning that first day, and it only got worse each day."

"Where did you get him again?"

"An Irish pub called *Shamrocked*."

She pulled out her phone and typed a few seconds. Shaking her head, she met my gaze. "There's no bar in the entire metro area called that."

I frowned, my stomach turning cold and queasy. "I'm sure that was the name of it."

She came over and leaned down across from me, propping her elbows on the table.

I couldn't bear the concern in her eyes. My eyes filled with tears and I swallowed hard. "I'm not crazy. I swear. It was *Shamrocked*, with a four-leaf clover in neon lights outside."

"I know you're not crazy," she scoffed, but the lines still creased her forehead. "What happened after I left? Let's retrace your steps."

"Okay." I sniffed. "Yeah."

"So we were at the *Crown* until about eleven o'clock. I left because I had to work. You were hanging out with Morgan and Tammy, right?"

"Yeah." They were our friends from B.M. Before Marriage. Girl-friends I'd lost track of after college. "We had another round, and then closer to midnight, we decided to go to a new club. Tammy said she'd heard great things about it."

"Do you remember its name?"

I scrunched my eyes, trying to remember. "Not exactly, but it was only a few blocks away from the *Crown*. So we decided to walk."

Viviana frowned sternly. She hated it when I walked around the city streets at night without protection.

"We were laughing, having a grand time. The streets were well-lit and cars were still buzzing up and down the road. It wasn't too cold that night, either. Chilly, but not drag a scarf up around your face cold. We were there in like ten minutes."

"Ten minutes from the *Crown*," she mused. "Do you remember the street?"

"Perez Parkway. We came to the big intersection with... uh...

What's that street?" I knew exactly where I was—but I usually had no idea what the actual road names or numbers were after a few turns.

"Eighty-Eighth."

"Yeah. The crosswalk light was flashing, so Tammy and Morgan hurried across. I was a bit behind, and by the time I got to the intersection, the crosswalk turned red. I didn't think I could make it." Damn my short legs. "I waved them on."

Viviana's eyes narrowed and she started to straighten, pulling up her phone like she'd call them right then and there to give them a piece of her mind. "They left you?"

"The bar was right there, and there was a line. I figured I'd catch up pretty quick."

"But you didn't," she said softly. "Did you?"

"I..." I sighed and shook my head.

"How drunk were you at that point?"

I shrugged. "I could walk and talk fine, but I was buzzed. We were mostly loud and crazy, laughing a lot, you know? But I wasn't staggering, falling-down drunk. I watched the cars a minute, and I needed to pee. Bad. Standing there in the cold didn't help. I started looking around on my side of the intersection, and I saw the neon four-leaf clover just a ways down the street."

Pulling up the map of the city on her phone again, she frowned. "Left or right as you were looking at the intersection?"

"Left."

"You're sure?"

I nodded. "Yeah. I started jogging a little, desperate for the bathroom. The street was darker, but it wasn't far. I mean, I was able to jog there without dying."

"A feat." She chuckled, knowing my hatred of any kind of exercise. Which was why I had thick calves and couldn't wear her killer knee-high boots, not to mention the rest of my generous curves, but oh well. Her laughter died and she met my gaze, her brow furrowed again. "There's no bar showing up on the map."

"Maybe it's new? Though the building was really old. Nice, but old. Dark, rich wood, and it had a gigantic fireplace alongside the wall. It was so cozy and warm, and the ladies' bathroom was clean and pretty. They even had a silver tray of lotions and fancy soaps."

Some of her frown lessened. We always judged an establishment by how nicely they treated their female customers in the bathroom.

"Were there other customers inside?"

I tried to remember. "Maybe a couple? I don't really remember. It wasn't loud like the *Crown*, thankfully, but there was some kind of Irish tune playing in the background. The bar ran along the length of the back wall, a real old-world polished look. I wasn't going to get a drink, but the bartender winked at me, and he was so cute. I couldn't help myself."

"Yeah? What'd he look like?"

"Shoulder-length black hair, adorable dimples in his cheeks and the greenest eyes." I sighed. "I thought, what the heck, one drink won't hurt, right?"

"What'd you order?"

"I asked what he recommended, and he told me it was a rule. The first drink you ordered in an Irish pub had to be Guinness."

She grimaced. "Ugh. I hate beer."

"I do too, normally, but I swear, that was the best beer I've ever had in my life."

She narrowed her eyes. "Maybe he roofied you."

"No, I don't think so. I mean, I felt fine. The mug was frosty cold and the beer went down really good. I even drank the last few swallows at the bottom." Usually, beer warmed too much for me to drink the whole thing. "Anyway, he wandered off to help someone else. There was a guy hunched in the corner closest to the fireplace. I didn't get a good look at him, but he seemed pretty grumpy. Even growled a curse at the bartender once, but he laughed and slapped down another drink for him. I was looking around, taking it all in. There were shelves behind the bar with all kinds of whiskey and bottles, with mirrors and lights to showcase the alcohol. But then I noticed him. The gargoyle."

I got goosebumps remembering. "My eyes ran over him and jerked back. It was like he was staring at me, silently willing me to see him. It was so weird. The bartender came back and saw me looking at it, and his eyebrows arched up. He got pretty solemn at that point. He'd been lightly flirting up until then, but after he saw me looking at the statue, he changed."

"Like worried, scared, mad, what?"

"I don't know. Like... solemn. He quit smiling but he wasn't rude. I asked him for another drink, but something different, and he jerked his head up at the statue and said 'I'll give you a shot of his favorite.'"

"What was that?"

I snorted. "It wasn't even alcohol. It was a shot of espresso in a little cup. He brought it from the back."

"Espresso. At... what time was it? Midnight?"

I huffed out a laugh. "Yeah, probably. But man, it was so good. Thick and syrupy almost, but not sweet. Just straight, heavenly coffee. I saluted the statue and kind of laughed, and drank the whole thing. But the gargoyle kept staring at me, and it was weirding me out. I asked the bartender to cover it up, and he tossed a cloth napkin over its head. That was a little better, but I swear, I could still feel it staring at me."

I shuddered a little and sipped my tea. I really didn't care for herbals at all. What was the point if there wasn't caffeine in it? But the warmth did soothe away some of my inner turmoil.

"What happened after that?"

I set the cup down and shrugged. "I don't know. It's all kind of foggy."

"So he did roofie you!" She surged up and started to dial 911 on her phone. I grabbed her wrist.

"No, I don't think so. Honestly. I never got a bad vibe from him at all. Just that creepy gargoyle. I didn't have anything else to drink there." I didn't want to think the cute bartender could have hurt me. I tried to remember that morning I'd woken up here. I hadn't been completely naked. I wasn't sore. Surely if I'd had sex, even drunken sex, after so long, I would have felt a little tenderness? But I'd felt fine and there wasn't any evidence that I'd been hurt or assaulted in anyway.

I just couldn't remember.

"But you don't remember what happened after that? How did you get home? Did he call you a car?"

I closed my eyes, fighting down my panic. "I don't know. I can't remember walking into your house that night. I don't remember going to bed. I don't remember feeling sick or scared or bad. Just that fucking gargoyle staring at me, and then I woke up the next day and it was beside me."

"In bed?"

"Yeah." I cringed. "I don't remember bringing it home, but then I don't remember coming home at all. Maybe I stole it."

She set her cup down and marched toward my room. By the time I managed to hop down off the too-tall bar stool, she strode back with the gargoyle in her hands. She threw open the front door, set him outside, and then slammed the front door shut and locked it. "There. Now we're going to get some sleep, and first thing tomorrow, we're going to go find this bar and return him."

She came back to me and cupped my face in her hands, searching my eyes. "Are you sure you weren't assaulted that night? Maybe I should take you to the hospital and get you examined."

"I'm fine. I didn't hurt the next morning. I was a little hungover, but I'd had quite a lot to drink. I didn't feel any worse than I expected to feel."

"Humph." She wrapped her arm around me and we walked down the hall. I hesitated outside my room, staring at the canvases propped up all around the room. While the gargoyle wasn't here to torment me any longer, all the paintings he'd inspired were. The three other men. The image of the church ruin and the statue. For the first time in my life, I regretted my skill. Because staring at that huge gargoyle glaring back at me, demanding his freedom, was too fucking real. He scared the crap out of me.

"Come on." She tugged me to her door. "You're sleeping with me tonight."

"Are you sure?"

"It'll be like the good old days when we used to sleep over at each other's houses."

Her bed was cushy soft with dreamy pillows and silky sheets topped with a fluffy down comforter. Yet I couldn't close my eyes. I was afraid he was there, waiting for me. The gargoyle. Doran. The man with the broken nose, standing in a lost, forgotten church graveyard.

I shivered and Viviana tucked the comforter around me and snuggled close with a giggle. "See? Just like old times."

I laughed, trying to relax a little. "You used to tell me about all your conquests, even back then. So who's after the gorgeous Vivi now?"

"A guy at work. His name's Michael."

"Not boss man?"

"Oh no. Boss man likes me too much as his assistant to risk boning me and messing up our relationship entirely. Michael's a hotshot fresh out of law school."

I gave her a fake gasp. "A younger man? You cradle robber."

"You didn't ask who *I* was after. You asked who was after *me*."

She kept talking about how the new guy was trying to get her attention, and I drifted off to blissful sleep.

3

"Riann."

The low, growly voice was insistent, stabbing the back of my mind like a hot poker. I recognized it. The same jerk had been yakking in my head ever since I brought that fucking gargoyle home. "Give it a rest, you hulking block of stone. My fingers are cramping, my eyes are burning, and my head is pounding like a jackhammer took up residence behind my eyeballs. I can't paint anymore."

Doran cupped my cheek in his huge palm, rough with callouses but incredibly tender. "It's not safe. You've been marked by Faerie. You've got to find us, love. Now."

I yawned and nestled my face deeper into his caress. I loved his rough brogue, even when he pissed me off. "Why? Why is it suddenly so important that I find four guys I've never met in real life?"

"You won't believe me."

I forced my eyes open and rolled over enough to look up into his face. He squatted down beside the bed, but his size was still intimidating. His shoulders blocked out the moonlight from the window. I knew his face, now, after so many dreams. It wasn't a face that would stop traffic because of his beauty. Far from it. But there was a certain majesty in the heavy brow and jagged nose. The kind of majesty a scarred lion king wore as he glared at the latest batch of young challengers, running away with their tails tucked between their legs, without ever unsheathing his claws.

"I don't believe in ghosts. Let alone fairies."

"Oh, but you will, love. Mark my words. You will."

"How did they mark me?"

"You walked into Warwick's pub. No ordinary mortal should be able to cross that threshold unless you have dealings with Faerie."

"Who's Warwick?"

"The asshole who flirted with you in front of me."

"The cute bartender?"

"Bollocks." He glowered at me. "He's not *cute*. He's a fucking leprechaun."

I laughed. I couldn't help it. "Leprechaun? Like pot of gold guy?"

"The only pot of gold that bastard has is the fool's gold he keeps in his pants. Which is where he'd better keep it, while he stays out of yours."

I knew this was a dream, but that pissed me the hell off. I sat up and jabbed a finger into his chest hard enough he grunted. "You don't get to tell me whose pants I can and can't get into. No one does." That was only one of the many reasons I'd divorced my husband. I wasn't going to have a man order me about. Ever again.

"You want to fuck Warwick?" Despite our argument, his brogue was lyrical, his voice almost sing-song, roughened only by his deep bass. "Fine, have the bastard. But I'll fucking kill him, so I will."

"Why? For fucking me? You have no right."

He leaned closer, his eyes flashing like dark blades. "I'll kill the bastard because he'll hurt you. He's a fuck 'em and leave 'em kind of guy."

"Sometimes that's exactly what a woman wants."

I tried to say it lightly, but his eyes narrowed. "Somebody already hurt you. Who? Tell me, so I can kill the motherfucker."

"It's over and done with." I sighed, staring at the necklace around his throat. A thick silver chain held what looked like a pebble, with a hole bored through the center so the chain could slide through. The whole necklace looked incredibly heavy. "Besides, I wouldn't want you to kill anyone just because they hurt my feelings."

"I'll kill anybody who looks at you sideways."

Taken aback, I looked into his eyes, seeking the truth, and yeah, a murderous glare darkened his eyes. I had no doubts whatsoever that he'd kill someone as easily as taking out the trash.

"Right, that's the perfect metaphor." Relaxing his intensity, he dropped his gaze to my lips. "I'll take out the trash for you. Anytime, day or night. I'm your guy."

"Why?" I reached out and touched the harsh planes of his face. His jaw was rock hard and grim, but his lips were soft as I ran my thumb over his mouth. "Why me? How did I get into this?"

"I saw you, and I knew you were the one who could free me and bring us all together."

I rubbed my eyes, so weary and foggy. "Bring who together? Free you? None of this makes sense."

He blew out a heavy sigh and leaned forward to brace his forehead against mine. "I'm sorry, love. I know I'm pushing you hard. I have reasons. You're the key, Riann. Without you, everything is lost."

"I have no idea what you're talking about."

"Find me. Go to Warwick if you must. He's a slimy bastard, but he'll help you as much as he can. Maybe he can explain things better than I do."

"We're going to see him tomorrow morning. But I don't need to find you. Vivi put your statue outside on the front porch."

He grunted. "That little statue is only a representation of me, a connection to this world. Don't go to see him in the daylight. It'll be a waste of time."

"What's that supposed to mean?"

"You'll see, so you will."

I ran my fingers over the planes of his face. He was as hard as the carved statue, but warm. Living flesh, not stone. "Why are you trapped in a gargoyle?"

"I'm cursed. Only you can free me, but you can't do it alone. You have to bring the treasures together."

"Treasures?"

"The stone, spear, sword, and cauldron. I've given you our names in this cycle, and what we look like. I don't know where the others are, but they'll be drawn to find you. They should be on their way to you now. You'll recognize them when you see them. But beware. Demons be coming for you, too."

Great. Fantastic. This dream was just getting better and better. Not.

I slid my hand around his nape and squeezed hard enough he lifted his head a little in warning. Then I snagged his bottom lip in my teeth.

His hands locked on my upper arms with brutal strength. I thought he'd throw me aside for the audacity of nipping him, but then he hauled me closer and opened his mouth on a ragged groan. Giving himself to me.

Oh yeah. I released his lip so I could slide my tongue into his mouth. He tasted like dark, smoky whiskey with a coffee chaser, like I could get drunk just from kissing him. I slanted my head to fit my lips to his better and ran my hands down his impressive shoulders. Broad, powerful, heavy muscle, like a living gargoyle.

Need roared to life in me. It'd been so long since I'd had a man in my bed, and my ex hadn't been all that great in the sack, either, at least the last few years. I had a feeling that Doran was going to blow my mind, and I couldn't wait. I lay back and tugged him closer, pulling him down with me.

He lifted his head, eyes glittering in the moonlight. "Are you sure?"

"Yes. Please. Make love to me, Doran."

With a rough groan, he buried his face against my throat and breathed deeply, dragging my scent into his body. I didn't know how, but I could feel my scent ease something inside him. Like ice on a sore muscle, heat on a throbbing ache. He rolled his eyes up to look at my face, and slid lower on my body. He nibbled on my tank top, giving it a playful tug with his teeth, and I groaned, arching my hips up. I'd love it if he seized the material in his hands and just ripped my clothes off.

His eyebrows rose, and his hands fisted in my shirt. I held my breath, my eyes flaring, braced for the sound of ripping cotton.

A scream tore through the dream, and I bolted up like someone had goosed me with a taser. "What? What's wrong?"

Vivi pointed at the side of the bed. "It's him. How'd he get back in here?"

I turned to look and froze.

The gargoyle statue we'd locked outside stood on my side of the bed. Very close. Leering.

"Fuck."

4

Vivi marched down the sidewalk that ran along Perez Parkway, my hand clutched hard in hers. She dragged me down to the intersection where I'd lost our friends that night. The dance club was dark and empty on the other side of the road. No surprise, since it was fucking eight o'clock in the morning. All sane people were still in bed this early on a Saturday. But after we'd found a freaking gargoyle statue staring at us—that we'd deliberately locked outside—we hadn't been able to get back to sleep.

Just as I'd done Monday night, we turned up Eighty-Eighth and started walking. It was freaking snowing again and the wind sliced through my parka.

"How much further?" Vivi asked through chattering teeth.

"Not far. I kind of remember that tattoo shop. There were a bunch of motorcycles parked out front that night and loud music blasted out. It was pretty cool. Maybe I should have gone in there instead of the bar."

Vivi snorted. "You're too much of a baby to get a tattoo."

"Hey," I growled. "I resemble that remark."

Finally, I saw the four-leafed clover sign, though in broad daylight, it didn't draw my attention like that night. In fact, the whole building looked pretty sad. The roof sagged and the sidewalk was cracked and buckled. The building itself was a plain brick square with a glass window front, which was, of course, cracked.

"Are you sure this is it? I thought you said it was nice."

I'd been in lots of bars and clubs that looked fucking fantastic at night and sad and lonely during the day, but this old falling down structure took the cake. In fact, I was pretty worried the roof might come crashing down on us. In the dream last night, Doran had told me it'd be a waste of time to come back during the day, but I hadn't expected it to look so completely different.

The front door was unlocked, so we went inside. The odor of moldy wallpaper and ancient dust burned my nose. Cracked linoleum covered the floor, not the beautiful black and white marble tiles. Everything was coated in grime. The gorgeous, shiny wood of the bar was caked in old paint and a thick layer of dust. The fireplace hadn't seen a fire in decades.

"I don't understand," I whispered. "This is nothing like I remember."

"But this is the place?"

"Yes, but not like this. Not abandoned and crumbling and dirty. It was beautiful."

Fucking sick to my stomach, I followed Vivi back outside. She didn't voice her doubts, but I knew what she had to be thinking. Something had to be wrong with me. I was either on drugs, or suffering some kind of delusion. Maybe the bartender had roofied me that night. But surely any drug he could have given me would have worn off already.

"May I help you, ladies?"

I looked up and relief flooded me. "It's you! The bartender. See, Vivi? I'm not crazy."

He inclined his head politely, but kept his gaze locked to my face. "I am known to occasionally tend bar."

"Is your name Warwick?"

"You've heard of me, then."

Confusion flickered through me. Did he recognize me or not? He looked like the bartender from that night, but Doran said he was a leprechaun. I didn't believe in little men in green suits and pointy ears who guarded a pot of gold.

He coughed and covered his mouth, to hide a smile, I thought. Eyes narrowed, I watched him. If he was Faerie, as Doran had said, could he read minds? To test it out, I focused on him. :*Doran said you'd better keep your pot of gold in your pants.*:

The wide-eyed look on his face was comical and worth a dozen buckets of gold. :*I have no such designs on the treasurekeeper.*:

Now it was my turn to choke on surprise and try to smooth my face when Viviana narrowed a hard look on my face. Treasurekeeper? I had the extremely uncomfortable realization that maybe... just maybe... the gargoyle in my dreams was real.

"What's going on here?" Viviana retorted. "I have a sneaking suspicion that my friend was assaulted in this establishment."

Warwick turned to her and bowed again. "Never, beautiful lady. No harm would come to any woman in my presence."

"There's something fishy going on. This place looks nothing like what she described to me, and she can't remember how she got home that night. That's definitely suspicious. Only her promise to come here and track down the truth kept me from calling 911."

"There's no need for the authorities," he said smoothly. "If you both would come back tonight, I think you'll be more impressed with the premises."

"I think I took something that night from you that I shouldn't have."

Warwick shook his head slowly. "Oh, no. He definitely should be in your care."

Frustrated, I rubbed my eyes, exhausted and near tears. "He won't let me sleep. I don't have any peace. I don't fucking understand what's going on."

He took my hand and kissed my knuckles. His touch was soothing, his palm warm, but it didn't feel intimate. Bummer. Until that crazy dream with Doran last night, I'd entertained the idea of finding the sexy bartender for my first post-divorce fling. But now I felt like only a casual acquaintance. Maybe it was because Vivi was with me. She couldn't help drawing men like bees to honey.

"Come back tonight with the token. I'll explain everything that I'm able."

"What token? The statue?"

"No." He frowned a little. "You had to have a token to… cross."

Token? What the fuck? This was getting weirder by the moment. Other than the gargoyle, I didn't know what he could mean.

He looked around, his shoulders tensing. "Beware. He's in the city. He knows the conduit has been found, though I don't believe he has pinpointed your location yet."

"He who? What's going on?"

He stepped closer and gripped my arm firmly, though he didn't hurt me. "You are the conduit. If they lose you, they'll never be able to free Doran."

"They who?"

"The four Irish treasures. Has he told you nothing?" He looked around again, his face tensing. "It's not safe to talk here. Come back tonight and I'll explain what I can. But you have to have the token to cross again."

He pulled away and strode up the steps and through the door to the building so quickly that we could only stare at the door and each other, back and forth. Vivi ran forward and pushed the door open again, but no one was there.

I stood in the doorway and watched her look around a minute, and then it dawned on me. "It's no use."

She stomped back over to me. "Why?"

I pointed at the dust that lay thick on the floor. Only two sets of shoes tracked through the ramshackle building. My Converse soles, and her heeled boots.

"But we saw him come inside."

For the first time, I heard uncertainty, and even a bit of fear, trembling in her voice. I squeezed her hand and tugged her back outside. "All we can do is come back tonight."

"You believe him. Even though nothing he said makes sense."

I thought of Doran in my dream, how his statue had been waiting beside the bed when Vivi woke me up. He was real. And if *he* was real...

"Yeah. I believe. Though I don't understand one fucking thing yet."

5

Slumped, I sat at the island in the kitchen waiting on the kettle to whistle. All the way back to her place, she'd put me through the Vivi Inquisition trying to figure out what token Warwick had been talking about.

"And you didn't stop anywhere else, after you left Morgan and Tammy?"

"Nope." My eyes ached, but I didn't want to sleep. Doran would start after me again, and though I wouldn't mind continuing that dream from this morning in the slightest… there were too many things I didn't understand. My nerves shimmered with tense anxiety. It felt like a massive thunderstorm hung over the house crackling with lighting, without a single drop of rain.

She poured hot water into two cups, gave them a stir, and set a cup in front of me. Hot chocolate, yum. After the chilly and fruitless trip this morning, some chocolate was definitely on my must-consume list. "You don't have a secret Irish ancestor in the family tree, do you? Like dear old Great-Grandma Molly who passed along the family's holy shamrock or something?"

I snickered, shaking my head. "If only it was that easy. I guess I could have some Irish ancestors, but I don't know anything about them. Newkirk is Dutch and we immigrated to America in the early eighteenth century. Beyond that, I have no idea."

"What did you wear that night?"

My cheeks burned and I focused intently on my cup. With my curvier body type, I was usually trying to hide my body, not flaunt it or dress up in something sultry. Not like her. She could make a pair of sweatpants look sexy. Besides, I'd been married long enough that I'd forgotten how to dress up for clubbing. At least that was what I'd told myself.

And yeah, it stung that my gorgeous friend had no memory of what I'd worn that night when she'd been with me. It wasn't like we were talking a month ago. "Black jeans and that corset top you gave me."

"Oh yeah. You looked great. You put your hair up too, right? And you wore my silver bangles."

"With the matching earrings." If my wardrobe was sadly lacking from years in the corporate world, then my jewelry collection was downright miserable. "I put them back on your dresser."

She headed down the hallway toward the bedrooms. "I've got an idea."

I picked up my cup and followed.

"Let's pull out what you were wearing that night and see if we can find this token he's talking about."

Sure. That sounded like a plan. "The jeans are in the hamper in the bathroom."

She ducked into the bathroom and I sorted through the hangers in the closet until I found the top I'd worn. Just looking at it made me blush. It was so not me, Riann Newkirk, the married customer service rep. No, I'd been the sexy artist who couldn't wait to taste her freedom. The emerald-green velvet bodice had hugged my curves and nipped in my waist enough to look sexy, without making me feel like a stuffed sausage all night. The girls had looked fucking fantastic with the extra lift and support. Though I hadn't gone out with the goal of picking up a man for a one-night stand, I'd gotten a couple of appreciative looks that had boosted my self-confidence to the stars.

With the outfit laid out on the bed, I set my cup of hot cocoa on the nightstand and pictured myself walking down the street toward *Shamrocked*. Eyes closed, I felt the brisk air on my face. I'd been buzzed, my emotions high and light, having the time of my life. I could have skipped and hopped down the sidewalk with joy. In fact, I did, at one point. My friends had giggled, but I didn't care. I was too happy. I'd swung myself around like I was dancing—

And promptly fell on my butt.

They'd roared with laughter, almost falling down themselves. I put my hand out to get up, and...

My eyes flew open. "Oh! I found a coin that night!"

I dug into the pockets of the jeans, front and back, more frantic as each one ended up empty.

"The hamper," Vivi said and we raced to the bathroom. She beat me of course. Laughing, she dumped all the dirty clothes out on the floor and we slung them aside piece by piece, until a coin lay on the tile. "A penny? That's the token?"

I gasped, my eyes widening. "You see a penny?"

She frowned. "Yeah. What do you see?"

I picked up a rough golden coin that looked old enough to have seen Stonehenge built. The carvings were faded by time, but I could make out a Celtic knot on one side, and a face on the other. A woman, I thought, but it was hard to tell as worn as the coin was.

"Oh," she breathed out. "Now that you're holding it, it looks different. It looks like an old gold coin."

Watching her face, I laid the coin down on the tile and removed my touch.

"Back to a penny." Wide eyed, she met my gaze. "How is this possible?"

"Magic?" I shrugged uncomfortably. "I don't know."

She looked at me like she didn't know me. Me, her friend for twenty years. It made my stomach tremble. "Where did you find it?"

"I was dancing around like a fool after we left the *Crown*," I whispered. "I slipped and fell. I didn't even see it. My hand slid into a couple of inches of snow piled up at the edge, and there it was."

She sat back sharply on her heels and stood up. "Wow."

My stomach plummeted and the sweet chocolate I'd drank suddenly burned like acid. I didn't want to lose her friendship. I'd be lost without her. Even if I gained Doran and whatever else was going on. But if this coin was magical, and Doran was real, and Warwick really was a leprechaun... then he'd warned me about demons too.

She offered her hand and pulled me up to my feet, but she didn't let go of me right away. "Think about it, Ri. What are the chances that you'd fall in the right spot? That you'd feel that coin in the snow if you couldn't see it? That you'd pick it up? That you'd need to use the bathroom, and you'd miss the traffic signal, and our other friends would go off and leave you? Let alone that your asshole ex would finally sign the papers after fighting to get you back for months. Why that night? It gives me chills to think about it."

"Yeah." I rubbed my arms briskly. "Me too."

"You know what this means, right?"

She grabbed me suddenly and lifted me up off my feet, whirling me around in the bathroom like we were dancing a waltz. "My best friend has four Irish treasures to claim for herself! You're going to be rich!"

Laughing with relief that she wasn't too weirded out, I hugged her back but squirmed in her grip. "Put me down, you idiot. The treasures aren't worth money. I'm as broke as ever."

She gave me a leer that would do the gargoyle proud, but she did set me back down on my feet. "You won't be poor in men, honey. And one of them will keep you satisfied, isn't that what you said?"

I laughed, but a little uneasily. I'd only managed to gain my freedom from one jerk. I sure wasn't going to saddle myself with another asshole, let alone four.

6

It was ridiculously hard to pick out something to wear to a Faerie pub. I didn't want to be disrespectful—if that was even a concern —but I didn't want to look like I was trying too hard, either. I finally settled on my second-best pair of dark-colored jeans (since I'd worn my nicest Monday and hadn't done laundry because I'd been painting like a maniac) and a nice sweater. It was too fucking cold to even think about wearing a dress, and I'd gotten rid of all my business casual clothes when I left my corporate job.

So, jeans. At least I wore a nice pair of ankle boots that were a little dressier than my beat-up Converse. I slipped the coin into my pocket and then stared doubtfully at the gargoyle. He was too heavy to carry around. Should I bring him? Warwick only said to bring the token. If Viviana drove, I could leave the statue in the trunk, but she hated driving in the winter mess on the streets and usually kept her Mustang in storage. I couldn't risk the driver changing his mind and driving off with my gargoyle in the trunk.

It made me feel vaguely guilty to leave him on the nightstand, though. Especially going to see Warwick, a man I'd already hinted I thought was pretty cute.

Stupid. To be worried about a gargoyle's jealousy. He was a fucking statue and he was already haunting me in my dreams. It couldn't get much worse. Right?

I paused at the door and looked back at the gargoyle. "Nothing's going to happen with the leprechaun, okay? So you can stop glaring at me."

Stepping out of the car Vivi had called, I stared up at the old building and tried not to feel self-conscious. But standing next to a goddess with effortless beauty would make anybody feel like a plain wallflower. She wasn't even trying, not really. She'd gone with black jeans and a luxurious black sweater so soft it might as well have been made of mink instead of yarn, but with her glorious hair down around her shoulders and a little bit of makeup, she looked like she was headed to a premier movie event.

Her eyes glittered with excitement and she squeezed my hand. "Let's see that magic, Ri."

I waited a minute as the car drove off. The driver looked back at us in his rear view mirror, likely checking Vivi's ass out, but maybe concerned about leaving two women alone in front of such a disreputable-looking establishment. The four-leaf clover sign glowed, but otherwise, there was no sign of the pub I'd visited last night. There wasn't even a single light on inside.

I slipped my right hand into my front pocket and wrapped my fingers around the coin.

The difference made us both gasp. It was like going to the eye doctor for a routine exam, and looking through the different test lenses to get to the right prescription. Touching the coin brought everything into focus, though nothing had seemed blurry to my human eyes. Warm light shone in the windows. The sidewalk was lined with crushed white stone and not a single crack marred the straight and even walk to the door. No windows were busted out. The perfectly straight roof was lined with cedar shakes, and the quaint white door welcoming us inside gave the building a cottage-in-the-woods feel. Even the traffic seemed distant and muted. I turned to look back over my shoulder, and then wished I hadn't. Headlights moved up and down the road, but it looked like they were underwater and creeping very so slowly they were barely moving at all.

Goosebumps raced down my arms as Vivi pushed the door open and we stepped inside.

As before, an Irish jig played softly in the background. Our heeled boots rang on the marble tiles. A fire crackled in the giant stone fireplace, and Warwick grinned behind the polished bar. Exactly as when I'd come here alone.

"Wow," she whispered. "I can't believe it's the same place."

"It's not." Smiling, he made a come-hither motion with his hand and started drawing two pints of Guinness. "You've crossed into Faerie."

"How do we get back?"

"The same as you came in."

I sat down in the same seat I'd used before and Vivi sat on my right. "How'd I get home that night?"

He quirked his lips and a dimple appeared in his cheek. "I whisked you home with a thought. I didn't want you roaming the streets, alone and vulnerable, let alone lugging our heavy friend through the snow. Crossing back to your world the first couple of times can take a toll on the unsuspecting human."

I narrowed my eyes, searching his face. I didn't remember taking my clothes off.

Setting our frosty mugs before us, he arched a brow, his smirk deepening, but he didn't deny or confirm my suspicions.

Vivi took a hesitant sip of the beer and made a pleased hum. "You're right, Ri. This tastes better than anything I've ever had before."

That soft sound coming out of her luscious lips had been known to bring men to their knees. So color me shocked when Warwick focused on me instead. "Right, how may I assist you, treasurekeeper?"

"First of all, what does that mean? Treasurekeeper?"

"You're the conduit, the one who can bring the treasures together. What has Doran told you?"

"He said there's three men I have to find: Keane, Aidan, and Ivarr."

Warwick nodded. "The cauldron, spear, and sword. Doran is the stone. The four treasures of Ireland. Do you know the history of the treasures and how they first came to be?"

I shook my head and he sighed. "They teach nothing of the old ways any longer. According to legend, the Tuatha De Danann brought four treasures with them when they came to Ireland. The Stone of Destiny, which declared the true king; the Spear of Lug, sometimes called the Slaughterer; the Sword of Light, from which no one can escape its light; and the Cauldron of the Dagda, from which none ever left unsatisfied."

"I've heard parts of that, yes, but you make it sound like objects. Doran made it sound like his friends were the treasures."

"They are. Over the centuries, the stories changed. Parts were lost, and some were forgotten on purpose to protect the treasures. They were given to protect Ireland in times of great need, and are reborn cycle after cycle, heroes of old come again. But... something happened several cycles ago. For the first time, Balor of the Evil Eye managed to defeat the treasures. He cursed Doran with his own strength, imprisoning him in his gargoyle shape forever. For several cycles, now, the heroes come into this world but cannot be complete. Either they can't locate the conduit, or they can't free Doran, or both. Meanwhile, Balor and his minions have only gained in strength while the treasures fade away. It's been over a hundred years since the treasures were last gifted to your world. Someday..."

His words trailed off and the corners of his mouth tugged down.

"They won't be born at all?"

He tipped his head to the side. "They're not really born, like humans, but aye. They won't come into your world at all. The cycle will end, and your world will be lost to the demon horde forever."

Wow, talk about pressure. I took a long pull from the mug, letting the beer slide down my throat. Damn, that was good shit. I could almost camp out here day and night just to drink my cares away. "But why me? I'm not even Irish."

"You must have some Irish blood, even if it's generations old. The Ireland we knew thousands of years ago doesn't exist the same way any longer. The old world faded away, just as the Tuatha De Danann have faded. Humans have no need for Faerie any longer, so they say."

"So what's Riann supposed to actually do?" Vivi asked. "We can't fight demons."

My heart swelled in my chest. She'd said *we*. She wasn't going to leave me to figure this out on my own, even if it involved some evil demon horde.

"Of course not. That's what the treasures do. The most important thing is to find the three treasures who are free. They're close. In fact, you've seen one of them already."

My eyes widened. "Other than Doran? Who?"

"Aidan was here the same night you were." Warwick tipped his head to the end of the bar. I remembered a man sitting there, his face in shadows. His disposition had been sour, to say the least.

"I have a feeling they're not going to be too keen on me showing up and telling them we've got to go find Doran."

Warwick swiped a cloth across the bar, not meeting my gaze.

"Yeah, that's what I thought."

"You have to understand how devastating their defeat was. How terrible their loss. They lost the conduit to the greatest evil we know."

The conduit—like me.

I shivered, wrapping both palms around my mug. "Are the conduits always women?"

"Always." Warwick chuckled a moment, but his amusement faded to a hint of concern, his brow furrowed. "The treasures are used to sacrifice and war, violence and death. Their conduit was the only hope and pleasure they had in this weary world, and they lost her, cycles ago. That loss has changed them. They're... harder, now, and it's been so long since the last cycle that they've forgotten what they once were. Their hearts are as stony as Doran's statue. They won't want to risk exposing their hearts and souls to a conduit again. It... hurt them. Terribly. And once hurt..."

Yeah. That I completely understood. "So what happens if I can't get them to come with me to find Doran?"

Warwick leaned forward, holding my gaze. "You must find them. You must free him. Or you'll die."

7

I drained the mug and slammed it down on the bar. Without even looking at me, Warwick swiped it up and poured me another draft while he stared at Viviana. My best friend wasn't going to take any pity on him. He might be a legendary leprechaun but he was still a man, and she'd eat him for lunch. There was a reason she worked for the best defense attorney in the city. In a matter of minutes, she'd have him by the balls.

Usually I enjoyed watching her work so effortlessly, but this time...

It was a silly thought. It made no sense. But all I could think was *I saw him first.*

With her elbow braced on the bar, she drew circles on the polished wood with her other hand. "So does she have any powers that she can use or call to force these obstinate men to help her?"

"With practice, she can call all the powers of Faerie to her will. She's the conduit. We know how important it is that she receive what she needs in order to reunite the treasures. Especially after their defeat."

When he turned to me, I almost fell out of my chair with surprise. His eyes gleamed, whether with amusement or interest, I wasn't sure.

How could he be interested in me, with Viviana right beside me? It was like comparing a candle to the heat and warmth of the sun. "The Tuatha De Danann aren't supposed to interfere in the mortal realm, beyond giving gifts for our own amusement, but over the centuries, we've become quite adept at circumventing our own rules."

I had a sneaking suspicion I knew where he was going with this. "You helped Doran, didn't you? Against the rules."

"Aye. After he was trapped, I created the miniature statue, so he could interact with his conduit and pull her to his side. Though I'd practically given up hope that anyone would ever step into me pub and see him for what he truly is."

My eyes widened with sudden realization. "You left the token too, didn't you?"

He inclined his head. "Guilty as charged. I can't help it if the purse split open and dropped me precious gold all over this cursed city. Eventually, I hoped the magic would call you and you'd pick up one of the coins. I knew you were close, though I admit, I'd almost given up hope."

"How long have you waited for me to find a token and step into your pub?"

He turned aside a moment, fiddling with bottles that lined the bar. "Honestly?"

"No, Pointy Ears, she wants you to lie to her," Viviana retorted.

I burst out laughing. I couldn't help it. *Pointy Ears.*

Warwick scowled at her, and his cheeks reddened. "I do not have pointy ears, thank you very much. I've been waiting nearly five years for you to find one of the tokens I scattered throughout the city."

My mouth fell open. Five years? That was almost as long as I'd been married, if we'd made it through to our next anniversary.

It made an odd kind of sense, though. While married, I never would have gone out clubbing or wandered into an Irish pub. Jonathan was too uptight to go drinking. Let alone allow me to go out on a girls' night to drink and party. I'd barely picked up a paintbrush in that entire time, so even if I'd found Doran, he wouldn't have had a medium to speak in my head until I actually heard him. It was freaky, how close I'd come to never stepping foot into *Shamrocked*. Never finding Doran's statue. Never meeting Warwick and learning the history of the treasures and what my role was.

I still didn't know what my role involved, exactly, other than finding the other three treasures. "Do you know where they are?"

He nodded solemnly. "You do too. You've seen the place. You felt their pull."

Surprised, I tried to think of anywhere else I'd been. Other than Vivi's condo and this bar…

"You said something weird." She turned on the barstool, searching my face. "You joked about getting a tattoo. You'd never said anything about that before."

Oh yeah. That biker tattoo place down the road. My eyes widened. "They're the treasures? A motorcycle gang?"

Warwick dropped his elbow onto the bar and braced his chin on his hand, smiling with that wretched dimple. "I'd hardly call three men a gang, now, would you?"

A highly inappropriate thought popped into my head.

A thought that never would have occurred to me before I'd stepped into this bar and seen a glaring gargoyle on a shelf. Or had a leprechaun wink at me.

Because I could certainly think of one kind of gang that would involve three men. Or four. Or maybe even five.

Gang *bang*.

My cheeks fired up as red as Vivi's hair.

Warwick threw his head back and roared with laughter.

"What?" She glared at me and then the bartender as he gasped for breath. "What'd I miss?"

"Nothing," I said hurriedly, avoiding his gaze. I hopped down from the barstool and almost twisted my ankle in the process. Damned high stools. "What do we owe you for the drinks?"

"Nothing, nothing at all." Still chuckling, he propped his chin back on his hand, his green eyes dancing with mirth. And yeah, heat. Even though he looked at me, and not my beautiful friend. That was going to take some getting used to. Maybe he winked and flirted with all the treasurekeepers.

I didn't like that thought.

At all.

Neither did he, evidently, because in a flash, he frowned instead of smiled. *:Not once in all of my five hundred and seventy nine years have I wished I was a cursed gargoyle. Until you.:*

I'd promised Doran that nothing would happen. Besides, I didn't know how to respond. I wasn't used to having men interested in me. Especially when I was with Vivi.

"Let's go," I told her, still avoiding his gaze. I didn't like knowing that he could hear my thoughts. How deeply could he eavesdrop into my head? It was creepy and invasive. I wanted to be alone with my fears and insecurities, rather than waving them around like dirty laundry hung out on the street for everyone to see.

He came around the bar and took Vivi's hand. With an extravagant bow, he pressed a kiss to her hand. "Farewell, beautiful lady."

As he came toward me, I tensed. I wasn't sure what to say or do. My hormones were out of control. It'd been a long time since I'd made love. Hard. Loud. Sweaty.

It would be all too easy to let an image fill my head of brilliant green eyes above me. Or below me. With Doran's rough palm sliding over my skin. His fist in my hair.

Both of them. Holy fuck, I was going to spontaneously combust.

I hadn't even met Keane yet—the man with the sensual lips and the knowing heat in his eyes that said he knew a thousand ways to get me off and would take his sweet-ass time doing so.

Fuck. I was in serious trouble. I had no idea how to deal with random hookups. I'd entertained the idea of picking up a man for a night of fun, but couldn't justify taking a stranger into Vivi's house. It was too risky. I didn't trust men. At all. Especially after Jonathan had made our split-up so ugly.

Let alone several *different* men.

:What makes you think it would be a random hookup?: Warwick asked

silently in my head as he reached for my hand. *:I could go bespell any human woman that caught my fancy. That would be random. You, Riann, are destined to be their treasurekeeper, but you can keep me treasure anytime you want.:*

He pressed his lips to the back of my hand, the same as he'd done to Vivi. But surely he hadn't lightly touched his tongue to her knuckles.

Slowly straightening, he rolled his eyes up to mine, that damnable dimple still flashing in his cheek. "If you carry the token, you can call me to your side at a moment's notice. You won't have to come back here for information, unless you're thirsty for Guinness, of course."

I drew myself up proudly, determined to ignore the magnetic pull of his emerald eyes. "I'm not going to call you for help."

"Sure, you are?" He gave me another wink before turning to move back around the bar. "Cheers, then. I wish you well."

He had to have done that on purpose, turning around to give me a good long look at how well he filled out tight black pants that seemed to be painted on his thighs and ass. I dragged my gaze up to his face as he turned back around and could only hope I wasn't drooling.

"Though I think you do be telling me lies."

8

Shivering, I pulled my jacket up around my chin and stared at the blacked-out windows of the tattoo shop just a block from the pub. A skull was painted on top of the black, with crossed swords rather than bones. Exactly as in my painting. Not freaky at all. Gulp.

Heavy-metal music thumped through the door and motorcycles lined the front. Way more than three, so how many people were inside?

"Are you sure about this?" Vivi asked beside me. "I mean, I'm down with whatever you want to do, but this place is shady as hell."

I agreed. We really had no idea what we were walking into. I thought about leaving. Vivi could call for a car. We could wait in *Shamrocked* with that nice warm fire and another pint. But I'd have to deal with that smug I-told-you-so look on Warwick's face. Worse, I didn't want to go home and look at my scowling gargoyle and have to tell him I chickened out. These guys were his friends. I was their treasurekeeper. The *leprechaun* had told me so.

I almost started laughing hysterically. What the fuck had I gotten myself into?

"You still have the pepper spray in your purse, right?"

She patted her pink sparkly purse. "Never leave home without it.

But if there's a bunch of assholes in here, then one little bottle of pepper spray won't get us out."

I sighed. "Let's hope we don't need it. Worst case, I'll call for Warwick to whisk us away."

"He was *so* into you."

My cheeks heated despite the brisk winter air. "I think it's just this treasurekeeper thing."

"Hmm, no, I don't think so. That makes it more complicated. After all, that puts him in competition with four men. Well, three and a gargoyle." She chuckled and bumped my shoulder with her elbow playfully. "Look at you go, girl. You're killing it now that you finally got rid of the asshole."

She'd never liked Jonathan, but she'd said her piece and then kept her silence until I told her how unhappy I was. Then Vivi was all over it, giving me a place to live without question. I hadn't told her half the shit I'd lived the last few years. I didn't want to break her heart.

"So what's the plan?"

I grimaced and shrugged. "Get out alive? I don't know. I guess I want to see how much Doran told me is true, and if I can get them to believe me."

"And when they don't?" She asked lightly.

"I make them believe me. Somehow."

I stuck my hand out to grab the doorknob, but the door cracked open by itself. Weirded out, I tried to tell myself it hadn't been shut all the way. Music poured out in a clash of drums and screaming guitar. Taking a deep breath, I pushed the door open the rest of the way and stepped inside.

The front room was set up like a tattoo parlor, or at least what I imagined one would look like, with a customer service desk and a couple of workstations on either side. Artwork covered the walls, all very graphic and bold, mostly with a Gothic touch. Lots of skulls: roses with skulls, skulls with snakes, and skulls with crosses. The quality of the artwork was really good. One of the snakes arched up off the wall, eyes flashing, and at first glance, I really expected it to strike us as we walked by. It looked that real.

Light gleamed from beneath a door marked "Office." I laid my hand on the door and felt the wood thumping with the music a moment, and then it flew open so quickly I jumped back into Vivi. The door crashed into the wall. Someone killed the music, but my ears still throbbed with the memory of that bass. Several round tables filled the room, and a dozen or so men all suddenly turned to stare at us.

"Wow, way to go, Ri," she whispered a little too loudly now that the music had stopped. "You definitely got their attention."

"I didn't do it," I whispered back. "I barely touched the door."

A bearded man with a big, burly chest pushed up out of his chair. He wore a leather vest and faded jeans, tats all over his arms and throat. He took a swig from the long-neck bottle in his hand and then said, "We're closed."

"That's not one of them, is it?" Vivi whispered.

Shaking my head, I scanned the other men in the room. They all looked like biker guys, with leather jackets or vests, jeans, and thick-soled boots. A bit rough around the edges, but I didn't get a bad vibe from them. A few men sat in the back corner, where it was darker. Something tugged deep in my stomach when I looked at them, but I didn't head over right away.

I focused on the man who'd stood up. He looked from me to Vivi and back, his eyes getting a dazed look in them that told me he didn't deal with a lot of women. Or maybe he was just easily fazed by the opposite sex. "Uh, you…" He stammered. "Do you ladies… uh… need some help or something?"

With Vivi solidly at my side, I gave the man the cutest smile I could muster. "Aye, in fact, we do. I'm hoping you can help me find someone."

"Here? Are you sure you got the right place?"

The trick was knowing which man to ask for. Of the three, who was the leader, if Doran wasn't with them? I decided to go with the meanest-looking man I'd painted. "I think so. I'm looking for Aidan."

The man's eyes flared and he gulped. "What does a lady like you want with the Slaughterer?"

Slaughterer? Fuck. Aidan's picture floated in my head again, that vicious scowl, the swords crossed beneath the skull. Aidan was supposed to be the spear, but the deadly blades kept flashing through my mind.

A chair scraped across the floor, drawing my attention back to the darkened corner as a man stood up. He wore a black leather jacket, the same as in my painting, but it didn't have the skull and crossed swords painted on it. He turned to face me, but stayed in the shadows. His shoulders were broad, but he had a way of standing slouched and casual, as though he wasn't dangerous, even though I sensed coiled strength hidden under that leather jacket.

"Are you Aidan?" I asked softly, trying to focus on his face despite the shadows.

"Who wants to know?"

His voice sent chills of dread trickling like icy fingers down my spine. Flat, dead, hard, his tone said he wasn't to be fucked with. He'd cut a man who looked at him sideways. "Me."

He laughed roughly and sat back on the table with casual masculine arrogance that set my teeth on edge. "Right, little girl. If it's me you're wanting to talk to, you can come on over and we'll have a grand chat." The lascivious tone on that last word told me he didn't mean talking.

Little girl? Rage shot through me and I stiffened, my chin tipping up. I might be short, but the fuck if any man was going to call me a girl. Or talk down to me. Or make me feel small, ever again.

Vivi grabbed at my arm. She knew all too well that'd piss me off. I shook her off and marched over to the table, my eyes locked on the asshole's face. As I neared, I could make out a trimmed beard on his jaws, short cropped brown hair, and baby blue eyes that looked so at odds with the deep furrow between his eyes and the fierce slant of his lips. He wore a plain white T-shirt under the jacket and he sat sprawled and careless on the table, arms crossed, that smug smirk on his lips despite his ferocity.

His eyes glittered with amusement, but there was a hint of darkness, too. A bit of recognition, maybe even dread. He had to know I was the treasurekeeper, even if he had no clue who I was. Electricity hummed in the air as I neared him. Surety ringing like a gong in my head.

I was supposed to be here. I was supposed to find him.

Even if he was an asshole.

I don't know what he thought I'd do. Maybe poke him in the chest, or slap him, or laugh in his face. All things I was tempted to do, sure. But I wanted to shock that smirk off his face. I wanted him to regret making fun of me, especially in front of his friends.

Even the way he sat on the table pissed me off. Knees spread, legs wide, taking up too much space. Typical man, putting his package on display.

So, I cupped that bulge in his pants and gave him a good, hard squeeze. Enough that his shoulders jerked and his nostrils flared wide as he sucked in a hard breath. "Hmm. Not bad. But I guess I should have asked for Keane instead."

I let go of him and stepped back, eyeing the two other men at the table. One chuckled, his head tipped back so he could see me without standing up, baring the long line of his throat. He didn't have the red stripe down his face that I'd painted, but I'd know those full, sensual lips anywhere. The other man had to be Ivarr. He smirked too, but his amusement was quiet, more solemn, and his eyes gleamed like burnished antique coins when he met my gaze. He waved both hands, warning me off. "He's Keane. Not me."

Keane kept his head tipped back, smiling up at me, his chair rocked back on two legs. On one hand, I wanted to kick the chair so it'd dump him on his skull. But on the other, his mouth was definitely tempting. His blond hair was wild and shaggy, giving him a wild, disreputable look that was doing some crazy things to my libido.

"I know better than to call any woman little girl. Let alone..." His eyes tightened and pain flashed over his face like lightning, gone so quickly I doubted that glimpse I'd seen.

"Do you know who I am?" I asked softly, leaning over him.

Solemnly, he nodded, but he didn't sit up or move away. "Are you knowing where Doran is?"

"Not yet."

Aidan let out a disgusted growl. "Then why the fuck are you here bothering us?"

"Yeah, I can see that you're definitely in the middle of something serious here." I peeked at Keane's cards and snorted. "You guys should fold already. He's got four of a kind."

Blowing out a sigh, Ivarr tossed his cards on the table. "Utter bollocks."

I met Keane's gaze and the corner of his mouth quirked up, making his mouth even more tempting. He had a garbage hand, certainly no four of a kind in sight. Though I wasn't sure why he wore black leather gloves indoors while playing poker. "What can I do for you, my lady?"

I wrapped my fingers around the strong column of his bare throat, feeling his pulse, the way he swallowed as I leaned down closer. He still made no move to free himself, or avoid me. In fact, he licked his lips, a sultry heat burning in his eyes.

It shook me to my core. I wasn't the kind of woman who walked up to a stranger and groped or kissed a man. Yet that was exactly what I wanted to do. My fingers itched to stroke down the hard column of his throat and down into his shirt. My fingers wanted to walk down his pectorals playfully and settle over his cock. He'd have a big one. Something in me knew that already. A phantom memory, that wasn't quite mine, floated in the air between us. I knew if I pressed my mouth to his, I'd taste honeyed whiskey on his tongue, and he'd like it very much if I dug my teeth into his bottom lip.

Shuddering, I straightened and pulled away, avoiding his gaze. Was that Doran, planting memories in my head? But how would he know what his friend tasted like? Maybe they were lovers. Or maybe a previous treasurekeeper's memories were trying to take over in my mind. Or maybe Warwick was fucking with me, using his powers of Faerie to confuse me. I backed away but ran into a hard wall of flesh.

Aidan. He didn't touch me, but loomed over me, his breath hot on the back of my neck. "Where do you think you're going, *little girl*?"

Keane tipped his chair down to all four legs. "Chill, Aidan."

"You think you can walk in here and touch my dick without giving me something in return?"

"I'm sorry," I stammered out. "I shouldn't have touched you in a sexual way. I'd have broken your fingers if you'd grabbed me like that."

Shuffling boots and whispers told me the rest of the motorcycle gang was quickly disappearing out the door. Not that I could blame them. I turned, looking for Vivi, avoiding Aidan's glare. She had her hand shoved down in her purse, ready to grab that pepper spray if I needed it. Bless her.

"You were there," he growled, his voice thick with emotion. Dread, anger, I wasn't sure. "Warwick got to you first."

Bracing myself, I looked into Aidan's eyes. Such a killer blue, both frosty ice and yet blazing with heat. "He said you were at the pub too when I walked in."

He leaned down, tipping his head slightly as he studied me. "If I sample these luscious lips, am I going to taste Guinness? Or leprechaun?"

I huffed out a laugh and ducked around him, moving quickly toward Vivi's side. "Only Guinness, asshole. Are you going to help me find Doran or not?"

Aidan sat back on the table and held his hand up, counting off his fingers one by one. "You don't know where Doran even is. You don't know who or what we are. You certainly don't have a fucking clue what we're doing. How dangerous it is. Or you wouldn't be here." He slammed his hand down on the table, making me jump. "Don't you get it, *treasurekeeper*? We're doomed to fail. The fae love nothing more than fucking with mortals, giving you a crumb of hope, only to laugh as a bigger, meaner creature swoops in and devours you while you cower over the bait that betrayed you."

"So what am I supposed to do?" I retorted, blinking away tears. "Doran won't let me sleep. I've painted a dozen pictures of you all this week alone. If you won't help me…"

"Go home," he growled so deep and vicious that his voice cracked. "This is no life for the likes of you."

Keane stood and took a step toward me, but Aidan flung out his hand and stopped him. "She's not for you. She's not for me. She's not for any of us."

"But—"

"I can't bear for another woman to die on me." Aidan retorted, his face dark with fury. He was shorter than the other man, but definitely the more dominant of the two. Keane ducked his head slightly, giving way before his friend's anger. "Die she will, and us too. Again. Over and over and over. I can't fucking take it."

I wanted to hate him, but the agony shredding his voice stole my breath. My heart ached for them all. Warwick said they hadn't even been reborn for a hundred years, so how many times had they already suffered and died? How bitter and hard would I be, if I'd watched my friends and lover die over and over again?

He looked at me and his eyes blazed with brutal intensity. "It's safer for you if you stay away from us. Hopefully you haven't picked up enough fae taint yet to draw the demons to you. I'm sure Warwick will do what he can to keep you alive as long as possible. Who knows, with a leprechaun at your beck and call, maybe you'll get lucky and outlive us all."

"You won't help me?"

The blazing intensity in his eyes suddenly dimmed, and he looked weary and defeated, centuries of loss and battle and heartache stacked on him brick by brick. "I can't, *mo stór*. I've seen shit the likes of which I pray you can't even contemplate. Go on with you now. I hope you have yourself a grand life."

9

Sitting at the island in Vivi's kitchen, I stared dejectedly at the ancient coin I'd laid on the granite.

I didn't want to have to call Warwick for help. I didn't want him to wink and laugh and be I-told-you-so smug, or worse, cute and sassy. One would piss me off, and the other would tempt me. I couldn't be tempted when Doran was locked away somewhere bellowing in my dreams for me to come free him.

With a sigh, I dragged my gaze up to Vivi as she moved around her kitchen. "I'm making a midnight sandwich. Do you want one too?"

It wasn't quite midnight—but I'd never turn down a snack. "Duh. I wouldn't miss one of your sandwiches."

Some people slapped mayo and paper-thin processed meat on white bread and called it good, but not Vivi. She bought the good, thick turkey breast sliced off the bone and smoked provolone from the most expensive grocery store in town, and always picked up fresh Italian loaves, or, in this case, buttery croissants. Plus fancy whole-grain spicy mustard, leafy green lettuce, and tomato slices, with huge blackberries as big as my thumb on the side. She sat down beside me at the island and we ate in companionable silence.

"I freaking love you," I said around a mouthful of sandwich.

"I do make a mean sandwich and a pretty decent cup of coffee."

I huffed out a laugh. "The best, actually. But I'm not even talking about the food. Or the fact that you gave me a place to stay so I could get away from Jonathan and quit my job that was making me so miserable. Or even for sticking with me while we went to see a leprechaun."

"I never thought I'd get to cross off 'meet Pointy Ears' from my bucket list."

I laughed again, shaking my head. "And then you marched into the lion's den with me and faced down a motorcycle gang."

"I had pepper spray if we needed it. Besides, most of them didn't strike me as being very gang-like."

Except Aidan. She didn't say his name aloud, but yeah. He was the only scary one we'd met tonight. Without him... I couldn't get the other two treasures. He was the key.

I yawned so hard my jaw ached, but I knew it was no use. If I slept at all, Doran would be growling and rumbling in my dreams, telling me to hurry up and find him.

"You need some sleep."

I sighed. "I know. But I think I need to paint first. The clues I need are in the paintings."

"If Doran can give you the clues, why not just tell you where he is and be done?"

"He doesn't know where he is. Other than his friends' faces, I don't think the actual paintings are coming from him at all, other than his urgency."

"Then who, or what, is giving you these clues?"

I shrugged uncomfortably. "I don't really know. I've always called it my Muse, but maybe it's something else. Faerie magic. Some destiny I never knew. It's like I'm... remembering."

"Like you're reincarnated?"

I grimaced, shaking my head. "I don't think so? But I don't really know. It's more like someone whispered everything I needed to know in my ear when I was born, and it's there in my head, but I can't remember it. I can only get close to that memory if I have a paintbrush in my hand. It's like… losing myself. I have to shut down everything, the world, myself, the art—and just let that voice speak again. It's scary, though, because it feels like I'm losing myself. Like maybe I'll snap out of it, but I won't be me anymore. Does that make sense?"

"Like you're becoming something else? Someone else?"

"Sort of."

She pushed her plate away and turned on the barstool to face me. I turned, too, taking her hands in mine when she reached for me. "Why do you think we're friends? I mean, really? What brought us together?"

I'd often wondered myself why the tall, beautiful, sophisticated redhead would ever be friends with a dowdy short geek like me, who'd rather paint or read a book than dress up and go on a date.

She gave me a sad smile, her eyes shimmering suspiciously. "You've always had a kind of magic about you, but you don't see it, do you?"

"Me?" I scoffed and pulled back involuntarily. But she squeezed my hands harder, refusing to let me go. "Hardly."

"Not leprechaun magic, exactly. But magic. You get a look in your eyes, like you're seeing the world in a way that I can't possibly understand, even though I want to. And when you pick up a brush and paint that vision that only you can see, it's truly magical. It's like you're letting us mere mortals peek into this incredible secret world that exists in your head. You're like a deer in the woods, barely seen, tiptoeing carefully through the underbrush so you don't make a sound. Sometimes I'm afraid if I move too quickly that I'll startle you, and you'll be gone."

I squeezed her hands firmly. "Me, leave you? Never happening."

"That's why I hated Jonathan so much," she whispered, but her eyes flashed with a wicked promise of pain and lots of it, on the man who'd hurt me. "Every single day you were with him, it was like watching a beautiful flower wither and dry up, locked away from the sun. He kept you shuttered and safe in that normal, boring, little life, and it was all a lie. You deserve so much more than safe and normal. You deserve fairy tales and adventure. Remember when we were kids? We'd go on adventures in the woods behind the trailer park, looking for the lost castle and the forgotten prince. We'd slay dragons and..."

My ears roared with rushing winds, like I was falling into a deep, bottomless well.

Of course.

Her words brought back childhood dreams and games that I'd forgotten so long ago.

"Ri? Are you okay? What is it?"

I slammed my hand down on the coin and closed my eyes. *Warwick, I need you.*

Something warm and hard suddenly pressed against my back and he whispered in my ear. "I thought you'd never ask."

10

I hated asking for help, especially from an extremely sexy leprechaun, but I had to admit that Warwick made himself extremely useful. By the next morning, I had an abandoned warehouse at my disposal, set up with more blank canvases than I could possibly paint in a month and all of my completed paintings set up around my work area as a reminder of what I was doing. He even set up a comfortable bed for me to collapse on when I was exhausted—and he managed to resist making a single sexual innuendo or inappropriate remark.

How could he, with my gargoyle glaring right beside me?

I was too busy to even think about sexual innuendo. I painted for hours. Fell into a stupor on the bed. Guzzled coffee or gobbled sandwiches and soup when Vivi insisted I eat. And then started painting again in a frenzy. Everything inside me was breaking apart, floating away...

And sliding into perfect place.

Vivi took off from work to help photograph each painting and spent hours on the Internet searching for churches near our hometown. Because I was fairly certain that those games we'd spent as children, wandering around the countryside surrounding Lake

Taneycomo, looking for the abandoned castle, hadn't been games. And the lost prince... Had to be my gargoyle. Why he might be locked up in the Ozark Mountains... I had no idea. But everything in my gut insisted that was exactly where he was.

My legs trembled with exhaustion when I finally laid the paintbrush down. My eyes throbbed with a brutal migraine splintering through my skull, but I was done.

Silently, Warwick whisked an office chair up behind me as I started to sink to the floor and Vivi immediately started taking pictures.

"I recognize parts of this." Her voice rose with excitement. "The way Taneycomo curves in the background—remember? We could see that bend from the top of Noble Point."

Noble Point had been one of our favorite places. Each summer, we'd built a watchtower at the top and pretended we were Riders of Rohan, ready to light the fires to call the armies to war. You could see for what seemed like thousands of miles in all directions. "Was there a church anywhere near there? I don't remember one."

"Let's find out." She stepped over to a folding table one of them had set up, and Warwick pushed me over so I could see. On top was a large map with red and green circles dotted across the surface. "The green circles are old churches that I know have closed and could be considered abandoned. The red ones are churches too, but they're still open as far as I know."

"Which one's the oldest? With crumbling stone walls and an old cemetery nearby?"

She consulted her meticulous notes. "Not all of them had notes about a cemetery, at least that I could find. It looks like the oldest church in the area is Our Blessed Lady of the Lake." She lifted her gaze to mine, her eyes shining with excitement. "It's near Noble Point too. Let me pull up the images online and see if it strikes a chord."

I tried not to be too excited, but my heart pounded and I held my breath, waiting until she turned her laptop around so I could see the pictures.

The church was definitely old and made of stone, but it wasn't falling down and abandoned.

"This isn't what it looks like today," she said hurriedly, seeing the doubt on my face. "This photo was taken in the nineties and they closed the church to open a new one. The website even says they reused a lot of the stone, but the original foundation is still there. That could be what you're looking for."

I looked over at the gargoyle sitting on the floor near my paint area. Before I could ask, Warwick fetched him over for me and set him gently on my lap. I felt pretty fucking ridiculous turning a stone statue around so he could see the images on the screen. I felt even stupider when I started talking to him. "Do you recognize it? Is this where you are?"

Warwick whistled soft and low beneath his breath. "That's a fine piece of magic I pulled, if I do say so myself. If he can hear you, that is."

"Oh, I think he can hear me just fine. I can't hear him, though, unless I'm sleeping."

"So maybe you should take a nap then," Vivi suggested. "You look like hell. Get some sleep, and we can decide how to proceed next."

"Thanks a lot," I gave her a wry grin, but I nodded, my eyes already trying to glue themselves shut. "The next big hurdle is figuring out how to get Aidan on our side."

Warwick chuckled. "That's the easy part."

"Oh really, Pointy Ears?"

He gave me a heavy-lidded smoldering look as he tucked his shoulder length hair back behind his very-not-pointed ears. "Aidan talks a mean game, but I guarantee the thought of me helping you—without him—has been eating him alive."

I frowned. "I'm not going to deliberately try and make him jealous. That kind of petty shit—"

"No, no, that's not what I meant," he broke in. "You're the treasure-keeper. *His* treasurekeeper. Well, theirs, at least." He looked away a moment, his shoulders tight. "He can't pretend that he doesn't know where you are, now. He can't pretend that he doesn't need to be by your side. That you don't need his assistance. Because you do. And it's his own damned fault that he's not here helping you. That I'm here in his place... like I said, it's eating him like a cancer."

I glanced over at Vivi and she tipped her head to the door, silently asking me if I wanted her to leave. I hesitated a moment, my fingers stroking over the statue in my lap, but then I gave her a slight nod. Her lips curled up and her eyes flashed with amusement, glee, and a whole lot of I-told-you-so. "I'm going to head home for a bit and get some sleep too. Call me when you come up with a plan for busting Aidan's balls."

My eyes were still gritty and sticky, like I needed to sleep a week, but my brain was firing super-sonic fast. There was so much going on that I didn't understand. I stood on a precarious ledge over a rushing, dark, freezing-cold river that would suck me down at a moment's notice.

A river that gleamed like the dark emerald of Warwick's eyes, even though he didn't look at me.

"What do you mean, I'm *theirs*?" I asked softly, watching his reaction, waiting for him to turn around and face me again.

He tipped his head to the side and lifted his shoulders in an elegant, casual shrug, even though he still refused to look at me. "The treasurekeeper is female. The treasures are male. They're drawn to her, and only come into their power fully when they're united with her. In this century, I'm sure you have no difficulty understanding what that generally means."

Now it was my turn to drop my gaze, in case he dared turn and see my reaction. I studied the gargoyle in my lap, turning him over so I could see his face. The crooked, broken nose. The fierce expression staring up at me. If I closed my eyes, I could hear Doran's rough growling voice whispering to me. His hands sliding up to cup my face as I pulled him down to me. It'd only been a dream, but it had felt right. Natural. Like my body already knew and recognized him.

When I met the other treasures, I'd felt that same instant physical connection. Not merely physical attraction, exactly, though I was certainly attracted to them as well. It was a sense of belonging and completion, like I'd been missing a part of my soul all my life, and hadn't even realized it until I found them. I'd dared to squeeze Aidan's junk and wrapped my palm around Keane's throat while trying really hard not to lock my mouth over his. Even though I'd just met them— it didn't seem that way. It felt like I'd always known them. The only thing that had saved Ivarr was the table between us, and the fact that his two friends were closer to me. If he'd been sitting there in Aidan's place, I would have touched him too.

I didn't think I'd be able to *not* touch him. Any of them. It was like a compulsion. A need to be in their personal space and breathe the same air as them and warm my skin with their heat. All four of them. Gah. I couldn't quite wrap my mind around it. Let alone five…

Am I actually considering it? Five, even four, men?

Shivering, I bit my lip, wondering what Doran would say if I admitted to feeling the same deep-seated need to touch the flirtatious leprechaun. The only man who was willing to help me find him.

"I'm not helping you to put you at a disadvantage, or to make you feel as though you owe me." The unusually solemn tone in Warwick's voice drew my gaze back up to his. At least he was looking at me again, though the corner of his mouth quirked with a wry twist of resignation. "It's been my pleasure to be at your disposal, and I expect nothing else in return."

I had to remember that he picked up on my thoughts. It was… disconcerting, to say the least. "Because I'm the treasurekeeper. I get it. You must feel the… pull of magic too."

"Not at all." When my eyes flared with surprise, he quickly said, "That is, I feel a pull, aye. And it's magical. But it has nothing to do with you being the treasurekeeper."

Skeptical, I searched his face, trying to decide if he was being truthful. The fae were famous for not being able to tell a lie, right?

Though in the fairy tales, they usually tiptoed along that line and used it to their advantage. He certainly seemed to be the kind of guy who'd love making Aidan or Doran green with envy.

He chuckled and came closer, though all he did was sit back on the table in front of me. "Well, that's certainly a bonus I'm not regretting in the slightest, though I do feel a twinge of guilt about making poor Doran jealous, when he's been imprisoned in stone for so long. Aye, we fae cannot tell a lie, though that doesn't mean you always hear the unvarnished truth, either. It's easy to lie with silence or pretty words that are meaningless, and if you want my silence because the truth is too painful, I'll give it."

I shook my head. "I don't want lies, or silence, even if it's uncomfortable. I'm just trying to wrap my head around what all this means. Are the treasures fae too? Immortal or mortal? Are they reincarnated the same every time? Am I reincarnated? Or am I... me?"

"They can and do die. In fact, they have died the last several times they were reborn. Though that's not the best word. They're not born as babies. One moment they're in Tír na nÓg, the Otherworld, living the life of celebrated heroes who saved the mortal world numerous times over many thousands of years... and the next, they're here, for a very short time. They come into this world knowing what their destiny is, and aye, that burden has become almost impossible to bear after so many times. They're fully cognizant of how much they've lost and endured every cycle. Those memories are still there, even after a period of rest beyond the veil. In many ways, it would be easier for them to die immediately and return to that haven, rather than toil in your world and wait for a brutal death. In that regard, I admire their valor a great deal, despite Aidan's reluctance to step in and help you directly. He could have given up and ended it a decade ago, but chose to remain and fight, even if that meant watching you or his brethren die again. Doran has been trapped for centuries now, unable to even return to the Otherworld."

He reached out and lightly touched the back of my hand resting on the gargoyle. I turned my palm and entwined my fingers with his, and the same familiarity pulsed in me, like a melody that'd been playing in my head, though I couldn't remember the lyrics.

"You are uniquely Riann Newkirk, mortal through and through. You have whatever memories and magic you pull to you as your destiny unfolds, but you are not reincarnated or reborn as a previous treasurekeeper."

"Then why does it feel like I know you, and them, when I just met you?"

He lifted my hand to his mouth and softly brushed his lips over my knuckles. "You know them because they're your destiny. Only you can bring the treasures together and bring the world back into balance."

"And if I fail...?"

"Then you die. The treasures die. And your world slides more fully into Balor's grip. The light grows dimmer every day, and if we lose you and the treasures again..." His lashes fluttered down over his eyes and he pressed the back of my hand to his cheek. "I fear the treasures will be lost forever. Balor is too strong in this world. He'll imprison all four of them, as he's trapped Doran, rather than allow them to return to the Otherworld. Your world will be overrun with demon spawn."

I swallowed the lump in my throat. It slid down into my stomach and lay there cold and heavy like a ball of lead. "Balor is...?"

"Balor of the Evil Eye, the Fomorian king of demons. He wants the treasures' powers as his own, and if he gains access to them, your world is doomed."

His cheek was soft against my hand, not rough with stubble at all. Such a small thing, but a stark reminder that he wasn't human. His hair was even softer, like the delicate down on a baby duck. I'd never dated a man with long hair. I liked it. A lot, actually. I pushed my fingers deeper, loving the way the strands curled around me, clinging to me. Begging me not to stop. I thought it might be all in my head, but as I touched him, his hair grew longer, magically spilling down his shoulders, a thick, black wave of silk, called by my touch. As if...

He leaned closer, letting his hair tumble forward over my arm. "As if grown simply for your enjoyment, aye. If you want my hair trailing behind me on the floor, I can make it so."

The thought of all this black silk sliding over my skin made me shudder. I wanted his hair falling down around me like a curtain, sleek and soft, smelling like—

I leaned closer and lightly touched my face to his hair.

He smelled green and fresh and lush, like a jungle of flowers and fruit, bursting with life. His skin smelled even better. Warmer, richer, like chocolate and furs before a fireplace, soaking in the heat. His pulse beat strong and steady against my mouth. I opened my lips and touched the tip of my tongue to his skin.

In a heartbeat, he scooped me up and strode toward the bed in the corner. My heart hammered, with anticipation and anxiety, both. I clutched the gargoyle to me, afraid to look into his stony face. Afraid to close my eyes and see Doran grimacing in my dreams, accusing me of being unfaithful. Of betraying him. He'd already threatened to kill Warwick, for fear that he'd hurt me.

But how could I be unfaithful… when I'd never met him outside of a dream?

Was this all an impossible dream?

Warwick lay me down on the mattress but only sat beside me. I stared up at him, relieved, but also disappointed. His lips quirked, revealing his dimple and the wicked twinkle in his green eyes. "I would never dare climb in bed with a gargoyle, unless he invited me."

My cheeks blazed and he laughed, his eyes glowing with warmth. I shoved the gargoyle off my thighs to the mattress beside me, though yes, the statue was still in bed with me. Glaring.

"You wondered if I was only interested in you because you're the treasurekeeper."

Biting my lip, I nodded.

He leaned down and braced one forearm beside my head. His hair fell down around me, like a black silk curtain. Exactly as I'd pictured before. "You stepped into *Shamrocked*, an unknowing, mortal woman. Granted, you had to have some excellent luck to find yourself crossing into Faerie, but I didn't know you were the treasurekeeper. Not until you saw Doran on the shelf."

My eyes widened. Yeah, I remembered that. We'd been chatting and laughing, and I'd let myself think about taking home this insanely sexy, laughing bartender. The better to kiss my old life goodbye, right? I was a free woman, the first time in years. I did hesitate at the thought of taking a stranger to Vivi's house without her approval. That was the only thing that kept me from scribbling my phone number down on a napkin for him. Or simply asking what time he got off work. I'd sat there drinking Guinness and imagining what it'd be like to have another man in my bed. A man not my ex-husband, for the first time.

And then bam. Everything had changed.

I stared up at him, my lips parting with surprise. He really had been attracted to *me*.

Riann.

Not the treasurekeeper.

He lowered his head and sampled my lips in a soft, delicate nibble. His breath sighed out and he lifted his head enough to look into my eyes again. Emerald starbursts swirled in his irises, spinning and sparkling in a dizzying array. "Alas, I dare not indulge in more than a sweet morsel to tie us over. You would regret more until you've freed Doran and hear his opinion of me directly from his lips."

He made perfect sense. But that didn't stop me from surging up from the pillow and trying to kiss him again. Deeper. I wanted to taste the dark hollows of his mouth. Feel his tongue stroking mine. Would he taste like exotic fruits and dark chocolate too? Or would he taste like whiskey? Or something else entirely?

His eyes spun brilliant green arcs throughout the room. I felt his mouth again, the softest touch. His whisper against my lips. "Sleep, *mo stór.*"

My eyes were so heavy. I fought to stay awake. To touch him. Taste him. It was like swimming up through miles and miles of ocean. My arms were so tired. I started to slide into darkness. Too fast. My nerves shrilled with fear, my stomach pitching. I had too much to do. I couldn't sleep—

Doran's arms closed around me, his grizzled cheek rough against mine. "Now it's my turn, *mo stór.*"

I clutched his neck and burrowed deeper into his embrace. "Don't kill him. Please."

"I wouldn't dream of it, love."

I breathed deeply, inhaling his scent. He smelled like... a hot summer night with a thunderstorm rumbling on the horizon. A bit of ozone burn in the air, mixed with the musky smell of a man who'd been hard at work battling monsters.

He huffed out a laugh and pressed his mouth to my shoulder. "You have quite the imagination where your nose is concerned."

I rubbed my face against him, curling against his solid chest. He felt so safe and strong. Like nothing would ever get past him. Nothing would ever hurt me while he held me. "Why have you changed your mind about Warwick?"

"I'm going to kill Aidan instead."

I lurched up enough to search Doran's face. His brow was heavy with deep grooves down his forehead, but there was a tiny hint of amusement in his eyes. "He wouldn't help me."

"Which is why I'm going to fucking kill him."

"You're teasing."

One eyebrow arched and his big palm slid up my back, pressing me closer to the heat of his body. "Am I, now. Because I assure you, if any harm comes to you because his head is up his arse, he'll beg me to kill him before I'm done."

Even in the dream, my body felt heavy with exhaustion. I tried to lift my head so I could kiss him again, but my muscles didn't want to work. "I think I know where you are."

His big hand kneaded my nape, making my muscles relax even more. "I knew you would find me. Now fetch Aidan to your side, even if you have to shoot him. It'll do you no good to come to me without them."

"I don't have a gun." My words slurred, but I hoped he could understand me. "I don't know how to shoot."

"You don't need a gun to wound Aidan. Take something that

belongs to him. He'll come for it soon enough. Though he may succumb to his jealousy before you can worry about it and come after Warwick."

"I kissed him," I whispered. "Just a little. Don't be mad."

His lips roamed up my throat to my ear. His breath hot. "You kissed me too, so all's well, love. But I'd rather you not fuck the leprechaun until I can join you both."

That made my eyes pop open a moment. "You would?"

"Aye, or you can have a go at us one by one. It's up to you, love."

I nuzzled back into his embrace, my face against his throat. His pulse heavy and strong against my cheek. "I'd like that."

"Which one?"

I drifted deeper into sleep, but I could still feel his arms around me. "All the above."

12

I'd never stolen anything before.

Dressed in black jeans and hoodie pulled up over my head, I casually walked up to the tattoo place and scanned the motorcycles parked in the front. Even standing outside the building, I could feel the treasures' pull. They were here. Inside. Just feet away. The men I was destined to bring together. Destined to love, if Warwick could be trusted.

I'd better be able to trust him. I needed him to tell me how to drive the motorcycle, once I figured out which one was Aidan's.

I touched the coin in my pocket—though I honestly didn't think I needed to any more. *:Which one's his, Pointy Ears?:*

:How am I supposed to know? I'm not his treasurekeeper.:

I blew out a sigh and walked up to the first bike. They all looked pretty much the same. Fairly heavy machines with big, thick tires, chrome pipes, and black leather seats. I stretched out my hand, intending to touch the leather seat, but it didn't feel right. Holding my hand out, I walked down the row. There. This one was Keane's. I was sure of it. I could see him flying through the night, leaning into the curves, revving the engine ever higher with a vicious smile on his face. The next one was Ivarr's. He was the sneaky one. He hung back, quiet, casual, reserved. You'd never suspect him, until it was too late, and you realized he'd let the air out of your tires, or stuck gum to your seat before you sat down.

The next motorcycle was Aidan's. It was a little lower than the other two, a bit of a wider seat. It looked... meaner, somehow. I didn't know anything about motorcycles, but it wouldn't surprise me if his had more horses under the hood. I touched the leather seat and could hear the low, rumbling growl of the engine and see Aidan's lips curled in a vicious snarl.

:This is it:, I told Warwick as I threw my leg over and climbed onto the motorcycle. It felt wide and heavy between my thighs. Very much like straddling a man. A very thick, muscled man. It made me shiver deliciously. It'd be way better if Aidan was sitting behind me, his powerful arms locked around me as he drove us flying down the highway toward Doran.

Warwick pressed against my back, his arms coming around me to grip the handlebars. "How about me instead?"

I leaned back against him and scooted my butt back so I could feel his erection hard against me. "Yeah. That'll do just fine. How do we start this thing?"

He stretched out a finger and a pop of green energy surged from his fingertip like a lightning bolt. Energy spun down into the motor and it roared to life, rattling and shaking beneath me.

Oh. Sweet. Heaven.

That was fucking fantastic.

He laughed against my ear. "Now you know why I changed my mind. I want to be *here*," he ground against my buttocks, "rather than drive from afar."

"Oh yeah."

He revved the engine, making the glass rattle in the windows with the deep throaty roar. Unless they had the music cranked again, someone inside should hear the distinctive rumble of the motorcycle. Hopefully Aidan would recognize the sound of his own bike.

"He will," Warwick promised. "Plus, he should feel you close. If nothing else, he'll be twitchy, impatient, and unable to concentrate."

He tipped the bike upright, still revving the engine so loudly he didn't try to talk in my ear. *:I'll disappear when he makes an appearance. Make sure you entice him to follow. I'll keep you safe, though. Don't worry about trying to drive. Just hold on.:*

"Hey! What the fuck are you doing?"

Show time. I looked over my shoulder as Aidan came charging out of the tattoo place, a fierce scowl on his face. I blew him a kiss and then turned around, leaning low over the handlebars. I couldn't see Warwick any longer, but he was still a heavy, if invisible, weight against my back. My hands moved, giving it gas, and my thigh shifted, like I was tapping a pedal. I relaxed into it, not fighting his control. The tires squealed on the pavement, the smell of engine and gas and rubber filling my nose as we tore across the parking lot. We shot across the road, leaning hard side to side as he guided us through traffic.

The bike rumbled between my knees, stirring my lust ever higher. Fucking hell. I'd never been so turned on, and here I had two guys interested… and nothing I could do about it, until I found Doran and freed him from the curse.

:They're coming,: Warwick whispered in my head.

Yeah, I could hear the roar of motorcycles behind us. Deep in the pit of my stomach, I felt a tug, an awareness. The treasures were in hot pursuit. Exactly as we hoped.

WE LEFT THE MOTORCYCLE PARKED OUT IN FRONT OF THE WAREHOUSE. Vivi had argued with me for hours, but I'd finally convinced her to stay home. I didn't need her to get in the middle of this, especially if Aidan was nasty. I had to protect him from her wrath—until I got through to him. Because if she saw him being mean to me, she might never forgive him, even if I did.

I'd gone back and forth in my head about whether Warwick should be present or not. He didn't demand to stay, though his eyes had narrowed and his lips flattened out in a displeased slant when I first mentioned it. I felt kind of bad, but I decided to let him stay, so I could use his presence to keep Aidan on edge.

:Use me,: he purred in my head. *:I love it. You can ride me like that motorcycle anytime.:*

Great. As the three surviving treasures stomped into the warehouse, my cheeks blazed fire-engine red.

Aidan strode straight toward me and belligerently bent down to shove his face close to mine. "What the fuck do you think you're doing?"

His game was obvious. He thought to scare me. Drive me away. But even though he was furious, the air vibrated between us, singing with joy as his proximity. He didn't scare me. In fact, I'd never felt more energized and powerful. He was magnificent in his fury. His eyes blazed, his jaws clenching, the muscles twitching in his cheek.

I grinned and batted my eyes, watching his face flash. "I'm kidnapping you."

"What the fuck is that supposed to mean?"

Keane and Ivarr stood behind him trying not to grin.

"Doran told me to shoot you, but I didn't have a gun. So I improvised."

Aidan turned that fierce look on Warwick, who lounged like a negligent, bored lord of the manor in the office chair off to the side. Which, of course, he'd positioned in front of the makeshift bed.

"What's the leprechaun got to do with it?"

I still didn't completely understand the dynamics between the four friends, but I had the strongest connection with Doran. There was a reason he'd been the one imprisoned away from the other three. He was their leader, their rock, the one who kept them together. His only concern about Warwick was that he'd hurt me, but he'd proven he was willing to do whatever he needed to help me. To stay with me. Even if that meant sharing my attention with Doran, and ultimately, the other three treasures.

So if Doran was okay with it…

I sauntered over to Warwick, dropped down into his lap, and looped my arm around his neck. "He's mine, too." The strangled look on Aidan's face almost made me laugh. Gently, I added, "I've come to an understanding with Doran. I hope I can come to that same understanding with you."

"What," he rasped out, "understanding?"

Warwick's hand playfully stroked down to my knee, his other hand toying with my hair. "I won't do more until Doran is free to join us."

"Do more." Aidan strode over and planted his hands on the arms of the office chair, leaning down close into our space again. He gave Warwick a hard look meant to intimidate, but my leprechaun smirked at him and lifted my hand to his mouth. He kissed each knuckle like it was a priceless artifact. "What have you already done?"

My heartbeat quickened, but not because I was afraid. Aidan glowered at me, his lips curled in a vicious snarl, but his pulse hammered so hard in his throat that I could see it. I could almost hear his thundering heart.

I focused on his lips. "I kissed him."

He wasn't going to make it easy for me. A man like him never would. But he didn't push up in disgust and walk away, either.

I cupped his cheeks, smoothing my fingers over the straining line of his jaws. I rubbed my thumbs in the harsh frown lines, easing away some of the fury burning in his eyes. But the emotion that replaced his anger made tears burn in my eyes. Agony. Hopeless, desperate agony.

"If I let you in, I can't lose you. I can't. I won't survive it. I'll surrender to Balor myself and hand my weapons over to his minions so they can chop me into a thousand pieces. I won't be reborn again."

I brushed my lips against his and his hands clenched on the arms of the office chair so hard that plastic cracked. "What happened to the last treasurekeeper?"

"She died. And it was my fault."

13

He straightened, without getting his full kiss, and averted his gaze, as if he couldn't bear to even look at me.

"What happened?" I asked softly.

"I was jealous. I wanted our treasurekeeper to myself. Balor used that jealousy to entrap Doran. He surrendered to buy her time to escape, but the demons fucking killed her anyway and we lost Doran too. It feels like it happened yesterday, even though it was nearly five hundred years ago. We've been reborn several times since, and we fail. We fail and we die, because we can't free Doran. Without him, we're nothing, and it's entirely my fault."

Unknowingly, I'd put him in the very worst position imaginable. I'd made him jealous, again, by bringing Warwick into the mix. But I couldn't bring myself to regret that decision.

"It's too late for me to give up Warwick to have you," I whispered, my throat aching. But he had to have the words. He had to understand the depths of my emotions.

Warwick didn't say a word, but his hand tightened on mine and I felt a surge of emotion from him. Not words, exactly, but relief and desire and overwhelming, aching need to hold me close and never let me go.

He was the only reason I'd been able to get this far. The only reason I had any hope at all of finding Doran. So if Aidan couldn't deal with that...

Aidan nodded, still not looking at me. "Perhaps if I'd not been a dick that night in the pub and spoken to you then, it might not be too late now."

"You knew, then? And you didn't say anything?"

His lip curled with disgust. "Aye, I knew. I was a fucking coward. I saw you staring at that statue and I felt the stirring of magic in my bones. But you laughed and smiled at the fucking leprechaun, and I couldn't bear to watch you die. I thought I could avoid you and keep you safe. Keep you out of our mess. But then you came to see us."

"And she stole your ride," Ivarr finally spoke, pulling my attention to the other two treasures. "That was fucking brilliant. The one sure way to piss him off and get him to chase."

Now that he had my attention, Ivarr strode closer and went down on one knee before me. "You haven't touched me yet, treasurekeeper. Do you not feel my pull?"

Using the tip of my index finger, I traced the neatly trimmed line of beard along his jaw and around his chin and mouth, then back up the other side. His eyes gleamed like dark-gold honey, sucking me in. Making me wonder if his lips would taste as sweet. I leaned closer and his breath sighed out, his chin tipping up to me. I didn't kiss him immediately, but brushed my cheek against his, inhaling the scent of his skin. He even smelled like thick golden honey, sticky sweet and warmed by the sun.

He chuckled, a warm, inviting sound that made me want to laugh too, even though I had no idea why. "Honey doesn't have a smell."

My eyes flew open and I backed up enough to see his face. "You can hear my thoughts too?"

"We all can. We've been touched by Faerie. We've walked the green, green hills of Tír na nÓg and tasted the nectar of the old gods. We aren't human any longer."

I shot a glare at Aidan's back, but Ivarr cupped my cheek, his thumb brushing over my lips.

"Don't be mad at him. We have to listen to hear, and he quit listening a very long time ago."

"I was fucking sick of hearing Doran bellow in my fucking ear," Aidan retorted, but without real heat. He even turned around, watching as Ivarr and I touched each other for the first time.

"Magical," Ivarr whispered. "I forgot how wondrous it was to touch the treasurekeeper. I feared we'd already lost you in this cycle. That maybe you'd never be gifted to us again."

I leaned in, holding my breath. The softness of his lips against mine made me shiver. He opened his mouth against mine, inviting me to taste him. I slid my tongue into his mouth and tasted the sweet honey directly from his tongue. His kiss was like drinking molten sunlight. I could feel his energy pulsing through me, heating my body, sizzling through my bloodstream, straight to my core.

I lifted my mouth and stared into his eyes. "No darkness can stand against your light."

"Not with you and my brethren at my side. My light hasn't shined in hundreds of years. Not without Doran, and not without you."

Keane stepped up and laid a hand on his shoulder. "My turn."

Ivarr scooted to the side, but pushed his head and shoulders up under my left arm so the heat of his body ran down my left side. Evidently he didn't mind Warwick's thigh in the way either.

Staring up at Keane, the image I'd painted flashed through my mind, the red stripe down his forehead and nose.

"The war stripe of my clan," he whispered, his eyes flaring. "You saw that? I haven't worn that stripe in a thousand years, at least."

"You should warn her," Aidan said, his voice gruff.

"No one walks away unsatisfied," I replied, trying to keep my voice light and teasing, even though I didn't really know what that meant exactly.

"It means..." Keane went down to his knees in front of me and leaned in, giving me a playful, sultry look. His dirty-blond hair tumbled down over his forehead and his whiskey-brown eyes gleamed almost as brightly as Ivarr's dark honey. "You'll like my touch very much indeed."

"What's that supposed to mean?"

"My touch is orgasmic." He held up gloved hands and waggled his fingers. "So is my kiss. You can touch me, that's fine. But when I strip these gloves off or touch you with my mouth, you will climax over and over, until I can finally break away from the contact, or you simply can't come any longer."

"That sounds fantastic and also terrible at the same time."

He huffed out a laugh and nodded. "Aye, that's the perfect way to say it. I'll blow your mind, but if I can't stop touching you, I'll risk pushing you too hard, too far. Even pleasure can become pain when it's given in excess." Staring up at me, he sighed, a frown tugging his luscious full lips down. "It's been a fucking eternity since I touched a woman, treasurekeeper. I won't be able to control my gift much at all, at least for awhile."

Holding my breath, I leaned toward him. "My name is Riann."

Braced for a cataclysmic eruption, I lightly pressed my lips to his. He made a pleased hum against my lips and opened his mouth slightly, his tongue gently tracing my bottom lip. I opened for him, letting him stroke inside my mouth. So tender and gentle. I relaxed against him, softening. It was just a kiss. Not a mind-blowing...

He turned his head slightly to fit his mouth more fully to mine, and something tightened inside me. Like a current suddenly blazed to life, burning a line of power from my mouth deep into my core. My nerve endings jerked awake, screaming with sensation. My breath oomphed out against his mouth as he slid his tongue deep.

My back arched, my hands scrambling at his shoulders, his hair. Warwick shifted beneath me, too, easing his dick more fully beneath my buttocks. A torment. To have him there, so close, but not inside me. To feel such an incredible surge through my body. I gasped into Keane's mouth, shaking as climax poured through me. It felt like my fingertips lit up and I was spinning rainbows through the room. I shook and groaned and writhed on top of Warwick's lap, while Ivarr pressed closer, his mouth on my shoulder, sharing in my bliss.

It went on. And on.

My muscles started to cramp. A massive charley horse seized my right thigh. My eyes burned and I threw myself back so hard I almost cracked my head into Warwick's nose.

Panting, I stared at Keane. His lips were swollen and full, his eyes smoldering with lust. He leaned back toward me and I slapped my hand onto his chest, holding him back. "Oh no. I think that's plenty until we find Doran."

He gave me a dark, heavy-lidded look so hot that my shirt should have gone up in flames. "Are you sure?"

I nodded jerkily. "Definitely. I promised him I wouldn't do more than kiss any of you until we found him. And if you kiss me again..." I gave a little wiggle on Warwick's lap, making him groan.

Keane laughed and backed away. "Yeah, right. Maybe you should let me do it again, though, just to watch the leprechaun squirm. It'll be worth it."

We all looked at Aidan, and he let out a low growl. "Did you steal my wheels just to kiss us?"

I didn't need any of them to tell me not to push him. Aidan would touch me in his own time—or not at all. It was his choice. "I know where Doran is."

"Well, that's fucking grand." He retorted so sarcastically I wanted to punch him. "But how do we fucking free him once we find him? Did you think in all these cycles that we've been reborn, that we never managed to find him? We have. It fucking sucks to stare up at his statue and be unable to wake him from the stone slumber Balor cursed him into. Do you know how you're going to wake him?"

"I'll figure it out when I see him."

"Motherfucker. You don't have a fucking clue, do you."

Irritation made me surge up out of Warwick's lap. I stomped over to my paintings I'd lined up against a makeshift wall. "The answers are here. We just have to decipher them."

The four men joined me. Ivarr let out a low appreciative whistle. "You painted these, *mo stór?*"

"Yes. What does that mean? *Mo stór?*"

"My treasure."

"But you're the treasures."

Ivarr and Keane looked at each other and shrugged, but it was Aidan who surprised me by replying, "And you're *our* treasure."

14

I was nervous about the guys meeting Vivi. I knew it was stupid. I knew she'd never do anything to deliberately hurt me, like flirt with my boyfriend or come on to him. Even if I had four or five boyfriends. It wasn't her I was worried about.

It was them.

Jonathan had made a pass at her once when he was drunk. She'd clubbed him over the head with her purse and he'd hated her afterwards. But the point was—he'd still done it. Maybe all men were weak when it came to gorgeous women. Maybe I wouldn't stand a chance once they saw her.

It didn't matter how often they called me "treasure." Not once they caught a glimpse of my red-headed goddess best friend.

She strode in before the sun rose the next morning bearing a to-go carrier of several cups of coffee that I knew she'd made at home. Her hair was loose about her shoulders, shining like gorgeous red velvet, and she'd donned plain blue jeans—that looked painted on her ten-mile long legs. She hadn't put on any makeup, but she didn't need to for her perfect skin to glow.

Meanwhile, I'd pulled my dark hair back in a ponytail, my eyes were puffy and red with exhaustion, and I wore a shapeless hoodie and dark jeans. Yeah, they were as tight as hers and I filled mine out plenty, thank you very much, but I had to be honest with myself. If any healthy male had his choice—

A hard hand grabbed my arm and spun me around. I crashed into an equally hard chest and Aidan's mouth came down on mine. He inhaled my mouth, one hand sliding behind my head to clutch me tightly to him. The smell of leather engulfed me, partly his jacket, but his scent too. Leather and gunpowder, the clash of swords and war. Panting, he lifted his mouth and pressed my face into his neck, squeezing me so hard I could barely breathe. His pulse thundered against my cheek. *:You're ours, Riann, as no other woman could ever be. And if you think I'd rather look at some random woman than you, then you'll be snatched up and kissed like this again until you know that you're the very breath I need to stay alive.:*

My eyes burned. I slid my hand up beneath his jacket and clutched a handful of his shirt in the small of his back, softening against him. He was so hard, vibrating on the edge of violence, uncomfortable to even lean against. Prickly and sarcastic, rude as hell.

And mine, all mine.

He huffed out a harsh laugh, dropped a kiss on my head, and loosened his fierce hold on me. But now that he'd put me here against him... I didn't want to leave.

"Good morning," I said to Vivi, turning my head enough to see her without leaving his arms.

"Good morning to you too." Her eyes danced with amusement as she set the drinks down on the table. "Looks like you've been a busy girl."

"You have no idea."

"So, what's the plan?"

"I've shown them the paintings and the maps, so we have a rough idea of where we're going. The only problem is that they don't know how to free Doran once we find him."

She handed me a cup, and though I loved leaning against Aidan, I loved her coffee, too. After yet another sleepless night, I needed caffeine more than I needed to hear his heart beat beneath my ear. I didn't move away from him entirely, though, and he kept his arm looped around my waist, his hip pressed to mine. "There aren't any clues in your paintings?"

"Not that we can tell. The paintings are more clues to his location, not how to free him."

"What about your dreams? Anything there?"

I sighed. "I haven't slept in forever, and the last dream…" My cheeks heated, making her snicker. Even Aidan cracked a smile. "Let's just say Doran hasn't been too interested in telling me how to break his curse."

"Well, all we can do is try with what we know. Should I rent us a big car for the drive down? Maybe an SUV?"

Aidan shook his head. "We've got that covered, as long as you don't mind catching a ride on the back of a motorcycle."

Despite his demonstration a few minutes ago, my stomach did a queasy flip-flop at the idea of Vivi clutching one of my guys around the waist as we drove down the road, her face on his back.

"Excuse us a moment," he said to Vivi, and then he cupped my cheek and dragged me back against him in another toe-curling kiss. He claimed my mouth like he was staking his territory, stealing my breath and crushing my lips beneath his, his tongue deep in my mouth. He slid his fingers up into my hair, messing up my ponytail, twisting his fingers just enough to make me feel his strength. To wonder what it'd be like to have him gripping me so firmly in bed, trapped beneath his weight.

I groaned into his mouth and he lifted his head, his eyes glittering like clashing swords. :*There will be no more worrying in this regard. You're ours. We're yours. End of story. Trust me to keep your faith and heart intact.*:

Sagging against him, I made no protest when he took the cup from my hand and held it for me. It was a miracle I hadn't poured the whole cup out on the floor. Now that would be a travesty.

He flashed a grin at me so quickly I almost missed it and shifted me around toward Vivi again.

She looked around, up at the ceiling, over at my newest painting, a smile on her lips.

"It's safe to look now," I said, though my words were slurred.

Laughing, she turned back to me. "Whatever's going on, you should definitely keep doing it so you get more kisses like that."

Aidan lifted his chin toward the door as my other two guys came in. "Here's Keane and Ivarr. They've arranged our escort." To them, he asked, "Are they ready?"

"They'll be here in ten minutes," Keane replied. He sniffed the air and his eyes lit up. "Is that coffee I smell?"

Vivi held out the carrier. "Help yourself."

He knocked back a long drink and sighed like he'd sipped nectar of the gods. Meanwhile, I was mesmerized by the way his throat moved as he swallowed. There was something so raw and sexual about him, even when all he did was take a drink.

"And the other things we discussed?" Aidan asked.

"Done as you ordered," Ivarr replied.

"What?" I asked.

"Precautions in case we don't come back." Aidan said it as casually as if he'd said I should grab an umbrella, it might rain. "The leprechaun too?"

"He agreed."

"What are you talking about?" I demanded, pulling away from the hard warmth of Aidan's body.

He looked at me, his eyes grim. "If we can't free Doran, we don't walk away. We die. But this time, we're taking steps to ensure you do walk away. Warwick will see to it."

I couldn't breathe through pain that ripped through me. Aidan's memories flickered in my head like pages turning in a book. Death, after death, after death. His head chopped off. A sword through his heart. Crawling across the ground, gasping, his lungs filling with blood, trying to reach her.

The treasurekeeper, the one he'd loved so much that he'd lied to Doran, accidentally betraying him to Balor's curse.

Blood and darkness, pain and loss. My chest hurt so bad I started to slip to the floor, though he caught me up against him.

"Ri? Are you okay?" Vivi's hand touched my cheeks, fluttering like a small bird. "Here, sit down."

They helped me sit in the office chair, and Aidan crouched before me, holding my hands. Lines of pain and regret bracketed his mouth and eyes. "I didn't want to share that with you. I'm sorry, Riann. I tried to shield you from the darkness of my failures."

"How many times have you died?" I cried, wiping my tears away.

"Too many times to count."

I closed my eyes and I saw her again, the woman he'd loved. She'd been small, too, like me, but otherwise, we looked nothing alike. She'd been fragile and perfect like a painted porcelain doll, her golden hair in ringlets about her face. "What was her name?"

"Cassandra, and she was far from perfect. Beautiful, aye, but..." He blew out a sigh and dropped his gaze our clasped hands.

It was Ivarr who continued the story. "You'd think that a legend like ours would be good, right? That we'd call the best treasurekeepers possible to our side. That good would always triumph. We'd send the demons back to hell and the people would cheer. But that rarely ever happened, even before we lost Doran. People are people. Some are good. Some are evil. Some are selfish, vain, and heartless. Unfortunately, we were given a treasurekeeper that liked us to fight over her affections rather than work together. She was a distraction, not a conduit. A true weakness. And it cost us our friend and leader, and destroyed our bond."

"It was my weakness, and we'll speak no more of it," Aidan growled, more like himself. He gave my hand a squeeze. "I intend to see this treasurekeeper survive whatever darkness we meet trying to free Doran. So we will do all that we can, and if the situation becomes dire, as it has so many times in the past, Warwick will whisk you away to safety."

"No. I don't want to leave you."

"You will. You must."

"Aidan—"

He shoved his face close to mine, his eyes frosted over glacial blue.

"You. Will. Leave. I can do whatever I must. I will die. Gladly. If only I know that you're safe."

I leaned into his space too, bull dog to bull dog, my eyes just as fierce. I hoped. "No, I won't. Because we're going to free Doran this time."

"You can't possibly know that."

I softened my stance enough to press my forehead to his, cupping his cheeks with both hands. "I do. I know it. I will it to be so."

"But—"

"I wouldn't argue with her," Vivi said, shaking her head. "Once she's made up her mind, she won't change it."

Even when I'd decided to marry a man who made me miserable. She was right in that regard. It'd taken almost five years to make me finally open my eyes and admit that I'd made a mistake.

Doran was different. They all were. Jonathan never would have been willing to talk about sharing me in a million years, even if the guy I wanted had saved my life a hundred times. Let alone with four guys. They were willing to make concessions for my happiness, bending their pride, swallowing their ego. Even Aidan.

Even when Warwick materialized underneath me, popping me up into his lap and making me let out a startled squeal.

Apparently that was the most hilarious sound they'd ever heard. Aidan somehow ended up falling back on his ass he laughed so hard. "Very funny, Pointy Ears."

"I thought so," Warwick replied smugly.

I stood up and Warwick and Aidan both snapped to their feet immediately. "Now let's go get my gargoyle."

15

Stealing Aidan's motorcycle had been fun—but flying down the freeway toward Lake Taneycomo behind him on the same bike was even more fun. Since I *had* stolen his bike, he guilted me into riding with him on the trip down Interstate 65. We rode at the point of the vee, with Ivarr and Keane on either side of us. Warwick rode directly behind us, and then the rest of the motorcycle gang roared along behind. Vivi hadn't hesitated a moment when the guy we'd first talked to at the tattoo shop offered her a ride behind him.

I was curled against Aidan's back, my arms tight around his waist. He'd insisted on helmets and the heaviest coat and clothing I owned, and it was a good thing. I was still chilled to the bone. I forgot the wind would whip around us, even with his broad back to serve as a windbreaker. :*I'm surprised your friends came along for the ride.*:

:*They're more than friends. They've helped us on quite a few jobs.*:

What kind of jobs? They'd been playing poker and they rode motorcycles.

I felt his amusement echoing in my head, even though I couldn't hear him laugh. :*There's a reason our club is named Demon Hunters.*:

Oh wow. I tried to imagine one of those bearded guys going after a demon and couldn't quite picture it.

Aidan sent a hard chill through my mind like a blade shining as it was drawn from its sheath. *:They're here for your protection. We're going to need all the help we can get to make sure we keep you safe.:*

My teeth started chattering, and it wasn't just from the chilly wind slicing through my parka. *:We're going to fight demons* now?*:*

:If you're right about Doran's location, absolutely. Balor will have set at least a few guardians to make sure we have as difficult a time as possible trying to set him free.:

Well, fuck that all to hell. It never occurred to me that we'd have to fight the demons to *free* Doran. I thought we needed him free to fight whatever war was coming.

Aidan's shoulders tensed against me. *:We've been fighting this war for thousands of years, and losing. That's why I wanted you to let Warwick take you to safety, if—:*

:Don't say it.:

:Not saying it won't change the reality.:

I hated the brutal reality he kept trying to convince me was our future. Hugging my thighs around him tighter, I slipped my right hand down and squeezed his dick like I'd done that first day. Yeah, he was rock hard, even though I sat behind him. *:You don't get to die until I've had this inside me at least a million times.:*

"Yo," Keane yelled over at us. "She gets to ride with me on the way home."

"Not fair, ye fucking bastard," Ivarr retorted. "Besides, Doran'll be all over her when we free him."

My cheeks burned. I didn't think they'd notice if I groped Aidan a bit, but at least Ivarr agreed we'd be freeing Doran, rather than Aidan's grim prediction.

We pulled off the interstate and started the winding path up and down the steep, wooded, narrow blacktop road toward Noble Point. A sense of familiarity hit me, a surge of homesickness that I hadn't expected. I didn't have the best relationship with my parents, now divorced and remarried with new families that had never felt like mine. They'd left the area long ago, and I didn't have anyone here I'd ever cared to come back to visit. My best and only friend was Vivi, and we'd escaped to college and then decided to live in Kansas City, far from the trailer park where we'd grown up and the rich kids who'd made fun of us.

We'd never looked back.

But these wooded hills stirred something deep inside me. A longing for something I hadn't realized I missed. Or maybe that ache was for Doran, my prince I'd searched for as a child. What if he'd been waiting nearby, frozen in stone all this time, wondering why I'd abandoned him? The thought fucking wrecked me.

We paused at the top of Noble Point while Vivi consulted the map to get our bearings. Aidan felt me shivering, and tugged my hands up inside his jacket. She stepped off the bike and came over to me, turning the map around so we were oriented with the lake behind us.

"It looks like we could drive back around this side of the hill, but it's a couple of miles out of our way before the road curves back down to the bay below. Do you remember that one trail we used to take home from school? I think that'll get us close, and then maybe we can just cut through the woods."

We'd always taken the quiet, wooded routes home from school, both because we loved the outdoors, and to avoid the bullies. "Yeah, that trail is just over there, I think."

Aidan signaled the rest of the riders and they cut their engines. I climbed off his bike and hopped in place a little to get my blood flowing. Excitement coursed through me. We were close. We had to be.

My smile faded as I watched them arm themselves. Like in my painting, Aidan pulled two curved sheaths out of the storage saddle on his bike and belted them around his waist. Then he slipped on a backpack with the gargoyle's head poked out of the top. I wasn't sure if I'd need the statue or not—but it didn't seem right to leave my connection to Doran behind.

Ivarr had an actual broadsword strapped to the side of his bike that he slung over his back. Keane had some kind of massive gun that he locked against his side. He saw me watching and winked at me. "Flame throwers work great on demons, as long as I don't catch the forest on fire around us."

My stomach clenched with dread. I didn't want any of them to get hurt. Let alone... I swallowed a massive lump in my throat and put on a bright smile. "So what weapon did you bring for me?"

"Me," Warwick slid up beside me and looped his arm around my waist. "I'm your most secret, deadly weapon of mass destruction. You point, I fire."

I gave him a suspicious look, hoping that he didn't intend to just whisk me away like they'd planned. I'd be royally pissed. Like seriously. Furious. I thought that very hard at him, but his eyebrows only lifted innocently, his eyes sparkling like faceted emeralds.

The other guys carried a motley assortment of sawed-off shotguns, blades, and Vivi's biker had a wicked-looking battle axe in one hand and a dagger in the other. I thought she'd come close to me and Warwick, but when she met my gaze, she shrugged and stuck close to the guy she'd been riding with. Naturally, he gave her a besotted grin. Hopefully she'd be safe enough with him.

The trail we'd used as kids was overgrown enough that we had to walk single file. Aidan took the lead, with me behind him, and Warwick on my heels. There hadn't been much snow or ice, thankfully, or the trail would have been treacherous. Some snow still packed against roots and rocks, but nothing on the hard-packed ground of the trail. My thighs ached by the time we made it to the curve that lead away from the lake and toward the trailer park where Vivi and I had both lived. The lake lay through the trees to our left, and though the leaves were gone, there were enough pine and cedar trees that we couldn't see the waterline.

"It's a bit steep," Aidan said, concern lining his brow. "It might be slippery."

Ivarr scooped me up in his arms, making me squawk like a strangled chicken. "Put me down."

Ignoring me—but giving me a huge, hopeful smile—he started down the steep terrain littered with stones and dead fall. "Aidan had you all to himself for three long hours. Though I'll warn you, if you grab my junk while we're hiking down to the lake, I can't guarantee we won't end up flat on our backs, sliding down into the water."

"Hold up," Aidan called softly.

Ivarr paused and Keane and another guy moved around us, slipping their way down the slope. "Let them scout ahead. See if anything's lying in wait."

My anxiety ratcheted up a notch as I watched Keane weave through the trees. If something happened to him... to any of them...

Ivarr shifted me in his arms, lifting me higher so I could put my face against his throat. "None of that, now, treasurekeeper. We have a duty to see to your safety, first and foremost, but secondly, to eliminate Balor's minions in the mortal realm. You can't keep us from this duty, but trust me when I say that each of us is a formidable weapon that'll make any demon hesitate, even our human comrades."

"And if... when," Aidan corrected himself when I leveled a narrowed look at him, "we free Doran, we'll be damned near invincible."

A low whistle floated up toward us, and Ivarr continued moving downhill. I glanced back over my shoulder, and saw Vivi safely in her guy's arms too. In fact, she was staring up at him with a stunned look on her face. Aha. Maybe my gorgeous friend had at last met her match.

I studied the man carrying her. He wasn't the normal slick, handsome, expensively dressed man she normally went after, but speaking from experience, that wasn't a bad thing at all. He was strong, and tall enough that he didn't have difficulties carrying her, even though she was nearly a foot taller than me, and he certainly handled her like a priceless artifact. Mr. Rough and Tough had turned to putty in her extremely beautiful hands.

We cleared the trees and stepped out onto a pebbled beach.

"Vivi, left or right?" I asked.

"Um... left."

"Do you feel anything?" Ivarr asked me softly. "Any hint that we're going in the right direction?"

"Not yet. Is that bad?"

"Not necessarily. He's been cursed a very long time. We might have to be nearly on top of him before you can feel his pull."

I could have asked for Ivarr to put me down, but I liked being in his arms. He didn't make me feel weak, but treasured. There was a difference, and if I got to touch him in the process, then we both won. As long as none of the others got mad at him. Though I'd already seen enough of their good-natured jokes and ribbing to suspect that they'd just come right up and take me from him if it was a big deal.

Except for Aidan. I had a feeling he would watch from afar, and if I wasn't careful, he might start to stew a little. Especially once we freed Doran. It was something I'd have to keep an eye out for, so that we didn't go down the same jealousy and betrayal situation that had led to the curse.

In a few minutes, we found a faint trail that led up a small hill. Keane called down, "There's a ruin up here. This might be it."

I squirmed and Ivarr set me down. I hurried up the hill to Keane and paused a moment, looking at what remained of the old church. Breathing hard, I scanned the churchyard, looking for anything familiar. A single lone tree stretched skeletal branches into the dull gray sky. A little creepy, but nothing like the trees crowded close in my painting, trying to devour the gargoyle statue. And of course, no statue. Just a small square foundation made out of cement blocks and an overgrown flagstone path.

The motorcycle guys fanned out, looking for anything suspicious. I took a deep breath and headed down to the old church, even though I knew the truth.

"Doran's not here," Aidan said, his tone flat. "This isn't right."

I didn't want to admit that I was wrong. It had to be this area. It had to be a church. An old church.

Old church.

My brain itched like I was on the verge of something momentous. A massive surge of inspiration.

My name. My name is Newkirk. Kirk is Dutch for church.

I whirled and dragged the map sticking out of Vivi's pocket. "You said they took the stone from this church and built a new one. Where is it?"

She pointed to one of the red circles a bit further up the bay. "Here. It's still called Our Blessed Lady of the Lake Church."

"We need to go there."

None of them questioned me or voiced any doubts. They didn't say, *"But Riann, you painted an old ruin, so how could Doran possibly be at a brand-new church built just a few years ago?"* Aidan jerked his head toward the beach and immediately, the guys headed that way, Keane scouting ahead as before. My eyes burned, my heart thumping too hard against my ribcage. This had to be it. I had to be right. I couldn't bear it if we'd come all this way, and they'd believed in me. Trusted me. And I'd been wrong.

The pebbled beach narrowed, trees marching down close to the water's edge. A little bit of ice crackled at the shoreline, but the man-made lake flowed like a river and was too fast and deep to freeze over completely. The winter temperatures hadn't been cold enough, and spring was just weeks away. In fact, as I ducked beneath a low sycamore branch, I saw buds, ready to burst forth as soon as it warmed a bit more. Roots and stumps made treacherous hurdles for someone with short legs, but with Warwick on one side and Ivarr on the other, they offered me a hand when I needed it to hop up and over a downed tree.

Aidan jumped across a ditch and paused, looking back at me, worry grooved deeply in his forehead. "Be careful. It's too far for you to jump."

I rolled my eyes. "Yes, Mom."

Arching a brow at me, he waited, one boot on a thick dead tree that made a sort of bridge over the narrow inlet. Warwick helped me up onto the log. Holding his hand, I eased out over the ditch. Well, it was actually more like a small creek than a ditch and several feet across. How the fuck had Aidan jumped over this thing without even getting wet? Let alone carrying Doran's statue on his back.

At least the log was fairly wide and I had good balance. Warwick held my hand until I was just a few feet from Aidan and then let go. Aidan stretched his hand out, reaching for me.

Something wrapped around my ankle and jerked me off the log.

With a startled screech, I fell into freezing cold water, but it wasn't that deep. I struggled to my feet in knee-deep water. My clothes were soaked through. Fuck. That'd be a problem in this weather. I hadn't brought a spare outfit. I scanned the water, but didn't see anything suspicious or scary. Aidan shrugged off the backpack and came bounding down the creek bank toward me, his eyes fierce. A short sword in each hand.

Someone bellowed, "Alarm! Attack!"

And suddenly I was flat on my back again, dragged through cold water, spluttering, my head slipping beneath the surface of the frigid water. My shoulder crashed into a rock, pain shooting down my left arm. My ankle throbbed. What the fuck had me? I couldn't see anything. It was all I could do to keep my head above water. And then I couldn't. Water closed over my head. So fucking cold. Taneycomo was below fifty degrees even in the hot Missouri summer, and even worse in the winter.

I tried to feel down my leg to get free, but whatever had me was still moving too quickly through the water. I couldn't sit up against the drag. Something dark swooshed over the top of me, gliding by like a shark. Only the flash of a silver blade told me it was Aidan. A red cloud suddenly filled the water and the vise clamped around my ankle released me as quickly as it'd dragged me off the log.

Freed, I swam toward the surface, my lungs burning. I shivered so hard I bit my tongue. My arms and legs trembled, making my movements clumsy. I wasn't going to make it. I'd die a foot away from air.

A blaze of green light hit the water and parted it like Moses split the Red Sea, clearing a shallow path toward me. Letting me breathe. Warwick. He came running toward me on a glittering green bridge of magic. Coughing and spitting out water, I managed to shove my numb arm up so he could grab my hand and drag me up out of the remaining water into his arms. I looked for Aidan, and then wished I hadn't. Because the thing that had grabbed me was like some horrific bad dream.

Long sickening-pink tentacles twitched and writhed in the water. I thought it was some kind of freak octopus, but it had a horse head.

A horse with tentacles.

:*Kelpie*,: Warwick said in my head. :*A big one, too. He'll need help with it.*:

Ivarr came toward us at a dead run, his long black coat flapping behind him like wings. He leaped, lifting the sword high above his head, and light poured out of his chest. Only this light sustained him in the air so that he flew over the lake. With one stroke of his massive sword, he hacked a deep slice into horse's neck, almost lopping off its head. Though it hung there, flopping, screaming out a strident whinny.

Aidan surged up out of the water and finished the job. Still twitching, the tentacles folded up like a writhing nest of thick snakes and sank into the deep channel.

Warwick carried me to shore. I was shivering so hard my muscles were cramping up. Vivi touched my cheek and hissed. "She's ice cold. We've got to get these wet clothes off her."

"I didn't. Bring. Spares."

"Give her to me," Keane demanded, shoving the flame thrower out of the way.

I would have groaned if could get my muscles to cooperate. I'd already tasted his kind of magic and I didn't think I would be able to survive climaxing on top of hypothermia. Surely there was another way to warm me up.

Pulling me toward him, though Warwick still held me too, Keane locked his mouth over mine. I braced for the surge of desire. Instead, he breathed fire into me. Glorious heat. Tiny sparks spun through my blood stream, cascading brighter and hotter. It hurt, too, like I'd swallowed a gallon of scalding hot coffee, but it was heavenly at the same time. My skin started to heat, like I was sunbathing. Hot enough that Warwick must have felt it too. I heard the catch in his breath, and felt a subtle shift of his grip on me.

:*We're both going to come when the magic peaks*,: Keane warned in my head. :*Pointy Ears, too, if he's touching your bare skin. But you'll be warm and dry and hopefully not scorched.*:

Um, yeah. Scorched would be just as bad as frozen.

The fire coursed through my body and settled deep in my groin. Liquid heat pooled there, making my muscles ache. My pussy clenched, and I couldn't hold back a moan. I hurt, but with need this time. I hooked an arm around Keane's neck. My other hand was tangled up in Warwick. His hair, it felt like. Maybe his shirt too. As desire crested in me, magic flared deep in my stomach in a spinning circle. Keane and Warwick were like spokes of the wheel, but the hub was inside me. The wheel tried to spin, but some of the spokes were missing. It wobbled, off balance and incomplete, yet the magic rolled through me and spun back toward them in a stronger wave.

I was the conduit. I magnified their power.

If we could find Doran and make the wheel complete…

No wonder Balor wanted the treasures broken apart and crippled.

No wonder the kelpie wanted to drown me. Though I didn't have any power of my own… I made the formidable treasures even stronger.

The wave of power hit Keane and his fingers tightened on my cheek as he groaned into my mouth. Warwick pushed against me, sandwiching me between him and Keane, and I thought I'd die with bliss. Now I trembled from head to toe, but with pleasure. I'd never really thought about having two men in bed at the same time, but now that I felt them shaking, coming against me, even though they weren't inside me, I wanted it. I wanted it so badly that a very horny part of my brain insisted it'd be a grand idea to take them down to the ground right here and have my wicked way with them.

"Right, so Ivarr and I are out there saving your cute arse, and you're too busy coming all over each other to even say thank you."

Keane released my mouth but I sagged against him, nestled between him and Warwick. I finally managed to get my head to turn, enough to look at Aidan, and while he wore a fierce scowl, his eyes weren't frosty. They blazed like blue fire.

"She was cold," Keane said. "I warmed her up."

"Fucking eejits," Aidan retorted, shaking his head. "Did it not occur to you that the leprechaun could have bathed her in magic and taken away the chill with a thought?"

Warwick rubbed his mouth against the top of my head and let out a pleased little sound that made my inner muscles tighten all over again. "This was more fun. Though I will bathe us now so we don't stink of sex as we go free the gargoyle. I don't want him to beat me into a bloody pulp for touching her."

Green light spilled through me. I heard tinkling chimes and his scent rolled over me: a green, lush jungle, sweet fruits and flowers, bright and colorful and glorious.

They set me on my feet between them. My clothes were dry, even my parka. My hair was fluffed out like I'd stuck my head under a dryer. I'd lost the ponytail holder somewhere. Warwick doused himself and Keane, and then dumped green magic over Aidan too, so he was dry after diving in after me.

He came closer and I threw my arms around him. He squeezed me tightly enough I grunted, unable to breathe. But again, this was a good pain.

"I thought I fucking lost you," he whispered roughly against my ear. "Don't fucking do that again."

"Are there going to be more kelpies ahead?"

"The fuck if I know. Probably worse things, to be honest."

Great. I blew out a sigh and pulled back enough to see his face. "Thank you. And you too, Ivarr. What you two did was incredible."

Ivarr smiled cheerfully. "At least we know you're on the right track. No way would a kelpie be camped out in this random lake in Missouri if it wasn't guarding something important."

"You did kill it, right?"

His smile slipped to a grimace. "Hopefully, aye. But even beheaded kelpies can sometimes work their twisted dark magic and sprout a new head."

"Maclin, Taz," Aidan called, and two of the motorcycle guys came over, one of them handing over the backpack carrying my statue. "Watch our backs and keep a close eye on the water. We don't want that fucking kelpie sneaking up on us. Keane, Smith, take point again."

Vivi came close, gave me a hard hug, and then looped her arm through mine. "That was scary."

"Yeah, tell me about it." Even though she was walking beside me, she kept looking off to her right, where the biker dude strode a few paces away. He kept casting furtive glances her way too. I lowered my voice. "So what's his name?"

"Hammer. I know, it's stupid, but I kind of like it. I kind of like him."

For the first time in my life, I heard anxiety in her voice. Like she was afraid of upsetting me, or disappointing me. Or worse, that I would judge her choice and think less of her. When she'd done nothing but blindly and faithfully support me through all my mistakes and missteps my entire life. My throat ached, but I forced a lightly teasing tone to my voice. "I like him too. He reminds me of a big teddy bear."

Her breath sighed out and she patted my hand on her arm. "Yeah, that's the perfect metaphor. He is like a cuddly teddy bear, though he can be a grizzly when he wants to be."

"With a name like Hammer, who's a member of the Demon Hunters Motorcycle Club, he's going to whip some serious ass to protect you."

"And bring all his friends over to drink beer and play poker and watch sports on television."

I laughed. "Sounds fun. When do I get invited?"

"Oh, honey, you're already invited. Unless you're too busy trying to beat five guys off you with a giant stick."

"About that giant stick—" Ivarr said, way too loudly, making all the guys laugh.

My face burned so hot even my ears crisped. "Don't even go there."

16

"This can't be it," Vivi whispered beside me.

I didn't say anything aloud, though I agreed. This church was one of those mega-churches with soaring steel-beam construction, big enough to house a couple of gymnasiums, shopping center, and probably a couple of coffee shops and delis too. I couldn't imagine any of the old stone from the quaint little country church we'd just left being reused in such an ultra-modern facility. Let alone would I expect to find a giant stone gargoyle inside.

Disgusted with myself, I started to turn away, but the smaller gargoyle on Aidan's back caught my attention. Just as he had that first night in the pub, the statue stared at me and wouldn't let me go. Aidan backed closer to me, and I reached out and laid my fingers on top of the gargoyle's head.

My vision flickered and I wasn't seeing the gargoyle in the backpack any longer. It was dark. Silent.

"Doran?" I whispered, straining to feel him. "Where are you?"

"Can you hear him?" Aidan asked.

"No." It came out closer to wail than I cared to admit. "I can't see anything. Wherever he is, it's dark."

"Then he's not outside. Do you hear anything? Listen for the smallest sound. A ticking clock. Anything."

I closed my eyes and tried to sink deeper into the stone, putting myself wherever he was. "No voices. No music."

"How about a heater or fan? Anything man-made?"

I held my breath, waiting. There was a faint scratching sound. Not rhythmic or consistent. I listened a few more minutes and then realized what it was. I'd heard that sound often enough as a kid. "A mouse. It's either in the walls, or making a bed in something."

"Right, now that's something, sure," Ivarr said. "I can't imagine this brand-new fancy church having a mouse problem. Maybe an outdoor building then. Do you smell anything? Can you smell through the connection?"

I took a deep breath, but all I smelled was the lush, fruity flowers of Warwick's scent.

He chuckled. "Backing out of the nose zone."

I waited, trying to breathe normally as I filtered through the various smells around us. My eyes still saw darkness—but my nose was smelling Aidan's leather jacket and a hint of Vivi's perfume. I closed my other hand on the statue and leaned closer, until my forehead touched the stone. I concentrated on the cold stone against my skin. The intricate carvings of vein and muscle in his straining shoulders and forearms. The more delicate structure of his wings. I ran my finger over the bump in his nose and I was there. In that dark room. With a mouse. And the smell of gasoline, oil, and hay. Old cut grass.

My eyes flew open and I let go of the statue so I could see. "An outbuilding for lawn mowers."

Without waiting for a signal, Keane and the other scout raced ahead of us looking for anything like that. Aidan strode after them, so rapidly that I had to jog to keep up.

"Slow down a bit," I gasped. "I want to touch him and see if I feel anything else, but I won't be able to see."

Warwick and Ivarr came up on either side of me as I put my hand back on the statue. That way if I fell trotting after Aidan, at least one of them would be able to catch me. But then they lifted me between them and we were all running. I couldn't see, but I guessed that Keane had signaled them.

Then I felt him. Doran. It was like he reached deep into my stomach, fisted his hand in my intestines, and dragged me straight toward him. I fought the urge to throw up, the sensation was so intense. Someone threw open a door hard enough it crashed back, making me flinch. I let go of the statue but I still couldn't see much, because we stood inside a dark metal shed. I smelled the gas and oil, just as before, and there were two large lawn tractors, but I didn't see a seven or eight-foot tall gargoyle anywhere.

"Where is he?" Aidan asked softly, turning around to check me.

The fist in my stomach twisted and jerked down toward my feet, making me groan. I pointed at the ground. "Down. He's down. There. Somewhere."

Ivarr and Keane pushed one of the mowers back against the wall and kicked debris aside.

"Here," Ivarr said, his voice tight with excitement. "There's a trap door. Move that other tractor back."

Keane pushed the other mower out of the way and Ivarr lifted a large trap door. Wooden steps led down into a hole in the ground.

"We have to go down there?" Vivi asked, her voice shaky.

Neither of us liked holes in the ground much. I reached out and she took my hand, squeezing tightly. As kids, we'd taken shelter from tornadoes in a dank hole in the ground very much like this one. At least it wasn't warm enough for the snakes and creepy crawlies to be out.

Ivarr drew the heavy sword and held it in both hands before him. Soft golden light surrounded him in a nimbus and he stepped down into the hole. "It looks like an old storm shelter that they're using for storage now. It's piled with junk. Hold on."

My jaws ached, my teeth clenched together with anxiety. I gripped Vivi's hand so hard my fingers cramped. My pulse thumped in my head, driving me nuts. It seemed like an eternity before Ivarr's head popped back up and he held his hand out to me. "*Mo stór*, your prince awaits."

My heart leaped. I met Aidan's gaze, and he nodded, almost smiling, but his eyes were still guarded and reserved. They'd found Doran before—but hadn't been able to free him. He wouldn't get his hopes up, only to have them dashed again.

"Keane, go ahead of her. The rest of you, spread out around this building and this hole. If anything tries to seal our exit off, we need you to raise the alarm. It's our only way out."

I started down the first step, but Vivi still clutched my hand, and she didn't budge. Her face was pale, her palm clammy against mine.

"Panic attack," she whispered, her voice shaking. "Give me a sec."

I looked around for her biker guy. "Hammer, right? Yeah. Please take care of her."

"No, Ri—"

I firmly placed her hand into Hammer's and let go. "There's no reason for you to suffer a panic attack. This is my fight. Stay up here and stay safe."

I took a deep breath and went down after Ivarr, clutching his hand. Aidan and Warwick followed, the leprechaun's green magic spinning jewels through Ivarr's golden light. Broken planks lined the earthen walls, with sloped shelves still holding mason jars coated in dust so thick they had to have been left here for decades. Someone's old root cellar, no doubt, and the summer's canning haul preserved forever. A jumble of broken furniture was stacked around the perimeter. The smell of dust and decay made my nose itch.

In the center of the cellar stood something twice as tall as me, covered in a dusty canvas. My heart pounded. It was the right size from my paintings. Keane and Warwick took a corner of canvas and pulled it back carefully, trying not to sling dust everywhere.

I gasped. A soft sound of recognition. The same fierce glare, busted nose, straining shoulders, and clawed feet from my dreams. His wings were tucked around him like a cloak. Even hunched down, he was still a foot taller than Aidan, and twice as wide. I stumbled forward and reached up to touch his face.

Cold, hard stone without a hint of life.

Tears spilled from my eyes. "What have you tried in the past, so I don't waste our time?"

Aidan grimaced. "Everything."

"You're the key," Keane added. "That's all we know. The treasure-keeper was the trap, and the treasurekeeper is the key to unlocking it."

"Don't think I'm weird, okay?" Aidan's eyebrows arched but he only nodded, silent as I touched the statue. I laid both hands on the gargoyle. I touched his nose. His face. Ran my hands across his shoulders. I pressed both hands over his heart—at least where I guessed it would be—and closed my eyes, willing him to come to life. Willing him to breathe. Move. Anything.

Nothing.

I stretched up on my tiptoes and pressed my lips against his jawline. Aidan gave me a boost up so I could kiss the cold, stone lips. But my stone prince still didn't come to life.

"What about blood?" I asked as he set me down.

He shrugged. "Tried it, each of us. We've all touched him at the same time. But nothing works."

"Give me the smaller statue, but this time I want to hold it."

He turned around and Warwick helped me lift the heavy statue out of the backpack. I sat down on the ground in front of the real-life statue, with the miniature copy on my lap. I closed my eyes and laid both hands on the smaller statue.

Chills raced down my arms. "I can see myself. He's there, looking at me. I can feel him."

"Then why the fuck can't he tell us what we need to do?" Aidan muttered.

I closed my eyes and concentrated on the statue in my lap. I sank into him. Willing myself to become stone, so I could feel what he felt. Maybe hear some stray thought or clue. But the rustling sound was annoying. It kept distracting me. It sounded bigger than a mouse. Ugh. If it was a rat…

I opened my eyes and searched the corner where I heard the noise. Two beady, red eyes flashed back at me. "I think there's a rat over there."

The sound of drawn steel made my teeth ache. "That's no rat."

Ivarr and Warwick both blazed brighter, driving back the darkness to reveal a hairy hunched shape. It looked like a big rat, or maybe an opossum, a light gray with a nasty pink tail. But it had big ears and shiny teeth, more like a badger or beaver. It was gross, but I wasn't immediately alarmed.

"How many?" Aidan asked in a low voice, sliding closer to me.

"Ten over here," Ivarr whispered on my right.

"The same," Keane said on the other side of Doran.

Warwick backed up against me from behind. "Same here."

"Fuck." Aidan growled. "Warwick—"

"Aye."

"What are they?" I asked, still not sure why they were so worried.

"Imps," Aidan replied. "If there's anything you can think of to try and break the curse, you'd best do so now. And fast."

I gulped and looked up at his grim face. "What's wrong? Why are imps so bad?"

Keane flipped a switch on his flame thrower and it roared to life, dripping liquid fire from the muzzle. "Imps like to eat people. But they won't touch you, *mo stór*."

17

E at people? Fuck.

I scooted closer to the gargoyle, with the smaller one on my lap, wracking my brain to think of a way to break the curse. I set the smaller statue beneath the larger and looked at them both together. They were exactly the same. But why did I feel Doran so much better —and see through the larger one's eyes—when I touched the replica? Was it because of Warwick's magic that had created it? I couldn't think why that'd make a difference. My hands trembled and I caught myself nibbling on the skin on the inside of my thumb nail, a bad nervous habit I'd broken long ago.

I brought up each painting in my mind, flashing through them again. I couldn't think of anything that would help. I had the treasures. I had found Doran's hiding place. No other clues were there.

I came back to the small statue. The connection I felt when handling it.

A sudden flash of heat blasted through the small room and something screeched. The stink of burning hair filled my nose. Aidan lunged and scuffed behind me, his breathing loud. The sound of his blades sinking into flesh made my stomach heave. Or maybe that was the smell of blood mixing with the charred hair.

"Ow! You little slimy motherfucker," Ivarr growled. "My sword isn't much use against something so fucking small. They're too damned fast."

"Keep the light as bright as possible," Aidan said, his voice tense. "It'll slow them down a bit. Keane, you're really going to have to burn as many as you can."

"Right, I'm on it." Keane managed to sound cheerful, even as he roasted a bunch of little hairy monsters with a flame thrower. "At least as long as the fuel holds."

"How long?" Aidan asked.

"Twenty, maybe thirty minutes."

"You heard him, Ri. That's your ticking clock. Then Warwick's getting you out of here."

I bit back the arguments and entreaties. He'd only ignore me. My best bet was to figure out how to break Doran's curse. Then it wouldn't matter how long Keane could roast the imps and keep them back. I pressed my lips to the little gargoyle again. I touched his nose. I closed my eyes and prayed. I hugged him. I yelled at him.

And the stone glared back at me, silent and frozen.

Tears burned my eyes. I risked a quick look around to see how the guys were holding up. Blood ran down Aidan's cheek and he held his left arm awkwardly, clamped against his side like it was hurt. A chunk was missing from the sleeve of his leather jacket. Ivarr's shirt was bloody beneath his coat. Exactly as in my painting. Dirt and sweat streaked his face, deeply lined with exhaustion. It must tax him to have to keep the light so bright, and he'd also had to help kill the kelpie. Keane shot controlled bursts of flames from the weapon on his hip, but I could tell by the tightness on his face that he was worried. Seriously worried.

Warwick pressed against my back, one hand on my shoulder, his green magic spilling down over me. Shielding me.

We're running out of time.

I squeezed my eyes shut and remembered the last time I'd dreamed of Doran. He'd held me while I fell asleep. He'd whispered my name and stroked my hair, his voice so gentle and deep, lulling me to sleep.

Or the dream when he'd almost made love to me. It'd been so real. If we all died, I'd never have the flesh-and-blood version of that dream. I'd never get to capitalize on the heat in Aidan's blue eyes, or the sultry curve of Keane's luscious mouth. Or feel Ivarr's light bathing my naked skin in a golden glow. Or wrap myself in the black silk of Warwick's hair.

A tear slipped down my cheek and dripped onto the miniature gargoyle. I didn't remember picking him up again. I sniffed and wiped the dampness off him, my finger settling in the hollow of his throat below his Adam's apple.

His naked throat. There wasn't a necklace. The heavy chain, with the stone pebble dangling from it. That'd been in the dream.

I looked up at the larger statue, and he wore the necklace. The chain was as thick as my wrist and the circle was white against the darkness of his stone body.

Scrambling to my feet, I touched the round stone hanging from the chain. The white circle lay on *top* of the statue, not a part of it, even though the chain itself was carved into stone. The round part didn't feel like rock at all. In fact, it felt like bone. *Brittle* bone. I slammed the meaty heel of my palm against it, but it didn't break. I needed something harder.

Aidan cursed beneath his breath. I spared a quick glance at him and I couldn't hold back a cry. Two imps clung to his back, biting him, sinking those long beaver-like teeth through the leather coat like it was nothing. He grabbed one of the hairy beasts by the neck, slung it down on the ground, and stomped it into a bloody smear, but the other one sank teeth into his neck just below his ear, making him bellow.

"I'm out." Keane pulled the flame thrower off his shoulder so he could use it like a club. "The ground's shaking. I think the imps called for reinforcements."

I didn't want to know what kind of reinforcements a bunch of hairy ravenous monsters might call from the depths of the earth. But I had the answer when the dirt wall burst open. A tall, putrid pea-green scaly thing pushed up out of the ground.

"Pooka!" Aidan whirled around and glared at me. "Get the fuck out of here, Riann. Go!"

I picked up the miniature statue and shot a glare at Warwick. "Not yet."

With all my strength, I slammed the smaller statue against the bone-colored disk hanging from Doran's throat.

18

The disk cracked. I slammed the base of the statue down on it again and again, breaking the circle free of the chain. The corner of the miniature statue broke off too, but all I cared about was that ivory disk.

A deep, low growl rumbled from the depths of the ground, and an earthquake heaved me up into the air. I slammed back to the ground, too hard, knocking the wind out of me. The light winked out. I called for Ivarr, but I couldn't hear anything because my ears were still ringing. I coughed, choking on dust and dirt and the stink of something that smelled like roadkill baking on the asphalt for days in August.

I pushed up on my hands and knees, blinking furiously. Something stared back at me. Close. Two red beady eyes blinked. Stained teeth as long as my thumb flashed in the darkness.

My first instinct was to scramble to my feet, but I made myself hold still, staring back at the imp. It tipped its head and made a chirping sound that wasn't scary. In fact, it might have been kind of cute. But then I realized that it was only calling its friends over to share the tasty morsel it'd found. Two more imps joined the one watching me. I didn't dare look away to see where the guys were. I tried to use my senses, but my ears were still ringing. Surely they were okay. An earthquake wouldn't hurt the three treasures who'd already defeated a giant horse octopus and twenty or more hairy dog-sized rats.

The three imps suddenly quivered. Cowering, they scurried backwards into the darkness.

Grinning, I relaxed a bit and rocked back on my heels. "Whew. That was close. Is Ivarr okay?"

Aidan didn't answer. Neither did Keane or Warwick. I could hear heavy breathing behind me, so my ears were improving. The hair at the base of my skull prickled. If it wasn't my guys...

Doran. *I did it. I freed him.*

Heart in my throat, I whirled around and froze.

The pooka stood just paces away, drooling as it looked at me. Lanky hair like seaweed clung to its head and it reeked even worse than the imps. It looked like a green Sasquatch, mostly scaled, but with uneven patches of mossy hair.

Near the stairs, Aidan and Warwick both fought another pooka, barely holding it back. Keane cursed and yelled on the other side of the room, swinging his empty flame thrower like a bat. Ivarr lay on the ground behind him. He wasn't moving.

It took me a moment to realize the large gargoyle statue was gone. Chunks of stone and rubble was all that left. A small cry escaped. Oh fuck. I'd broken him. I'd shattered Doran into a million pieces. *How the fuck am I going to put him back together again?*

"Treasurekeeper." I jerked my gaze back to the pooka, surprised that it could speak. "Evil Eye has promised a great reward for you. Especially if I bring you back alive."

"Bring me back where?"

It grinned, licking slug-like lips that made me shudder. "He never said I couldn't taste you first."

I backed away, carefully, feeling for each step so I didn't fall over a chunk of Doran. A sob tore through my throat. *Doran.*

A massive taloned paw dropped onto my shoulder and jerked me back against cold, hard stone. "You called, *mo stór?*"

19

That voice. It rumbled like granite boulders tumbling down the side of a mountain, but underneath, it sounded like Doran. The man who'd whispered in my head, driving me to paint nonstop for days.

I started to turn to him, tears dripping down my cheeks, but the pooka let out a terrible shriek that made me clamp my hands over my ears. It sounded like a massive train derailing, metal screeching on metal as it came off its tracks. The other pookas came to join it. They bared blood-stained teeth, their long knife-like claws shredding the earth with anticipation, eyes glittering with hatred.

Aidan stepped up beside me and laid a hand on my shoulder. Keane dragged Ivarr up and they limped over to us. Ivarr lifted his head, and both he and Keane reached for me.

All four treasures. Touching me.

The wheel blazed to life inside me, spinning with Ivarr's golden light. All four spokes. Whole. Balanced. Complete.

Then Warwick stepped closer, sliding his hand around Aidan so he could touch me too. Warwick's green magic poured into the wheel, making it spin faster. Brighter. A wave of power exploded out of me. Their power, finally united once more. I trembled as the magic poured into me, swirled around the wheel, and then surged out, a constant, massive flow. I didn't try to direct it, even if I could have. That wasn't my job. Just as when I painted, I surrendered to the muse, or in this case, the treasures, and let them use me as their conduit.

Power slammed the pookas back into the bowels of the earth. Doran's voice crashed like a massive thunderstorm. "Tell Balor that the Stone of Destiny lives and breathes again. The treasurekeeper is ours. The curse is broken!"

He snatched me close and surged up the stairs and out of the storage building. His wings unfurled and he launched into the air, clutching me against him. I twisted toward him and hooked my arm around his neck, burying my face against him. For one thing, he smelled good, like wet stone after a summer thunderstorm. But I also fucking hated heights. If I looked at how high we were, I'd probably throw up all over him.

He still felt like hard stone, but now he was hot to the touch, breathing, muscles moving beneath my cheek. His heart thundered against my ear and I felt his emotions as my own. He flew in a slow circle, drawing in deep breaths of fresh, crisp air, reveling in the sunlight. He wanted to soar as high as possible and roll crazily across the sky, his joy bubbling out on a vicious shout, but instead, he tucked me close and drifted back down to the ground to land with a gentle thud.

He set me on my feet, facing him. Even crouched down, his head was higher than mine. He was a deep, gun-metal gray, just as in my paintings, with black, inky eyes. And yeah, he had a fierce glare, a busted-up nose, huge claws, and leathery wings.

I leaped up to throw both arms around his neck anyway.

He enfolded me close, mindful of his claws. "Riann Newkirk, treasurekeeper, you are victorious this day. You broke the curse that held me trapped in stone for hundreds of years."

His shape flowed beneath my hands, gargoyle's hide fading away to a man's skin.

A very *naked*, very large man, who held me a foot off the ground and tucked me tightly against him.

"Doran!" Keane ran up and gave him a friendly slap on the back. "You're as mean as ever, I see."

Doran grinned and punched him in the shoulder hard enough that the other man grunted and took a half-step back. "Now that's a grand way to say welcome back."

Ivarr joined in, throwing an arm around me and one around Doran to draw us into a group hug with Keane laughing in the middle.

"Hey, now, if there's going to be naked hugging, then I'd rather have *mo stór* between us."

"Pointy Ears!" Doran bellowed. "Rustle me up some clothes."

Warwick laughed in my head, giving me images of Doran dressed like what I'd first thought of when someone said leprechaun. *:What would you like to see him in?:*

I snickered. "Um, you'd better be more specific if you don't want to be dressed in a green suit and pointy ears yourself."

While they made increasingly vulgar suggestions about what my leprechaun should dress him in, I looked around for Aidan. He hesitated a few paces back, frowning, like always. Mean, furious, fists clenched at his sides. But all I felt from him was abject longing and deepest shame.

He wanted to join us. He wanted to laugh and joke and hug his best friend who'd been lost for hundreds of years. But his own guilt kept him locked away. It'd been his fault that Doran had been cursed in the first place, and pride kept Aidan from approaching. He'd rather choose to be ostracized than learn that his friend hated him for his part in the curse.

:Aidan.: I waited until he met my gaze, his icy blue eyes narrowed. I held my hand out to him and he flinched. *:Come here.:*

Glaring at me, he stepped closer and clamped his hand over mine. The other guys quieted a bit, automatically stepping back so Doran saw him beside me.

Tugging a black T-shirt down over his chest, Doran looked first at me, an eyebrow arched. "What do you think, love? Am I acceptable?"

My eyes blurred with tears, but I quirked my lips and gave him a hopefully sultry look. "You were perfectly acceptable as the gargoyle, but honestly…" I paused, and deliberately let my gaze trail down his body. He'd settled on tight, black jeans and the plain T-shirt, which hugged every muscle and bulge to perfection. "I much preferred you naked."

The other three guys roared with laughter, but Aidan didn't even crack a smile as Doran stepped closer. He cupped my chin and bent down to murmur against my lips. "That can be arranged, love. As soon as we're somewhere safe." Then he straightened and leveled a dark look on Aidan. "I told her I was going to kill you."

Aidan's eyes flared and he swallowed hard, but to his credit, he didn't step away or back down. In fact, he nodded and took a deep breath. "Aye, I figured as much."

Doran took a step closer to him and dropped a heavy hand on his shoulder, sliding his big palm up to the back of Aidan's neck. While Aidan stood there, grim-faced and braced for a killing blow.

Squeezing him hard enough that Aidan bared his teeth, Doran leaned down with an equally fierce glare. "Ye bleedin' shite." Then he dragged him tight in a vicious hug. "The next time she fucking asks you to do something, I don't care what it is, I expect you to help so she's not forced to steal your wheels to get you to act."

Aidan pounded him on the back, his voice muffled and hoarse. "I'm sorry."

Those two words echoed between them. Aidan meant it a thousand times over, for everything from the curse, his betrayal, the pain and torture of their deaths since, and finally, his refusal to help me when I'd asked. And Doran knew it, without demanding a complete explanation. That was enough. For him, and for me.

He scooped me up and gave me a toss in the air, making me let out an embarrassing gasp. I told myself it was a gasp, not a screech. Or worse, a squeal.

"Pointy Ears, take us home."

20

Home to Warwick meant *Shamrocked*. I sat at the bar once more, in my seat, but the bar was crowded with my men.

The bikers had stayed behind to make a more leisurely trip home, and I wasn't surprised at all when Vivi stayed with Hammer. The way he went roaring off into the sunset with her arms clutched around his waist, her red hair whipping behind them, told me I might not see my best friend for quite some time. I hoped she had a grand time, and I couldn't wait to be her bridesmaid.

Warwick set a frosty pint in front of me and then bent down, elbow on the bar, chin in hand, a smile flickering on his lips as I drained the whole thing. "I swear, you have the best Guinness in the world."

Doran sat on my left, his right hand jammed into the waistband of my jeans against my lower back. Enough to be possessive—but not crude. At least not yet. He slammed back a shot of whiskey with the other three guys and roared, "Another round, Pointy Ears."

Warwick arched a brow at him, but grabbed the bottle of amber liquid and poured each of them another round. "Considering I was the one who made it possible for you to connect with Riann through the statue, I suggest you remember my proper name."

"Or...?"

Warwick winked at me and gave a casual toss of his head that sent his black hair shimmering down his back. His hair reached his buttocks now. Every time I looked at him, I swore his hair was longer. "Or the next time you ask for clothes, maybe I'll tie a bright red bow around your dick and forget the rest."

"Speaking of dicks—" Keane began.

"Shut your fucking mouth," Aidan broke in.

But Keane refused to drop it. "She's grabbed Aidan's twice now, but she made me and Warwick come already."

"Is that so?" Doran turned enough to give me a heavy-lidded look that made me stammer.

"Only kissing, as I promised. Except I did grab Aidan's junk. He was being... difficult."

"Was he now," Doran said in that low grumble that made my insides quiver. "I hope you gave him a good hard squeeze then."

I gulped and Aidan laughed. "Aye, she did. Though somehow, I never did learn whatever lesson she was trying to give me. I guess I'm too hard-headed. She'll likely have to grab me again, many times."

Doran seized the waistband of my jeans and lifted me up onto the bar in front of him. This time, I did squawk. I couldn't help it.

"I'm going to need this lesson, too, but first, I feel the need to show you how much we treasure you. All of us. Aye, lads?"

"Aye," the rest of them said in unison.

I had no idea what that meant, but the fire burning in Doran's eyes told me it was going to be good. Very good indeed.

"Your Highness, Warwick Greenshanks, Prince of the Summer Isle, would you be so kind as to dress *mo stór* in something more... accessible?"

Prince leprechaun? I looked over my shoulder and he bowed low, though his emerald eyes remained locked to mine. "It will be my great pleasure, Your Highness, Doran Stoneheart, Prince of the Windswept Moors."

I jerked my head around to search Doran's face. "You're a prince too?"

"We all are," Ivarr said. "Except Aidan. He's actually King of the Fallen Dells."

Aidan grunted sourly. "They're called the Fallen Dells for a reason. There's no kingdom left. Balor destroyed it all thousands of years ago."

Before I could ask the other two guys what their formal names were, Warwick snapped his fingers.

I suddenly found myself sitting bare-ass naked on top of the bar, except for the emerald-green corset top I'd worn the first night I found my way into *Shamrocked*. I reflexively started to close my thighs and cross my arms over myself, shocked and yeah, embarrassed. But Doran was sitting between my thighs already, and I didn't want him to think I was afraid. I wasn't, at all. But it was one thing to flirt and tease and kiss, and entirely different to suddenly be so exposed in front of five men. One of which I'd only known in my dreams. Besides, I wasn't exactly one-hundred-percent confident in my own body. Being married to a passive-aggressive asshole had put a dent in my confidence. I was too short, too chunky—

"Now that is a sight worth enduring a dark curse for hundreds of years," Doran whispered, his voice a low, deep rumble that made me shiver. He caught my hand and lifted my trembling fingers to his mouth, pressing a kiss on each fingertip. "May I treasure you, love?"

Oh, fuck, his voice. So deep and growly, goosebumps raced down my arms. But he waited. Looking at my breasts lifted up by the corset, down my nipped-in waist, and finally settling on my pussy, open and bare, and yeah, aching with need. I was wet and more than eager. I just hadn't expected to end up on top of the bar with them all looking at me.

My cheeks blazed but I glanced over to see the other guys' reaction. Ivarr leaned back against the bar, putting his impressive package on display like Aidan had that day at the tattoo parlor. But where Aidan had done it to try and piss me off, Ivarr hoped I'd be tempted to give him a good squeeze while Doran treasured me, whatever the fuck that was.

Keane licked his lips as he circled Doran, coming around to my other side so he could prop an elbow on the bar and look up at me. His hair tumbled down into his eyes, his mouth soft and lush and so damned tempting as he very deliberately stripped off the gloves so he could touch me.

But I wouldn't need his kiss or his touch to come in record time.

"Um, what does *treasure* involve?"

If he meant to take his clothes off and fuck me on the bar, I'd be down with that. Even if the others watched. Especially if they watched, even though the thought made me blush.

Doran stood, kicked the barstool out of his way, and dropped to his knees in front of me. "It involves me licking this sweet pussy until you come, while any man of your choice kisses you and touches you. Then Aidan can slide up here and take my place while I kiss you. And then Ivarr and Warwick. Keane'll go last, because once he touches you with his magic lips, you won't be able to take more."

My eyes were probably almost as big a silver dollars and I was pretty sure my mouth hung open.

He leaned toward me, his eyes locked to mine. "After treasuring comes fucking, if you're up to it, yeah?"

"Yeah." I swallowed hard, trying to string words together. "Please."

He cupped my knees and pushed my legs up on the bar, knees bent, opening me fully to him. "Lean back into Warwick, love. He's got you."

And so I found myself draped back on top of a lovely old-world bar in a Faerie pub while a gargoyle ate me out and a leprechaun kissed me. Warwick cradled me against him, supporting my head with one hand so I could twist around and reach his mouth. His hair tumbled down over his shoulder to pool on my breasts like black silk. Doran took a deep, broad stroke with his tongue up the full length of my slit, making me arch up off the bar. His hands gripped the backs of my thighs, pushing me wider, holding me still. Just enough force to make me revel in his strength. Like when Ivarr had carried me, I didn't feel weak or scared or intimidated, even though Doran was holding me down.

I felt…

Treasured.

Doran licked every inch of me—except my clit. He wasn't a man afraid to get dirty, either. He buried his face against my drenched pussy, using his chin and nose to rub and push on every sensitive inch of me. He slid a thick finger into me and stroked and twisted and pushed harder. Filling me up. Drawing a ragged cry from my lips. I snagged a handful of Warwick's hair in my left hand and gripped the back of Doran's head with my other. He finally sucked my clit into his mouth and I lost it. My hips twitched and I shook beneath his mouth, struggling to free my legs. But he kept me spread wide on the bar, my body open so he could plunge his tongue deep. He groaned against me, tasting my cream, and that set off a whole new round of tremors.

Someone lifted my thigh and pushed his shoulders underneath my knee, draping my leg across his back. I forced my eyes open and Aidan flashed a dark, hungry look at me as he lowered his mouth to my flesh. Doran came up on my other side and tugged the corset lower, so he could slip his fingers down inside. He lifted my breasts out, pillowing them on top of the corset.

"Look at yourself, Riann. Look how gorgeous you are. Your nipples are lush and hard, eager for my mouth. Begging me to lose my mind and sink balls deep into you, even though I promised you could have us all treasure you first."

I looked down my body. My breasts exposed, my nipples rock hard. Aidan between my thighs, ice blue eyes flashing up at me a moment before he sank his tongue deep inside me.

Ivarr moved closer, his eyes shining with his inner light. "May I treasure your nipples, *mo stór?*"

I groaned, my head dropping back against Warwick.

"Was that aye or nay? Doran?"

Doran laughed and rubbed his face against my left breast, rasping the tender nipple with his stubble. It made me shudder on another cry. Again, as Ivarr leaned in and inhaled my other breast. While Warwick kissed my neck and lightly bit my shoulder. I arched up against Aidan's mouth and came again, but this time, I yelled so loudly my throat hurt. When I could finally open my eyes, I realized I'd squeezed my thighs around Aidan's head so hard I'd probably killed him.

I loosened my fierce leg-grip and he sank his teeth into my thigh, his mouth wide, biting hard enough to leave the indention of his teeth in my skin. So then Ivarr and Doran both pressed their teeth into my breasts. Not as hard, but definitely enough to make me shudder and hurt my own ear drums again. I gripped the back of Doran's neck and tugged until he looked up at me. "Please, I need you."

Aidan immediately stepped back so Doran could stand between my thighs. But his fucking jeans were still on. Still zipped.

As soon as I thought it, Warwick waved a finger and Doran's clothes disappeared.

"Thank you," I whispered. Looking at him took my breath away. He'd had a hard life. You could tell from all the scars on his body. His face had been smashed or beaten, his shoulder was scarred, an ugly puckered scar on his side that looked like an arrow or sword had sank through him. Not to mention all the cuts, scrapes, and claw marks that crisscrossed his body in old, thin, white scars. Yet he was Stoneheart, the formidable Stone of Destiny that led the four great treasures of Ireland. And he was mine. All mine.

"Let me guess. All those scratches are from your previous treasurekeepers, because I'm pretty sure I'm going to leave marks on your back when you finally get inside me."

He gripped his magnificent cock and gave himself a slow pump, watching the way I licked my lips. "Tear me up if you'd like, love, but I can promise you that not a one of these scars is from any previous treasurekeeper. Except this one."

He briefly touched his left pectoral muscle, but I didn't see any scar there.

"You, Riann. You have left a deep wound in my heart that only you can fill. You found me when everyone else had given up. When countless others failed. You went against my own friends and bent them to your will in order to save me. You painted day and night, fighting your own exhaustion to find me. So if you have any wish at all, I will meet that need, or die trying."

My bottom lip trembled, but I managed to say, "I have a wish."

His eyes flared with intensity and he stepped closer, leaning down over me. "Aye, love, what is it?"

"I want to see the rest of my treasures jacking off while you fuck me. And then I want Keane to kiss me so we all come together at the same time."

Doran tugged my ass closer to him, his eyes blazing with heat. "That can be arranged, love. Lads, you heard *mo stór.*"

Their clothes disappeared in a flash of green magic, giving my eyes a feast of powerful, muscled men. Aidan had full-color sleeves tattooed on both of his biceps down to his wrists. Ivarr had roses and skulls inked across his chest, with a heavy sword that looked like it'd pierced his heart. Only instead of blood, rays of light burned from the wound. I turned my head to see what Keane had tattooed, but at first glance I didn't see any. He turned around enough to flash a gorgeous colorful back tattoo, so intricate that it'd take hours to explore it all. Something I intended to do at my leisure.

Aidan shot a glare at Warwick. "That's my favorite leather jacket. I had best get it back."

"Not if I'm keeping it," I told him.

He leaned closer, a snarl twisting his lips. "Do you think I'd give you the jacket off my back?" I nodded and dropped my gaze to his dick. He huffed out a laugh. "Right, yeah, so I would."

"Warwick? Do you have any tattoos?"

"Fae skin doesn't take to ink, sadly."

It dawned on me that I wouldn't be able to see him. Not if he was behind the bar. "Can you come around where I can see you?"

"I've got a better idea." Suddenly my head popped up, supported on his chest. He lay flat on his back on top the bar perpendicular to me. And yeah, turning my head, I could watch the way his long, graceful fingers stroked over his erection.

Doran made a low sound that drew my gaze back to him. "Are we all arranged to your satisfaction, love?"

My cheeks colored, and I nodded, reaching up as he came down to me so I could entwine my arms around his neck. "Does this bother you?"

He frowned. "This?"

"Um… Having them all here. So I can watch them."

A smile broke the grim lines of his face and he reached down to position himself. He rubbed his dick against me, making sure to nudge my swollen clit. My legs trembled, my breath catching in my throat. "Never. You're the conduit, our hub. It's only natural that we center around you every chance we get."

He sank into me, taking his time, thrusting only an inch or so, before easing back out. I wanted him, definitely, but I hadn't had a man of such size before. After coming twice already, my clit was so damned sensitive that I couldn't stay still. By the time he was balls deep, I was the one sweating and shaking, when he'd been imprisoned for hundreds of years.

He lowered his chest against me, bracing one forearm on top of Warwick beside my head. "I've had lifetimes to lie in darkness and plot all the wicked pleasures I'd give the lucky treasurekeeper who managed to free me. Granted, I didn't expect she'd be able to bring Greenshanks to heel, but aye, you did, and here he is, lying beneath us both."

"What kind of wicked pleasures?"

He slowly pulled out of me, making me writhe and gasp and quiver all over again. "Look at your treasures, love. Look at the way they stare at you, wishing they were inside you. Wishing we could all be inside you at once. Aching to come in you. On you. Marking you as ours. Would you like that, love?"

I liked it so much that I couldn't even manage to nod my head. I couldn't think. Not with Doran thrusting back inside me. Warwick's stomach lifted in a slow roll, his fingers working his dick so close to me. Keane's breathing, already ragged, his eyes glowing with heat as he came closer, hoping for that kiss. His eyes locked on my mouth.

I stretched out both hands, one for Keane, and the other toward Aidan and Ivarr. I wasn't sure which I had, until golden light crept up my arm, wrapping me in the warmth of liquid sunlight. His dick was like a thick, red-hot iron rod in my hand.

Green magic swirled to life inside me, meeting that golden warmth. The wheel spun, the spokes gaining speed, lifting me up, power cascading higher and higher. I was going to come apart. I'd break into a thousand pieces. Like the gargoyle statue.

"Now," Doran whispered, and Keane pressed his mouth to mine.

I shattered. His breath oomphed out with mine and I felt his magical gift of pleasure spilling through me, and then spinning out to the rest of them. With a guttural cry, Doran thrust deep inside me like he was going to split me open and look for another curse to break. Ivarr groaned, his cock jerking in my hand. I felt hot splashes of cum on my arm and shoulder from him and Aidan. Keane kept his mouth locked to mine, spilling on both me and Doran. Hopefully he didn't mind. Warwick lasted the longest, and I had to admit, part of me was disappointed when his cum was exactly the same as the other men's, rather than green sparkles, though it was pretty impressive that he managed to get some on my breasts.

Doran dropped his weight against me, grinding me into the wooden bar.

I lay there, gasping for breath, my entire body throbbing with pleasure, covered in cum and sweat, and I started to laugh. A good laugh. The kind of laugh I hadn't had in a very long time. Probably since I'd been a kid running barefoot in the woods, looking for my lost prince.

And now I had him. Them, rather. All five of them.

Doran nuzzled my throat. "I love to hear that sound on your lips, *mo stór*, second only to that delightful sound you make when you come that nigh busts my eardrums."

Blushing again, I thumped him on the shoulder. "Where are we going to live?"

"Anywhere you'd like. The world is ours, love."

"Both worlds," Warwick added, his fingers stroking my hair. "I would love to show you the Summer Isle." He sat up, helping me upright between him and Doran, and he chuckled against my ear. "If you'd like green sparkles next time, I can certainly accommodate that. In fact, I can spin rainbows every single time you fuck me, and you can have my pot of gold anytime you wish."

"Aye," the other men said, grinning and slapping each other on the back.

"I think it's time for another drink," Doran said.

"And, um, maybe some clothes?"

Warwick snapped his fingers, giving us back the clothes we'd been wearing, except I kept the corset top and gained Aidan's leather jacket. He scowled, but only a little, and his eyes gleamed like sapphires.

Setting up a line of shots, Warwick gave Doran the bottle of whiskey and then leaned closer to me. I still sat on top of the bar, but everything had changed. It was like picking up Warwick's token and looking at *Shamrocked* through new lenses again. Only this time, I was the one who'd changed.

I ached with the deep, pleasant throb of a well-used pussy. My sensitive clit rubbed against my jeans and made my breath catch every time I moved. And yeah, the corset was way lower than I'd ever dared to wear it before. The brown of my areolae peeked out over the sweetheart neckline. I examined my hands, and slipped my fingers up inside the right jacket sleeve to touch my forearm, remembering how Ivarr had come on me just a few minutes ago. I guess treasurekeepers absorbed that magic, because I didn't feel sticky or gross, and there wasn't any residue left, other than a soft golden shimmer on my hand and a hint of green on my chest.

"Are you well, treasurekeeper?"

"Very well. Fantastic, actually. It's just a lot to take in. I mean, I just had sex with five men on top of a bar."

"Technically, it was three men, a gargoyle, and a leprechaun."

He slipped his arms around me, drawing me back against him. His ridiculous hair spilled into my lap and I combed my fingers through the silky strands, shaking my head ruefully. "You really are going to grow your hair to the ground, aren't you?"

"Aye, of course. We will do anything for you, Riann. Anything at all, just to see you smile. Even if that means stealing the formidable spear's jacket or motorcycle again."

Aidan leaned in, a fierce scowl on his face, though all he said was, "Promise me that the first time you let me fuck you, that you wear that jacket and nothing else."

I batted my eyes at him. "Deal."

"And let me watch. Or better yet, let me participate, right here all over again." Warwick laughed against my ear. "Me lovely thousand-year-old bar will never be the same."

∼

CONTINUE RIANN'S STORY IN LEPRECHAUNED.

Four hot Irishmen sitting in a leprechaun's bar...

All staring at me like I'm his pot of gold.

Oh yeah, I'm one lucky woman.

But everything isn't rainbows and lucky charms with my four Irish treasures. Warwick may have helped me break the curse trapping Doran as the stone gargoyle, but the guys don't trust the leprechaun. At all.

Worse, demons are pouring into our world unchecked despite the four treasures being reunited. I am their treasurekeeper, the conduit that allows their magic to flow, but there are disturbing holes in my memory.

Someone doesn't want me to remember...

And these whiskey-drinking, tattoo-loving, motorcycle-riding badasses are quick to leap to the conclusion that I've been lepre-conned.

LEPRECHAUNED

LEPRECHAUNED

HER IRISH TREASURES

Four hot Irishmen sitting in a leprechaun's bar... All staring at me like I'm his pot of gold.

Oh yeah, I'm one lucky woman. But everything isn't rainbows and lucky charms with my four Irish treasures. Warwick may have helped me break the curse trapping Doran as the stone gargoyle, but the guys don't trust the leprechaun. At all.

Worse, demons are pouring into our world unchecked despite the four treasures being reunited. I am their treasurekeeper, the conduit that allows their magic to flow, but there are disturbing holes in my memory. Someone doesn't want me to remember...

And these whiskey-drinking, tattoo-loving, motorcycle-riding badasses are quick to leap to the conclusion that I've been lepre-*conned.*

For my Beloved Sis.

Thank you to Sherri Meyer
for all your help and late night edits!

1

Life with the four Irish treasures wasn't going to be all rainbows, pots of gold, and lucky charms.

Barely a week ago, I'd woken up in bed with a stone gargoyle statue, and my life had not been the same. Now I sat in a leprechaun's bar with five gorgeous men at my beck and call.

Great, right? What more could a girl want?

For one thing, a bed—for sleep. I'd been painting for days, trying to find clues to Doran's whereabouts so we could break the curse. I hadn't slept much at all. I'd almost died in Lake Taneycomo, we'd freed Doran, and the four treasures had brought me back to *Shamrocked* for some incredibly hot sex on top of the bar.

I wasn't complaining. Far from it.

Though after what seemed like hours later, they were still drinking. Still laughing and catching up on all the battles the other three men had been in while Doran lay trapped. And I was falling asleep slumped against the bar.

I could go home… except my current home was only a room at my best friend's house. Viviana had taken me in when I'd left my ex-husband. I didn't have my own place, and I sure couldn't bring four or five men home to her guest room.

Bleary-eyed, I propped my chin up and turned to Warwick behind the bar. "Do you have a place where I can sleep?"

A gentle chime rang through the bar, cutting through the laughter immediately. Doran, Aidan, Ivarr, and Keane immediately set their drinks down on the bar and gave Warwick their full attention.

"Last call, gentlemen." He tipped his head my way. "*Mo stór* needs her beauty sleep."

I almost cracked my jaw yawning so hard. "Sorry to end the party."

"It's sorry we are that we lost ourselves in tales rather than seeing to you." Doran came closer, pulling me gently into his arms. He was still gigantic even in his human form. His massive hand cupped my entire head, and his body was just as hard as the stone statue. "Let's be off to bed, lads."

"Uh." Ivarr gave a sheepish glance in Aidan and Keane's direction. "She won't be wanting any part of our loft."

"Fuck." Aidan grimaced, the formidable crack he always had between his eyes deepening into a Grand Canyon crevice. "No way can we take her there."

I yawned again, snuggling up against Doran's mighty chest. "Where do you live? It can't be that bad."

"Above the tattoo parlor." Keane tugged on his gloves, preparing to step back out into the real world. No one ever went away from him unsatisfied... which meant his touch was orgasmic.

Every muscle in my body shivered with the delightful memory of his touch and kiss. But yeah, I was too tired to even think about round two now.

"It's a place where a bunch of men sleep in between battles," Aidan added. "Not just us, but the rest of the Demon Hunters men who don't have a place of their own. It's a motherfucking dumpster heap."

"The warehouse?" Warwick offered. "It's mostly empty, plenty of space, and there's a bed she can use to rest."

Doran's chest rumbled beneath my ear like distant thunder. "Riann needs to rest in comfort and safety. Not in a war camp or an empty, cold a warehouse, for fuck's sake. What have you bleedin' idjits been doing with yourselves all these centuries? Have you no gold or property accumulated to accommodate *mo stór* for even one night?"

"We invested everything in weapons," Aidan retorted. "You were gone. The treasurekeeper, dead or lost. Cycle after cycle after cycle. We focused on killing as many of the fucking demons as we could and called that good enough until we were slaughtered to start anew."

I was so tired their words started to blur, and I could barely mumble myself. "I'll just sleep here. Even though you're as hard as a rock."

Doran shifted me in his arms, cradling me like a baby. "Have you no mortal bed here, Greenshanks?"

"Only the bar, sorry to say."

I blinked fiercely, trying to pry my eyeballs open. "How about the Summer Isle?"

No one said anything. For a moment, I thought I really had gone to sleep. But no, they were staring at me.

"Faerie be a dangerous place, *mo stór*," Warwick said.

I frowned. "You said you'd love to show it to me someday. Why not now?"

"Damn me traitorous tongue." He smiled apologetically at the other men as he wiped the bar and removed their drinks. "Sorry, lads. I didn't mean to put that bee in her bonnet."

At least being confused helped me wake up a little more. Not to mention hurt. Maybe he'd just thrown out that offer earlier, not ever intending to take me to his home. A polite lie thrown out casually in a conversation. He hadn't meant—

:Never,: he whispered in my head. :*I meant every word.*:

"Then why?" I whispered, blinking back tears. My eyes were gritty. I wanted a bath. I wanted to sleep for a week.

"Most mortals never set foot into Faerie at all," Doran said. "This here bar be fairly safe. I sat on the shelf watching Warwick's trade for centuries, and only a handful of humans ever found their way inside. They all went home after a pleasant pint. But this place is on the fringe of Faerie. One foot on either side of the veil, so to speak. It's understood to be neutral."

"Aye, so it is," Warwick replied. "I've served fae both dark and light, though mark my words. If Evil Eye asked for a pint, I'd throw him out, his terrible eye be damned."

"There be rules," Aidan said with a grim slant to his lips. "Fae be fucking dangerous at any time, but in their own land, it's naught but trickery and illusion."

It took a few minutes for my exhausted brain to finally read between the lines. *They don't trust the leprechaun. Even though we just fucked on top of his bar.*

Warwick had helped us free Doran, and in the beginning, he'd been the only one willing to help me. I'd had to fucking steal Aidan's motorcycle to get his attention. All I'd had to do was walk into *Shamrocked* accidentally, and Warwick had been on my side, eager to help.

Too eager?

Why didn't they trust him enough to allow me to go to his home?

I lifted my head, forcing my bleary eyes to focus on Warwick. The sexy bartender who'd been my first introduction to Faerie. The leprechaun who'd started growing his hair down to his waist—and swore it'd be to the floor if I wanted it—simply to please me. *:Why don't they trust you?:*

:It's complicated. Let's just say my reputation precedes me.:

Doran looked down at me, his eyes narrowed. "What is it, *mo stór?*"

And it dawned on me.

:They don't know that you can talk in my head.:

:No,: Warwick answered. *:They cannot hear our conversation despite their own spokes in your mind.:*

:Why?: I asked again. *:How is this possible?:*

:You're mo stór. *Remember that, no matter what happens. You be treasure for me too, Riann Newkirk.:*

Which wasn't an answer at all.

2

I really had to sell a painting soon, because I was going to owe Viviana a fortune after all this was said and done.

I had to use the credit card she'd given me to rent a hotel room for a few nights. I knew she wouldn't mind in the slightest. I did text her first, though I wasn't surprised when she didn't answer right away. After we'd freed Doran, she'd ridden off into the sunset on the back of Hammer's motorcycle, her glorious red hair blazing like a banner.

She probably would have told me just to take everyone to her house, but that would have been awkward as hell once she came home. She hadn't said how long she'd be gone, but I imagined at least the weekend. She made a fantastic salary and had always been frugal with her money—though she did have a weakness for designer clothes. I knew she could afford it, but I still felt like shit for using her card again.

Growing up poor had affected both of us, though in different ways. I still wondered if part of why I'd fallen into marriage so quickly had been a desire for financial stability. I'd even given up my painting to work a job that I hated because it was the sensible and financially smart thing to do.

Vivi had made it her life's goal to become indispensable, wherever she worked. She was certainly indispensable to me. My only friend, my rock that had gotten me through the horrible divorce. A place to live while Jonathan dragged me through court over and over and over. Money for an attorney I couldn't afford, even at a fraction of the price I'm sure she would have made on anyone else, likely as a favor to Vivi or her boss.

She loved the challenges that came with working for the best defense attorney in Kansas City. Perhaps even the state. I'd certainly hire him if I ever got into legal trouble, though I didn't currently have two pennies to rub together.

I was running on fumes by the time we got checked in to the local Comfort Inn. At least we'd have free breakfast in the morning. I couldn't even muster amusement at watching Doran react to modern technology. Sitting on a shelf in a leprechaun's bar, the gargoyle hadn't seen many motorcycles, elevators, or cellphones.

I'd managed to get a suite so we had two queen beds and the couch pulled out into a full-sized bed. Hopefully that would be enough surface space for anyone who didn't want to share a bed.

I zombie-walked my ass into the bathroom to take a shower, while Aidan, Keane, and Ivarr played rock, paper, scissors to decide who got to sleep with me and Doran, because evidently they thought there'd be enough room for another unreasonably large man's body in addition to the massive gargoyle. A queen-sized bed had never seemed so small.

Standing under steaming hot water, I tried to wrap my brain around everything that had happened. In a matter of days, I'd begun painting again like a mad person, driven mercilessly by Doran to find him and break the curse trapping him as the gargoyle.

Before that, I'd been pretty alone in the world, other than my best friend since childhood. My ex, Jonathan, certainly didn't count. I didn't have much family, at least not that I remembered. Most of my childhood was hazy, as if I'd blocked it out for a reason.

I'd never felt like I fit anywhere.

Vivi was my only family.

Now I'd suddenly gained *five* lovers.

Who was this person? Not boring, geeky Riann, that was for sure. I'd rarely ever had boyfriends growing up. At least, I didn't remember any before my ex-husband. I suppressed a shudder as I turned off the water and toweled dry. I was free of him, and my new men were nothing like him.

But are you sure? A tiny part of my mind whispered.

What did I really know about them? I'd only met Doran in person a few hours ago, though he'd been haunting my dreams. I couldn't deny the intense pull I'd felt for all four of the treasures from the very beginning. Going so far as to grab Aidan's junk the first time I met him, simply because he was being an arrogant ass.

So unlike me.

It was unlike me to do any of this. Paint like a maniac again. Go off on adventures. Fuck some men I just met on top of a bar...

My cheeks blazed as I looked at myself in the steamy mirror. I'd asked them to come on me while Doran fucked me. Even the leprechaun. I'd enjoyed being ravished on top of that bar. Of having cum from five men on my skin.

Me. The plump, short, mousy unemployed, broke painter.

Now they waited for me outside the flimsy bathroom door. I didn't have a change of clothes. No money. No job. No place to live.

Plus there were undercurrents between the four men and Warwick that I didn't understand. It made me feel uneasy, as if something important was unsaid between the five of them, and I didn't have a clue what it was. Other than Vivi, Warwick had been the only one to help me. If they decided they needed to try and force me to choose them over the leprechaun...

No. Doran had welcomed him into the fold, so to speak. I wasn't going to doubt their dedication to me the very first night we were all together.

But we aren't all together, I couldn't help but think as I stepped back out into the room clad only in the basic hotel terry cloth robe. Warwick wasn't here. They hadn't wanted me to go to his homeland in Faerie, though surely it would have been more comfortable. Certainly more spacious. Not to mention free.

"It's decided," Doran said as I paused at the foot of the bed. "We have a plan."

Ivarr lay beside him on the bed, bare chested but still in dark boxers. Evidently he'd won the right to join us. Good. I hadn't had a lot of interaction with him yet. Of the four treasures, I knew the least about him. His black skin contrasted with beautiful amber eyes that glowed with his brilliant light when he smiled.

Taller than the other three men with a lanky, lean frame, Ivarr was the Sword of Light, from which no one could escape. When he'd helped Aidan with the giant kelpie in the lake, a golden beam had shot out of his chest. He'd flown toward the battle on nothing but light.

Beside him, Doran seemed to take up two-thirds of the bed. A big man, both wide and tall and thick. Giant platter-sized hands and feet. Crooked hooked nose. Hulking shoulders. Very much the gargoyle from my dreams even in human form.

I glanced over at the other bed, and Keane sent a smoldering look at me. He had the sheet pulled up over his lap, so I guessed he didn't have a stitch of clothing on. Also, no gloves. Gulp. Though I couldn't blame him in the slightest for not wanting to sleep with tight leather on his hands.

That put the grumpiest man of the lot on the couch. Despite the comfortable temperature in the room, Aidan had retrieved his leather jacket that I'd "borrowed." Rather than pull the bed out and take up all the space in the room, he'd chosen to simply kick back on the couch with his head on the armrest and his still-booted feet propped up on the opposite end. His eyes were closed, his face shadowed by one arm over his forehead, but I didn't buy that he was asleep.

"After a few hours' rest," Doran continued in his deep, floor-rattling rumble. "We'll sort out our resources so we may secure permanent living quarters that are both safe and comfortable."

Sort out resources? I couldn't help but frown. "Does that mean you'll have to sell some of your weapons and stuff?"

"Aye," Aidan replied in a flat, bored tone.

I really didn't know any of them too well yet, but Aidan was never bored. Never not sarcastic with a bite to his voice. It sounded to me like Doran was making him sell off some of his equipment to fund a place to live. For me. "I'm sorry. Vivi was helping me list some of my paintings to sell too."

One icy baby blue eye cracked open in the shadowed recesses beneath his arm. "Why the fuck would you be sorry? I don't give a rat's ass about mortal weaponry. We have a conduit now. We shouldn't need an extensive human arsenal to push out the demon horde."

"Oh. You sounded... not mad. I took that to mean you're upset."

He huffed out a laugh and slammed his eye back shut. "Only that I am denied the pleasure of tucking that glorious ass back against my dick while you sleep."

Now it was my turn to let out a laugh, though it came out more like a strangled groan.

"That's my pleasure tonight," Ivarr drawled, sitting up to offer me his hand.

It was both an *"oh, shit,"* and *"fuck yeah"* moment. Did I take the robe off? Or keep it on? We'd already fucked. Well, Doran had been inside me after treasuring me on the bar, which meant he'd driven me insane with his tongue. All of us had climaxed thanks to Keane's wicked talent.

But it was one thing to have sex, and another to actually sleep in their arms. Like looking into their eyes, breathing the same air, relaxing enough to sleep, safe and secure. I did trust them. Obviously. Or I wouldn't be here. I'd almost died to free Doran. I had no doubts whatsoever that they'd always take care of me, if for no other reason than to keep their magic intact.

I was their conduit. I was the hub at the center of the wheel, four spokes spinning around me, casting out powerful magic to drive back the forces of darkness. They wouldn't risk that, especially after losing the treasurekeeper before when Doran was cursed.

Deciding to keep the robe on just for my own peace of mind, I took Ivarr's hand and let him help me crawl up into the middle of the bed. Both he and Doran turned on their sides, giving me a little more room, but it was still wall-to-wall muscle. Heat. Rock-hard temptation all around me.

I ended up facing Ivarr, so it was Doran against my back. His gigantic hand splayed across my abdomen, snugging me back against his heat. With his arm around me, I was almost completely encased in muscle. He was just that big. It made me feel like a baby bird tucked under her mother's wing.

No safer place in the world than under Doran Stoneheart's mighty arm.

Curling our clasped hands against his chest, Ivarr just looked at me with those beautiful golden eyes. "Such a treasure. We are truly blessed, Doran."

"Aye."

That single word rumbled through me, vibrating me from head to toe. How could he say that—when he'd been trapped for hundreds of years, a giant gargoyle statue forgotten in a root cellar near a church?

He rubbed his mouth against my ear. "I'd suffer the curse another thousand years just to hold you again, *mo stór*."

Blinking back tears, I curled my other hand around his wrist, holding them both. "No more curses, please."

"What was your life like before you heard Doran's call?" Ivarr asked. "If you're not too tired."

I was feeling less like a zombie after the shower, though I didn't think the alert brain would last long after the week I'd had. "I lived with Vivi. She took me in after I filed for divorce."

His eyes flared and he glanced up at Doran. "You were wed before?"

Shame tightened my throat. "Yeah. For five years."

"Did you love him?"

His question shouldn't have startled me. People got married because they fell in love, right? But I honestly couldn't remember being happy with Jonathan. I must have been once. Before he hit on Vivi. Before he made me feel so small. "I guess so? At least in the beginning."

Doran lifted his hand to my chin and turned my face toward him, leaning back to make room for me to turn enough so my neck wasn't strained. "I detect unpleasantness in your voice, and your mind is nothing but thick tar when you think of him. Does this man yet live? I will be only too happy to pay him a visit."

Aidan growled. "Let's each collect a body part from this wanker."

"No, no," I said hurriedly. "I don't want anything to do with him ever again. The divorce was bad enough."

Doran's eyes glittered with malice. "Tell us, *mo stór*. I want to know this story."

My stomach churned, my eyes burning with tears. "I don't like to talk about it."

His stony face softened, and he brushed his lips against each of my eyelids. "Very well, *mo stór*. We will talk of it another day but talk we must. If this man broke your heart, we must take care to heal it and not injure you further."

Relieved, I turned toward him and buried my face against his chest. His big fingers stroked my hair, trying to take away some of the hurt. But he couldn't soothe that pain away.

I was scared. Terrified, actually. Once they heard my story, they'd think less of me. I certainly did. Why had I married such a jerk? Deliberately? Especially when I couldn't remember a single good time?

When I couldn't remember if I'd ever even loved him?

3

I slept so hard and long that I woke feeling a bit like Rip Van Winkle. Sunlight streamed in through the windows, but I couldn't tell if it was morning or afternoon. For a moment, I didn't remember where I was.

Then I turned my head and found gleaming golden eyes shining back at me.

"Good afternoon, sleepy head," Ivarr said. "Feel better?"

I stretched, groaning as blood started flowing through my lethargic muscles. "Ouch. I'm actually pretty sore. I feel like a herd of horses trampled me while I slept."

His lips quirked, a dimple popping up in his cheek. "Doran does tend to have that effect."

Heat flooded me. Embarrassment, yeah, a little, but also desire. The memory of him thrusting deep inside me made my breath catch on a soft, ragged sigh. I couldn't recall feeling such overwhelming pleasure before.

A twinge of unease nagged me. Not that I wanted to dwell on my ex-husband's skills—or lack thereof—in the bedroom. But when I tried to remember...

"What has put that look on your face, *mo stór?*" Ivarr asked.

"Nothing," I said brightly, sitting up enough to fluff the pillows up beneath me so I could see the entire room. "Where is everyone?"

"They went to give Doran a tour of their weapons cache to decide what to keep and what to sell. They've been gone a few hours."

I was vaguely surprised to find myself still wrapped up in the hotel robe, though it was gaping open a bit after sleeping. I didn't really care to put the corset top back on—but the rest of my clothes were at Vivi's. While I'd certainly felt sexy in the green velvet that hugged my curves and made the girls look fantastic, it was an outfit to wear to the club. Not something you wore during the broad daylight at a cheap hotel, without feeling like you were taking the walk of shame home for some new clothes. Though that did make my lips quirk.

Me, Riann the geeky painter, taking one hell of a walk of shame back to get some clothes. Oh yeah.

"Aidan grabbed some things for you from your friend's house," Ivarr added.

Eyebrow arched, I watched him get up and fetch a bag to lay on the foot of the bed. "How did he even know where she lives? I never took him there."

Ivarr snorted. "Aidan is part bloodhound. He could track you to the coast and back now that he knows your scent."

Hmm. Maybe. Though he could have asked Warwick where Vivi lived. Would he have stooped so low as to ask the leprechaun? Warwick had whisked me home that first night, and then I'd called him for help to secure the warehouse and move all my painting supplies so I could work on finding Doran's location.

Either way, it was a very considerate thing for Aidan to do. Even more so because he generally wasn't the warm-and-fuzzy kind of guy.

"I can nip downstairs for some coffee if you'd like," Ivarr offered. "It's not as good as what your friend made, but it's better than nothing."

"That'd be great, thank you."

He leaned down, bracing his forearm on the headboard. "My pleasure, *mo stór*."

His eyes gleamed with soft golden light that seemed to flow into me, filling me with sunshine and warmth. It felt incredible, like an internal hug and a thousand compliments all wrapped up into an exquisite chocolate candy that dissolved on my tongue and sweetened my entire body.

I cupped his cheek, tracing my thumb along his jawline, enjoying the roughness from his stubble. "You really are incredible."

He closed his hand over mine, moving my fingers so he could kiss each fingertip. "Nothing compared to the treasure of your heart."

I tipped my head back, offering my mouth silently, if he wanted a kiss. He did indeed. His soft lips nibbled against mine and the sense of glow intensified. As if I was swallowing a warm, thick glob of honeyed sunlight. So good. I could feel that heat spreading through me as if I'd thrown back a shot or two of fine Irish whiskey.

He lifted his head, his eyes sparkling with faceted rays of sunlight.

"Wow," I breathed out. Too bad I hadn't brushed my teeth yet. I would have gladly opened up for a deeper kiss.

"You give me that power, *mo stór*. My light had all but died out before we found you. I'll be right back."

Warm sparks danced through my blood as I watched him leave. Double wow. His ass filled out his jeans just as spectacularly as his kiss had lit me up. Shaking myself out of a dazed stupor, I got up and dragged the bag into the bathroom. Aidan had even thought to grab my toothbrush. Bless his grumpy heart.

At the very bottom of the bag, I found the worn gold coin that had allowed me to step into *Shamrocked* the first time. Did I still need the coin to enter the pub? Or would it look like the old run-down abandoned house again? As long as I was with the guys, it probably didn't matter. They were the lost magical treasures of Ireland.

I was just the human lucky enough to be their conduit.

Though holding Warwick's gold coin made me feel a little more magical and less like a basic human. I slipped the coin into my pocket, determined to carry it with me as a good luck charm. Hopefully more of that magic would find me.

Freshly scrubbed and dressed in my favorite faded, paint-streaked jeans, I found Ivarr waiting for me with the promised cup of coffee. "I wasn't sure how you liked it, so I brought some packets of creamer and sugar."

I ripped open some packets of the dried creamer and stirred them in, but they did little to help the bitterness. It was still caffeine. "What's on the agenda today?"

"I called Aidan while I was downstairs, and he said they're going to be another couple of hours. What would you like to do in the meantime?"

"I'd like to head over to the warehouse and get some of my paintings listed for sale. Vivi got me connected with an online art gallery. I just need to finish uploading the pictures."

Then, if I still had time... I'd see if the muse had anything new to say.

4

———

We grabbed some fast food on the way to the warehouse. Munching on salty fries, I got the first canvas loaded to the gallery's site. I chose to sell the painting I'd done of the gargoyle in the creepy church graveyard, but I couldn't bear to part with the portraits of each of the guys. I put an insanely high price on the church one, thinking it probably wouldn't sell anyway, but if it did, it would solve my immediate cash problems.

I definitely needed to prepare something new to sell. Painting for myself was one thing. Painting for profit... I wasn't sure what would sell anyway. In a perfect world, I'd paint whatever I wanted, and it would sell like hotcakes. I snorted, shaking my head. A fairytale for sure.

To warm up and get my creative juices flowing, I started by painting Ivarr. The way he sat so casually and easily, a warm light in his eyes. A ready smile on his lips. Golden energy rising up like a nimbus around him.

Nice. But I wanted to go deeper. Something more challenging. "Would you take your shirt off?"

He winked at me as he tugged his t-shirt over his head without hesitation. I painted him sitting, facing me. Turning away. The long, lean lines of his back. His graceful, gentle fingers. The black flap of his coat rising around him like wings as he flew out over the lake to help Aidan. The heavy longsword held in both of his hands over one shoulder.

His light pushing back the imps in the cellar. Shining. Always shining against the darkness. Slowly dimming.

Until he kissed me. Which lead me to thinking about his mouth. The delicious, rounded curve of his ass.

"No fucking fair."

I jolted at the vicious tone near my ear, whipping my head around to see that Aidan had joined us, along with Doran and Keane. "Hello to you too."

He scowled at me, even as he leaned in and pressed a hard, searing kiss to my lips. "I'm next."

"For what?"

Eyes narrowed, he tipped his head to the canvas. "I want you to paint me next."

I turned to look at the painting and squeaked. Oh shit. Heat scorched my face. When had I asked Ivarr to take his pants off...? Or had I just painted him from a place of imagination? I peeked over at the bed and another wave of heat flooded my cheeks.

Just as in my painting, he lay on the mattress. Stark naked. The long, beautiful, lean lines of his body on full display. His cock erect, his fingers wrapped around the base. Eyes burning like twin suns. Shoulders and neck corded with muscle, as if I'd been tormenting him for hours.

Maybe I had. Shit.

I dragged my gaze up to his. His lips curled in a sensual smile. Not frustrated or angry at me for tormenting him in the slightest. Only that shining sensual heat, promising to fill me to bursting with all the light and energy of the sun.

"Sorry," I squeaked out again. "I don't remember asking you to... uh..." I waved my hand vaguely in the general vicinity of the bed. "When I paint, the muse takes over."

"My pleasure, as always, *mo stór*." He chuckled softly, releasing his dick as he sat up. Casually naked, dick out, even with his friends now in the room. As if it was the most natural thing in the world. "Any luck, Aidan?"

"Not as lucky as you," he huffed out, scanning the other canvases. "You did all these this afternoon?"

I turned, surprised to find three other canvases, all featuring Ivarr in increasingly fewer clothes. Most of them didn't have his face or his eyes, just the glorious lines of his body and the same warm golden tones against his shining ebony skin. "I guess so." I shrugged uncomfortably when Aidan turned another piercing look on me. "When the muse takes hold, I don't remember much. I just paint."

Keane let out a low whistle as he looked over the canvases. "Very impressive. I agree, I want to see what your muse thinks of me."

My cheeks were pretty much on fire at this point. Though yeah, I wanted it too. Now that they were all here, close to me, I could feel a pulse in the air. As if the wheel needed to spin. Magic needed to be released.

Oops. Not a good word choice with one gorgeous man naked and three others wishing they could join him.

Doran let out a low rumble that made my blood heat even more. "We brought food, though now I'm not sure that any of us wish to eat dinner."

I met his gaze, not surprised to see his eyes heavy and dark. "What are the... uh... rules? Like how does this all work between you?"

His eyes narrowed, creating a chasm in his forehead almost as grim as Aidan's. "There are no rules, *mo stór*. What you want, you take. Whenever and however it pleases you."

5

Such a novel concept.

The thought flickered in my brain, but for a moment, it felt like someone else's. Someone who had not had much of a say in what happened. Especially in the bedroom.

Not me.

Though the sense of unease rolled back through me, churning my stomach. As if there was a trap buried ahead, just waiting to swallow me up. I hadn't been happy with Jonathan. In fact, I'd been miserable. I didn't remember having great sex with him. Or even good sex. Or even... bad sex.

Why can't I remember?

Aidan seized my arm and dragged me over to the table. Only he didn't sit me down in a chair. He picked me up and plopped my ass down in the middle of the table. Then he planted his palms on either side of my hips and leaned down into my space. "Who am I going to kill tonight?"

Startled, I leaned back a bit to gain some space. "I'm sorry? What?"

Doran sat gingerly in one of the chairs, as if expecting it to explode into a thousand pieces. His head was still higher than mine, and the snarl on his lips told me this was very serious. "I feel the unease spiraling through you, Riann. We all do. So you'd best start spilling some truths to your treasures so we may better protect you."

Evidently, it was serious enough that Ivarr scooped up his boxers so he wouldn't distract me further. He and Keane both came closer to the table, and though it was rectangular and not circular, I could feel the wheel flaring to life with their nearness.

Magic spilling through me. Spinning out with ever-increasing power. The four Irish treasures, and me, their treasurekeeper, the conduit for their magic. It had been so beautiful feeling them all come together around me, both for their magic, and when we'd fucked at *Shamrocked.*

I couldn't bear to lose that sense of belonging and rightness so quickly.

My eyes burned, but I didn't want to cry. I didn't even know why I felt like everything was crumbling away. They'd done nothing to indicate they were upset or unhappy. "I guess I'm having some PTSD from my marriage."

"Tell us about him." Aidan's voice softened, all the hard edges and scowl gone from his face. That shocked me more than him picking me up and dropping me onto the table. He wasn't ever soft or gentle or kind. Was he? That made my eyes swim even more. "Start with something easy, *mo stór.* What's the fucking bastard's name?"

"Jonathan," I whispered. "Blake."

Aidan pressed a gentle kiss to my forehead. "And where did you meet Jonathan Blake, *mo stór?*"

It wasn't a trick question. It should be easy to answer. But it was like pulling open the drawer in a filing cabinet and finding only empty manilla folders. The spots were there, perfectly labeled and organized. Just... empty.

I gave him the most likely answer. "College, I think. Vivi went to UMKC, and I went to the Kansas City Art Institute. I think I met him at an event."

"You think?"

I closed my eyes, scanning those mental folders again. Concentrating fiercely. "I don't remember exactly."

"Where did you go on your first date?" Doran's low rumble made me shiver.

"I didn't date much. I was busy painting or hanging out with Vivi." All true. "I didn't have a lot of experience with guys."

Aidan's mouth brushed my ear, his hot breath making my hair tickle my skin. "I didn't ask you about guys in general. I be asking about Jonathan Blake. The man you married."

"I honestly don't remember. I must have blocked it from my memory."

His hand came up around my nape, pulling me against his chest. "Or those memories were taken from you."

I breathed in his scent. The fresh, clean scent of his cotton T-shirt. Dark, luscious leather sprinkled with the bite of gunpowder. So good. I couldn't be upset or scared with the Slaughterer on my side. Surrounded by his friends. My lovers.

Then why did my stomach clench on another pulse of dread? "Who would have done such a thing?"

"Describe him for us," Doran said. "What did he look like?"

"He's about five foot ten. He always called Vivi an Amazon because she was taller than him. Brown hair. Brown eyes. Average build." It dawned on me that he'd asked what he'd looked like—as in the past. "He's still alive as far as I know. In fact, he finally signed the divorce papers after fighting me for nearly a year."

Doran shook his head slowly. "I'm sorry to say that the man you might have loved is dead, Riann. He is no more."

"How?" I whispered numbly. "How could you know that? Surely someone would have called me."

Aidan heaved out a heavy sigh. "Changeling."

I searched his frosty-blue eyes, surprised by the hint of regret in his tone. "What's that?"

"Sometimes a fae swaps himself out for a human, whether baby or adult. One sure way to identify a changeling is a suddenly ravenous appetite."

I tried to laugh, but it sounded like a choked sob. "I don't remember him eating that much."

"He didn't eat food." Aidan leaned closer, pressing his forehead to mine, his grip surprisingly gentle on my nape. "He ate your memories. That's why you can't remember meeting him. Falling in love. Even bad memories. They're gone, destroyed by the fae who stole your husband's life."

I jerked back away from him, forcing another harsh laugh. "You must be mistaken. I didn't know about any of this fairy stuff then. I hadn't found *Shamrocked* or met Warwick. I didn't even bring Doran's statue home until a week ago. When did this fae supposedly take Jonathan's place?"

"You won't be able to remember." Keane's usually sultry voice was somber, echoing with grief. For me. For the memories that I'd lost. "We'll have to ask Viviana if she noticed a particular event or time when the man you married suddenly seemed different."

"But I remember certain things," I protested, still unable to wrap my mind around the idea. "We were married for five years. I was so unhappy, hating my job, hating my life. I wanted…"

Bits of flimsy, wispy images fluttered through my mind. Tattered and worn and thin. I'd been going to the Institute. I'd always intended to be an artist. I'd worked really hard to get accepted into the program on scholarship, because I sure didn't have the money for tuition.

Jonathan would have known that I wanted to be an artist. Yet that was the first thing I'd given up. He'd never come right out and forbade me to paint, but he'd ridiculed and belittled me, or implied I was hurting our future together by neglecting a "real" career. Slowly making me feel worse until I gave in.

Until I gave up my dream. The one thing I had always loved.

Tears trickled down my cheeks. Vivi had tried to tell me early on in our relationship that something was wrong. But after he hit on her…

I hadn't wanted him around her again. I hadn't trusted him, and I hadn't wanted to expose her to any more of his bullshit. In my own stupid way, I'd been trying to protect her from the man I'd married.

The man I was stuck with. Evidently, he hadn't been a man at all.

"Warwick said *he* was in the city and that I had to be careful." I swiped at my cheeks, determined not to break down. "Was he trying to warn me about Jonathan even then?"

Aidan's baby blues darkened at my mention of the leprechaun's name. "When did he warn you about him?"

"When Vivi went with me to find the bar. She was worried that I'd been roofied because I couldn't remember how I'd gotten home. But the bar wasn't there—only an old, falling down house. I thought I was going crazy, but then Warwick was there. He told me to come back that night and to be careful."

"That's one thing I've been meaning to ask you, *mo stór*," Doran said. "How did you get into *Shamrocked* in the first place?"

"I accidentally found one of Warwick's gold coins on the sidewalk in the snow. It was in my pocket."

I couldn't see Keane and Ivarr behind me, but I had the feeling they were all four looking at each other with the same suspicion as the glances Aidan and Doran shared. "What? He said he'd been leaving his coins all over town, hoping that I'd find one."

Aidan snorted. "A leprechaun is never parted from his gold. I'd sooner believe that Doran gave up his gargoyle to shift into a pink unicorn than Warwick accidentally on purpose dropping a single coin for you to find."

"I wouldna mind a pink unicorn," Doran rumbled. "They have beautiful sharp horns on their heads."

"Did Warwick say how long he'd been trying to reach you with his coins?" Ivarr asked.

The sick feeling increased in my stomach. "About five years. I thought it strange at the time because that's how long I'd been married to Jonathan. But surely it was just a coincidence."

Aidan dropped down into one of the chairs with another disgusted sound. "Did you ever wonder where the word conned came from, *mo stór*? Lepre*con*. He conned you. He conned us all."

6

I didn't believe him.

Warwick hadn't conned me. He couldn't have. Not after he'd helped me, saved my life, and then participated in that decadent scene on top of his bar in his pub. That hadn't been fake. It hadn't been a lie.

I wanted to reach out to him and ask, but with all four guys watching me, I didn't want them to leap to any conclusions. I sure wouldn't be able to hide that I was talking to someone else, and the last thing I wanted was to imply that I trusted Warwick more than I trusted them.

I trusted all five of them. I didn't believe for a moment that Warwick had anything to do with me being hurt in any way.

"I hope for the sake of your heart that the trust you've placed in Greenshanks isn't misplaced." Though the heavy skepticism in Doran's tone told me he sided with Aidan. "You were marked, and much earlier than any of us suspected. A changeling has damaged your memories for years. That you were able to distance yourself from the creature and still manage to find the rest of the treasures and break my curse is nothing short of a miracle. Let's eat first, but I'd like as much information on Jonathan Blake as we can find."

"Agreed." Keane rummaged through the bags of Chinese takeout and started passing containers around. "Give me a few minutes on a laptop and we'll know what color underwear the gobshite's wearing."

Aidan helped me down off the table and I sat between him and Doran. A little numb. A little heartbroken. But also oddly relieved. I'd known something was wrong with the marriage. I hadn't felt like myself in so long that coming to Vivi's was like being reborn again. Finding parts of myself that I'd forgotten or had lain dormant in those years. Waiting for a little sunlight to blossom again.

I only partially listened as the guys filled Ivarr in on whatever equipment they'd sold to raise cash. Instead, I focused on the leprechaun. *:Warwick?:*

:Aye, mo stór? *Are you needing me despite having the treasures at your beck and call?:*

I had to be careful. If Aidan's suspicions were right, then I didn't want to accidentally betray us to Warwick. But I refused to believe he'd betray me. Not after what we'd been through. *:What do you know about my ex-husband?:*

I ate several bites of cashew chicken before he answered.

:There be restrictions placed upon me that I must abide, though it distresses me greatly.: His voice whispered through my head, trembling with anxiety and emotion. *:You're on the right track. Keep pushing for answers, Riann. That's all I can say.:*

Confirming that something fishy was up. But not necessarily something Warwick himself had done. *:Aidan said Doran would sooner give up his gargoyle than you'd give up your gold.:*

:Sometimes there be greater treasure than gold at stake. Remember what I told you last at Shamrocked.*:*

You be treasure for me too.

I blinked fiercely, trying to keep my emotions under control.

:Hold on to that, love,: Warwick whispered. *:Be wary. I cannot say more.:*

"Have you a place in mind to live, *mo stór?*" Doran's deep rumble shook me back to their conversation.

"Not really. I'm happy anywhere."

"We could travel," Keane said wistfully. "I'd love to see the homeland again."

"That's one thing I still don't understand," I said. "Why are the Irish treasures here, in Kansas City, Missouri, of all places? I would have thought you'd be reborn only in Ireland."

"We go where the war dictates," Aidan replied in between mouthfuls of noodles. He ate like he hadn't had a meal in days. Maybe he hadn't. I couldn't remember seeing him eat until now. "Before Doran was cursed, we had long periods in Tír na nÓg, and we were only reborn to Ireland. But once we lost him, we kept getting spit out to your world quicker, over and over and over. We haven't been back to Ireland in centuries. The demons be here, so this be where we return."

"You've been fighting them awhile this time?"

He had an even bigger mouthful of lo mien, so Ivarr picked up the conversation for him. "Time is a funny thing when you've been reborn so many times, but near as I can remember, we've been back six or seven human years."

So close to when I'd come to Kansas City and married Jonathan. Another coincidence? I didn't think so. Why had Vivi and I been so set on coming to Kansas City? She was so smart that she had scholarships to go anywhere. She'd chosen UMKC, because I had finally gotten a full-ride scholarship from the Kansas City Art Institute.

Another coincidence? Or divine magic at play to bring me where I needed to be?

What were the chances that I'd grow up near Doran's hiding place? That I'd have wandered the hills around the lake looking for a lost prince? That I'd come to Kansas City to study art—the very thing that helped me find him?

The talent that Jonathan had immediately squelched as soon as we married. To prevent me from finding Doran?

"I wasn't always in the same location," Doran said, startling me out of my reverie. "I believe I was sent to that cellar because you were near."

"Right," Aidan mumbled around a mouthful. "The last time I physically saw your gargoyle was in a dead-end, closed subway tunnel in New York City in the eighties."

I couldn't help but rub my temples, trying to follow. "Wait. You're saying that you weren't physically placed in the church cellar until…"

"Until you were there," Doran replied. "My prison was not of this earth, but in an immortal plane similar to Tír na nÓg, the Land Beneath the Sea, or Over the Waves, or countless other names for Faerie. My prison appeared physically wherever the treasurekeeper was, but then faded away until she could be born again."

"So are the demon things here only because I was born here?"

Aidan pushed away from his empty container, though his eyes narrowed on mine, as if he'd snag the rest of my cashew chicken if I dared leave a bite uneaten. "Not at all." I felt a little better, until he added, "The demon fae be everywhere now. Your world is nigh overrun with them."

I pushed my container over to him and he didn't hesitate to dig in. "But that can't be possible. I've never seen any of these creatures before. How can they be everywhere?"

"You were married to one," Doran said. "Yet you did not know. How many times have you passed a changeling on the street and not noticed?"

Ouch. Blow straight to the heart. Had I really not noticed that Jonathan wasn't human? Could you live with someone, share a bed with him, and not realize the truth? If so… "We're fucked."

Aidan flashed the biggest smile I'd seen from him. "Exactly so."

"But do you see the imps and pookas here in the city? Or are they all these changeling things?"

He shrugged. "All of that and more. Fae cast a glamor so mortals can't see their true nature. You might see a cat on the street, but it's an imp. Or a tall, muscled man dressed in a suit headed to the office, but it's actually a pooka. They can mask their ravenous nature until they accomplish their goal."

"And their goal is…"

He shoved another huge mouthful of cashew chicken in answer. I winced. Eating. That was their goal. If we'd failed to free Doran in the cellar, the imps would have eaten us. Well, Aidan had supposedly arranged for Warwick to get me out of there if things went badly, but I would have been furious if he'd whisked me away while the rest of them died.

"Aren't you finished yet?" Keane shot a frown across the table at Aidan. "Axel is set to meet us at the shop for some reconnaissance."

Aidan grumbled around the last mouthful and pushed away from the table. "Why didn't you say so? Call if you need us. Otherwise, we'll meet you at the hotel later tonight."

I would have asked for a goodbye kiss from them, but he was still chewing up that last mouthful, and a kiss from Keane would have sent me into a screaming climax. Though he did give me a sultry wink, promising to bring that magic to play later at the hotel.

Oh yeah. I was going to need to do some in-depth painting of him next. I looked over the table at Ivarr with a questioning lift of my eyebrows. "Sorry you had to miss out on their fun to stay with me all day."

"Hardly a punishment, *mo stór*. I loved every minute with you, though I do have one request."

My cheeks heated, remembering every graphic detail of his body. "Yeah?"

"I want to watch you paint Doran next."

7

I set up another canvas as Doran stripped down to his skin. Ivarr already sat on the bed, propped up with pillows like he was getting ready for a really good show. At least he'd kept his boxers on. The sight of two beautiful, powerful naked men would have been my undoing.

"I can't remember ever posing for a portrait before," Doran grumbled more like Aidan. "Are you sure you want my hulking beast on your canvas, *mo stór?*"

It dawned on me that the gigantic man was nervous. He thought it highly unlikely that I'd find him as attractive as Ivarr. Granted, Doran's body shape was completely different, even when he wasn't shifted into the gargoyle. His shoulders were massive. His barrel chest huge. His arms too long. His hands and feet massive. His thighs like giant pillars of cement. Even his facial features were large in proportion to Ivarr's, and the busted nose certainly didn't help disguise the heaviness of his brow.

Add in all the scars and cuts to his big body...

And I was spellbound. I'd thought of him as a majestic lion before. An aged king who'd fought off dozens of challengers over the years and had the battle scars to prove it. He wasn't handsome in the traditional sense. But there was a definite sense of royalty in the proud tilt of his chin. Grace in the way he moved despite his size. Even more telling, in my opinion, was his gentleness. He had never handled me in a way that made me afraid.

Aidan could grab my arm and haul me around like the impatient asshole he was, but Doran would never handle me that roughly. He didn't dare because of his size. Aidan's harshness was all a bluff anyway. I knew beyond a shadow of a doubt that he wouldn't ever hurt me.

Doran's gentleness wasn't a bluff. He would never fail to guard his actions and movements around me to ensure my safety. He was just too big and strong to ever forget his own strength.

I grabbed the blank canvas I'd put on my easel and took it back to the others stacked along the wall. I needed something bigger for Doran. I wanted to capture his full majesty, like a king on his throne. The gargoyle on his perch. If they had perches? I really wasn't sure.

I came back with the largest-sized canvases that I'd purchased, one in each hand. Because once I got started, I didn't think I'd be happy with only one painting. Unless...

Unless I ended up leaving one of them unfinished so I could get into bed with them.

Because yeah. Just staring at the two of them, so different yet so similar, waiting for me. In bed... This would be some of my fastest painting ever.

I cocked my head to the side, envisioning what I wanted to do. "You know how gargoyle statues are on the tops or sides of buildings? Watching for evil? That's what I want you to look like, only on the bed."

Doran cast a concerned look at the bedframe, as if afraid it wouldn't hold his weight. It wasn't anything fancy—but Vivi had insisted that I should have a comfortable place to rest in between paintings. She never would have bought something cheap and flimsy, so I was pretty sure whatever frame the mattress sat on would hold up.

Climbing on the foot of the bed, he crouched down over his feet.

Knees splayed wide, those big hands gripping the edge of the mattress like it was a roof of a building. Braced on the very edge, his forearms immediately caught my attention. All that strength. The corded lines of muscle and sinew and ligament drawing my eyes up the length of his arms to massive, bulging shoulders and his thick, muscled neck.

Gulp. I picked up my brush and sank into that image, capturing every muscle with loving detail. With Ivarr in the shadows behind him to adequately reflect exactly how large Doran was. Ivarr's eyes began to gleam with his golden light, casting more of Doran's face into shadow. Though I caught the gleam of his eyes. The flash of his white teeth in the darkness. Sharper than I imagined. More like a wolf. Or a bat, maybe. His? Or the gargoyle's? Or just my crazy muse? I wasn't sure.

"May I ask for something myself, *mo stór?*" Doran's rumble deepened, rattling the very foundations of the building.

I nodded, though I didn't look up from my work.

"Paint yourself into the next one. And when you're done, put yourself here. With us."

8

I couldn't remember painting myself before. When I looked at myself, I didn't see anything interesting enough to capture on a canvas. But I wanted to be in this picture. I could see it so clearly.

Me, standing in the gargoyle's shadow. Dressed in something white, flowy, and elegant despite my short, curvy body. Reaching my palm up to the gargoyle's cheek. Pressing my lips to his. Watching the stone flow away to reveal the man beneath.

The bedframe groaned as Doran shifted his weight. I focused on him rather than the painting in my head. Instead of perching at the foot of the bed, he'd moved up to the headboard and reclined against it like a throne. One knee up, his elbow casually braced on it. His other leg bent slightly, his hand casually on his knee.

His thick cock jutting up in silent invitation.

I stared a moment, captivated by the memory of him inside me. Filling me up. Pushing me higher than I'd ever flown. Had I ever climaxed so hard before? I couldn't remember—but maybe those memories had been destroyed by the changeling too.

I couldn't dwell on that thought without making myself ill again. I had no idea when Jonathan might have been replaced. When I might have had sex with my ex-husband—versus a changeling fae creature that had devoured my memories.

My brush moved over the canvas, seemingly with a mind of its own. I was there in that painting. The white gown flowing around me. My head falling back with exquisite pleasure as I lowered myself onto his cock. His big body a fortress, a place of safety that I could always turn to. My mighty protector.

Golden light flowed through the vision, shifting my perspective. Ivarr's beautiful body curled around mine. His arms supported me as I rode Doran. The light in the darkness. The truth cutting through the lies. With Ivarr's light, I would always see through any illusion. I would know...

My eyes closed, holding the thought close like a secret in the depths of my heart. I would know if anyone lied to me. Even Warwick.

Tension bled away from my shoulders, softening the heavy sense of dread in my stomach that I'd been trying to ignore. I didn't doubt Warwick's honesty in the slightest, and I refused to believe that he'd conned me. But now I would have that confirmation if I ever needed it.

I painted in long, broad strokes. Hurried. Throwing paint onto the canvas with abandon. I wanted to finish it. Quickly. So I could slide into that vision and bring it to life.

I dropped the paintbrush with a clatter. I didn't wear a flowing nightgown, but when I pulled the shirt over my head and wriggled out of my jeans, I didn't hear a single word of complaint from the men waiting for me on the bed. Doran lifted me up effortlessly, setting me on my knees between his splayed thighs. He didn't ask anything of me, choosing to sit and wait for me to decide how quickly I wanted to proceed.

As soon as I focused on Ivarr, he rose up slightly from his reclined position beside his friend, though he, too, simply waited for my direction. My pace. My rules. It was so shocking to me, which unsettled me all over again. It made me suspect there were dark things in my head that the changeling may have feasted upon. Horrible things he'd done to me, just so he could devour those dark memories.

They knew it, reading the slight waver on my face. Or sensing the unsettling pit in my stomach.

"If Greenshanks had anything at all to do with that sickness swirling in your stomach, I'll see him drawn and quartered." Doran's grim rumble pushed back some of the uneasiness threatening to overtake me. "Though I hope for your sake that he be as innocent as you believe."

I moved closer to Doran, reaching up to cup his heavy head in both my hands. "When you first started talking in my dreams, I didn't believe you. I didn't believe *in* you. But I do now. I believe in you. In all of you. And I believe in Warwick too."

Doran leaned his mighty head down against mine, resting his chin on the top of my head. "Then I believe in him too, *mo stór*, because I, more than any of we four, have been saved by the incomparable strength of your heart."

I leaned forward and pressed my lips to one of the deep grooves in his shoulder. He had so many scars. So many battles. I couldn't comprehend how many times they must have died to save the world that didn't care about them in the slightest. He wore the impact of all those lives deep in his flesh. Physical proof of all the times he'd fought and died to save the world.

His skin quivered against my lips, a soft sigh escaping his lips. I raised my head, stunned to find the scar had smoothed away. His flesh looked whole and unmarked once more.

"Such power," Ivarr whispered. "You truly are magical, Riann."

"It's not me," I replied, shaken. "It's *your* magic. I'm only the conduit."

"A conduit can change the flow through it," Doran said. "Transform it into something else. It's been so long since we were all four reunited with our treasurekeeper, methinks the fae magic is so relieved and excited to be used again that it's expanding your ability."

Me. Magic? I certainly felt magical in their arms. Especially when they looked at me with such burning desire. Vivi was the beautiful woman who drew men to her like bees to honey. I'd never been magnetic like her. I was the quiet geeky artist with paint smeared on my cheek. Too shy and awkward to even think about dating much.

But they both looked at me like I was a miracle. That certainly felt magical to me.

I rose up over Doran's hips and slowly began to take him inside. His big hands settled on my waist, supporting me while I worked him deep. He was a big man in all ways. Sweat beaded on my forehead when I rocked my hips. I didn't try to take him balls deep. Not yet.

I'd entertained the possibility of having Ivarr inside me at the same time, but I didn't think I could bear any more sensation. Though he pressed his lips to mine. The gentle glide of his palms over my back and arms brought my skin to life. His heat warmed my back, just like in the painting I'd been working on. Solid muscle everywhere. Safe.

So safe.

Climax rippled through me, a wave that started gently, like their touch, but built to a crashing crescendo. Shattering me up against a crystalline ceiling that exploded into a million stars. Doran's guttural sigh pushed me higher, his big hands squeezing me harder against him. His hips thrusting, lifting me up, driving me into a higher level that made me claw at his shoulders.

Panting, I sagged against him a moment, trying to catch my breath. "No offense, big guy, but I'm going to need to start with one of the other guys next time so they get a turn before I'm unconscious."

"I'm not complaining," Ivarr nuzzled my neck, still curled around my back. Soft golden light shimmered all around him. "Your pleasure always pushes me over the edge. Though I'd love to be inside you too."

It hadn't really dawned on me until now. I had four men in my bed. No, five. We'd been intimate. They'd come on me. Yet only Doran had ever actually been inside me. As Ivarr said, he wasn't complaining. But I was going to have to come up with some kind of system. No matter how eager I might be after so many years, I was only one woman after all. Human, even, compared to supernatural Irish treasures and a fucking leprechaun.

Doran rolled slightly onto his side, letting me settle between him and Ivarr. "Flip a coin next time. Though not Warwick's gold. Aidan'll never trust it not to favor the leprechaun with every toss."

The bed was too small to get very comfortable between two large men, one of which resembled a massive stone gargoyle even in his human form. "Is there bad blood between them?"

"Not that I know of," Ivarr replied. "Aidan isn't the trusting sort to begin with."

I huffed out a sigh and closed my eyes. That was the understatement of the century.

9

Freshly showered, I sat on one of the hotel beds while the guys argued over who was getting the bathroom next. I hated to keep spending Vivi's money, but maybe we should have gotten a couple of rooms. One shower for five people—especially large, rowdy men—was a challenge. I hadn't seen many cars in the parking lot, so hopefully there weren't a lot of guests that'd be filing noise complaints.

Aidan and Keane had brought several bags of fast food with them—as well as what looked to be the entire whiskey selection from the liquor mart on the corner. As long as they kept the noise down to a dull roar, I didn't mind them drinking, though I couldn't help but dwell on the fact that we could have gone to *Shamrocked* for all the alcohol they could want.

Except that was where Warwick was.

Absently tracing the coin in my pocket, I played back scenes from before we'd freed Doran, trying to tell whether Aidan had been so suspicious of Warwick all along, or if his distrust was more recent. Simple jealousy—the same trouble that had befallen their former treasurekeeper, ultimately leading to Doran's capture? Or something deeper? But they'd lived for thousands of years. Surely even Aidan wouldn't hold a grudge that long.

He flung himself down on the bed beside me with a vicious scowl. "No couch for me tonight or I'll be ripping new assholes in all of you."

Ivarr winked at me, sultry golden heat shimmering in his eyes. "Fine by me. She painted me earlier today."

Aidan snorted. "Is that what you're calling it now?"

Blushing, I elbowed him hard in the ribs and concentrated on my phone. "I did paint him, and Doran too." And more, of course.

I texted Vivi. *Are you free to talk?*

She replied back almost immediately. *Sure. Give me 5.*

"So," Aidan drawled, waiting until I met his gaze. "Jonathan Blake. You ready to hear what we found?"

My stomach immediately quivered with dread. "If you can tell me in five minutes or less. I need to call Vivi."

Aidan held up his hand and started counting off his fingers. "Born in Kansas City thirty seven years ago. Lived here all his life. Everything about him checks out until you guessed it." He arched a brow, waiting for me to finish his sentence.

"Until five years ago."

He nodded. "He job hopped around town off and on for years, never anything substantial but basic and expected for a loser of his caliber. One day, he was an assistant manager selling shoes and then the next, he started a business named Solobrex worth a hundred times more than he ever made in his life, coincidentally around the time you and he must have started dating."

"Solobrex," I said slowly. Even the word tasted bad on my tongue. "I never was sure what he did there exactly. He owned it?"

"Nobody's sure what Solobrex does." Sitting in the rickety office chair, Keane gingerly scooted closer to the bed. "That's what makes it a good front."

"A front for what?" I asked. "Jonathan was a lot of things, but I wouldn't call him a smart, brave, or strong man. He wouldn't have been smart enough to be involved in money laundering, let alone anything illegal or risky."

Aidan let out a low grunt. "Exactly. You just described the man to a T. I still can't—"

Keane broke in, "Didn't you say you needed to call Vivi? It's been five minutes."

"Yeah." I stared down at the phone screen, trying to get a grip. Keane might have interrupted him but I knew exactly what Aidan had wanted to say. How could I have ended up with a man like Jonathan? If he wasn't smart, brave, or strong... what had ever attracted me in the first place?

"I'll walk you down to the lobby if you want," Keane said. "If you want some quiet for your call."

Doran was humming in the shower—but it sounded like giant boulders rolling down a mountainside. Ivarr, acting as bartender, started a discussion—aka argument—with Aidan about what they were going to watch on the television. Which had to be at maximum volume.

"Yeah, that'd be great."

I started to get up out of bed, and Aidan's hand clamped down on my forearm. I expected him to boss me around. Tell me to be careful. Demand I return to bed—and him—as soon as possible.

Instead, he leaned up from the stack of pillows against the head-board and kissed my forehead. "Forgive me, *mo stór*. The thought of you being unhappy or worse for a single moment makes me want to commit mass murder on a global scale."

Blinking back tears, I leaned against him a moment, soaking in his heat. "I don't know why I married him either. I'm hoping Vivi can tell me."

My phone rang, so I picked up her call as Keane opened the door. "How are the lovebirds?"

She laughed, and I couldn't help but smile with her. Her joy was too contagious. Tall, brilliant, and drop-dead gorgeous, she'd always had her choice of men. Yet a bearded, thick bear of a man on a motor-cycle had won her heart rather than the slick men in suits that she worked with. I didn't know much about Hammer other than he was a member of Demon Hunters, the motorcycle gang that rode with my guys.

"Absolutely delightful. And you?"

"Great for the most part." Keane led me over to a set of chairs that looked like museum pieces from the seventies. "Just a few things I wanted to go over with you, if you have a few minutes."

"Hmmm. Sounds alarming. What's wrong?"

I sat down in the avocado-green chair. Keane, bless him, moved away closer to the front door, giving me a little privacy while still remaining close enough to protect me if needed. "Nothing's wrong exactly. Just... I'm trying to remember. About Jonathan."

"Oh," she said softly.

"Before I tell you what the guys suspect, was there ever a point where you thought he was an okay guy? And then he changed to be the asshole that we both hated?"

Silence weighed heavily between us while my heart thudded heavily.

Finally, she said, "I didn't understand what you saw in him, but I thought I was being too harsh. No man would ever be good enough for my best friend."

I slumped in the chair, my heart sore and bruised in my chest. "See, that's just it. I don't know what I saw either. The guys asked me about him, and I couldn't answer. Why did I marry him? Why did I think I loved him? Did I ever really love him at all? I don't even remember how we met."

"You had this whole story about how you went to get sneakers and the salesman was teasing you about having paint on your hands. You mentioned you were a student at the Kansas City Art Institute, and then later that day you ran into him on campus. He was dying to see some of your work. Seemed sketchy to me but you were charmed. You honestly don't remember?"

"I don't remember anything," I whispered, blinking back tears. "The guys think... that... well... Do you know what a changeling is?"

"No." She drew the word out. "Something involving Faerie?"

"Yeah. Like he was human and then something fae took his place."

"He seemed human to me, but I guess Warwick looks human enough too."

"Exactly. They think Jonathan the human was swapped out at

some point for a creature of Faerie. But if you never noticed a difference, maybe he wasn't ever human."

"Surely you would have suspected something right away, then."

I blew out a shaky sigh. "Would I, though? I didn't have any experience dealing with men. I never had a boyfriend. I'd resigned myself to always being your kooky friend with too many cats. Some creepy fae in a human suit shows a little interest in me, and I'm in over my head."

"You'll always be my kooky friend, though I don't think one can ever have too many cats."

I laughed a little. It was better than crying. "When did you have concerns?"

"Uh...." She hesitated before admitting, "When you introduced him to me. There was just something about him that set my teeth on edge. I told myself that I was being too overprotective, but there were a lot of red flags right away."

"Like what?"

"The way he talked to you versus everyone else. He oozed snake-oil charm when talking to me, but then casually told you to go make him a sandwich. Or to get him a drink. Or to stop talking. The first time you did what he said, I could only stare, my mouth hanging open in shock."

I grimaced, my stomach churning. "Really? Ugh."

"Again, I tried to rationalize it. Maybe you were into being told what to do. Not my kink, you know? But you didn't enjoy it. You weren't smiling. You weren't laughing. The light in your eyes started to die and it was horrible to see." Her voice thickened as if she was in tears. Which made my lips wobble too. "I tried to get you alone to see if you were okay, but he was always there at the house. He never let you go anywhere alone. School was crazy and then I started working for Boss Man. You know how demanding he is. Time slipped away despite my best intentions. I even stopped by your job a few times, but the energy there was even worse. I hated that place. It sucked the air out of me every time I went inside. I hated the thought of you working there every single day."

My eyes widened. "I worked there too. Solobrex, I mean. Jonathan insisted that I needed a regular full-time job rather than indulging in my little hobby. I'd forgotten how awful that place was."

"You didn't remember that you worked there until just now? How is that possible?"

I whispered the ugly truth. "The changeling was feeding on my memories."

"Oh, honey."

I swiped my tears away. "That's why I can't remember dating him, how I fell in love with him, or our wedding. I don't remember anything specific. Only generalizations for the most part."

"For the most part?" She repeated softly.

I swallowed hard and forced myself to say the words out loud. "I think he may have hurt me sometimes. On purpose. So he could feed on my pain, and then later feed on my memory of it too. A kind of perfect crime, I guess. Hurt me, cause damage, and then destroy my memory of that damage. Where's the proof?"

"Your body remembers."

I shivered, my eyes closing. "Yeah. Sometimes. Like an invisible fog that I don't realize is there until I'm in it and feel how cold and nasty it is. It sneaks up on me."

"Ri, honey, make sure you're communicating with at least Doran. They might trigger you unexpectedly and not know how to handle it."

"Yeah." My throat tightened but I nodded, even though she couldn't see. "I will. They've been great so far. That's how I started to realize that things must not have been right at all with Jonathan. Simple courtesy, asking my opinion, making sure I'm okay. That shouldn't surprise me."

Arms closed around me. Keane leaned down over the back of my chair, his cheek to mine. He didn't say anything. He didn't have to.

"I'm so angry." Her voice vibrated with low, quiet fury. "Not only did he sexually assault you, but then he took away your memory of it, so you couldn't even work through the trauma. What can I do to help? Make a list of therapists? Drive around the city until I can find him and run his ass down? Hire a hitman?"

I couldn't help but laugh. "I love you, but I'm pretty sure I've got four hitmen more than eager to hunt his ass down."

"I love you too. I'm so sorry, Riann. I wish I could have done something as soon as I suspected things weren't right."

"It's not your fault. How could you possibly know what we were dealing with that long ago? We had no idea any of this existed."

"He targeted you from the beginning." Keane's voice carried a sinister edge though he didn't increase his volume. "That you survived long enough to find us at all is a miracle."

"Doran said I was marked by Faerie. I thought my first interaction with anything fae was at *Shamrocked* but Jonathan marked me years before."

"How did you finally break free of his hold?" Vivi asked. "And what kept him from forcing you to come back?"

Chills raced down my arms. Shivering, I pressed back against the chair, tugging Keane's arms around me tighter. "I have no idea."

10

More than a little shellshocked, I said goodbye to Vivi. With cold fingertips, I fumbled to put the phone back in my pocket. My hand didn't seem to want to work. Keane closed his fingers over mine and gently took the phone from me.

"I'll take it for you, *mo stór.*"

"Thanks," I whispered, my throat aching.

I didn't want to cry.

I wanted to scream. Break things. Punch Jonathan's smug face into a bloody smear and light his house on fire. Smash his windows. Slice his tires.

I wanted five years of my life back.

I didn't want to remember all the horrible things he might have done to me. I just wanted those wasted years spent hunched over a computer in a grim, dim cubicle. Rushing home to cook his dinner and wash his clothes and clean his house. And worse.

My mind flinched away.

"Shhh." Keane swept me up against his chest. "I've got you. You're safe now and always."

I burrowed my face against his throat and breathed in his scent. Warm, spiced rum with a thread of something smoky winding through it. A hint of pipe or smoldering peat. In a flash, I sat beside a cheery fire on a cold, snowy night, wrapped in furs and sipping my hot drink. Not cold at all. Because the heat of his eyes promised to keep me warm forever.

Aidan threw open our room's door. "What the fuck happened?"

Keane carried me inside and leaned down to place me on the bed, but I clung to him, hiding my face against him. He finally shifted around to sit on the bed and hold me across his lap. "Some of her memory's returning."

A large, very gentle hand settled on my back. I knew before he spoke that it was Doran. "What do you need most, love? What can we do this very moment?"

I tightened my fingers in Keane's shirt, clenching my jaws. Fighting to keep my rage controlled. My mind leaped from thought to thought like stray sparks lighting up a bone-dry forest.

All the chores I'd done around the house. While my husband did absolutely nothing. The cooking, cleaning, laundry, errands, grocery shopping... Everything that a household needed done. Plus work. The job I'd hated so much. No time to paint. No time to see Vivi. No time to do anything but slave for him.

Work. I needed to tell them.

"Solobrex," I ground out. "I worked there too. It was awful. I didn't remember until Vivi told me."

Doran's giant hand smoothed up and down my back. The bed dipped and another man pressed against my side, enveloping me in the rich scent of leather. Warm, golden light bathed over me, trying to take some of my hurt away. But this hurt couldn't be soothed. Not this time.

In fact, the golden light of truth only made me see more clearly.

"Everything was gray. The cubicles, the carpets, the walls. All very modern and expensive, I'm sure, but uniformly gray. Like a prison. I didn't know Jonathan owned the place and I can't remember exactly what I did. Only that I hated it. We weren't allowed to hang any kind of artwork or personal items in our cubicles. I made the mistake of taking in a plant that Vivi had given to me when we got our first

apartment in Kansas City. Just a common pothos, but it'd thrived in
our dinky basement apartment. As soon as I took it to my cubicle, it
started to shrivel up. The tips of its leaves browned and blackened.
The roots rotted, even though I didn't change the watering schedule."

I laughed, but it sounded harsh to my ears. "I hated everything
about the place, but the pay was great. Too great to leave, he said. I
had to make my car payment and help with the rent on the new
condo. I'd never cared about money before. I didn't care about invest-
ments or retirement accounts or any of the other stuff he told me to
do. I just wanted to paint."

My voice broke.

The one thing I'd given up.

Resolute, I lifted my face from Keane's throat. "I was that fucking
plant. I rotted and withered every moment in that place and with him,
yet I couldn't leave. I didn't even know anything was wrong. I just felt
so bad all the time. I was trapped but couldn't see the bars and chains.
Not until it was too late."

"Aye, you did know." Doran knelt on the floor between the two
hotel beds, yet he still managed to tower over us. "You fought every
moment to stay alive, love. So you could find and free me. Do you
think a normal human could have survived a changeling's appetites
for so many years? Only a survivor would have made it out alive, and
you did, Riann. You broke free of something that should have been
impossible to escape."

Rage bubbled up inside me. "It shouldn't have happened. Not to
me, not to anyone. I'll never be the same. I'm damaged and hurt and
he's still out there. Unharmed, untouched, probably laughing his ass
off about how much he got from me. I'll never know everything that
he stole from me. How can I when I can't remember? Did he take
memories of my childhood? What if he'd destroyed my memories of
Vivi? She's all I've ever had."

"Then let's go get him." Doran's voice rumbled the floor. "Let us
bring his head on a platter. Or is it other body parts you'd rather
have?"

I wasn't normally a vindictive person. That was Vivi's area of expertise. She hadn't been joking when she'd offered to find Jonathan and run him down with her car. She'd never done anything illegal—to my knowledge—but she'd deliberately chosen to work for the best defense attorney in town, and not just because the pay was great.

But staring into Doran's dark eyes...

I wanted nothing more than to take him up on his offer.

He swept me against his chest. The hallway outside our room blurred with his speed. He pounded up a flight of stairs, following Ivarr's golden light. Threw a door open and carried me out into the dark. His chest heaved, his back arching. His head thrown back, neck and shoulders straining. His body quivered as the gargoyle erupted.

Black leathery wings swept out from his back. His skin thickened and grayed, turning into the weathered granite. Clutching me against his chest, he ran toward the edge of the roof and leaped off into darkness. For a moment, we dipped, falling, my stomach tumbling in a queasy roll. Then his wings caught air and we soared into the sky.

Cold air stole my breath, but I was too exhilarated to care. Cars moved below us like little toys. Someone shouted and pointed up at the giant black thing streaking across the sky. Ivarr's golden light soared ahead of us, probably drawing even more attention. But I couldn't find it in myself to care.

:*Not to worry*,: Ivarr said cheerfully in my head. :*I'm blurring our images with my light. They see us—but they can't tell what we are.*:

The roar of a motorcycle drew my attention back down to the road. Two bikes wove in and out of traffic, following us along the ground. Aidan and Keane raced ahead, turning back to the north. It took me a few minutes to realize where they were leading us.

The grocery store on the corner. The gas station where I'd filled up my car on the way to the job I hated. The two-story condominium buildings arranged in a horseshoe facing concrete pond. The fountain had been shut off for the winter, though the water wasn't frozen.

I recognized the giant, ugly cement toad in the center. I hated that thing. It reminded me of Jabba the Hut. Why anyone had thought it deserved to be displayed in public was beyond me. I'd been forced to see it every day going to and from work. The frog was even visible from the kitchen window, so every time I did dishes, I had to stare at the ugly monstrosity.

This was our old neighborhood. When I'd been Mrs. Jonathan Blake.

I hadn't been back here in a year, even to get the rest of my stuff. I didn't want it. I didn't want anything that reminded me of my old life. Not the year-old SUV I'd been paying for or the racks of business casual clothes I'd worn to work.

Doran rumbled in my head. *:The fountain is a portal to the Other-world, right outside your door. How did you escape him, love?:*

I swallowed hard. *:I don't know. I remember getting out of an Uber at Vivi's. I was barefoot and in my pajamas. I had my wallet, my phone, and a couple of changes of clothes in a bag. My old clothes from college—nothing I'd gotten in the last few years. I left it all behind.:*

:Fuck.: Aidan's voice clashed like swords. *:The portal's wide open. Stay clear until we can disable it.:*

Wide open—like for creepy crawly creatures to start pouring into Kansas City? I suddenly had visions of giant green pookas and those nasty rat imps swarming the streets. *:What does that mean?:*

Doran spun away from the fountain in a slow, wide circle. *:Even humans could accidentally stumble through an open portal.:*

Ivarr swooped lower, casting his golden light over the bulbous creature's face. My heart pounded with anxiety, terrified he might get sucked through. *:Some of the dark fae use portals like this to lure in food. One way in, no way out. From the fat frog, I'd say there's some kind of bog on the other end. Is it warded?:*

Armed with both of his short, curved swords, Aidan circled the fountain, testing how closely he could get without triggering the trap. *:Yeah. It's so heavily warded that I can't feel where it starts. It's going to take all of us to shut it down.:*

Sighing, Doran swept lower, looking for a safe place to deposit me. *:I'm sorry, mo stór. I meant this to be a quick and satisfying resolution to your dismay, not yet another battle that may risk your safety. We dare not leave such a portal unguarded and open.:*

:What can I do to help?:

:*Nothing,*: he said firmly. :*Let your treasures handle this threat.*:

Lightly, he set me down on my feet in the parking lot beneath a streetlight. :*Okay—*:

I fell. Something jerked my legs out from under me. I grabbed at the lamp pole, but it was too late. I skidded across the pavement on my ass, feet pointed straight at the damned fountain.

Not again. I don't want to nearly drown...

My feet slammed against a parking curb. Something popped in my lower right leg with a sickening crunch.

I screamed, my stomach clenching with the pain. I flung my arms up, reaching for Doran. I couldn't see him, but I heard the flap of his wings. He seized me, talons digging into the waistband of my jeans. Another hand in the back of my sweatshirt. He heaved with a loud roar, but it was like I suddenly weighed ten thousand pounds. His wings pounded the air, his talons screeching through the ground, leaving deep grooves in the concrete and grass as we tumbled closer to the fountain.

Not even the mighty Stoneheart could lift me off the ground.

11

---

*I*f Doran can't fly me out of this...
   I couldn't even finish the thought.

Aidan and Keane grabbed hold of Doran's left arm, Ivarr on the right. Every impressive muscle straining, all four of them fighting to keep me out of the fountain. Yet nothing could stop our slide toward the circular pool.

I closed my eyes, trying to relax and let the magic flow. I was their conduit. They couldn't lose me. I couldn't bear to lose them either.

The wheel spun in my mind, pouring out streams of gleaming, sparkling light. The spokes were balanced. Magic flowed, thick and free despite my terror, though I couldn't help but notice the absence of Warwick's green power mixing with ours.

Aidan's magic clashed like swords with the force of thunder. Ivarr blazed like a captured sun. Keane blazed with all the might of immense hunger, fueling our will. Doran's wings pounded the air, his big body straining. But it wasn't enough.

:*It's no good,*: Aidan said. :*I tried smashing the center but the magic just bounces off.*:

:*Same.*: Normally Ivarr's voice flowed like honey through the magical wheel, but now he rasped, hoarse and strained to the breaking point. *:We'll have to disable it from the other side.:*

The spinning wheel squeaked. No, that was me. *:What's on the other side?:*

Grim silence echoed through the spokes. Great.

Ivarr thought the frog fountain meant a bog. That wouldn't be too bad. Surely.

Famous last words.

Doran managed to lift me up a little so at least I didn't crash feet first into the decorative ring around the pool. My breath oomphed out, my body bending over the concrete edge. I gripped the ledge, straining to stay out of the icy water. *:Don't let go!:*

:Never,: he swore.

My arms quivered. My leg throbbed so badly I was afraid I'd broken it. I stared down at the water, dreading the shocking cold. A thin sheet of ice ringed the outer edge but the rest of the fountain was still open water. I couldn't see my reflection in the cold, dark murk. How deep was it?

My hand slipped. I pitched forward, even though Doran threw his considerable weight backward, trying to haul me back. My clothes tore. Hands gripped my arms. Aidan's forearm locked around my throat. His breath panting in my ear, straining—

I hauled in as much air as I could. Icy cold bathed my face. Shards stung at my skin like shattered glass. Everything rolled and pitched, my head down, my feet up. But then the world was upside down too. Head spinning, I fell *up*. Panting, I stared up at a gray, stormy sky. Cold and wet, it took me a second to realize I wasn't underwater. The fountain was gone.

So were my guys.

I jerked upright, my heart in my throat. "Doran!"

I twisted around, looking frantically for any sign of them. He swore he wouldn't let go. *:Where are you?:*

Silence echoed in my head.

The magical spinning wheel was gone. I couldn't feel them. Anywhere.

Panic tightened like a noose around my neck. Panting, I looked around for anything familiar. The condos and fountain were gone too. I sat on a small grassy island, though I could feel water seeping into my jeans. Everything was wet and muddy. The ground squelched beneath my hands and knees as I shifted my legs beneath me, panting with pain. I could move my toes, and my knee was okay. Hopefully I'd just sprained my ankle. I didn't think I could walk, but I couldn't sit here either. Waiting.

Waiting for whatever dark fae had set the trap to come along like a spider and feast.

Waiting for my treasures to show up and save me.

Waiting...

My whole life had been spent waiting. I'd spent five years waiting for something to change. For something to wake me up. Shake me out of the stupor I'd fallen into once I married Jonathan. I'd waited five years to make my escape from him, though I still couldn't remember exactly what had finally rattled me enough to wake me up.

I wasn't going to sit here waiting to die.

Though I had to be smart too. Smarter than I'd been when I married Jonathan. Smarter than when I'd let my rage sway the guys into heading back to the home I'd shared with my ex. What had I hoped to gain? Sure, it would've been great fun to watch Doran tear a new hole in his hide. I'd love to see Aidan pound my ex into a bloody pulp.

Instead, I'd ended up separated from my guys in some kind of swampy trap.

Gingerly, I crawled closer to the edge of the grassy island. Muddy water circled the knoll, and as I got closer to the edge, my hands sunk deeper into the sludge. Up to my elbows in thick slime that smelled like a sewer backup. A thick gray fog stretched out before me, muting the landscape. I couldn't tell if there were more little islands in the swamp. I couldn't see dry land. A house. Nothing.

I crawled forward another inch, and this time, my right hand kept sinking. There wasn't anything beneath, no mud or roots that I could feel. Perilously close to dunking my face into the swamp, I reared back, struggling to pull my arm up out of the sticky muck. My hand finally popped free, and I carefully backed up to the more solid grassy area.

Trying to stay calm, I spun around slowly, straining to see beyond the fog. A way out. A path. Anything. I closed my eyes and concentrated on sounds, but it was strangely silent. I didn't hear any insects or birds. Just the frantic pant of my breathing.

This wasn't a natural swamp at all, or I'd be eaten up with mosquitoes. I'd hear chirps and croaks. Not silence.

Shaking with cold, pain, and exertion, I crawled back to the highest point of the little island. I pushed up, keeping my weight off my sore leg, wavering as I hopped around, trying to see if a higher vantage point would help. The same gray fog encircled me, as if the cloudy, overcast sky stretched down to the water in a thick, gloomy dome.

I started to lose my balance, so I dropped back down to the ground, crying out as my other foot bounced awkwardly on the ground. Pain shot all the way up above my knee. Not good. My shoe felt too tight. A little ice and some ibuprofen...

A sob slipped through my lips. I had to get back first.

"Riiiiiiiiiian."

My name drawled out like that. I instantly knew who it was.

My stomach heaved.

:*If you can hear me, he's here. Jonathan. The changeling. My ex. He's here.*:

12

My stomach heaved and a chill sweat broke out on my forehead. Torn between fight or flight, I wasn't sure what to do. Squeeze my eyes shut so he couldn't bespell me again? Or keep my eyes wide open so I could protect myself? I had no idea how I'd fallen into his control before, so how could I protect myself now?

Shiny black tips of his shoes appeared in my line of vision.

Like driving past a horrible car accident, I was compelled to look at the carnage. Black dress pants, speckled with mud. He wouldn't be pleased about that. He'd always been very particular about his appearance. Vivi said it was because he was an average-looking man with a receding hairline. He thought by always looking like a bigwig that he could fool people into believing he was important and powerful.

He *had* been powerful. He'd managed to keep me from leaving for five years, even when I was miserable.

A heavy gold watch glittered on his wrist. He wore a tasteful blue patterned silk tie. Impeccable white dress shirt. Beautifully tailored jacket that looked like something Vivi's Boss Man would wear into court.

Bracing myself, I looked up into his face, terrified but also weirdly eager to see what happened. If his eyes would glow with magic or if there'd be something outwardly visible that would betray what he really was.

But no, he looked the same, like a basic, boring businessman. Well-dressed but not particularly remarkable. His brown hair was trimmed short on the sides, longer on the top, carefully swept to the side to disguise his growing forehead. His brown eyes seemed human enough. He didn't glow with power.

In fact, he managed to look... sad. Pained. As if he truly had missed me.

Lying bastard.

"It's been so long. How are you, Riann?"

I blinked, trying to figure out his angle. How should I play this? Maybe *he* didn't know that *I* knew he wasn't human. Did he know about the treasures? That Doran was free?

"Fine," I finally said, trying to play dumb. "What happened?"

He grimaced and brushed at a speck of mud on his thigh. "Well, it seems as though you returned to our previous home."

"Yeah. I was going to key your car. How did I get here?"

His eyes flared, his lips curling with amusement. A break in his careful mask. Jonathan Blake would never have been amused at the thought that someone might damage his Porsche. "I think you fell and hit your head on some ice."

Playing along, I frowned. "Really? I don't like it here. I want to go home."

"Of course, honeybun."

Instant revulsion washed over me. That horrible pet name struck a raw nerve that jangled from my injured leg to the top of my head. I couldn't believe that he'd called me that for years, and I hadn't immediately run for the hills as fast as I could go. Absolutely ridiculous.

Unfortunately, I'd betrayed myself. Riann Blake wouldn't have looked at him with that kind of instant disgust.

"Ah." His smile changed, somehow managing to look regretful. "I see that we have a bit of a problem after all. How much do you remember, honeybun?"

I tipped my chin up and crossed my arms over my chest. "Everything, snookums."

Which was a lie. We both knew it. Though he twitched at the equally dumb pet name I threw back at him.

"Excellent. I'm relieved to know that you'll cooperate fully."

I arched a brow at him. "I never said that."

"Oh? Well, I'd hate to wake up the guardian of this little oubliette I set up for you. But I will if I must. I'm sure he's extremely hungry. I'm surprised that he hasn't already woken, but I did want to ensure I had time to question you before he feasted."

I resisted the urge to look around the grassy island in search of this guardian. Maybe it was out in the water? Some kind of swampy tentacle thing like that disgusting kelpie in Lake Taneycomo? Great. What I wouldn't give for my treasures to suddenly fall through a magical portal with their swords and blazing light, ready to tear off the horse creature's head.

Hairs prickled on my nape and my spine itched with the urge to jump up and defend myself. Even though I couldn't walk. I didn't think Jonathan knew that. Yet.

I gave him a suspicious glare. "What do you want?"

"You have certain information that I need. Despite my best efforts, you've been able to hide that knowledge from me."

"Is that why you destroyed so many of my memories?"

He swept his hands out before him, his shoulders shrugging. "Staying on the mortal plane takes a great deal of energy. Your memories served me well, and yes, I enjoyed flipping through the mental scrapbook of images and events from your past. Worthless little bits, granted, but amusing just the same. You won't miss them."

I swallowed hard, my eyes burning. I did miss those memories. I barely remembered my childhood with Vivi, playing in the hills looking for the lost prince. If I'd been able to remember those summers when I first found the gargoyle statue...

"You knew," I whispered, my voice shaking. "You knew about Doran all along."

"Of course. That's why I found you in the first place, treasurekeeper, and why those memories were destroyed first." He squatted, his brown eyes warm with entreaty. "You have the knowledge buried inside you."

I swept away angry tears. "What knowledge?"

"How to defeat Evil Eye once and for all. The key to his ultimate defeat is written in your very soul. That's why he's always so determined to kill the treasurekeeper as quickly as possible. Why Stoneheart was captured and imprisoned. Not to weaken the treasures. To weaken *you*."

"Me? That's ridiculous. I don't have any power."

"Compared to the original treasurekeepers, yes, that's true. Very little of the original magic is left. But there is power in you. It calls to every fae in this bloody city. Why, I did you a favor."

"Give me a fucking break," I snapped. "Feeding on me was no *favor*. Keeping me miserable and unable to figure out why for five years..."

His deep-throated chuckle cut through me like a razor-sharp knife, revealing the true creature hiding beneath the human suit. His eyes glittered with mirth at my suffering. Sharp white teeth flashed. Outwardly he still looked the same, but chills crept down my arms. "Oh, honeybun. Truly, I forgot how amusing you are. Of course, you were miserable. Misery makes for a delectable feast and doesn't leave a single scar."

"I have scars," I whispered, each word tearing my throat.

"Indeed." He licked his lips, making me shudder. "It cost me a great deal of effort to keep you hidden, honeybun. Do you honestly think you could have survived on your own in this city without me? Evil Eye's minions roam the city at will, sniffing the wind, looking for any sign of you. They would have dragged you kicking and screaming down the nearest portal, and your beloved Stoneheart would still be lying in the bottom of some forgotten cellar prison. Or worse, the meddling leprechaun would have finally tracked you down."

"Warwick?" My voice shook. "What does he have to do with any of this?"

Jonathan threw his head back and laughed again, holding his stomach as if I'd told the funniest joke he'd ever heard. "Oh, that's rich. So sweet, little honeybun. Have your treasures not warned you about a leprechaun's true nature? It takes a special breed to play the game of neutrality between dark and light fae."

I drew a shuddering breath despite the ache in my chest. I didn't want to believe Warwick might have been capable of hurting or betraying me. He'd said himself that *Shamrocked* was a neutral place. He'd served fae both dark and light, though he'd sworn he would throw Balor out.

Could that have been a ploy to make us think he was on our side? Fae couldn't lie, right?

You be treasure for me too. Hold on to that, love.

Something rumbled through the ground beneath me, making the whole island quiver.

"Ah, times up. Fhroig awakes." Jonathan slapped his thighs and stood, though he bent down, offering his hand to me. "Come along, honeybun."

"Where? I won't go back to my old life with you."

Nodding, he sighed regretfully, though he couldn't disguise the sharp glint of his teeth, his tongue flicking out to taste my scent on the air. "Does it matter as long as you're not devoured by Fhroig?"

"Yes. I want to know exactly where you're taking me."

"This time, I'll take you to my true home."

The grassy knoll rocked, making me gasp. It was almost like... breathing. "Where's that? Hell?"

"Once he awakens, even I can't stop him." Jonathan looked at something behind me and grimaced. "We must go now."

I wasn't falling for that trick. Of course, there was a horrible frog creature coming. I wasn't going to take my eyes off the monster in front of me. "What are you? Was Jonathan ever human? I need answers, or I'm not going anywhere with you. Especially not to some unknown place you won't even name. It's probably even worse than this nasty swamp."

"I said I would take you to my true home where you'll even be safe from Evil Eye's minions."

Sure. Until he decided to kill me himself. Or worse... What if he started feeding on me again and managed to destroy the memories of my guys? If he made me forget that I was the treasurekeeper?

I can't lose them again.

He took a step back, lifting his hands palm out before him. "Stand up slowly, Riann. He's not fully awake yet."

A horrible squelching sound behind me tightened my shoulders. I had to look—even if it was some kind of trick. Ever so slowly, I swiveled my head around. Two gray, muddy lumps had pushed up out of the soggy grass. Maybe two or three feet tall. Fatter at the bottom where they sat on the ground but generally rounded at the top. I didn't see any limbs or eyes or mouth.

That's not too bad. Right?

One of the lumps moved, slinging droplets of muddy water that my mind registered on my cheek and arm. It opened. Blinked.

The two lumps. Were eyes. Red eyes with vertical black slits. Looking at me. Almost like a frog or crocodile submerged in water except for the very tip of its eyes. Three feet apart or so. Which would make the creature's mouth...

I distinctly felt the ground moving beneath my hand. No, it wasn't ground at all. Grassy roots and mud—that covered a giant frog head.

"When his mouth opens, you're dead," Jonathan whispered. "Not even I can save you. I don't know how long it'll take for you to be digested, but I guarantee it won't be a pleasant way to die."

"And having you devour my memories and hurt me for years is such a better alternative?" I retorted in a low voice, slowly backing away from the creature's eyes. How far away was his mouth? Frogs had long, elastic tongues. I needed to be as far away as possible...

"My pillars still stand on the plain where Evil Eye was first defeated. You'll be safe enough there until you can tell me how to kill him once and for all. You know that fae can't lie."

Though that doesn't mean you always hear the unvarnished truth, either. Warwick had said so himself.

The ground started to collapse inward just feet away. The mouth. A thick, pasty pink worm wriggled beneath the muddy grass.

Die inside a nasty frog hole. Or go with my ex-husband changeling to his home somewhere in Faerie? I was under no illusion that he'd simply let me go when he got what he wanted—even if he was right that I possessed some secret knowledge he needed. I had to assume it was a protected place in the Otherworld where even Warwick couldn't find me. How would he even know where to look?

I didn't know who this asshole was. Let alone where he was taking me.

Desperate, I glanced back at Jonathan. He offered me his hand. Impatient, perhaps even nervous, he snapped, "Hurry. We must go. Now."

Why didn't he just grab my hand and whisk me away? Warwick could have snapped his fingers and we'd be sitting at his bar, waiting on Doran and the guys to show up.

Warwick. Of course. I jammed my hand down into my jeans pocket, fumbling to find his coin. Cold metal against my fist.

:I need you.:

A thin curtain of green suddenly flared around me. Jonathan's mouth sagged open, jagged teeth clashing with fury.

Warwick's arms close around me. I smelled his lush, flowery scent, his long black hair tumbling around me like the finest silk. "Bloody hell, Riann. I thought you'd never call me."

13

Green and gold fireworks flashed all around us. Clutching Warwick, I didn't even look around. I didn't care where we went, as long as it was away. With his arms around me, all my suspicions faded away to nothing.

This was right. Safe. I felt as safe in his arms as I did in Doran's embrace. I didn't care what they thought about leprechauns in general. I didn't care what Jonathan had tried to imply about Warwick's neutrality. He'd come to my aid, exactly as he'd promised, when no one else could.

"Thank you," I whispered, lifting my head from his chest.

"Greenshanks at your service, *mo stór*." He leaned down to gently kiss my forehead. "Welcome to the Summer Isle."

His home in Faerie.

Color assaulted my senses, so bold and vivid that I could hear and taste what I was seeing. Pink sky tasted like cotton candy, sweet and melting on my tongue, but it sounded like high, sweet flutes trilling a gentle melody above the noise all around me. Purple and red flowers tumbled in a crashing crescendo that tasted like pops of cayenne and curry against the sweetness of the sky. Giant yellow platters sang a deep, bass melody and tasted like lemony sunshine. They looked like sunflowers, only with white centers instead of brown. Even the white seared my eyes with intensity, as if a million-watt bulb burned in the center.

I dragged my gaze back up to Warwick's face. A glimmering green aura hung about his head, tasting and smelling like fresh herbs plucked from the garden. The sweetness of mint, the bite of rosemary, brightened with lemongrass and grassy parsley. His long black hair flowed like ribbons of silky night through the green. His eyes glowed like golden suns, casting enough heat and light that I could feel the warmth of his gaze on my cheeks.

"Wow."

His lips quirked and he entwined his arm with mine. "Allow me to give you a tour, *mo stór*."

I took a step and my leg immediately gave out, pain shooting up to my knee again.

He caught me, sweeping me up against his chest. "Lady, forgive me. I didn't know you were injured."

My whole leg throbbed from my foot to my knee, making my breath catch in my chest. "When Doran set me down in the parking lot, something caught me and started dragging me toward the fountain. My lower leg jammed into a curb. I hope it's just sprained." My voice broke on the last part. Now that I was safe, I couldn't hold back the tears. "It hurts pretty bad though. I'm afraid it might be broken. At least I didn't hurt both legs."

He carried me toward an archway covered in flowery blue vines that added a deep bass trombone-like sound to the cacophony. Though as we neared, I realized the flowers were butterflies, wings fluttering gently. They didn't fly away as we passed through.

"The fountain was a trap keyed to you alone. If you'd driven there, it would have activated as soon as you stepped out of the car. Anyone could have been able to cross the portal unwittingly, but the magical trap engaged as soon as it sensed you nearby. Naturally, it was set to refuse access to anyone else once it caught you, in case you had assistance nearby."

Immediately, I thought of the guys. My treasures. Left behind, helpless to reach me... They must be frantic and furious.

Warwick laughed softly. "They are indeed, but have no fear. Time slows to a faint crawl in Faerie, almost nonexistent in the mortal plane. There's no rush to get you back to them."

One moment we were in a garden. The next, he was striding across soft white marble with vivid green and gold veins. The assailing noise and colors from outside faded away, leaving me drifting on a soft fluffy cloud of peace. Bending down, he set me on a velvety green chaise, carefully lifting my sore leg up to slide a pillow beneath. A small round table held a crystal pitcher that glistened with some kind of liquid, cups, a plate of what looked like cookies or little finger sandwiches, and a silver bell that tinkled when he gave it a quick shake.

"Let's see what ails thee." Kneeling beside me, he loosened the laces and gently worked my shoe off. Though I still hissed with pain. "What questions do you have while we wait for assistance?"

"If I didn't have your coin in my pocket, would you have still been able to come?"

"Aye, though having the coin made it infinitely easier for me to penetrate Fhroig's lair. It also ensured our effortless escape before the changeling could interfere without a need to expend all my magic. I could have reached you either way, but lucky indeed that you had me gold on your person."

I thought a moment, wincing as he carefully tried to roll my pants leg up. There were other questions I wanted to ask him. Hard questions. I wasn't sure that I wanted to know the answers. If he *had* conned me... I didn't want to know.

Did I?

He looked up from my leg, his face grave. "Before we explore your further questions, I must make it clear that your thoughts be loud in me head as the sounds outside be to you, even more so than on the mortal plane. Summer Isle be me lair, so to speak, in Faerie, as that bog be created for Fhroig. Everything here works its magic for me. If you'd rather have privacy for further conversation to protect your thoughts, then I recommend we wait to discuss your concerns back in the mortal realm."

Before I'd managed to free Doran, he'd told me that he wouldn't lie —unless I wanted a lie of omission. His silence, rather than the truth, if it was too painful for me to hear.

I didn't want his silence.

"How much did you know about me before I walked into *Shamrocked* the first time?"

Emerald green fire bursts flared in his eyes and he laughed softly, shaking his head. "Even now, you manage to surprise me. Not the question I expected first. I knew the treasurekeeper was nearby. Those of us with any access at all to the mortal world felt your ceaseless pull. But nary a one of us could find you. A curtain covered you, shielding your image and location from all eyes, even though we could still smell your scent and feel your magic. It wasn't until *he* came into me pub and threatened me that I knew exactly how imperiled you be."

My eyes widened. "Jonathan threatened you?"

"He did indeed, and I was bound to accommodate his wishes, to a point. In that regard, you'd be wise to heed what others have told you about leprechauns."

I opened my mouth to blurt out a denial, but the words wouldn't come. I hadn't expected him to agree with everyone telling me to be wary of him. Surely not. He'd just saved me. But had he been in on it from the beginning? No. I refused to believe it.

A chime sounded and Warwick stood, smoothing and straightening his clothing. I hadn't noticed how nice he looked. He wore a shiny silk emerald tunic with long, flowing sleeves and black pants that looked like plushy velvet. Chunks of polished emerald and gold decorated his hair and throat, and yes, this time, his hair hung down to lightly sweep the marble tiles as he turned.

He bowed low as a woman stepped through the garden archway. Airy layers of gossamer silk floated all around her, robe, cape, and maybe even wings, glistening with opal droplets. A bit shorter than Warwick, she seemed to glide over the marble without taking a single step. Her skin looked like polished copper, and a matching thick braid hung down her back and trailed the floor behind her like a train.

Her face was starkly beautiful. Hauntingly high cheekbones, delicate nose and mouth, wide, shining eyes, sprinkled with light and power. As if I stared too long, I would never be able to look away. Her eyes gleamed like captured stars but I couldn't tell a color. All colors of the universe sparked in her gaze.

Still bowing, Warwick said, "Thank you for coming, Your Majesty."

"Of course, cousin. You've done all of Faerie a great service in helping keep our treasurekeeper alive and well." She glided closer, a smile flitting over her perfect lips. "I'm Morgan, and you must be Riann, who managed to free Stoneheart from his long imprisonment."

I caught myself still staring at her. A queen, from the way Warwick answered her. I flushed beet red and quickly started to swing my legs over the side of the chaise. Should I bow like him, or kneel? Or fucking *curtsey*? Did people kiss her hand?

Her laughter tinkled through the room, and she quickly lay a hand on my sore leg, stilling me. "Lady Riann, please don't attempt to rise when you're injured, and please, no kissing of hands is required." She winked at Warwick, a dimple appearing in her smooth coppery cheeks. "Unless it's *your* hand being kissed, my dear."

Unsure, I settled back on the cushions, trying not to be awkward while she examined my leg. With my jeans rolled up, I could see the swelling. My foot looked like a balloon, and I'd developed an impressive black and blue cankle. No wonder I hadn't been able to walk on it.

Queen Morgan stared intently for several minutes. Long enough that I dared a quick glance at Warwick, trying to understand what was going on. I didn't feel or see anything happening, but I had no idea how magic might work here.

"It's very much the same as when you work magic." She straightened, brushing her palms off as if she'd gotten something on her hands. "That was some nasty work. You should drink as much honeyed nectar as you can take. That'll speed healing from the inside out."

Flushing, I looked back down at my *nasty* foot. It was still swollen and bruised.

"Oh, no, dear one." Shaking her head, she lightly touched a fingertip to my forehead. "I spoke of the lingering taint from the changeling. It was like a stain on your shining light and made you more susceptible to any dark fae influence. With Evil Eye running amok, you need all the magical protections at your disposal. Your foot will be as good as new once you drink some of Warwick's nectar."

"Oh. Thank you. For everything. Both of you."

"I ask only one thing." Holding my gaze, she leaned closer. Her eyes spun rainbows and diamonds through my mind. "The changeling's name, if you please."

14

My head spun. My stomach flip flopped. A cold, clammy sweat broke out on my forehead.

"Jonathan," I croaked out, shivering. "Blake."

The spinning rainbows flitted through my mind, dancing and bouncing like colorful fireflies. *:Not his human name.:* Morgan's voice fluttered through me delicately. *:His fae name. True names have power. Which one of our people did this to you?:*

"I don't know," I said aloud.

The dizzying rainbows and dancing butterflies faded away. I blinked up at her, my breath coming in soft pants. She brushed her fingertips lightly over my cheek and straightened, turning to Warwick. I had the sense of silent communication flowing between them, but I could barely keep my eyes open. Everything kept spinning. The marble room. Copper skin, rainbow eyes. Emerald green and black silk.

Warwick.

He cupped my cheek and pressed a cup to my lips. "Drink, love. This will help."

My brain shrilled something about never eating or drinking anything in Faerie, but it was too late. I'd already swallowed a mouthful of the sweet, cool liquid, and suddenly, my body demanded more. All of it. As if I would crumple into dust if I didn't drink the entire pitcher. With every swallow, my body felt heavier. I couldn't hold up my head. I couldn't keep my eyes open.

I must have slept, though I had no sense of elapsed time. Only the steady drum beneath my ear and Warwick's fresh, bright scent of green. His hands smoothing my hair. His lips against my forehead. His voice flowing over me, though I couldn't make sense of the words. It almost sounded like singing. A whole orchestra, notes rising and falling around us like birds on the wind. All the colors humming with vivid, pure notes, with a clear, high tenor rising over the top. His voice. Singing about...

I couldn't quite understand. But it felt like... love.

I opened my eyes and his lips quirked. "There you are. Feel better?"

"What happened?"

"The Queen of Faerie has that effect on mortals. Just being in her presence can make you lose track of everything you ever knew or thought. On the bright side, that gave the nectar time to heal your leg."

I looked down at my very normal-sized foot, no longer black and blue and puffed like a balloon. "Wow. I feel like I'm going to show up back on earth and a hundred years will have passed."

He smiled but it didn't quite meet his eyes. "Aye, it's possible to get lost in Faerie."

I reached up and twirled a lock of his dark hair around my finger. "I can see why."

"Would it be such a terrible fate to be lost with me?"

"Not at all." I lay my head back on his chest, turning my face against his throat. "Not if you're here."

"The never-ending temptation." He sighed against my temple. "Though you would never be complete without the treasures. I can't do that to you, even for an eternity of bliss, just you and I."

"Is that why the guys were worried about me coming here?"

He huffed out a laugh. "Indeed. Many a mortal has stepped into Faerie and refused to go back, and for much less than such a magnificent catch."

I laughed too, though my chest felt tight and I wanted to cry. "Especially with a changeling laying traps for me and those nasty creatures. Having Greenshanks all to myself sounds like paradise for sure."

"Now, love, even Aidan isn't nasty."

Grateful for his teasing—when he could have made me feel miserable—I play-growled and fisted my hand in his hair. Not to hurt him.

But to never let him go.

"Aye, love, never." He kissed my temple. "When you're ready, I'll take you back. Though I want to show you something first."

I lifted my head, still clutching his hair. "What?"

He stood, pulling me up to my feet with him. I held on to him, testing my injured leg, but it wasn't sore at all. "Wow."

With a snap of his fingers, my shoes and socks were back on my feet, my jeans dry and clean, and all the dried, caked-on mud disappeared. He tucked my hand around his arm and led me toward a stone wall covered with lush ivy. "I'd love to give you the complete tour, but I'm afraid the treasures be pounding on the door at *Shamrocked*, demanding entrance."

My eyes flared with surprise. "Really? Why would they go there?"

Warwick waved his hand and the ivy parted like a curtain, revealing a darkened hallway. The scent of rich, black loam filled my nose. Rather than stone or wood, the walls looked like a hand-carved tunnel with bits of roots and rocks caught in the dirt. "They can't access the portal, so they came to the next best thing. And, of course, they suspect that I'm a villainous traitor in your abduction."

I refused to ask. I knew his heart. Everything would make sense when we all sat down to discuss what had happened.

"This is the safest place in all of Summer Isle, perhaps even all of Faerie." We paused in what felt to be a spacious room or cavern, though it was still too dark for me to see the ceiling. "No one knows I have this, even Her Majesty. I keep it in the dark as much as possible, though I can't help but come and stare at it every chance I get."

I had no idea what he was talking about. Some kind of animal that only lived in the dark? A bat? He lifted his palm and light slowly brightened around his hand, illuminating an easel holding a canvas. It wasn't large, perhaps sixteen by twenty. Most of the canvas was dark with shadow, but in the center, a bright doorway gleamed with opalescent light that spilled over a girl, standing in the center. She wore a bright green coat. Not quite lime, but brighter than Warwick's emerald.

A silhouette stood behind the girl, dark against the pearly light streaming through the door. The shadowed shape of clothing was feminine, as if the person wore a floor-length formal gown.

"I love the light treatment." I leaned closer, trying to make out details of the girl, but she faced the darker, larger woman in the doorway. "Who's the artist?"

"You don't recognize it?" Warwick asked softly.

I jerked my head around, searching his face. "Me? I did this? But when? How?"

"This canvas was my first solid lead that you were near. I saw it on a student display in Crown Center and immediately brought it here to keep it safe."

Stunned, I turned back to the painting, trying to see my hand in its creation. I did tend to pull on gothic or strange elements, and the darker color palette was my style. But I felt no resonance when I looked at it. No sense of ownership or pride of creation. "When would I have created it?"

"The display was for the Kansas City Art Institute. I immediately tried to find you there, but the trail was cold. My guess is that I must have just missed finding you right after the changeling made his connection. You don't remember creating it?"

I shook my head. "I don't recognize it as mine. It could be, certainly, but I don't even have a faint memory of the concept, let alone the execution. I was only at the Institute a month or two before..." My heart ached, stealing my breath.

Before I'd given up on my dream and walked away from a full-ride scholarship at an art college. I couldn't remember any of the paintings I might have completed in that first semester. So where had this painting come from? Had I done it before I got to Kansas City? But then how did it end up on display?

"How did you find it?" I finally asked.

"The magic called to me."

Magic? What magic? I looked at the painting again. It was good. Captivating, sure. I loved the play of dark and light, and even the light had an otherworldly quality. It wasn't yellow or even white, but seemed to carry light like a prism. Amazing work—but not magical.

Not like colors so bright they touched my sense of taste and hearing. Not like a Faerie queen who could dazzle my mind or a drink that could heal my injured leg. Or turn a man into a gargoyle.

Warwick moved his hand closer to the painting so that more light spilled across the canvas. "Look at the wonders you have wrought."

As the canvas brightened, the shadows seemed to swirl and move. The light pouring through the doorway had movement, as if the woman was shooting rainbows through the doorway. In the dark silhouette of her dress, I could suddenly make out the flow of layers, very much like the gown that the queen had been wearing. Even a hint of tucked wings behind her back. Though her hair flowed loosely like a cape over her shoulders and down to the ground.

In the inner folds of her gown, a large cat blinked at me. Black cat, green-gold eyes, as large as the girl in the painting. For a moment, I could hear purring. Not from the painting, but inside me, a memory, perhaps. A cat curled on my lap, a thunderous purr rumbling through me.

The eyes winked out but the rainbows still flowed from the doorway, an active flow of light, spreading through the shadows in the border. Bringing to life more shapes in the darkness. Dark creatures with sharp teeth. Red eyes. Black sweeping wings and razor-sharp claws clattering on stone. Curling deep-purple tentacles writhing in the light. Flinching away from the rainbows—but still trying to reach the girl.

She held something in her hand, lifting it up toward the woman in the doorway. It glowed with golden light. A candle, maybe? Though as

I bent nearer, trying to see through the swirling rainbows, I realized it was a paintbrush.

Me. It had to be me. Even though I couldn't see myself in the girl's features or remember painting it.

Warwick's light dimmed and the swirling rainbows faded. The writhing shadows quieted. It was still a lovely painting, but the motion—the magic—stilled.

"Imagine seeing this in broad daylight," he whispered. "Even humans stared at it in wonder, though I doubt they could see the same magic flowing through every stroke. It still captured attention. I nicked the canvas immediately and brought it here to keep it safe, hoping I could find you before it was too late. But I couldn't see your face in the painting. I had no idea what you looked like or where you were. Only that you must be found and protected."

He sighed heavily. "I failed to find you in time. Your light was already stifled. I had to settle for leaving the coins throughout the city, hoping that you might still have enough magic to find one and break through to *Shamrocked* before they could kill you."

Stunned, I couldn't seem to form a coherent thought. Staring at that painting—that I had evidently created, but couldn't recognize— had broken something in me. Or at least derailed me.

That wasn't me. But it was.

I didn't paint that. I couldn't have.

But I did.

"I admit that I fell in love with the creator of this painting long before I ever saw your face. There's so much of you in this painting, Riann. Every stroke sings of the beauty of your soul. The way the light falls on your skin and sparkles in your eyes. Magic hums all around you, even though you're unaware. I was obsessed with you, but I didn't know where to find you. Until you walked into me pub."

I swallowed the giant lump in my throat. "And then I saw the gargoyle on the shelf."

He laughed softly, though it broke my heart. "I knew you were the treasurekeeper so it was no surprise. But aye, I felt the weight of Stoneheart's glare burning a hole in the back of me head as soon as he saw you. It's grateful I am for even a wee corner of your heart reserved for me."

I turned toward him, wrapped my arms around his waist, and leaned against him. Staring up into his eyes, I let him see exactly how much he meant to me. The way my heartbeat surged whenever I was near him. "You helped me when no one but Vivi believed a word I was saying, even though that meant we were able to free Doran. Instead, you could have whisked me here to your Summer Isle forever, and I would have loved you without ever even knowing about the treasures. Which only makes me love you more, Warwick Greenshanks."

Bending down, he cupped my face in both of his hands. Arcs of green sparked around him, a magical aura that warmed my skin. "And I love you, Riann Newkirk. I bring all the powers of the Summer Isle to assist you in any way possible."

He slid one hand up into my hair, tangling his fingers in a firm grip that made my lips part on a soft sigh. Desire coiled through me, sparked by his magic and the fiery green light in his eyes. He slanted his lips over mine, his other hand turning my head just so. Pinning me for a soul-searing kiss that stole my breath. And my heart. All over again.

His tongue stroked over mine, his grip fierce. As if this might be the last time he was able to kiss me. At least without Doran or one of the other guys watching.

:*Brace yourself.*:

I wasn't sure what he meant. Breathless, I clung to him. Sinking further into the glowing green magic that flowed around him.

Something crashed. Deep bellows and shouts echoed in my head. I opened my eyes, but I already knew where we were.

The dark cave and my forgotten painting were gone. I sat on top of the glossy wooden bar at *Shamrocked*. And four very angry men tore at the front door of the pub, determined to reach me despite whatever protections Warwick had on the place.

Aidan roared. "There's the bloody bastard! Your head is mine, Greenshanks!"

15

Frozen in horror, I watched Aidan barrel toward Warwick, a sword in each hand. Then it dawned on me.

Aidan couldn't see me. I was behind Warwick. Even now, he was protecting me.

I jumped down off the bar and ducked under Warwick's arm, sliding around in front of him. "I'm okay! He saved me!"

Aidan didn't slow his charge. Maybe he couldn't. He was the Slaughterer, the mighty Spear of Lug. Once he was revealed, there was no escape.

I threw myself at him, trying to slow him down. Distract him. He wouldn't ever hurt me, so if I could get in his way...

Smoothly, he hooked his arm around me and swept me behind him, throwing me backward so hard I lost my footing. Doran caught me up against him, his big hands cradling my face, turning me this way and that to make sure I wasn't hurt. Then he crushed me against him so hard I couldn't breathe.

"I died a thousand times while you were gone," he growled against my ear. "I fucking hate being so helpless. What happened, love? How did you get away?"

"I'll tell you," I finally gasped out. "But stop Aidan from hurting him."

Aidan swung both swords, hacking at the bar and knocking over bottles as his quarry dodged and rolled.

Warwick chuckled, a bright, cheerful sound that reached me over the thuds and crashes. "Don't worry about me, Riann. High Court fae are nigh impossible to kill on the mortal plane, even for the treasures."

His last few words were strangled. I pulled out of Doran's arms enough to see that Aidan had his forearm pressed hard against Warwick's throat, bending him backward over the bar. The other sword flashed in a downward arc toward Warwick's face.

I flung out my hand, instinctively reaching for him. To stop the sword. Somehow. I couldn't bear for him to be hurt. Ever. Especially not now.

The sword spun out of Aidan's hand, flipped around, narrowly missing his face, and shot over his shoulder toward me. Reflexively, I closed my fingers over the hilt as it thumped into my hand. The sword was surprisingly heavy. My arm trembled under its weight, forcing me to wrap my other hand around the hilt.

Aidan whirled, a fierce scowl gouging his forehead. "What the fuck are you doing?"

I stared at the sword. His sword. My mouth opened but no words came out.

Doran closed his fingers over mine, carefully removing the vicious blade before I dropped it and cut off my own foot. "I've never heard of such a thing. Nobody stops the Slaughterer."

Still glaring, Aidan stepped closer and took back his sword. "Humph. Evidently *she* does."

Shaken, I stared at him, not sure what to say. I refused to apologize for taking his sword away before he could hurt Warwick. Though I had no idea how I'd done it, or what exactly it meant. I was supposed to be the treasures' conduit. I didn't have any power of my own.

But I'd just taken the Slaughterer's magical weapon from his own hand.

I hadn't meant to cause any harm. Neither had Warwick. He'd

fucking saved me and then been attacked by a sword-wielding maniac.

Just as smoothly as he'd thrown me to safety, Aidan hooked his arm around me and dragged me up against him into a full-body hug. Keane and Ivarr joined him, holding me as tightly as Doran had earlier.

"I thought for sure that you were gone for good." Aidan's voice was hoarse and rough with emotion. "I couldn't bear it. I lost my mind, Riann. All that matters is your safety, and if he saved you, then I'll give the leprechaun three wishes."

"No offense but I'll not take you up on that deal." Warwick straightened his tunic and shook his hair loose about his shoulders. "Twas wishes that got me into trouble in the first place. Why don't you all sit down, and I'll tell you what I can, though I'll warn you now that I'm still under geasa."

Grudgingly, the guys let up their death grip on me enough to help put the bar back to rights. Though Doran didn't release my hand, as if afraid I'd disappear again. Already behind the bar, Warwick pulled a round of beers.

Doran lifted me up onto a bar stool, but stood behind me, his big body caging me protectively in front of him. "So, love, tell us if you will what happened once you passed through the portal."

"If I may…" Warwick broke in. "Let me begin the tale as I know it, because the events at the fountain were set in motion long ago." At Doran's nod, he continued. "As you know, we're on the fringe of Faerie, and so it's easy enough to move *Shamrocked* at will. With your statue on me shelf, I found that the pub would manifest near the treasurekeeper when she began to come into power."

"Wait, what?" I gulped. "I never came into power."

Aidan grunted. "You say that when you just yanked a sword from the Slaughterer?"

I turned toward him, peering around Doran's beefy biceps. "Okay, so yeah, maybe that was power, but I got that power from *you*. The treasures are reunited, right? So that makes us powerful."

Warwick shook his head. "A treasurekeeper calls the treasures to her side as her power grows. Granted, that power has been failing with Doran's capture, but you were calling them to you. It was no coincidence that *Shamrocked* was on this corner when you were nearby, or that the Demon Hunters just happened to set up shop nearby. We were all pulled by your ceaseless tide to be where you needed us. Then I found the painting, and I knew beyond a shadow of a doubt that you were in danger."

"What painting?" Keane asked.

"A painting of the treasurekeeper opening a door to Faerie," Warwick replied softly. "It screamed of magic, power, and danger all around. I took it to the Summer Isle for safekeeping but failed to find its creator. I followed the breadcrumb trail to the Kansas City Art Institute, but I was too late. She was gone."

"I don't remember painting it," I whispered. "I don't even recognize it as mine, though I agree it's done in my style. We're guessing that Jonathan must have gotten to me just before Warwick was able to track me down."

Ivarr sighed heavily. "Of course. The trail disappeared because the changeling was already feasting on your power. No wonder Warwick couldn't find you."

"I did what I could," Warwick continued. "I tossed me gold around the city, especially around the pub, hoping against all odds that she would find her way to us. One evening, a mortal man found his way inside with one of my coins. He took note of the Irish theme of the bar and jokingly dropped the coin on the bar, asking if I would give him three wishes. Me a fool, I agreed. Only to learn the man was no mortal at all."

My eyes flared with sudden realization. "It was Jonathan, wasn't it? The changeling Jonathan."

Warwick nodded. Sweat beaded on his forehead and I detected a faint quiver in his hand as he lifted his heavy mug for a long swig of beer. "He got his wishes. You can guess much of what he demanded of me."

"You couldn't warn her." Doran's chest rumbled against my back. "You can't say who he be. You can't take any action to stop him."

Warwick thunked the empty mug down on the bar. "Close enough. I did what I could without violating his geasa, but it wasn't enough. Year after year went by, driving me insane with worry and helplessness. I could do nothing but wait. Hope against hope, even as the magic died a little more each day. I went to every art fair and display I could find, hoping to stumble across another canvas, a clue to her identity. I had a vague notion that if I could point the other treasures in her direction that they'd be able to circumvent the changeling where I couldn't, but it was too late. The ceaseless tide of power that had called us here to Kansas City faded away."

"You said nothing," Aidan growled. "All these years. You could have told us something. Surely. If I'd known..." He slammed his mug down on the bar and bowed his head. "I'd like to say that I would have found you, Riann. I would have done something. But I fear that I would have been the same bull-headed idjit who refused to help you until you stole my ride."

Doran clamped a hand on his shoulder and dragged him closer so I could hug him. "You don't know that. You did what you could. All of you. You had no idea that I was in trouble."

"But I did," he mumbled, his voice cracking. "The treasurekeeper's always in danger. I pretended that if I didn't know, you would be alright. If I kept you away from me, you couldn't be harmed. Meanwhile you were raped and tortured by a changeling that you couldn't escape."

I shuddered. I had a problem with that word. My brain immediately rejected the idea. That wasn't me. I hadn't been raped. Or tortured.

I'd been miserable, sure. I'd wanted to divorce Jonathan, and even though I'd wanted to leave, I somehow never could. It made sense now that I knew what kind of hold that he'd had on me.

My mind had created scenarios and excuses while I lived with Vivi. Because I hadn't wanted to remember the truth. Some of that had been damaged memories, yes. But some of it had also been avoidance.

I had never been in love with Jonathan Blake—because that man didn't even exist. Any vague idea of a normal relationship had been me trying to survive while the changeling reeled me deeper into the trap I couldn't escape.

Closing my eyes, I leaned against Aidan, grateful for both him and Doran supporting me. I didn't think I could sit upright without their help. I'd just melt into a sobbing mess on the floor.

Ivarr stroked my back. Keane held my hand between both of his gloved hands, gently kissing my knuckles one by one.

And Warwick stood on the opposite side of the bar. A sad little smile on his lips.

I pulled my other arm free of Aidan and reached across the bar, offering my hand palm up. Warwick lightly danced his fingers over my skin but didn't immediately take my hand in his. As if he didn't have the right. Or he didn't want to upset the guys, especially Aidan.

"He saved me," I said out loud. "Jonathan was there on the other side of the fountain."

"What happened, love?" Doran asked.

"When I opened my eyes, I was on a muddy, swampy island. Jonathan came almost immediately. It was his trap. He said he needed something from me. Something he hadn't been able to find out in five years."

Lifting his head from my shoulder, Aidan searched my face, a heavy scowl creasing his brow. "Did he say what?"

"He wanted to know how to kill Balor once and for all."

Keane snorted. "Like Warwick said earlier, it's nigh impossible to kill a High Court fae on the mortal plane. It's even harder to kill one in Faerie."

"Balor's High Court fae?" I asked. "I'm not even sure what that means."

"All the Tuatha de Danaan and Fomorians are High Court," Keane replied. "Most Tuatha are light and most Fomorians are dark, but they intermarried thousands of years ago, so it's much more complicated than that."

Evidently I looked as confused as I felt. "Tuatha de Danaan are the ones who brought the four treasures to Ireland, right?"

"According to the legends, aye," Doran replied. "Though it's not as simple as that. Much has been lost over the lifetimes we've lived and died. I used to think that we were merely mortal warriors who were gifted magical powers by the fae, but maybe we were fae once upon a time. Or a mix of human and fae. The queen might remember, but that was long before even her time."

"Queen Morgan?"

Ivarr's golden eyes flared with streams of light. "So not all the old legends have died."

Sheepishly, I lifted my shoulder in a bit of a shrug. "I didn't know the legends. I met her when I was in the Summer Isle."

With a grunt, Aidan gave his empty mug a slight push toward Warwick. "Sounds like I need another drink for this tale."

Warwick refilled the mugs but not with his normal light-hearted wink and tease. In fact, he avoided meeting my gaze entirely.

:It's not your fault,: I told him.

:Aye, but it is. I failed you.:

:Never. You did what you could.: Out loud, I said, "Jonathan wanted me to go to his home in Faerie. He wouldn't tell me where it was or what his true name was. I knew that if I went with him, I'd be dead as soon as he got what he wanted, but the alternative was to stay and wait for Fhroig to wake up."

"Bloody hell," Aidan growled. "He put a trap on top of Fhroig's lair? That's some underhanded nasty shit that I'm not even sure Evil Eye would do."

"The island wasn't land at all," I whispered, shivering at the memory. "Fhroig started to wake up. His eyes popped up out of the ground, and a giant hole started to open up before us. Jonathan said that if the mouth opened all the way that even he couldn't save me."

Ivarr's eyes burned like lasers. "It's a fucking horrible to die because Fhroig doesn't kill you right away. He's magical. He can digest you while he keeps you alive, some say for centuries."

My stomach quivered with dread. "I guess Jonathan wanted me to suffer if he couldn't get what he wanted."

"That's what I don't get." Keane shook his head, his brown eyes almost as icy as Aidan's. "What could you possibly know that he hadn't already been able to get out of you? What's so important that he'd risk exposure on the mortal plane for five fucking years? Though I suppose that's but a blink of an eye for any fae."

"He said the key to defeating Evil Eye was written on my soul. That's why the treasurekeeper's always captured or killed as soon as possible."

Doran rumbled. "What else did the bastard say? Anything that will help us identify him?"

I closed my eyes, trying to remember exactly what Jonathan had said. "He'd been shielding me, both from Warwick and from Balor's minions. Then he said something about pillars."

A low, sweet chime rang through the pub. My eyes flew open, and I looked up at Warwick. Though his lips were firmly clamped shut and he didn't shake his head or give me any other clues, a light danced in his eyes.

"Can you remember exactly what he said?" Aidan asked.

The scene played back through my mind. The widening hole, something bubbling up inside it. Likely a giant, sticky tongue. Jonathan's urgent voice. "'My pillars still stand on the plain where Evil Eye was first defeated.'"

The chime rang again, longer, making goosebumps race down my arms.

"Holy fuck," Ivarr whispered.

The other guys just looked at each other. Even Keane's sultry lips were in a harsh slant.

"What?" I asked. "Who is it?"

Casually, Warwick picked up Aidan's mug and pulled him another draft. "I've been much more careful with me wards since that unfortunate encounter. Especially now that the treasurekeeper walks among us. In case you're worried that some unsavory fae might overhear."

"Eochu Bres." Doran's voice rattled the heavy mugs on the bar. "High King of Maige Tuired, better known as Pillars on the Plain."

A resounding gong-like chime rang through the pub for several seconds. Once it quieted, the silence seemed to echo and pulse with tension.

"Who's that?" I whispered faintly.

Aidan glowered at his mug. Ivarr shook his head. Keane tapped leather-clad fingers on the bar but didn't answer. I couldn't see Doran's reaction but from the grim tone of his voice, I figured it must be pretty bad.

Warwick leaned down on the bar in front of me, his lips quirked with a wry chuckle that didn't reach his eyes. "Only one of the most powerful fae kings to ever cross the veil."

Aidan grunted, shaking his head. "Not quite as hated as Evil Eye but a close second."

Great. Just fucking great.

16

Usually when the guys drank, the mood shifted to laughter and teasing. This time, nothing could shake the grim weight hanging over our heads.

Doran still clutched me, refusing to let me go for a moment. At least Aidan wasn't trying to chop off Warwick's head any longer. Definitely an improvement. Though I didn't think they'd be pals anytime soon.

"You said you met Queen Morgan earlier," Aidan said, pulling my attention to him.

"She came to heal me. Evidently I still carried some of the changeling's dark power."

He grimaced and gulped another long swallow of his beer. "Fucking bastard. Was he still feeding on you?"

Shuddering, I met Warwick's gaze. "I don't think so. He kept trying to get me to come with him, but I was able to refuse. I don't think I would have been able to keep my wits about me if he was still feeding on me."

"A changeling plants a sort of tether in their host, a connection that they use to feed on energy and emotions," Warwick said. "I could feel the darkness still in you, but his geasa forbade me from interfering with his magic in any way or even warning you that it was there."

"What activated it in the first place?"

He shrugged. "I have no way to know for sure, but usually it's something very small. A minor favor or request that gives the fae a foothold in your will. A sense of obligation that they take advantage of, though it could be as easy as giving the fae your full name."

My eyes flared. "He held his hand out to me in the oubliette but didn't touch me. I thought it was weird, though of course I was relieved. If I'd taken his hand…"

Doran's arms squeezed me tighter to his broad chest. "He'd have likely reactivated his link and you would have been gone forever."

I couldn't breathe, but I couldn't bring myself to care. "How did I get away from him in the first place?"

Everyone looked at Warwick. He even made scowling look pretty. "I have no bleeding idea. I wasn't there, remember? I was forbidden from searching for you or interfering with him in any way. I had to wait for you to find me."

"I wish I knew more about your legends and histories. Or how Faerie works." I rubbed my temples, trying to ease the brewing headache. "I'm so confused. I'm just a human, a mortal woman. Yet I'm supposed to have some secret knowledge to take out this powerful dark fae? How? Who's Bres anyway and why would he want to stop Balor?"

"Keane's the best storyteller," Aidan said. "Though we'll be here all night."

Keane huffed out a laugh. "I'll keep it short. Five minutes or less."

Ivarr thumped the bar. "I'll take some of that action. No way you can keep it under five."

"Done," Aidan said. "The leprechaun can mark the time."

"Luck you," Warwick drawled. "Time it yourself."

I couldn't help but snort. "What did you say?"

He winked at me. "Luck is better than any f-bomb."

Aidan rolled his eyes and pulled an antique watch on a chain. He flicked it open. "Go."

"When the Tuatha de Danaan first came to Ireland, Nuada was king." Keane began in a gentle, sing-song voice, not rushed at all. "He lost his hand in battle against the Fir Bolg and was forced to step down. They chose Bres to lead as king because he was half Tuatha de Danaan and half Fomorian, and they thought he'd bring the best of both sides together. But they were horribly wrong. Bres allowed the Fomorians more and more power. As their darkness increased, they began to enslave the Tuatha de Danaan, destroying their light. Until all the light courts banded together and demanded that Bres step down as king.

"He did at once—but he secretly went to Balor and began to raise an army with the goal of wiping out all the courts who opposed him, even if that meant selling out to Evil Eye. With Balor's help, Bres returned to retake Pillars on the Plain. Nuada had been magically restored to health, and with Lug's help, they killed both Balor and Bres. Ireland's future was secured for the light. Until the Tuatha de Danaan were later forced to retreat to the Land Beneath the Waves. Time?"

Aidan grunted sourly. "Three minutes."

"No fair," Ivarr retorted. "He skipped all the good stuff. Like how Balor locked his daughter in a tower to prevent her from filling the prophecy about his grandson killing him. Or how Balor's eye worked in battle."

I held up my hands, stilling their argument. "If they died in battle, why are we still having a problem with them now?"

"Oh that's easy," Keane replied. "Fae never really die. They may leave the mortal plane but they're immortal. They come back, just like we treasures come back in one shape or another. It's their power that brings us back."

I rubbed my temples harder, trying not to wail. "Then how are we supposed to stop the changeling from taking me again? Or stop Balor from trying to capture Doran or one of you? If they can't actually die?"

"Like I said earlier," Warwick said. "It's nigh impossible to kill a High Court fae, let alone an extremely old and powerful fae like Evil

Eye. Even other Tuatha de Danaan couldn't kill him for good. Our best bet is to weaken their power so much that they can't easily return to the mortal plane for centuries. Chopping off his head, putting out his eye, or even magically poisoning him won't actually kill a fae. It just slows him down."

"Are you saying that if the Slaughterer cuts off your head that you won't die?" Aidan asked in a soft, flat voice, more menacing because it wasn't his normal growl.

"Aye, that's exactly what I'm saying. It'll hurt me power, sure. *Shamrocked* would wink out of existence for a time. Summer Isle might sink beneath the waves. But I would still exist, and I will build my magic anew."

Aidan's hand reached over his shoulder toward one of the swords crossed on his back—as if he was going to test out the leprechaun's words. My heart pounded desperately, and I locked my fingers around his wrist. Not to stop him, exactly. Just to hopefully calm him. To remind him that I was here.

That my heart was invested in all of them. Not just him.

Aidan sighed and dropped his hand to the bar, my fingers still on his wrist. "I'll test your words another time."

"Don't be a bleedin' idjit," Doran growled. "You know his words to be true. I've vague memories of chopping off Evil Eye's head myself a few times. Yet here we are, back on the mortal plane, battling him again."

I fought to keep my emotions under wrap, but my voice quivered and my eyes burned. "There's so much I don't understand. There's no way to win this. I'll never be free of him."

Doran rested his chin on the top of my head. "I know, love. We've dropped a lot on you, and you've been through hell and back again in a matter of days. Some sleep will set you to rights. You will be free of him. We'll find a way."

I nodded, though inwardly I groaned at the thought of going back to the hotel with the small, rickety beds. Or the huge, cold warehouse. Or Vivi's. I was bone-deep weary and soul tired. Tired of being home-less. Of being in danger.

Of not being able to remember who I really was. What my life was supposed to be like.

"We've got you, love." Doran picked me up, cradling me in his arms. "The lads worked some deals earlier and when we were rushing over here, we got the final notice that the sale went through. We have a much better place lined up for us now. A home, if you like it."

I lifted my head, searching his face. "Really?"

"Absolutely. It's a bit of a drive outside of the city, though. Unless Greenshanks would be so kind as to whisk us there."

Warwick inclined his head. "I would be honored to assist *mo stór* in any way possible." He waited a moment, his eyebrows rising expectantly. "I merely need the location."

Keane opened his mouth but Aidan cut him off. "I'll do the deed."

Aidan leaned over the bar, his eyes fiercely intent. Slowly, he held his hand out to Warwick.

Holding my breath, I wasn't sure what was happening. Visions flashed through my head. Aidan seizing Warwick's hand, dragging him across the bar and trying to bash his head in. Swords clanging. Shouts and broken glass...

Warwick closed his hand around Aidan's. Silence hung between us for what seemed like an eternity. I wasn't sure what was happening. Some kind of silent arm-wrestling match? No, they weren't straining.

The bar disappeared in a dizzying flash of green and gold. My head spun a moment and I blinked furiously, trying to refocus my vision. Crisp nighttime air stung my cheeks. Stars dotted the velvet sky. I hadn't seen stars in forever. The city lights made stargazing impossible.

Doran strode up a few steps and I caught a glimpse of a wide porch with double doors swinging open. The interior of the house was dark but evidently he could see exactly where to go. He carried me through a few rooms while the guys flipped on lights behind us.

He paused, waiting a moment for Keane to catch up with us. He turned on the light, and I realized we were in a spacious bathroom. Scratch that. A dream master bath with a huge, tiled shower that two or three of the guys could use at the same time if they didn't try to kill each other. A dreamy soaking tub with jets. All done in expensive-looking creamy marble, though the gold-tone faucets were too ostentatious for my taste and outdated.

Doran set me on my feet. "Take a nice long soak, love. There are a couple of other showers in the house, so no one'll bother you and there's no rush. When you're ready to sleep, there's a bed just outside this door."

Keane winked at me. "It's the biggest bed I've ever seen."

Now that sounded promising indeed.

17

I wasn't sure how the guys had managed to buy a house so quickly, let alone one that was furnished. But I was too tired and grimy to care. I stripped out of my clothes and took a nice steamy shower, though I did spare a longing glance at the tub. Another time. I'd light some candles, maybe add some salts or a bath bomb. That sounded heavenly.

I wrapped a fluffy towel around my head. A thick terrycloth robe hung on the back of the door. It looked brand new. Maybe this place had been an Airbnb before the guys had bought it. If so, it was a high-end place. A pang of guilt struck me. It must have cost them a fortune.

I had nothing to contribute. I hadn't been to my job in weeks, and I'd only made a few lousy bucks in tips. Without Vivi's help, I didn't know what I would have done after leaving Jonathan. Disregarding the changeling complication, just leaving him had left me penniless. I'd made good money—I thought. But I'd been buried in debt.

Just another way he'd been controlling me, I supposed. A way to keep me dependent on him and my job in case I ever did think about leaving him.

I kicked my dirty clothes into the corner and opened the door to the master bedroom. I froze, taking in the scene.

Keane and Aidan made sense, for the most part, but they were both naked. Which short-circuited my brain. Both of them were covered in tats, which made me want to push them down flat on the bed and lick every single one of those ink marks. Ivarr and Doran were also in the room, though they were both at least partially clothed. Or I really may have spontaneously combusted. Ivarr stood with his back to me in the corner of a large window. He glanced over his shoulder at me, a warm, golden light flickering in his eyes. But he quickly turned back to staring outside into the dark.

Bare-chested, Doran filled up the doorway, one shoulder casually leaned against the doorframe. He gave me a slow once-over, his heavy, dark gaze hot enough to singe the terrycloth.

But it was the sight of Warwick sitting at the foot of the bed that made my throat tighten with emotion. They'd brought him—or allowed him to join us, at least. He wasn't excluded. Rightfully so, he was here. With us.

With me.

Doran made a low, rumbly sound that drew my gaze to him. "No expectations or pressure, love. If you want to sleep, you'll sleep as safe and snug as a bug in a rug. Ivarr and I be on guard duty tonight. We've had time with you already, and they have not." He pinned that formidable stone gaze on each man one by one. "What she says, goes. Don't make me come back in here and knock heads together, or I'll bar you from the bedroom until she specifically asks for your return. Understood?"

"Aye," each man replied.

Aidan, of course, wore a formidable scowl. He sat propped up against the headboard, arms crossed over his chest. Though he didn't spare a single glance at Warwick sitting so close. A few minutes ago, I'd been afraid they'd try to kill each other.

Now they sat on the same bed. Waiting for me.

A squeak escaped my lips which made a huge grin soften Doran's stony features. "Indeed, love. Call me if you need assistance."

Before I even thought about my next move, he shifted into his gargoyle. Impossibly wide, thick shoulders. Broad chest. Heavy brow, a large crooked beaked nose. Talons clattered on the floor as he turned and headed down the hallway, black wings brushing the ceiling and walls on either side.

"I'll be outside if you need me." Ivarr ducked out of the window and shut it before I even felt a draft.

My gaze hopped from Aidan's scowl. To Keane's sultry smile. To Warwick's innocent aw-shucks dimples. "Um. Not that I'm upset at all, but why are you here?"

Casually, he slung a long, silky curtain of black hair over his shoulder, drawing my attention to the heavy weight of his hair. Making me think about how incredible it would feel gliding over my skin. "Aidan and I have come to an understanding."

I dragged my gaze back to Aidan. "Is that true?"

He rolled his eyes. "I'm a right bastard, aye, but I wouldn't keep a man you love away from you. Besides, he saved you when we failed you."

I swallowed the lump in my throat and moved closer to the bed. "You didn't fail me."

"Aye, we did. You were in danger. Your treasures were unable to penetrate the trap. You were alone and vulnerable. Without the leprechaun, you'd be worse than dead."

His words rang with fury, his voice cracking with emotion. I crawled up onto the bed and slid up against him, dropping my head to his chest. "I'm okay. I'm safe."

Aidan rubbed his mouth against my hair. "Only thanks to him. So aye, Warwick Greenshanks be welcome wherever you are, as long as you care to have him."

I pulled back enough to look up into his face. "I love you too, you know. I don't want you to be uncomfortable or upset."

He huffed out a breath and reached up to loosen the towel holding my hair up. "I'm wrapped around your pinky finger, Riann Newkirk. Twist me into a pretzel, put my balls in a vise, whatever it takes. What's left of my heart be yours."

∾

AIDAN

I TWIRLED SOME OF HER DAMP HAIR AROUND MY FINGER, AND I couldn't help but think that my worst fear had come true.

The latest treasurekeeper had come into my life and wrecked it all to hell. She stole my ride. She drove me to take a risk, to try and find Doran one last time. To free him against all odds.

But worse, she made me fucking *care*.

She made me fucking love her.

Then she'd disappeared through that fucking fountain, and I'd gone insane.

Something broke inside me, letting out all the rage and fury I've been carrying through each lifetime. The hopeless battle raged on, life after life, generation after generation. Our light went out a little more each time, while the darkness only got stronger.

It wasn't fucking fair. None of it was.

We'd lost Doran for centuries. It wasn't even worth us coming back to try again to push back the dark. Not without him. This slip of a mortal woman traipsed into my life and demanded I let her into my black, withered heart. She'd taken up residence in my every thought. She was my breath and the beat of my heart.

If I lost her…

Grimacing, I forced myself to let go of her hair before I dragged her against me and demanded she let me inside. At least until this storm passed. Just once. A moment of safety. A moment of peace. Before the battle claimed my soul again.

"Something's not right," she whispered.

My worthless heart shriveled up and died all over again.

"Remember what you promised?"

Eyes narrowed, I stared back at her, not sure what the fuck she was talking about. She glanced back over her shoulder at the leprechaun. "Do you remember?"

The bastard gave me a devious, underhanded look that I fully deserved. Fucking hell. If the leprechaun had his way, I'd end up in a meat grinder.

Warwick snapped his fingers, and her hotel-style robe was replaced with my favorite leather jacket. And nothing else.

My jaws clenched, my teeth grinding together as I fought to keep myself under control. When we'd had a taste of her on top of the bar, I'd demanded that she wear my jacket the first time she let me fuck her. She'd agreed.

"Ah." Her lips quirked and she ran a hand over the opposite sleeve. "There's nothing like the smell and touch of leather on my skin."

I jerked my head at Keane. "You heard the lady."

Her eyes widened, her gaze darting over at the other man as he slid closer. Keane never took his leather gloves off—at least not until he was ready to finish his partner. Once he touched her with his bare hands, she'd climax so hard and long she'd be done for the night.

Fuck me. I couldn't wait to see her writhing between us. Gasping and crying with release.

Keane cupped her cheek in his leathered palm. "Are you too tired, Riann?"

"No, not at all. At least not now."

"How would you like us, then?"

She looked back at me, a shy, fragile question in her eyes that damned near made me crack my teeth with shame. That I had ever made her doubt herself, or how much she meant to us. To me.

"You want him, you got him."

I regretted the harshness in my tone, but I couldn't seem to keep my edges under wraps when I was with her. She exposed my weaknesses and regrets, making me throb like a rotten tooth or a shattered bone.

"I don't—"

I seized her chin and jerked her close. "Don't you dare fucking apologize or make excuses for how you feel. Ever. You want him. You got him. If I wasn't such a sorry bastard, I would have invited him to the shitty hotel in the first place."

Warwick chuckled. "Better yet, I could have whisked us to the finest hotel in town, though Evil Eye probably owns it."

"What? Balor actually owns properties?"

"Of course. He needs streams of income and jobs for his minions to blend in among the mortals. Most fae have stakes in human properties. You've probably noticed some in the past. They especially love grand old mansions with overgrown riotous gardens and massive, ancient trees. Or patches of thick forest in the middle of town where no forest should be. All the wild places that remain, caves and places of darkness, bottomless pits in the oceans. Different courts tend to buy and invest in different technologies or industries. Evil Eye prefers mining and mining equipment. Which is how he's able to move so many imps and pookas into human spaces without anyone noticing."

My dick was going to explode in agony if we didn't get busy. I fisted my hand in her hair, bunching up my fingers at her nape. Pulling, just a little, while I watched her reaction. Her pupils blew wide, her mouth softening on another one of those squeaky sounds that almost made me nut on the spot.

"Now you see why I was reluctant to bring the leprechaun along on this ride." I tightened my grip, twisting my hand tighter. "Do you want a history lesson on the economic impact of fae courts on the mortal plane? Or would you rather fuck?"

She bit her luscious bottom lip. "The latter."

I leaned into her, putting my face right up against hers with my meanest scowl and deepest growl. "Say it out loud."

"Fuck me. Please."

18

I couldn't be sure, given my Swiss cheese memory, but I was pretty sure no one had ever manhandled me in bed before. Not in a way that I enjoyed it. Doran and Ivarr had been extremely gentle and tender. Even the first time on the bar, everyone had been so careful with me.

Five men were a lot, and they'd handled me like I was delicate china that might shatter into a thousand pieces.

Aroused Aidan was way more. Like a million times more.

Doran's rumble echoed in my head. *:Tell him if he's too much, and he'll rein himself in. I won't allow you to be scared or uncomfortable a single moment. I'll throw his ass out on the curb first.:*

Evidently Aidan heard his friend's words too. His eyes narrowed to slits. *:If you're ever scared of me, really scared of me, I'll fucking slit my own throat.:*

I scowled back at him. "I'm not scared. Don't you dare hold back."

He looked over at Keane, who immediately gave him a subtle nod. I wasn't sure what Keane would be able to do if Aidan lost control of himself. I didn't want to find out.

Aidan gave that same look to Warwick. Surprised, I started to glance back over my shoulder to see how he responded, but Aidan's grip kept me from turning my head. He'd demanded the leprechaun get me out if things went bad when we went to free Doran. So it wouldn't surprise me in the slightest if—

Black hair tumbled down over my shoulder and a hard, muscled body loomed over me. His hands jerked my wrists behind me into the small of my back, effortlessly pinning me. "That isn't our plan at all, love."

All the breath left my lungs in a rush. Wide-eyed, I watched Aidan release me and lean back casually against the pillows and headboard. My scalp tingled where he'd gripped my hair, and my heart galloped ninety miles an hour. Hovering between a hell yeah and oh shit, my body didn't know whether to jump off the bed and race for the door, or turn into a quivering melted puddle on the mattress.

My breath came in shallow, soft pants that echoed in the room. Thoughts exploded and dissipated rapid fire through my mind. Aggressive Aidan wasn't a surprise. Aggressive Warwick was. What role would Keane play? From his sultry eyes and luscious, pouty lips, I'd always pictured him as a flirt, taking his time as he lazily kissed or stroked. A tease—but not dangerous.

But the molten heat blazing in his eyes threatened to obliterate me to dust.

"Yeah, that looks damned good on you," Aidan said. "Let me see more."

I wasn't sure what he meant. Take the jacket off? How could I when my arms were trapped behind me?

Warwick pushed my wrists up higher, lifting me into an awkward scramble on my knees. His other palm slid up to squeeze the front of my throat, arching my shoulders back against him. His fingers encased my neck. Letting me feel the strength in his hand. Making me work a little harder to breathe as he applied more pressure.

The subtle threat that all he had to do was squeeze and I'd be done.

I wouldn't be able to breathe. Not if he didn't allow it.

All very calm and controlled. I wasn't hurt. I wasn't scared.

In fact, I felt just as safe as I had with Doran and Ivarr—beneath Stoneheart's wing with Ivarr's gentle, warming light.

I was safe then. And I was safe now. Even with my hands pinned and my throat held captive.

Safer than I'd ever been in my entire life.

My lingering uncertainty and tension melted away. Unlike before when I was with my ex, I would remember everything from this moment. Every precious second was unforgettable. The deep grooves in Aidan's forehead from his usual scowl, the burning lust in his eyes. The light, teasing stroke of leather between my breasts as Keane stroked me. The slide of Warwick's silken hair against my cheek, smelling of the flowers and lush trees of his home in Faerie.

They weren't going to hurt me and then wipe my mind later. Despite the blazing heat in their eyes, they weren't going to feed on me.

"Are you sure?" Keane drawled as he stretched out beside my knees. Close enough that I could feel his breath tickling my bare thighs. "Because I'm ready to feast."

I hadn't meant to broadcast that thought. Evidently our connection was getting stronger, more effortless. Or maybe I just trusted them more as I healed from the past. Without the changeling's darkness spreading inside me.

"That's a fine idea." Aidan lifted his arms and folded his hands behind his head casually. As if he was settling back to binge a new show on Netflix. "See how many times you can make her come."

Rising on his elbow, Keane dropped soft, gentle kisses on my stomach. My muscles twitched, making me jerk involuntarily against Warwick's hold. Pausing, Keane looked up at me, checking in. Making sure I was okay. Now that I was more aware of our connection, I could feel their presence hovering in my head. Not to listen to my thoughts, not exactly. Just making sure that I was okay. More than okay. That I was enjoying every single touch.

Heat radiated from the spot he'd kissed, sinking deeper through layers of skin and muscle. Almost like a drug in my bloodstream. Liquifying everything it touched.

His lips quirked into a smug, sensual grin. "Would you like another hit?"

I'd known his kiss was powerful, but it hadn't dawned on me that he could kiss me anywhere and send that kind of energy pulsing through my body. If he ever put his mouth *there*...

My eyes squeezed shut and I shuddered, almost coming at the thought.

"Exactly," he whispered. "Especially if I take off the gloves."

A ragged, whimpery sigh tore out of my throat.

"Was that aye? I think that was aye."

I somehow managed to nod my head, even though my brain had already turned to mush.

Warwick released my hands, picked me up, and set me down over the top of Keane's face. My eyes flared wide. I sucked in a deep, desperate breath, like one final gasp for air before my head sank beneath the waves.

His lips closed around my clit, the epicenter of a massive climax that tore through my body. My lungs seized. Everything clenched down hard. Jerking and trembling under the assault, I still somehow managed to lock gazes with Aidan.

Who watched me thrash and flail like a starving wolf, waiting for his turn to feast.

Hands stroked over my body, spreading delicious heat. Bringing every inch of my skin to life. The rasp of leather, distinct from bare skin. Warwick's palm on my throat again, holding me upright. Keeping me from falling forward. Panting, I tried to lift off of Keane's face, to give us both a little breathing room, but he gripped my thighs, pulling me down harder. His tongue stroked and swirled, sending another wave of climax rolling through me.

The same. Another. I wasn't sure. It didn't seem to end, an endless, rhythmic rolling tide that lifted me higher and higher. I struggled against their grip. Trying to get away. Trying to get more. I wasn't sure. Sensation poured through me, surely too much to bear. Sweat dripped in my eyes. My thighs ached. My lungs burned. Yet my aching core squeezed tighter.

"Please," I gasped out. Not even sure what I was begging for.

Warwick leaned me forward. "Hold on for dear life, love."

I seized handfuls of bedding, twisting my fists for leverage. Not sure whether I needed to try and drag myself to Aidan, or shove back down Keane's body so I could take him inside.

Kneading my ass in both hands, Warwick pushed inside me on a long, smooth thrust to the hilt. While Keane sucked my clit into the heat of his wicked mouth. He breathed a long pulse of molten heat into me, another magical wave that crashed through me. Screaming, I buried my face in the sheet, bucking and shuddering in agonizing bliss.

Warwick leaned down over me, fisting his hand in my hair. Pinning my head down against the bed, which lifted my ass up higher. He thrust again, an endless stroke that made my writhe and sweat and babble incoherently. More. Enough. Please.

"Luck me," Warwick growled against my ear. "Which is it? Are you wanting us to stop?"

"Harder." I heard the word come out of my mouth but it didn't sound like me.

He laughed roughly. "Aye, love, with pleasure."

19

WARWICK

Gritting my teeth, I fought for control. Deep, hard strokes as she demanded. Rocking her body, grinding her pelvis down harder on Keane's tongue. Making her breath thud out heavily with each fierce thrust.

I wanted to make this last as long as possible. I might only taste her pleasure this one time...

I didn't think she understood the brutal reality of what it meant to be the treasurekeeper. What it meant for her treasures to be spun back to the mortal plane over and over in an endless war. Mortals were born and gone in the blink of an eye. Brilliant kaleidoscopes of emotion and beauty, yet gone just the same.

I could not bear to think of her dead and gone.

Let alone the thought of her inevitable suffering. Grief, when her treasures died as they always did, returning to Tír na nÓg. Her own brutal death as Evil Eye's grip tightened on her world. Whether together or one by one, the treasures would be destroyed, and without them, she, too, would die. This glorious light would wink out, and I would spend all eternity in darkness. Trapped like her painting that I'd stolen away to the Summer Isle.

Another wave of her pleasure slammed into me like a visceral punch in the gut. I grunted, wavering a moment on a towering precipice. Crystalline rainbows of magic danced around the bed, spinning out from her. Pure magic, the brightest light of her soul. And she had no idea.

I clutched her desperately, aching to keep her safe. Cursing myself for bringing her back to the mortal plane when I could have kept her forever in the Summer Isle. She wouldn't have to die. She wouldn't have to suffer her other lovers' death.

I could have made her forget it all.

But then she wouldn't have this. Keane's gift sending another wave of pleasure rolling through her body. Aidan waiting in the wings with his burning, ravenous gaze. Doran and Ivarr moments away, ready to rush to her rescue or join us at her request. As much as I yearned to have her safe forever in my domain, she wouldn't be fully happy without them. Without the incessant pull between conduit and treasures, she never would have found her way into *Shamrocked* in the first place.

She screamed, a wordless plea that made me shove deep, aching to fill her up. To be so deep inside her that she'd never forget me. Her magic rolled through me, leaving me shaking in release. Out of my head, bathing in her pleasure, I barely remembered to capture all the magic we released before we lit up the Kansas City skyline like the Fourth of July. Even if the changeling didn't dare attack four united treasures, I'd be a fool to mark our location for Evil Eye's minions. He had plenty of dark fae at his beck and call to send an entire army against us.

But it was too much magic for me to absorb. Straining to keep it contained, I pushed back as much as possible into Riann, giving her all that her mortal shell could hold. Treasurekeeper magic braided with leprechaun green and gold. Such a marvel to behold.

Panting in a sweaty heap, I fought to keep my face easy. My eyes bright, or at least soft and full of emotion. Not grim or full of dread, abject terror at the thought of watching her suffer and die.

She lifted her head, brushing hair out of her face. Hers, mine, a glorious tangle. "Help me up. I think I suffocated Keane."

"Nonsense." Still mostly underneath her, Keane let out a long, pleased rumble of satisfaction. "Now that was a feast indeed."

Blushing hotly, she heaved up to her hands and knees in an awkward scramble and flopped back down as if she'd used the last of her reserves. Indeed, as I assessed her condition, her mortal body felt paper thin despite the elixir she'd drunk in Faerie to heal her injured leg.

With a thought, I pulled an ice-cold glass of spring water into my hand and pressed it to her lips.

"Wait," Aidan barked, quickly sitting up and reaching for the glass. "What is it?"

She arched a brow at him and took the glass from me. "What does it matter? I'm dehydrated and dying of thirst. Thank you, Warwick."

Her eyes were shadowed and heavy, her face pale, though her tart tone made Aidan settle back against the pillows with a humph.

I inclined my head, a wry smile on my lips. "Providing hydration is the least we can do after such a precious gift, *mo stór*."

She drained the glass and handed it back to me with a glum look tightening her face. "I'm wiped out and only one of you actually... er..." Crimson flooded down her neck, drawing my gaze to the hint of luscious breasts beneath the leather coat she still wore. "If we were grading sex scenes, that's only a thirty-three percent completion rate. I'd fail for sure."

Sitting up to grab her by the lapels, Aidan dragged her closer to him, tucking her down against his side. "You couldn't be more wrong. For one thing, Keane blew his load just as hard as the leprechaun did. So you're two out of three in that regard. But you failed to realize that some of the points on this assignment are weighted more heavily than others. The three of us are fucking lightweights in that regard. The only one who matters is you. You fucking aced the exam, won a shit ton of extra credit, and now can skip a few grades and sleep for a fucking year."

"But—"

He glared down at her and jerked the sheet up around her. "No ifs, ands, or buts about it. You fucking rocked our world off its axis and then some. You're alive. You're breathing and smiling and screaming with pleasure just fine, thank you very much. When it's my turn, it's my turn, and I'll have your screams and pleasure then, too. For now, I'm grateful that you let me watch. I'm even more grateful that you're now going to fall asleep in my arms, safe and sound."

Keane crawled up the mattress to spoon her other side. Quietly, I rolled to the edge of the bed.

"Wait," she called softly. "Where are you going?"

Surprised, I paused on the edge of the bed and looked back at her. Eyes heavy, hair tousled, lips full and lush, cheeks and throat rosy, her skin gleaming with afterglow magic. "Did you want me to stay?"

A crestfallen look of sudden doubt swept over her face.

In the blink of an eye, I knelt over her legs and cupped her face in my palms. "Forgive me for ever putting that look on your face, *mo stór*. I would rather Aidan hack off my head for good than leave you a single moment. But if this is to be your home in the mortal plane, then I wasn't sure of my welcome. A visit is a fine thing but guests stink like fish after a few days."

She hooked her forearm around my neck and lifted herself up to press her face against my throat. "If you're not welcome, then I'm not either. You're more than a guest to me."

Aidan gave me a deceptively sleepy look. "I didn't take you for a fuck 'em and leave 'em kind of guy."

I couldn't help but laugh. "Sure, now, though I'm betting that one of you warned her I'd be exactly that sort."

She loosened her arm so she could slide back down to the mattress, though she kept a handful of my hair threaded through her fingers. "Actually, it was Doran who said it first. He said he'd kill you if you hurt me, and that the only pot of gold you have is what's in your pants."

I dropped down on top of her, though I shifted most of my weight down toward the foot of the bed, with only my upper body draped across her stomach. "Well, it's certainly true that I'm pure gold in me pants, but I assure you, I have plenty of gold elsewhere."

Laughing softly, she combed her fingers through my hair and gave a shy, soft look up at Aidan. The kind of look that cracked open the coldest, grimmest heart of stone ever to walk the earth. "You don't mind?"

His jaw worked. His eyes shot daggers. But he swallowed hard and cleared his throat gruffly. "Fuck no. The leprechaun stays."

20

I wasn't sure how long I slept, though my body insisted that years had passed while I lay sleeping. My muscles were so stiff that I winced as I sat up. I swung my legs off the edge of the bed and sat there a moment, waiting for my thighs to stop quivering.

I had a good solid ache in my core, but this muscle soreness was from that endless climax Keane had given me. While Warwick fucked me.

Just remembering made my cheeks scorch. Though there wasn't anything shy about my pussy. Like a cat, it woke up with a luxurious stretch and purr, wondering where the guys were. Whether we could go for round two with Aidan this time. How hard would I come if Keane took off his gloves?

I slowly shifted my weight off the bed to my feet, making sure I could stand. I wavered a little but managed to shuffle toward the bathroom. Sunlight poured in through the window, illuminating the bedroom that I'd paid little attention to last night.

The room was plenty big, even with a massive bed and a couple of chairs in front of a cold fireplace lined with large river rocks. I hadn't really noticed last night, but everything was wood. Even the ceilings. Was this house a log cabin?

The furnishings were nice but dated, as if someone had picked out a bedroom suite in the nineties. Huge cream-colored pieces with fake gold trim and knobs. Even the curtains were an odd paisley in green and maroon, though the fabric was heavy and expensive looking.

I scooped up the robe I'd used last night and hopped in the shower again. Now that I was looking and paying attention, I realized the bathroom was also outdated though pristine. The sink was a clamshell shape, though the tiles were timeless marble. Not a speck of mold in the shower and the glass door was crystal clear. Either the place was rarely used—or they had an excellent cleaning crew.

Back in the robe with my hair in a towel, I headed toward the bedroom, not sure what I was going to wear.

I shouldn't have worried. Aidan sprawled in one of the chairs, jean-clad thighs spread wide, plain white T-shirt, and of course, his leather jacket back where it belonged. A tray sat on the small table between the chairs with two paper cups and a box. The familiar duffel bag waited on the bed, probably with fresh clothes from Vivi's.

"Coffee?" I asked hopefully.

"You know it."

Not bothering to get dressed first, I sat in the other chair and picked up the paper cup, still nice and hot. I took a sip and closed my eyes in bliss. I wasn't sure what time of the day it was, but damn, I had really needed a shot of caffeine.

"Is it alright?"

I hummed out a pleased sigh and took another, longer sip. "Delicious. Thank you."

"When Red brought coffee to the warehouse, I didn't taste any sugar or flavoring, so I kept it simple."

I thought a moment, replaying that day in the warehouse. I'd been nervous for the guys to meet my gorgeous best friend. So nervous, in fact, that I'd been thinking some not very nice things about myself. To silence those negative thoughts, Aidan had grabbed me close and kissed me thoroughly.

Our first kiss. Two kisses, actually.

I couldn't remember him drinking any of Vivi's coffee. So if he hadn't tasted sugar or flavorings…

It'd been the taste of coffee on *my* tongue.

A man of few words, most of which were growled or cursed or muttered with a dark look. Yet he'd been the one to fetch me a bag of clothes, not once but twice now. Even more impressive, the clothes he brought made sense and went together. He'd picked up fresh coffee, made perfectly because of the way I'd tasted when we kissed.

"It's exactly right," I whispered. "Thank you."

"Figured you'd need to eat," he replied gruffly. "I'm sick of fast food, so I got something better."

Curious what he meant, I set the coffee down and looked in the cardboard box. Buttery, flakey croissants that smelled divine. Butter, yeasty bread, and… "Chocolate croissants? How'd you know that was my favorite?"

He smirked. "Lucky guess."

"Bullshit. I bet you texted Vivi."

"I don't even have Red's number. You look like a decadent, chocolate croissant to me. So that's what I got. I cleaned them out."

Now that was a compliment if I'd ever heard one.

I took a bite and fought the urge to shudder with bliss. So good. Washed down with cappuccino. The breakfast of champions. "So what's on the agenda today?"

He leaned forward, bracing his elbows on his knees, his hands clasped. "Our first priority is to get this place as secure as possible. One of us will be on the lookout every bloody minute we're here. Plus we're bringing in our weapons cache and several of the men offered to help guard the perimeter."

"Sounds like you're getting ready for war." I tried to keep my voice light, but the faint quiver betrayed me.

"We are."

"Because of me?"

He shrugged. "It's our purpose."

Sitting here in the quiet room with no distractions, I concentrated on him. In my mind, he was like a steel and concrete high-rise tower.

No windows. No doors. Infinitely strong and so tall that the walls disappeared into the mists above. I flicked my focus to each of my other men briefly. As soon as I thought of them, Ivarr's glow filled me, endless warmth and burning energy of the sun when needed. Keane's luscious purr of satisfaction backed with a formidable hunger that would never end. Warwick's lush green energy and riotous garden of colorful flowers.

Even Doran Stoneheart was wide open to me. As soon as he felt my faint touch, his gargoyle turned toward me, wings unfurling slightly, talons unsheathed, ready to leap into the air to rush toward my defense.

We were open to each other. Little bits of thoughts and emotion flowing between us on the same currents of magic that allowed us to communicate silently. I brought them together. They couldn't do their job without me, and I needed all of them to feel the spinning wheel inside me evened and balanced so the magic could flow.

Aidan was here, the closest to me, yet he was completely shut off. I couldn't sense any of his emotions. Could he—

"Aye," he said hoarsely. "I do. I listen to you constantly. You know why I'm shut off. It's for the best."

When he'd first kissed me, I caught a few images from him. War, death, pain, suffering. He'd apologized for letting any of that touch me.

Fighting back tears, I whispered, "I can't imagine how much effort it takes to keep all those memories locked away in such a massive tower."

He shrugged again and picked up his cup. "It's the least I can do."

I watched silently as he drank, draining the cup in a few long swallows. My heart ached for him, but I didn't know what to do. I didn't need to reach him or break those walls down. He was here. He was with me. He wasn't avoiding me any longer in some misguided attempt to spare me. The wheel was balanced enough to cast their magic when they needed it.

But was that enough? Or would I do more harm than good if I tried to get inside those formidable walls?

He thumped the cup down on the table so hard that the bottom edge crumpled. "You've done more than enough, *mo stór*. All I need you to do is survive as long as possible."

Pain splintered in his voice. Unspoken heartache after heartache. He had suffered so much through lifetime after lifetime, only to blame himself for losing Doran. Without their leader…

He'd taken on that role out of a sense of guilt. He'd carried their failures himself, an endless punishment. He died the hardest. The worst possible torment. He took the riskiest approaches when they tried to free Doran, paying his due over and over again. Wallowing in pain and death, deliberating trying to pay in suffering to bring Doran back.

Trying to make amends. To atone for his mistake.

My throat ached, my chest tight, but I held back the tears. I didn't want to add to his guilt by making him think he'd made me cry. But I couldn't sit here and leave him hurting, either.

I set my cup down, quickly stood, and dropped down into his lap before he could react. Straddling his hips, I curled up against him, nestling down into his body so I could put my face against his throat.

He swallowed, his heart thudding heavily against me. Rigid and tight, thighs and chest braced for impact or war. His hands settled on my back gingerly, as if afraid I might explode, a million jagged fragments that might injure him. Or tear that massive wall down.

"I don't care about that," I whispered against his skin, trying to soothe him. "You don't have to let me in. I just want to hold you."

"It's not that I don't want to let you in," he grumbled, rubbing his mouth against my hair. "I don't want to hurt you with all those memories. You're light, Riann. I'm darkness and pain and death. I'd rather die than let any of that taint you."

AIDAN

CURLED AGAINST ME LIKE A WARM, SOFT KITTEN, SHE BREATHED PEACE into my skin. Warmth into my stone-cold heart. Light into the deepest, darkest corner of hell that made up what was left of my soul. She smoothed my rough edges, de-razored the concertina wire, and took a jackhammer to all the concrete.

Without saying a word or even lifting her fucking pinky finger.

She hummed against my throat, a pleased little sound that made my dick throb beneath her. Which only made her wiggle deeper into my lap.

My eyes sealed shut so I could focus on every inch of her against me. "I'm starting to suspect that I was set up."

She laughed, her breath tickling my throat, her lips wandering over my skin. "How's that?"

"I hoped that you'd fuck me if I bribed you with coffee and chocolate croissants."

She breathed into my ear, her tongue flicking over those whorls. "You'll never have to bribe me."

My fingers dug into her back. I fought down the intense wave of lust threatening to obliterate me. Insisting that I rip the robe off her. Bare her flesh for my teeth and tongue. Drag her kicking and screaming to the most insane, intense climax—

"Yes." She punctuated that single word with a playful bite on my earlobe.

My entire body shook beneath her. Not because of her assent.

She'd heard. She'd seen what I wanted to do. Inside my head.

She'd managed to worm her way inside my own personal hell.

A vicious wave of regret crashed over me. I'd failed to protect her. I'd failed to keep her wholesome and light and clean.

Then a wave of mindless panic threatened to send me leaping to my feet, dumping her on the floor.

She'll see. She'll know.

She'll know the truth about me.

The selfish, jealous bastard who'd destroyed a legendary fellowship for a heartless woman. Who'd left his friend trapped in horrific darkness to try and save his treacherous lover. Who'd paid for that sin in blood and flesh for centuries to no avail.

All the deaths I caused. The pain I delivered and suffered.

She knew the general circumstances about how we'd lost Doran. But the reality of being spit back out to die over and over... The crushing defeats... The agonizing suffering that my actions had caused. Not just to me, but all of us.

Doran might have forgiven me.

But—

Her fingers stroked over my face, butterfly kisses over my eyes and nose, stroking away the cobwebs of dread. "There's nothing for me to forgive. I love you, Aidan. Here and now. That was another lifetime ago and it wasn't even me. Why would I keep punishing you for something that happened hundreds of years ago?"

"It was *me*, though." My voice cracked, raw granite crumbling to dust. "I betrayed us all."

"Balor—"

"No! Damn it all to hell. Me. I did it. I broke Doran's heart. That was fucking *me* and no one else."

She sat up sharply, squeezing the back of my neck to hold my attention. Her eyes blazed with a torrent of emotions, too many for me to name. "You think so little of Doran Stoneheart?"

My eyes flared with surprise. I couldn't track where this was going. I'd expected her to flinch away, shudder in horror, and withdraw to leave me eternally alone as I deserved. Block me from her bed and her heart.

Again, as I fully deserved.

Not challenge what I thought of Doran, the greatest hero to ever walk this earth. Let alone glare at me like a little spitfire.

"He's Stoneheart for a reason. His heart isn't fragile or easily broken. Let alone mine. I'm not a flimsy paper heart drawn on tissue paper, Aidan. I've been through shit too. I've lived in darkness for years. I have regrets. So many regrets. But I'm still here, still fighting and kicking and trying to make a life for us. Isn't it time you lived too?"

Weariness suddenly weighed me down. Mountains from the past. Guilt and shame and regret. My arms fell down limply against the chair. My head sagged back, and I slumped in defeat. "I don't know how to live, Riann. I only know how to die."

Staring down at me, her head tipped slightly to the side. I was too tired to try and read her emotions or listen inside her mind for clues to what she was thinking. For the first time in this incarnation, I felt as old as the earth itself. I'd seen it all, done it all, died every way imaginable. I just wanted it all to end.

"Then let it end," she said. "Let this be the last time you come back."

I blew out an endless sigh, my eyes falling shut. "Then the world falls to darkness. Evil Eye wins."

"Then let him have this worthless hunk of rock."

Despite my bone-deep weariness, I had to chuckle. "If only it were so easy."

"Why can't it be easy for once? We'll be dead and gone. Why must you keep coming back to fight a war that only you care about? Let someone else lead the battle next time. You've earned your rest. You've more than earned your paradise."

"When you die—"

She broke in. "Everybody dies. It's inevitable."

"You don't understand."

"Then help me understand. What happens when you die? Where do you go?"

My hands tightened on the armrests, making the wood creak. "Back to Tír na nÓg."

"Which is like a paradise, right? What I saw in Warwick's Summer Isle was beautiful."

A muscle ticked across my jaw. My teeth ached. "It's fucking hell, not paradise."

She cupped my cheek, smoothing her thumb over my lips. "Why?"

My eyes flared wide and I practically howled like a wounded beast. "Because you won't be there! Don't you see? You're mortal. You'll be dead and gone, and I'll still have to live eternity without you!"

21

I'd never been a religious person. I didn't know what I believed about the afterlife. It'd never really mattered to me, as long as I went to the same place as Vivi. I'd never really thought about what eternity would look like.

Let alone what it must have been like for him. Sent back over and over, for thousands of years, to die in a ceaseless, useless war. How many treasurekeepers had they known throughout history, if they received a new one each time they came back? Always a woman, meant to draw them together.

Then they died and lost her forever.

Never to see their lost love again.

None of them were waiting on the other side for them.

No wonder he'd been so reluctant to even speak to me, let alone get close to me.

I was no fool. I didn't assume I was the best treasurekeeper they'd ever had, let alone the one they loved the most. Why should I be any different compared to the dozens—or hundreds—of women who'd acted as their conduit? I wasn't special. I wasn't unforgettable. I certainly wasn't their greatest love in a thousand years.

"You're dead fucking wrong." He scowled at me but his voice

remained flat and even without his usual bite. "That's the problem, Riann. That's why I didn't want to be anywhere near you. I knew as soon as I turned to face you, that I'd be obliterated. You'd suck me in like a supermassive black hole and blast me to bits."

I grimaced, shaking my head. "That sounds terrible."

He huffed out a humorless laugh. "Agreed. That's why I stayed the fuck away as long as I could. But some ballsy-ass chick stole my bike and forced my hand. She dragged me back to reality and made me face what I had become without her."

"What's that?"

Without knocking, Keane stuck his head inside the room. "A whiny, mopey bastard wallowing in the past?"

Rubbing his knuckles across his forehead, Aidan grumbled. "Fuck off. I'm tired is all."

"Ah, is it help you're needing?" Keane's voice brightened, his eyes dancing with mirth. "Perhaps a bit of a show like last night to wake you up. Get you fired up and in the mood. Funny, though. I thought you were horny as hell this morning when you left to get coffee."

Aidan threw one of the cups at him. "Get the fuck out! You've done had your turn. This is my time."

"Tick tock, motherfucker." Keane winked at me, flashing a dimple in his cheek. "If you need assistance, *mo stór—*"

A low, vicious sound tore out of Aidan's throat. His body coiled beneath me, all tight muscle ready to start a war against his friend.

But I had other plans. So did he. I just needed to remind him.

I sat back on his knees, untied the robe, and let it sag open, slowly slipping off my shoulders. I didn't say anything. I didn't have to.

Eyes blazing, Aidan stared at my breasts. The long column of his throat worked on a rough swallow. His fingers gripped the chair, making the wood groan.

I turned to look at Keane over my shoulder, giving him a smile of gratitude for helping break Aidan out of his funk. "Bye, Keane."

He blew a kiss and quietly shut the door behind him.

Aidan didn't say anything, but his breathing quickened. I shrugged the robe off completely and sat there, letting him drink his fill.

It wasn't easy for me. I'd never been very confident in my body, especially compared to my gorgeous friend. Too short, too round, too shy and quiet.

"You won't be quiet for long."

His gruff voice sank into me. Goosebumps flared down my arms. I shifted slightly, feeling the rough denim of his jeans beneath me. The rock-hard outline of his cock, so close, but so far away. My core burned like molten lava, aching with emptiness. As if my pussy couldn't remember what it felt like to be filled up with a man, despite the great sex I'd had just a few hours ago.

At this rate, I was going to leave a damp spot on his jeans.

He huffed out a laugh and lifted his hand toward my face. The pad of his thumb stroked over my bottom lip, ungentle and rough. The hand of a warrior, calloused and worn through centuries of wielding those swords.

"I'm no Keane with his soft, magical hands. I'm no Ivarr with his glowing warmth. I'm certainly no Doran. I might be as hard as stone, but I'm not as stalwart and honorable. Even the leprechaun has me beaten in that regard. At least he plays by a twisted set of rules that he never breaks."

He gripped my chin, digging his thumb and fingers into my jaw. His voice dropped into a basement growl that made my spine tingle. "I'm a hard, jealous, bitter man, Riann. I want to break myself into a thousand pieces in your pretty little cunt. Claim every inch of you as mine, at least once. Sweeten my lousy disposition on your screams and feast on the honey that pours out of your body every time I touch you. I want to take you where no one else can or will and then see if you'll still open your arms and love me."

With a jerk, he released my chin and dropped his hand back down to the chair. His jaw flexed, muscles ticking. His eyes blazed. The chair creaked beneath his grip, as if any second it would explode into kindling.

Trembling, I stared at him as his words sank into me. My heart pounded. My nipples ached, rock hard and standing at full attention.

Adrenaline jacked through my veins, fine hairs rising up along my nape.

I waited a moment to be sure. I'd been hurt before. I was sure of it, though I couldn't remember exactly what Jonathan the changeling had done to me. Surely I'd been scared of him. Terrified he would eventually kill me if he wearied of trying to learn whatever secret I supposedly had buried deep inside me. Enduring the torment in hope that I would somehow escape, long before I even knew about the four Irish treasures waiting in the wings for me.

I'd known the horror of being helpless. Trapped. Unable to protect myself from a man.

I didn't feel any of that fear now. Not with Aidan.

Only anticipation.

I didn't say anything as I scooted back on his knees. The skin around his eyes tightened, another muscle tick across his jaw, as if he thought I might leap up and run as hard and fast as I could.

Instead, I reached down to unbutton his jeans.

Eyes heavy, he watched me fumble with the zipper and pull at his clothes with increasing desperation without saying a word or lifting a finger to help me. My breathing rasped loudly in the room. Skin hot, eyes fevered, I couldn't think of anything but getting him inside me.

His cock finally sprung free, nice and thick and long enough that if I hadn't had Doran already, I'd be a little hesitant about taking Aidan inside me the first time. I crawled up his body, my breath sighing out in a rush as I pushed him inside me. Lungs burning, I twisted and swayed my hips, working him deeper.

Seating him all the way inside me with a final, heavy thunk that almost made my heart explode.

Panting, I lay against his chest, my arms tight around his neck. Little twitches shivered through my body. I couldn't sit still. He was so hard and thick inside me. Unbearably full. I squirmed and wriggled until I groaned out loud. I needed more. Less. I wasn't even sure. Tension strained inside me.

"Please," I finally whispered, locking eyes with him.

"Please what?" He drawled in a rough rasp that made me shiver.

Which made me whimper, every nerve ending screaming with sensation.

"Touch me. Make me come."

He licked his thumb and slipped his hand down between us. Fingers splayed over my stomach, he worked his thumb down my slit until my eyes rolled back in my head.

"Jackpot."

The roughness of his thumb, the pressure, it was too much. Climax crashed through me, jerking my muscles like I was a puppet tossed aside in a heap of sweaty hair and boneless limbs. I lay against his chest, trying to catch my breath. I couldn't.

Not with him balls deep, as thick and hard as ever.

I gulped. Tried to get my jumbled thoughts together.

His fingers played in my hair, smoothing the damp strands away from my face. "That was for you, Riann. A sweet, juicy little appetizer. But the next one?" He tightened his hand in my hair, drawing a ragged sound from my throat. Part whimper. Part plea. For mercy. For more. I didn't even know.

He growled in my ear. "The next one's for *me*."

22

Between one breath and the next, I found myself slammed face down on the mattress hard enough that my breath whooshed out. My scalp burned and tingled from his fierce grip in my hair. Pinned, I lay there panting, trying to control my breathing. The last thing I wanted to do was hyperventilate or pass out.

Not before the best part of the scene.

"Stay," he hissed in my ear, his voice echoing with menace.

He released me and I heard the rustling of his clothing. I lifted my head, hoping to get a glimpse of rock-hard muscle covered in tattoos. Begging to be traced with my tongue.

A sharp smack on my ass startled me.

"I said stay. Don't move a fucking muscle, or I'll use your mouth instead of that glorious ass."

Too many thoughts bounced around in my head at once.

How surprisingly nice that smack felt. I'd never really thought about getting spanked before, but oh yeah, that could definitely—

My mouth watered, my jaws aching at the thought of taking him on my tongue. Straining wide around his meaty girth. Seeing how far I could take him down my throat before I gagged. That could—

And holy shit, my ass? Did that mean...? Did I want—

Cold goo dripped down my crack. Calloused fingers smoothing up and down between my cheeks. An embarrassing sound squeaked out of my mouth before I could stop it. My back arched, my hips automatically lifting my ass up into his caress.

I didn't know I was into butt stuff. Had I ever done anal? How had he known?

His forearm braced over my shoulders, his palm on the back of my head. Holding me down. His weight settling against me. My heart pounded so hard that black spots floated through my vision. Something stirred deep in my memory, uncurling a tendril of shadow before disappearing again.

Aidan's cheek pressed against mine, the rough stubble on his jaw bringing me back to the here and now. The rich scent of leather still hung around him, softening his harsher scent of gunpowder and war. He hadn't hurt me. He never would.

"Are you with me, Riann? If it's too much, we'll do something else. I'll still tear you up missionary style."

I couldn't help but laugh even as said pussy convulsed with sheer bliss at the thought. "I'm okay."

A low rumble vibrated from his chest. "*Okay* isn't what I'm after."

He wanted to be unforgettable. To leave a mark on my memory, maybe even my body, that I'd never be able to wipe from my mind. Of all my men, he was the most possessive. His jealousy had torn the treasures apart in the past. Their treasurekeeper at that time had reveled in his fierce attention, the strife that she brought among the four friends. She'd played them against each other, which had only worsened his darker tendencies.

His fear that he wouldn't be enough to hold my attention. That I wouldn't love him as much as I loved the others. Or worse, that I might be too intimidated by his darker urges. That I might be scared of him.

No, that wasn't quite right. He wanted me to be a little afraid. He wanted to stomp along the line between out-of-control lust and outright violence. Yet still be absolutely confident in my trust in him.

I let out a fragile whimper. Exactly the kind of sound that would excite him. While I arched my back again, lifting up my ass. Inviting him to do his worst to me.

He shifted up to his knees, keeping his forearm against my shoulders. "Doran's your safety net, yeah? You say his name, or reach for him in your mind, and I'll stop. We'll both hold you and keep you safe."

"I don't need Doran Stoneheart to keep me safe." My voice sounded breathy, my heartbeat still pounding like runaway horses. "Not when I've got the Slaughterer at my back."

~

AIDAN

I TRIED. I HONESTLY TRIED.

I tried to go slowly. To be gentle and tender and kind. Even when I didn't have the barest ounce of tenderness in my body.

Gritting my teeth, I fought the urge to bite her shoulder hard enough to leave marks in her flesh. To plunge deep inside her, drawing out a ragged scream. I didn't want to hurt her.

Lies. Lies I told myself.

I wanted to hurt her.

I wanted her to scream.

And still love me. Still desire me enough to beg me for more.

Keeping an iron fist on my lust, I tested her asshole with my fingers. Opening her up. Seeing how much she could take without telling me to stop.

Fucking hell. Another one of those sexy, ragged little cries came out of her throat and she arched into me. Begging for more.

I squeezed and kneaded her full, plump buttocks. Stroked the swell of her hips. The dip of her waist. Fighting to keep my big head in control. When all I wanted to do was spread her wide—

"Aidan." The plaintive cry of my name on her lips sent a massive fissure through the towering concrete defenses I'd built to keep her safe. "Aidan, please."

I reared back on my knees, pushing her thighs wide to make room for me. Filled my palms with her incredible ass, squeezing and pulling her open. Torturing myself with the sight of her puckered hole. Knowing how tight she'd be.

The sounds she made when I plunged my thumb inside to rub around her tight ring. Incoherent babbles and kitten mewls that made my dick throb. So easy. I could come on her ass right now and just watch the way my seed ran down her crack. But it would be so much better to be inside her.

I pushed against her asshole, kneading her cheeks, squeezing hard enough to leave fingerprints in her flesh. Her voice climbed an octave and her hands scrambled against the mattress, fisting in the bedding. Heaving like a freight train, I tried to pause so she could adjust. Even though it felt like all the veins in my skull were about to explode. But she moved. She fucking lifted her ass, inviting me in, and I couldn't stop.

I shoved deep, fighting through the tightness of her body. All the way. Balls deep. Her cries ringing in my ears. Her body shuddering beneath me. Captive. Pinned. I yanked her up by her hair enough to get my forearm around her throat. Locking her against me.

She struggled and twisted in my grip, her breathing as loud as mine. For a moment, horror strangled me. Regret churned in the pit of my stomach. If I hurt her... Drove her away from us...

One flailing arm managed to reach back over her shoulder. She snagged my head, pulling us tighter together—not trying to escape.

I sank my teeth into the ridge of muscle between her neck and shoulder. A primal bite to mark her as mine. A moment where I could hold her flesh inside me, as she held me. The taste of her skin in my mouth blew through the last remnant of my sanity. A burning fist of lust tore through my spine. Guttural sounds rattled my chest. I plunged deep, shuddering on a climax that seemed to reach inside my abdomen and drag my guts and organs out of my body.

Still spasming, I fell on top of her. Crushing her, I knew, but I couldn't have moved an inch if Balor himself strode into the room.

Sweat cooled on my skin. My heaving chest steadied. I had the presence of mind to loosen my fingers. To let go of the vicious grip of my jaws on her shoulder. She didn't move beneath me. Her hair was a tangled mess, still damp from her shower. I swept my hand over her face, trying to see if she was alright. Conscious. Injured. Terrified.

If she hated me now...

My hand trembled, trying to uncover her eyes. I had to see for myself that she wasn't afraid or hurt. That I hadn't ruined everything yet again.

Terror didn't twist her lips. She didn't glare at me with fury or recrimination. She didn't even open her eyes beyond a sexy, sleepy blink. Then she turned toward me, curling up against me with a soft little sound that blasted the last bit of concrete and steel encasing my heart.

Relief pulsed through me, making my eyes burn. I pulled her closer, trying not to squeeze her too hard. She needed to be able to breathe, not have her ribs crushed by an insane man who wanted to beg her.

Don't leave me. Don't ever, ever die.

"Aidan?" She whispered, her voice raspy and hoarse.

I made a low hum, my lips brushing her forehead.

She didn't reply. Wondering if she'd fallen asleep, I leaned back enough to search her face. Her eyes were open, though she stared intently at the ink swirling around my throat rather than my eyes. She bit her lip. Flicked a quick glance up at me.

My dick stirred. More than interested in round two.

Her cheeks reddened. Her teeth tugged on her lip. "Could you maybe spank me? Next time. If you don't mind."

My chest ached as if my ribcage was going to explode.

I was the tough guy. The meanest, baddest, motorcycle-riding bastard of the group. I couldn't go all soft and gushy. Even though what I really wanted to do was fall down to my knees beside the bed and beg her to let me worship her all over again.

Next time. I hadn't ruined everything. She'd let me fuck her again. In fact, she was already laying the groundwork for us to do it again.

"Harder?" I managed to say, though it came out harsher than I intended. My throat was too tight with unspoken emotion. Relief. Gratitude. Undying devotion for all time. "Or longer?"

She nodded. "Mmm hmm."

Then she nestled her head beneath my chin and promptly fell asleep.

Meanwhile, I wasn't ever going to sleep again for fear of missing a single moment with her. How long did we have before Evil Eye killed us this time?

Not fucking long enough.

23

I woke up briefly when Keane came back. Aidan left but Ivarr joined us. Then Doran and Warwick. Every time I woke up, a different man had joined me on the bed to cuddle.

It took me a couple of wake-up times to realize they were still wearing clothes. They weren't coming to see if I might be up for round three. Or was it four? I couldn't even remember.

Finally, it dawned on me that they were taking turns guarding me while I slept.

Of course, that melted my heart. But it also scared the shit out of me.

I wasn't safe. I wasn't ever going to be safe. Not while Jonathan was trying to get me back. His trap at the apartment had almost succeeded. The guys hadn't been able to come after me. If I hadn't been carrying Warwick's gold...

I shuddered enough that Doran made a low soothing rumble and tightened his arms around me. I snuggled closer to the broad granite planes of his chest, breathing in his scent. Wet stone after a thunderstorm, a hint of lightning still in the air.

"Do you think the changeling has other traps set for me?" I asked.

"I think it's highly likely."

I tipped my head back so I could see his face. I knew he wouldn't lie to me—but I'd rather see the open honesty in his deep, dark eyes for myself. "How do we stop him?"

He brushed my hair back from my face, tucking the strands behind my ear. "Our best strategy will be to stay one step ahead of him."

"Because we can't actually stop him."

He nodded solemnly. "Through you, we treasures have been blessed with more power than we've known for centuries, but he's nearly as powerful as Evil Eye himself. Our best hope is to weaken him enough to force him back to Faerie."

"How many times have you fought Balor?"

"Too many to count."

"Have you ever won?"

He lifted one mountainous shoulder in a careless shrug. "We've forced him from the mortal plane before, though not in the last several hundred years."

"Even then, he comes back, though. Right? So what's the point?"

"It's a mythical, legendary cycle. A villain rises. Heroes answer the call. Battles rage. Sometimes we live to fight another day. Most times, we don't, and the world slips deeper into darkness."

"What happens then?"

"I suppose we won't return to this plane any longer. There won't be any need. The spark of magic that we bring with us will die out, and the only magic left in your world will be Evil Eye's."

"So man-eating monsters will overrun the world?"

"Eventually. Though even Evil Eye doesn't want all of mankind dead."

My stomach pitched on a queasy roll but I managed to force out a laugh. "He's got to feed his imps somehow."

"Exactly."

That didn't make me feel any better.

"It's curious to me that Bres would be so invested in defeating Balor," Doran said. "At one time, they were allies."

"They're at war in Faerie?"

"Not that I'm aware of, though Evil Eye has been spreading his dark influence through the realms."

My mind felt muddled with too much information. Like a giant ball of yarn had unraveled and tangled up in my head. Everything I needed to know so that I could understand what we needed to do was here. But I couldn't begin to find the end of the string. Worse, if I did manage to find the end so I could pull on it...

I had a feeling I'd end up with a knot the size of Texas. Everything was supposedly gigantic in Texas.

"There's still so much about Faerie that I don't understand," I finally admitted. "Warwick mentioned High Court fae before. Are the courts like separate countries? With alliances or ongoing wars?"

Doran let out a low hum that vibrated through my ribcage. "Not exactly. I could try to explain what I've come to understand, but I think it'll be best explained by fae himself."

A light chime sounded in my head. It took me a second to realize that it wasn't an actual doorbell and that Doran hadn't heard it. I opened the metaphorical door to Warwick. *:Are you free to—:*

Materializing in a puff of green, he plopped down beside us on the bed. "How can I help?"

As I rolled over and sat up so I could talk, I had to bite back a groan. I'd definitely been sleeping too long. I was stiff and sore. Again. Whatever healing agent that had been in the elixir had definitely worn off.

Doran fluffed up the pillow for me. *"Mo stór* has questions about Faerie."

"Of course. I'll tell you anything that I'm not directly forbidden to share under a geas."

I sat back against Doran's side, his arm around my shoulders. Taking a deep breath, I held it a moment, letting all my thoughts churn, hoping they might naturally fall into some kind of categorization or natural order. "You said before that Aidan is the King of the Fallen Dells. He said his kingdom was called that because it fell to Balor thousands of years ago. Is that a realm in Faerie?"

"It was, yes. When the four treasures were first incarnated into mortal bodies, they were honored with their own Faerie realms and titles."

"He's a king and you're princes. Why?"

Doran gave me a wry grin. "I couldn't care less about titles and such. But in one of his human lifetimes, he was known as King Áedán. The name has been modified over his many lifetimes, but the title stuck."

"Do you actually have land somewhere in Faerie called the Windswept Moors?"

"No, not any longer. Once, yes, but it was so long ago that I can barely remember a rocky cliff with a grim-looking castle. Waves crashing against the rocks. The wind blowing in my face as I perched on the parapet."

"What happened to your home?"

"It faded back into the forgotten mists."

"Because of Balor?"

He sighed. "I'm sure that played a part, though he didn't explicitly raid the castle and burn it to the ground, if that's what you be thinking. Everything in Faerie is sustained by magic. As my powers faded over time, so did my place in Faerie. It is no more."

I frowned. "Like an island sinking into the ocean? Atlantis?"

"You're thinking of Faerie as physical ground and land," Warwick said. "That's not the way Faerie works at all. It's not a place on a map that you can go to. It's a dimension. An alternate plane of existence that few mortals are even aware of. That's how *Shamrocked* moved in the mortal world depending on where the treasurekeeper was located. You pulled that dimension of Faerie to you just by existing."

"But I walked in your garden. It was real. I could smell the flowers. I could touch them, see them. They were *real*."

"They're real, just as I'm real. But I do not naturally exist in the mortal dimension. There's a cost for me to be here, which I pay gladly," he added quickly, giving me a wicked, knowing grin. "The longer I'm here, the more power I must draw to remain. As I pull more power to this realm, Summer Isle will shrink, wilt, and eventually fade away if I don't return to sustain it."

I stretched out my hand and gripped his knee. "Then you must go back. I won't risk your home just so I can see you whenever I want."

He picked up my hand and pressed a kiss to my palm, his fingers stroking my knuckles. "Never fear, *mo stór*. I would pay any cost to simply see your face and hear your voice, but it would take decades of constant mortal life before I would begin to risk losing Summer Isle."

"I still don't really get how you can travel back and forth to Faerie if it's not a physical place. *Shamrocked* is a real place that I can see and walk into from the street." I frowned, remembering when I'd taken Vivi back in broad daylight, only to find an empty, abandoned house. "Though I guess it did look different. I thought that was your magic working to protect the bar. Was it… not actually there? Until night?"

"How good is your understanding of mathematics?"

My involuntary grimace made him laugh.

"Very well. I'll see if I can explain it in a way that you'll understand." He adjusted our hands so that my index finger pointed upward. "The tip of your finger is one point in this room, a three-dimensional space. The tip of Doran's impressive nose is another point in space. Once you know the two points, you can draw a straight line directly to his nose, right?"

He released my hand, and I moved my index finger straight up to lightly touch Doran's nose. "Of course."

"But when it's just the tip of your finger, a single point, you could go in infinite directions. Some you can see with your eyes or at least comprehend as a part of your physical existence. A point on the ceiling. A point on the floor. A point in the bottom of the lake where the kelpie's remains lie rotting. Some points you can't see with mortal eyes but you could at least imagine. Like a point on the surface of your sun. An impossibly distant planet in a galaxy you've never even heard of. Then there are places of mythology and legend born of magic, like the roots of Yggdrasil. The top of the brightest golden pyramid in Heliopolis. Or the Land Beneath the Waves, Tír na nÓg. These points lie in alternative, magical dimensions that I assure you exist, even if you've never seen them with mortal eyes or walked there with your own two feet as you did on the Summer

Isle. But if you have the power, and know a point in that dimension..."

Between one breath and another, the bed suddenly sat in the middle of Warwick's lush garden. Flowers tumbled down overhead in colorful curtains of fragrant blossoms. Everything was slow and stretched out, as if time didn't matter. Bright sparkles hung in the air, making it thick with glittering stardust and fragrance. My ears rang with heavy, slow notes. Chimes, or strums on a harp's strings, drawn out over infinity to enjoy every last nuance.

Ever so slowly, I turned my head and met Warwick's gaze. His emerald eyes flashed with spinning golden bursts of power, dazzling to behold. Sucking me down in a dizzying whirlpool of magic.

I blinked and we were back in the bedroom. My stomach quivered, my heart jolting in my chest, as if startled by the sudden change in gravity and time. Though I could still smell the spicy fragrance of flowers in my nostrils.

"Fae don't need to draw a line from point to point. We simply pull the locations together so they overlap, or they're so close they're part of the same dimension, at least for a time. Like a wrinkle, a small pocket of an alternative reality." With his other hand, he used his fingers to gather up the sheet, folding it into a messy accordion. "It's not a physical distance we travel but a fabric of space and time that folds, stretches, and bends to our will."

I took in a shaky breath. My heart skipped a beat, quickened, and then finally settled into its normal rhythm. "Wow."

They let me think in silence for a moment. Warwick holding my hand. Doran's thick arm around me, steading me. I looked up at him suddenly. "If your prison was in an alternate dimension, a plane like the Summer Isle, then theoretically, I should have been able to access it from anywhere here, right? I didn't need to drive down to the lake to find you."

"You were reaching me when you dreamed me. We were together. We touched. That was real, a shared dream where I wasn't trapped in stone. You made that possible. So aye, you could have freed me from anywhere. But sometimes you need a physical journey to reach a destination because it gives you the mental space and exercise you needed to make the leap."

"What's to keep Jonathan from pulling me into *his* reality?" My voice trembled and a chill crept down my spine. "Whenever he wants?"

Doran let out a deep, low growl that vibrated my bones. "That's why one of us will be with you always, ready to defend you at a moment's notice. Anything could be a trap like the fucking fountain. At least he doesn't know your current location, which makes the task more difficult. That's the main reason we chose this place outside of the city where none of us have ever been before."

Shivering, I closed my eyes a moment. Any moment, sucked away into Fhroig's lair. Or even worse. Trapped. No way to reach Doran. Jonathan was too smart to make the same mistake twice. Next time, he'd figure out a way to keep even Warwick out.

Not to mention Balor, who was even more powerful, bent on a hopeless, endless war that would end in my treasures' death. While I endured a changeling's nefarious attentions in Faerie for the rest of my mortal life.

Fucking hell. What kind of bullshit legendary story was that?

Warwick squeezed my hand gently, drawing my gaze up to his face. "It's not as bleak as all that. High Court fae agreed thousands of years ago on what they can and cannot do on the mortal plane. Granted, not all fae still abide by the old rules, but for the most part, elder Tuatha de Danaan do. I find it encouraging that you said the changeling offered his hand—but didn't touch you without your permission. That's an old rule put upon us long ago to give mortals free will."

"Plus, not all fae can move through the veil to this plane as easily as Warwick," Doran added. "The darker, lesser fae, like Balor's imps, can't bear sunlight and don't have enough power to penetrate the veil between without assistance. Which is the sole reason we've been able to keep your world from being overrun entirely despite losing ground to Evil Eye the past centuries. Even he needs time, resources, and power to move his fae army to the mortal realm."

Nervous energy pulsed through me. As much as I loved the idea of being able to lay around and cuddle with the guys as long as I wanted, I needed to *do* something. Anything. I couldn't wait like a sitting duck, picked off because I was frozen with fear.

Tipping my chin up firmly, I turned to Doran. "Isn't there a fight somewhere that I can help with? A nest of imps you need to drive out? Something I can do to help?"

A wide smile softened the formidable planes of his face. He leaned down, cupped my chin, and pressed his forehead to mine. "While I admire your indomitable courage, *mo stór*, leave the killing of imps to the Slaughterer."

"But isn't that what I'm supposed to do? I'm your conduit. I'm supposed to help—"

"Your gifts lie elsewhere," he broke in gently. "A thousand years ago and more, sure, the treasurekeeper went into battle with us. But we've lost too many treasurekeepers in the past, and I refuse to miss even one breath with you as long as this body lives."

"But—"

He squeezed my chin and gave my head a little shake. "Leave the killing and warfare to us."

My throat ached, my voice breaking. "I don't want you to die in this useless war against Balor and leave me alone the rest of my miserable life."

The door slammed open, making me jump. I pulled my chin free of Doran's fingers and turned to see Aidan glowering in the doorway, arms crossed over his chest. "You think so little of us, *mo stór*? A few dark fae be no match for your treasures now that we have you at our side."

Keane and Ivarr came in behind him. They were all dressed in black military-style garb. Aidan's swords hung on his back, the hilts poking up above his shoulders. Keane carried the massive flamethrower he'd taken to help rescue Doran, and he'd painted the red slash down the middle of his forehead.

Just like in my original painting before I ever met them in real life. *They're ready for war.*

24

KEANE

Wearing warpaint once more tapped into something I had lost long ago. A faint ghost of the mortal warrior I had been before I began to carry my immortal gift. Forgotten long ago, until she painted me in a dream.

The man I had been. The man I could be again.

Riann's gaze lingered on the red stripe, making me even gladder that I had painted it.

"This is your gift." I drew my index finger down over the red swatch of paint, pulling her gaze down my face to my lips. "Your artist's eye that sees through the mists of time, piercing even the veil to reveal long-forgotten truths."

Staring at my lips, she swallowed hard. A delicate shiver made her shoulders tremor. "Promise me one thing."

"Anything."

She dragged her gaze back up to mine. "*When* you get back from wherever you're going, I want you inside me when you kiss me."

"After I spank that glorious ass again." Aidan slapped me on the back. "Harder this time."

"Deal," she replied.

I had never been one to shirk my duties, especially when it came to war. I was as hungry for battle and blood as I was for sex and food. It was my nature to be ravenous in all things. But I involuntarily took a step toward the bed, my eyes burning like bonfires in my skull.

Aidan gripped my shoulder, dragging me back. "Not so fast, lover boy. We've got to clean out a nest first."

"Where?" Doran asked.

"Roanoke Park," Ivarr replied. "On the news this morning, they said the concrete that's been blocking the cave entrance for decades crumbled and cracked open overnight. Sure sounds like an imp party waiting for nightfall."

"Agreed." Doran lifted his arm from her shoulders and moved to the side of the bed. "How many of your men be ready?"

"All of them," Aidan replied. "Ten wait for us in the city, and five more are making their way separately to locations near here to keep watch for anything suspicious."

"Even Hammer?" Riann asked.

"Red and her beau are back in town."

She scrambled to the other side of the bed and grabbed her phone. "She texted me but I didn't hear it."

While she was quickly typing a reply, Doran pulled on pants and joined us. "What's your plan?"

"We head into the cave while the Demon Hunters guard outside," Aidan replied. "They're tough as nails and excellent shots but they don't do as well in dark or tight locations against fae, even lesser fae. I'd rather they pick off any stragglers that get by us and make sure we don't have a surprise attack from outside."

Doran lowered his voice, trying to whisper. "I meant the plan for *mo stór's* protection."

"Excuse me?" Riann strode toward us in a magnificent display of naked flesh. Eyes sparking with fury, her hair mussed and tangled from Aidan's manhandling.

I tried not to ogle her while she was obviously upset, but I couldn't keep my gaze from sweeping down her frame to drink in the full, delicious curves of her body. Her breasts would fill my hands. Not to mention her ass. No wonder Aidan hadn't been able to resist the urge to redden those lush cheeks at least a little. My mouth watered at the memory of her taste on my tongue. The heat and wet flesh over my face. I would gladly die every day for eternity as long as I could wake between her thighs again.

"As I said earlier, our powers deal in war," Doran said. "Your gift lies elsewhere. We won't risk you."

She marched right up to the big man and poked him in the chest with her index finger. "I can't stay behind twiddling my thumbs while you're in danger either. I won't."

He gently gripped her shoulders. "We're not the only ones who'll be watching the city for signs of dark fae activity. Anyone who knows about the treasures will come to the realization that such a cave collapse will draw our attention. If they know about us, then they know about you. If we take you with us, you'll be exposed."

"And if you leave me behind, I won't be protected. Right?"

"Warwick—"

"Is no match for an old, powerful fae like Balor," she broke in. "Not alone, and especially not when he's bound by the oaths he had to swear. Right?" Her head swiveled back toward the leprechaun. "No offense."

Despite being fully clothed, Warwick managed to look positively decadent in a careless lounge across the foot of the bed. His ridiculously long black hair swept out around him like a silken cape. He huffed out a laugh. "None taken, *mo stór*, and you're absolutely right. If the changeling showed up, there is very little that I could do. I couldn't raise a finger against him, even with your life at stake. A geas bound by a leprechaun's gold is unbreakable."

Doran glowered, Aidan looked like he was about to start spitting coffin nails, and even Ivarr's normally soft, golden light carried a glittering diamond edge.

"Let's think this through carefully," I said, lifting my hands in a soothing gesture. "She makes a valid point. This house is an unknown location as far as we know but he could track by scent, like you, Aidan. Could you find her by scent alone even if there wasn't a trail?"

He grunted sourly. "Aye. It would take me longer, sure, but I'd know almost immediately that she wasn't in the city. Evil Eye's focus be here and now, so I'd assume she'd remain close enough to return. I'd loop around the city in growing arcs until I picked up her scent. A few hours at most, and I'd have her location."

"There has to be a reason he didn't scoop me up when he had the chance." Riann gnawed on her bottom lip, her brow scrunched. "When I thought he was still human, he fought the divorce in court for almost a year. He knew where I was living and working, because I had to provide all that detail to the court. I didn't know anything about you yet. So why didn't he nab me then before I could free Doran and learn more about what was going on?"

Warwick joined us. "He wanted you to lead him to something that he believed would help him kill Evil Eye once and for all. Maybe he thought we had to be with you to unlock that possibility."

Her gaze focused on me. "When you were telling the story about Bres and Balor, you said they were allies. Why would Bres want to kill Balor now?"

"I would guess that he wants to protect Maige Tuired. Magic is slowly weakening across Faerie in all dimensions except Balor's. He takes more and more for himself, gorging on the magic and devastation of others. While the rest of Faerie fades, Dún Bhalair only grows stronger."

Warwick nodded. "Very true. Her Majesty says the veil thins more and more every day."

"The veil between my world and Faerie? What happens if that comes down?"

"Neither Tír na nÓg nor your world will exist any longer," Warwick said softly. "All realms will be absorbed into Evil Eye's domain."

"Let's assume that I really do have something that Jonathan wants, even though I have no idea what it is. He did argue over the property settlement several times. My attorney thought that was especially strange since I left with very little property of my own. He also kept demanding I come get my things that I'd left behind, but I refused. I told my attorney I didn't want any of it."

"He wanted you to trigger the trap," Aidan growled.

"Yes, probably, but he kept acting like I was lying about taking something. Could it be the painting you saved?"

"It does have a great deal of power in it," Warwick replied. "The longer you stare at it, the more you see, especially in light. Though I haven't dared study it much for fear of drawing Evil Eye's attention to it. If a High Court fae wants into my court, I won't be able to keep him out for long. I thought it best to suppress all traces of its lingering magic as much as possible."

A sinking pit of certainty weighed heavily in my stomach. "This cave-in is a trap. I don't think it's an imp nest at all."

"Oh there's gonna be imps." Doran shook his head slowly. "And pookas and likely redcaps too. The changeling be clever enough to get us to strike Evil Eye's minions and expose our treasurekeeper at the same time."

"A two for one with a cherry on top," Aidan added grimly. "We attack Balor and weaken his forces, or we die, or better yet, both. Either way, the changeling takes the opportunity to steal *mo stór*. That painting will be in the bleeding bastard's slimy hands before our bodies are cold."

"Every trap can be sprung." Riann's chin lifted, her shoulders squared bravely despite the faint quiver in her voice. "Knowing is half the battle, right? So what can we do?"

I looked from man to man, the cold dread in my stomach worsening. We all knew the truth.

Though I would give my last breath to spare her any pain.

Doran gave her a gentle push toward the bathroom. "Why don't you get dressed, love? The lads and I'll have a chat and see what we come up with."

She crossed her arms over her chest and spared each of us a hard look despite the growing pink in her cheeks. "Don't you dare try and sneak off to leave me behind."

"We wouldn't dream of it," Doran replied.

She didn't notice that his voice cracked like a thousand-pound granite boulder reducing itself into rubble.

25

S wiping tears away, I called Vivi as I pulled on my clothes.

"I hear there's some bullshit about to go down," she said. "How soon are you heading back into the city?"

"I don't know. I think the guys are going to try to pull some bullshit of their own."

Her tone sharpened and though I couldn't see her, I felt her intensity radiating through the phone screen. "Yeah? Let me guess. Spare you any danger, send you away, blah blah blah."

I sniffed and nodded. "Something like that. They think they're headed to a trap, so naturally they're trying to protect me."

I gave her the five-minute rundown, though not as good as Keane's story. I kept hopping around too much. "Do you remember me painting something that would have been on display in Crown Center? Probably soon after I entered the institute. It had a glowing doorway and a young girl standing in front of it."

"You painted a lot back then but I don't remember a door specifically. You usually painted forests and creatures."

I scraped my hair back into a sleek ponytail. "What happened to all of those old canvases? Maybe there's other clues in them that I'm missing."

"You took them all when you moved out."

I blew out a sigh and slammed my hairbrush down on the counter a bit too hard. "I guess they're all destroyed then."

"Well you certainly didn't have much of anything when you moved back in with me."

"What did I tell you that night?"

"Not much. You were too upset and I didn't want to push you too hard. You'd already been through so much."

"What, though? Had I told you?"

"You didn't have to say a word." Vivi's voice hardened. "I could see it on your face. You looked positively ill. Pale, drawn, exhausted. Huge dark circles under your eyes. You slept for a solid twenty-four hours. When you finally came out of your room, you seemed so much better that I didn't fight you when you insisted you didn't need to go to the doctor."

"That's how bad I looked?"

"Yeah. I was afraid you'd been assaulted." She paused, her voice catching. "Repeatedly. You wouldn't say anything, and I didn't want to trigger you. But you weren't right those first few days. Then you seemed to come out of a dark cloud. I was thrilled—though I was worried about your memory. I assumed you'd blocked most of it so you could heal in your own time."

"I don't know if I'll ever remember exactly what happened. I probably don't want to remember now." I gave myself a shake and stared at my image in the mirror. "I'm stronger now."

"Oh honey. You were strong then too or you'd never have survived as long as you did."

My throat squeezed around a giant lump. "I didn't feel strong."

"You were," she replied firmly. "And you are. You're the baddest bitch I know. Now what are you going to do about these blockheads who think they're going to send you away for your own damned good? Hold on a sec."

I heard a man's voice though I couldn't make out what he said.

"Hammer said we're headed your way. I guess the plan is for you and me to be shipped off together somewhere."

I nodded slowly as a plan began to shimmer in my mind. Not just any plan. Chills rippled down my arms. I hugged myself, briskly rubbing my arms. I could feel the magic humming around me. In the mirror, my eyes glittered like jewels. Their magic? Or mine? Did it matter?

"I have an idea. Can you bring a few things for me?"

"Absolutely—as long as it'll fit into my purse. Hammer says we've got to move quickly and we'll be on his bike."

"In my room, there should be a watercolor palette and a small pad of thick paper. Also a set of charcoal pencils."

"Done. Anything else?"

"That should be enough. I'm guessing the guys will have a bunch of weapons we can choose from."

"You got it. See you in about thirty minutes."

I bent down and rummaged through my jeans until I found the gold coin. Stroking my finger over the faint outline of a woman's face, I whispered aloud, "For luck."

26

I stared doubtfully at the huge black SUV. I might be mistaken but it looked like some kind of military vehicle. "Why can't I ride with one of you again? I like your motorcycles."

"You'll be safer inside a closed vehicle." Aidan jerked open the back passenger door. "This beast has bulletproofed glass and armored panels."

I scowled at him. "Which won't keep out a fae."

"Right," Ivarr said in a light, cheerful voice that didn't match his eyes. Normally shining with warm golden tones, his eyes were almost completely brown with only a hint of amber lightening them. "Which is why we've loaded the car down with salt and bare iron. They despise that shit."

"I've also put a glamor over the vehicle," Warwick added. "Most eyes will slide right over it without even seeing it."

They were sending me away. It was as obvious as the huge, crooked break in Doran's nose. All of them were walled off in my head. Concrete and granite, cold and hard and impenetrable.

Lonely.

They'd been taking lessons from Aidan in that regard.

A muscle ticked across his cheek but he didn't deny it.

"I see," I said softly.

"Don't make this harder than it has to be."

I looked from him to the other men. Keane couldn't meet my gaze. Warwick looked sus as hell, nervously twirling his hair into long, thin braids. Ivarr turned away so hard his black coat fluttered about him like wings. Doran offered his hand to me, but only to help me step up into the big vehicle. "We'll see you on the other side."

I blinked back tears as I settled into the seat. Vivi and Hammer were already in the front. "Don't lie to me."

"Tis not a lie, love. I'll find you, whether on this side of the veil or beyond."

I stared straight ahead so I wouldn't have to see the lie in his eyes. "Like you've found all the other treasurekeepers, right? Yeah, that's what I thought."

"I didn't want to spend eternity with any of them. Only you, Riann Newkirk, and find you, I will, so swears Doran Stoneheart." He shut the door hard enough the vehicle rocked beneath me.

"Drive," Aidan growled in a thunderous voice. "As hard and fast as you can. Don't stop for nothing until you're on fumes."

Hammer floored it hard enough the tires squealed. Vivi twisted around in her seat, offering me her hand.

I grabbed her hand in mine, squeezing gratefully. "I'm so glad to see you."

"Are you okay?"

Now that they couldn't see my tears, I indulged in a few moments of messy sobs. "I will be. Bleeding idjits." Which only made me cry harder because that was something Doran would have said. They didn't even kiss me goodbye. Even though they expected to die. "Tell me something good."

Vivi spent the next few minutes regaling me about the weekend she'd spent with Hammer. They'd ridden long hours through the day and night, just the two of them on his bike. When they got tired or hungry they pulled off the road. Quaint diners. Rustic cabins. No change of clothes until she bought something new.

"And not designer stores, either." She gave the beefy man behind the wheel a playful growl. "Only thrift stores. That was the rule."

I gasped and clutched invisible pearls. "Oh my. However did you survive without Prada or Versace?"

She nodded. "I know. It was quite the challenge. But it was fun. Besides, I was out of my clothes more than I was in them."

I plugged my ears and sang loudly, "La la la, I'm not listening to the gory details of your sex life."

Laughing, she snuggled up against him, peeking back at me over his shoulder. Her eyes glowed with happiness. Her hair was loose and casually tousled, rather than her normally smooth and perfect waves. No makeup. And she'd never looked more beautiful.

"Love looks good on you," I whispered, grinning.

"You too, honey. Even if they're assholes. Want to see what I brought?"

Sniffing, I nodded. She jerked her head toward the other passenger door. "Lucky for you I've been using my largest tote."

Gucci, of course, with plenty roomy for even the sketchpad. I pulled out my artist supplies. "You don't have any water by chance?"

"Check the rear cargo section," Hammer replied. "They loaded a ton of shit in the back. I'm guessing they would've thought to send water and snacks because they didn't want us to stop anywhere."

Dangling over the backseat to reach—cursing my short arms—I found a large case of bottled water, along with an arsenal of what looked like farming equipment in the back. Old, rusted spikes, the ends of spades and hoes, even a few crowbars. A case of cheap salt. My duffle bag. Of course, Aidan would have made sure I had something to wear.

Blinking back round two of waterworks, I focused on getting my paints ready. "You're going to have to pull over once I start painting."

Hammer groaned. "You heard the man. I can't—"

"Sure you can, babe." Vivi leaned up and whispered in his ear. I didn't look up but from the sounds I was pretty sure she was using her tongue more than her words to convince him.

I pulled out my phone. "What do you know about Roanoke Park?"

"Not much," she replied. "Is that where the action is going down?"

"Yeah. Evidently there's a cave in the park that had some kind of break in."

"Oh, I heard about that on the news," Hammer said. "The cave was walled off over fifty years ago because some kids got lost inside. At least that was the excuse. Now the concrete blocking the entrance was knocked down overnight. Some joggers noticed and called the police. I'm guessing it's being guarded to keep people out."

With the current news story, I found several images online. A rocky cliff jutted up from the ground, covered in moss and vines. A large tree grew to the side, branches stretching out over the hole like a leafy roof. Though in this picture, the hole was covered in cement. I'd have to do some modifications based on the time of year. The tree wouldn't have any leaves, and there'd probably be some ice and snow gathered in the ridges. Especially along the ground. Which way did the cliff face? Would the sun have melted everything already?

I'll have to guess. Trust the magic. Let my brush find the answers as I go.

"Okay, I'm ready to start painting. Can you pull off the road?"

He blew out a sigh. "I'll take the next exit. Though Aidan'll have my hide."

My lips quirked, my cheeks heating at the thought of what Aidan would do when he found out what I'd done. It wouldn't only be my face burning. "Let me worry about him."

"Are you hoping to paint a clue?" Vivi asked.

I shook my head as I lightly sketched out the cliff and tree. "Not exactly. I'm not even sure this is going to work. Give me a few minutes and then I'll tell you what I'm hoping to do. These aren't my normal mediums but I didn't want to worry about cleaning my brushes. Besides, even in that giant tote, you wouldn't have had room for my smallest canvas."

They let me work in silence. The sound of the charcoal gliding over the paper was soothing. Familiar. The smell of paper. The pigments that flowed across the page. My nape prickled and goose-bumps rose on my arms. My fingers tingled. I could feel the magic filling me as I breathed, flowing in and out of me, pulling me closer to the picture beneath my brush. I painted a tiny blue bird sitting on a limb and I could almost hear its song. A yellow butterfly floated like a delicate leaf. The sun showered the cliff in golden sparkles that spun in a slow dance that I choreographed with my brush.

My heart thudded heavily. I set the brush aside, letting the last strokes of pigmented water settle deeper into the paper. "I'm not sure that this will work, but I'm going to try and travel like the fae do. If I understood Warwick correctly, then fae can fold locations together without moving at all. If I had time, I'd experiment and see if I could take you to the Summer Isle first. Though I'm not sure that I could enter it without him."

:*My home is always open to you,* mo stór. *No ward could keep you out, even if that be my intention.*:

I laughed in my head, relieved that he could still hear my thoughts. :*Don't tell Aidan what I'm going to try and do.*:

:*Never in a million years. I quite like my head on my shoulders where it belongs.*:

A muffled rumble echoed through the concrete that they'd built between us. I could almost see Aidan slamming his fists on the wall, yelling with fury.

To be safe, I shut every mental door of my own, imagining myself locked inside four steel walls. Letting out a nervous giggle, I looked up at Vivi. "We need to hurry before they figure out what I'm up to. Hammer, can you grab some of the iron in the back? Maybe some salt too. I'm assuming you're both going, if this works, that is."

"You're not leaving me behind," Vivi said stoutly. "Not this time."

"There's a cave," I warned. She paled but tipped her chin up and gave me a nod. She hated dark, tight spaces. "Then it's a good thing I've got a big, beefy man who'll carry me. Right, babe?"

"Without question, Vee. I'll be carrying your cute ass straight to safety."

She rolled her eyes. "What are we expecting to see when we get there?"

"A trap. The guys think there's a nest of imps and other nasty creatures, like before—but that the cave-in was triggered by Jonathan to draw me out into the open."

Vivi's eyes widened. "The changeling? How do we stop him?"

This was the part that even my very best friend was going to balk at. "We don't."

"What? No fucking way, Riann." She grabbed at the still-damp watercolor, likely to rip it up into tiny pieces before I could try and use it. "You're not going to use yourself as bait. Or worse, a sacrifice. I won't allow it."

"I only need him to *think* that's what I'm doing. I'm the bait and trap together."

"Tell me the plan down to the last detail or I veto this whole thing."

"I can't," I whispered, shaking my head. "This is the kind of thing I don't dare even think of. Let alone say out loud. I'm not sure what's listening, even in my own head." I hesitated a moment, trying to decide how much would be safe to tell her. "The changeling had a... a... seed planted inside me. A bit of his darkness was still inside me this whole time. I think it's gone now, but what if it's not? What if he has some other way to read my intention? Then we're screwed before I can pull this off. The less you know the better. I don't even dare think it aloud for fear he or the guys might see what I'm going to try and do."

"If they wouldn't want you to do this, then I don't either. They love you. They only sent you away with us to keep you alive."

I swallowed hard. "I know. I love them too. But I can't sit back and let them die, even if that means I escape. I'll never be free anyway. Not as long as Jonathan can track me down. And trust me when I say I'd rather die a thousand times in every horrible way you can imagine than be forced to spend an hour at his mercy again."

Her lovely face firmed. Resolute, I nodded silently. She had my back. I had hers. Hammer would help keep her safe. I wouldn't even have to ask.

I just had to get us there.

27

Breathing deeply, I tipped my face up to the sunlight. There was still a bit of snow on the ground in places and the air was still too chilly to call it spring, but I could feel the promise of warmth and green growing things on my skin.

Vivi stood on my left, her arm locked with mine. Hammer had his arm around her waist. I wasn't sure if we all needed to be touching or not, but I'd rather be safe than sorry. Something buzzed in the corner of my mind, trying to distract me. Threatening me. That was Aidan. He still didn't know what the hell I was doing but he sure didn't like it, not one bit.

I fought the urge to reach out to him. Or to Warwick. I'd love to tell him what I planned. Talk through my options and make sure it would work. But I needed the element of surprise if I had any hope at all of succeeding. If all else failed, I had to hope he would make sure I died quickly rather than end up in Jonathan's control.

"Ready?" My voice sounded sure and loud. Too loud. Vivi squeezed my arm encouragingly. I stared down at my painting, letting the brushstrokes pull me in. This was *my* magic. My power. I only had to believe it.

Believe in the magic. Believe in myself. Easier said than done.

My heart pounded, waiting to see what would happen, if anything. As the seconds ticked by, I focused on the colors and the way they bled together, creating new shades. The intricate details my muse had been led to add to the painting that hadn't been in the grainy website photo. Sticks in the rocky cracks promised green plants in the spring. Stubborn plants that would bloom and grow despite the lack of soil. The lone tree with sweeping branches, shielding the dark hole of the cave. Wait. The concrete was gone. Had I painted the walled-up spot, or the hole? I couldn't remember.

Movement on the page drew my attention to the butterfly. Its wings flapped so that it dipped and danced against the darkness of the hole in the side of the cliff. The cheerful little bird on his branch bobbed his head, inviting me to come inside. Welcoming me.

A gust of air rattled the paper, making me clutch it harder for fear it would be swept away.

"Oh," Vivi gasped. "Riiiiiiiiiiiiiiii…"

My name drew out into an impossibly long syllable. The ground jolted beneath my feet, making my stomach pitch. I reeled slightly, my body sluggish as I caught my balance.

"Annnnnnn!"

The last syllable of my name ended loudly with a jarring crash that reverberated through my head. Hot air blasted past my face, stealing my breath. The stink of smoke and cooking meat—foul, rotten meat—made me gag. Keane's flamethrower. Metal clanged, swords hacking and swinging. Aidan. Ivarr. The ground shook, an earthquake rocking me off center. A bellowing roar made my ears roar. Doran's gargoyle.

I couldn't move for a moment, as if my physical body was still back at the SUV while my mind tried to focus on what was happening around me. Shaking my head took all my effort but helped clear some of the mental cobwebs. The cliff rose above us directly ahead. Chunks of concrete and rock lay tumbled on the ground. A handful of men stood outside the cave, armed with sawed-off shotguns and brutal hatchets. Another man lay on the ground, a policeman, I thought, from his uniform.

I didn't see Jonathan anywhere. Would he look the same? Or

would he take on another form to disguise himself? He could be one of Aidan's men for all I knew. I had no idea how often a changeling could take up another human body or what kind of limitations he might have. Warwick hadn't recognized Jonathan as fae when he'd first stepped into *Shamrocked*.

Though I suspected the changeling would keep Jonathan's body. It was another way for him to torture me. To remind me of our former connection. I couldn't remember much of what I'd lived through while married to him, but my body still carried an imprint of the haunting memory of pain and misery.

Another screeching roar rumbled the ground, making even the tough Demon Hunter guys back up a step. That didn't sound good. At all. I couldn't imagine Doran making that kind of sound, but it sounded big and furious.

Hammer offered me one of the rusty tools. A short trowel with a pointed, sharpened end. "Are you sure about this?"

I nodded stiffly, quickly folding up the watercolor and shoving the paper into my back pocket so I could wrap numb fingers around the wooden handle of the trowel. It wasn't sharp like a knife but I could probably do some damage with it. It wasn't my primary weapon. If it came down to close combat with an old garden tool, I was dead anyway.

Picking my way through the debris, I entered the mouth of the cave with Vivi and Hammer right behind me. I crouched down off to the side, hopefully hidden and out of the way until my eyes adjusted to the darkness. It smelled of old earth and dampness, sort of like the cellar on Summer Isle where Warwick had hidden my painting, though this cave smelled rank. As if some animals had been using the cave as their restroom, made even worse by the stench of smoke and burning flesh. Definitely some nasty shit.

I strained to see deeper into the darkness. Was it a narrow tunnel —or an open chamber? I couldn't tell. The roars and crashes echoed all around us, making me think it was more of an open space. My ears throbbed with all the noise, yet I couldn't see them. Surely Ivarr's light or Warwick's glowing green aura would be visible if they were so close.

I risked popping up for a better look, scurrying several feet forward. Water splashed up on my jeans. Gingerly, I stretched my toe out, testing for the depth. But I didn't immediately feel ground beneath my shoe, even though cold water inched up over my knee. Involuntarily, I shivered, remembering the kelpie dragging me down to the bottom of the lake. Would there be another horse octopus here? Guarding the nest?

"Let me check," Hammer whispered, coming up beside me. He carried a hoe on a long wooden handle, testing the water in front of us. He poked the stick around, and something brushed against my calf.

I bit my lip, trying to stifle a sharp inhale. "Don't move."

Vivi clutched me, shivering against my back. "What is it?"

"I don't know. Something touched me in the water."

Her breathing quickened, her fingers digging into me so hard I winced. "Oh shit. Not again. Can I use the flashlight?"

We'd found a slim emergency flashlight in the glove compartment. With her claustrophobia, we'd agreed that Vivi should carry it, though we'd only use it if we had no other choice. In a dark cave, a flashlight would be like a giant bull's eye marking our location. But given the situation, I didn't think we had a choice. She was about to hyperventilate—me too—and I needed to see where the guys were.

"Yeah, but be ready to switch it off quickly. We may have to make a run for it."

She fumbled a moment and then a ray of light shot out of the slim canister, surprisingly bright and strong for such a small flashlight. She aimed down at my leg, illuminating a huge hairy rat floating in the water.

I flinched back against her before I realized it was dead. Also, not a rat, but an imp. "At least we're in the right place," I muttered. "But where is everyone?"

Vivi kept the light low, shining along the surface of the water. We stood at the edge of a large underground lake. More dark shapes dotted the water. Some were still moving, though they were swimming toward the center island, not toward us. It made me think of rats bailing a sinking ship.

Two massive shapes wrestled in the center, wings flapping, jaws snapping. I recognized Doran's gargoyle immediately, but I wasn't sure what the other creature was. It looked sort of like a scaly bird only it had three heads. A giant red lizard-slash-buzzard with three sharp beaks and massive talons that screeched along Doran's stone hide.

Other creatures milled around the island. Imps and pookas I recognized from before. Knee-high rat creatures with massive knife-like teeth and giant green swamp monsters. Even bigger creatures that towered over Aidan and Ivarr, who stood back-to-back. Keane and Warwick fought another huge pack on the opposite side. I wasn't close enough to see their faces, but I could feel their grim urgency. Even though they'd walled themselves off from me, I could sense... pain. Blood.

They were hurt. They were fucking *losing.*

Then it dawned on me why they weren't holding their own.

They weren't using their magic.

Ivarr didn't glow with the bright light of truth. Even Warwick fought with a long, graceful sword in his hand rather than a flash of green and gold power. The Irish treasures had been reunited after hundreds of years, but they weren't using their magical powers that made them immortal through the ages.

Fury arced through me like a fiery bolt of lightning. They were protecting me, avoiding their magic in case Jonathan was waiting. They didn't want to expose me accidentally. Even if they'd sent me far away from them...

They'd rather die and be eaten by hairy rats and swamp monsters than risk even a faint trail of magic that would lead back to me.

Throwing my head back, I closed my eyes and spread my arms open wide. The giant wheel lay quiet and still inside me. I gave it a mental shove, trying to start the flow of magic through the spokes.

But nothing happened. It was just a wooden wheel, creaking and slowing down to a bare wobble.

Every other time I'd pictured the wheel in my head, it was already spinning and full of rainbows of light. They must have locked down the magic when they shut down our connection. Which made sense. If I was their conduit, and they cut themselves off from me, they'd cut themselves off from the source of their magic as well.

Aidan roared above the din of battle. "Don't you dare, Riann!"

Bile burned the back of my throat. My fingers trembled and I shifted my grip on the trowel so I wouldn't drop it. I'd been running for an entire year. Avoiding my ex-husband, dodging his constant demands, sensing the trap. I'd been right, of course, though I'd had no idea the trap had been magical. I'd had no idea he wasn't even human.

I'd been running. Not from him, but all the hurt he'd caused me. The dark memories hovered beneath the surface of my mind like giant sea creatures, waiting to swallow me. I didn't want to remember. I didn't want to think about how long I'd stayed. How easily he'd managed to trap me in the first place. It made me feel stupid. Weak. Like I was nothing. Like I didn't matter. Nothing I said or managed to do had ever mattered.

Which was only one of the many lies I'd believed for years.

No more. I wasn't going to run any more. Not from him. Not from my fears. I wouldn't be controlled by my dread and fear any longer. Not by him or anyone else. I dug deep down inside me, reaching for the artist. The confident woman who'd flirted with a cute leprechaun. Who'd dreamed of a man with giant hands and a broken nose and believed in him enough to go on a wild goose chase to free him.

The same woman who'd stolen a badass biker's ride for the sole purpose of infuriating him into a chase. Who was confident enough to mouth back to him, secure in the knowledge that his growling and snapping was all for show. The woman who'd bathed in the golden light of truth and wasn't afraid of ravenous hunger. Who painted with abandon and laughed with her friends and knew beyond a shadow of a doubt that they would always have her back.

As if she knew I needed even a small gesture of comfort, Vivi lightly touched my back. Reminding me of her presence at my side.

I took a deep, cleansing breath, letting all my fears flow away. All my doubts in myself. The lies I had been told, both by others and myself. All the half-truths and secret shames that held me back.

:The changeling'll be watching for the treasures' magic,: Warwick warned. *:It'll be like a beacon, calling him straight to you.:*

I gave the wheel a hard spin, willing the magic—*my* magic—to flow. Dazzling colors exploded around me, lighting up the cave in glittering rainbows. *:Good. I'm counting on it.:*

28

Magic surged through me like a geyser, raining down in crystal droplets of power. Ivarr's light blasted free, a formidable solar storm that incinerated through the nearest creatures. Lightning arced from Aidan's swords, cutting down the larger trolls like they were nothing but paper mâché. Roaring, Doran snapped off one of the winged creature's heads. But instead of tackling the other two, he whirled toward me.

All of them. Rather than fighting the fae, they started to cut a path through them to get to me.

A green and gold trail sparkled behind Warwick as he blurred. Time slowed. Or maybe I was seeing him through the fae magic I'd called, moving through dimensions where time didn't matter. His hair swept around him like a black cape, his eyes burning green fire. His mouth moved, but his voice echoed in my head.

:The changeling—:

Still stuck in that in-between plane between worlds, I turned my head ever so slowly.

Jonathan smiled at me, the same nondescript brown eyes and average stature of the mortal man I'd thought I married. "So we meet again, honeybun. Though I dare say that this time you won't be so happy with the outcome."

Ice crackled through my veins. I lifted the trowel slightly, drawing his attention to it. "I'd like to make a deal with you." My voice echoed in my head, high pitched but steady.

He smirked. "Ah, the old folklore still lives. Incredible. I suppose you'd throw garlic at a vampire and try to shoot a werewolf with a silver bullet too."

For all his bravado, I couldn't help but note that he didn't move closer. He didn't try to touch me. Maybe he couldn't without violating the old ways, or maybe he really didn't like the iron. Out of the corner of my eye, I tried to measure the distance between me and Warwick. He still moved toward me, but at a snail's pace. I could still see the cave behind him and smell the smoky stench, but everything seemed stretched out and thin.

As if Jonathan had lifted this spot up into Faerie. Or brought Faerie down to this cave, changing the rules of physics in the process.

Vivi threw something at Jonathan over my shoulder. "Eat salt, bitch."

Lightly, he stepped aside, though he shuddered and swept one graceful hand over his other sleeve, knocking stray particles away. When he looked back at her, the narrowed, dark slant of his eyes made me involuntarily push her backwards. Away from danger. I'd seen that look in his eyes all too many times.

"Stupid human plays stupid games. Control your pet, honeybun. You know what happens to your pets when they don't follow my rules."

I opened my mouth, unsure what I was even going to say. The words weren't there. Only a blank spot in my mind. Not empty—I could feel something swirling, fighting to break free. A crying, screaming tornado of fury and pain that had left a lingering, ghostly imprint on my core.

"Ah, I forgot." He lifted his index finger on his right hand. "Here. You can have that one for free. Such a tasty little morsel."

I knelt on the ground in perfectly trimmed green grass at dusk. I could still see, though the light was fading quickly. It was the in-between time between day and night, where the sun had slipped beneath the horizon but the sky hadn't darkened to full night yet.

"You have to go," I whispered urgently. "Please. I don't want you to be hurt."

A black cat stared back at me. I didn't recognize it immediately, even though I was talking to it like it was my pet. She was mine, I knew that now, though it was also like meeting her for the first time. Her eyes were golden with hints of green, reminding me of both Ivarr and Warwick. Staring back at me with large, sad eyes, she meowed plaintively, and I could almost understand her. If I listened hard enough—

"That's Vanta," Vivi said. "You couldn't ever tell me what had happened to her."

I didn't move, afraid to disrupt the vision and lose her again. "You see her too? You know her?"

"She was your cat before we moved to Kansas City. She was roaming around in the woods behind the trailer park. As soon as she saw us, she started running toward us, yowling and purring like she'd been waiting for us." Her voice softened with awe. "For *you*. Now that we know... She recognized you, Riann. She'd been waiting to find you."

My breathing sawed in and out of my chest. Jagged edges slipped and sliced inside of me. Something bad had happened to her. My stomach churned and clammy sweat dotted my forehead. I wanted to turn away, bury my face in my hands, and sob.

Her rumbling purr grew louder. She rubbed against me, twining around my leg, insisting that I pet her. Hold her. She was heavy and large in my arms, her black fur silky against my cheek.

"What happened to her?" Vivi whispered.

I flinched. On my hands and knees in the garden, I vomited into the grass. Wailing. Sobbing. Begging him to stop. She hissed and clawed at him, but she couldn't get away. She wouldn't leave me.

He'd killed her. Not just once but over and over. My mind reeled with the snippets of horrible nightmares. All the evil, cruel ways he'd devised to torture us. Because that was exactly what it was. He tortured and killed my cat, to torture me.

So he could feed on my pain and fear.

Night after night. The same horror.

Vivi's arms tightened around me. I could feel her solid body against my back, her hands smoothing my hair, her voice. Trying to calm me, as she'd done when I'd first come to her house in the middle of the night. For weeks, I hadn't been able to sleep without waking up screaming and sobbing, though I couldn't remember why.

"You killed her," I rasped. "Over and over. Then you took that memory from me, so I wouldn't leave. So I couldn't warn her. Did you resurrect her just to kill her again?"

"Oh no, honeybun. She did that all on her own. That's how much she loved you. Which only made each night's feast more sumptuous."

Vanta's purr rumbled louder. She looked into my eyes, and I finally saw the magic spiraling through her. She was no ordinary cat. She'd been trying to tell me the truth about my husband and why I was in Kansas City. All the things I needed to be doing to find my treasures. But he got to me first when I was away from her, and once that seed had been planted, she hadn't been able to save me. She'd been trying to wake me up from the unending nightmare, even if that meant she was killed and tortured too.

She head butted me softly, rubbing her cheek against mine. Then she was gone.

I brushed my tears away. "I remember now. I remember how I got away."

"Ah, yes, I would love to hear how you escaped." His smile widened, all white, perfect teeth and glittering eyes of malice. He didn't have to say so that he could prevent me from escaping again.

I didn't mind telling him. In fact, I *wanted* to tell him. I wanted him to know what had saved me. Besides, I needed to delay. Warwick wasn't close enough yet.

"You were finished with her. With us." I shuddered, not ready to look at the full memory in all its gory detail. "You were in the shower. I was locked inside the bathroom with you. So I wouldn't hurt myself trying to get away, you said. You hadn't wiped the memory away yet. I was huddled on the floor in the corner, as far away from you as I could get. In that moment, I knew the full scope of what you were doing. I knew that you would make me forget again. That it would happen over and over, and I had no hope of remembering. I'd tried to leave messages for myself before, but you'd always found them."

Under the guise of taking a shaking breath, I risked a quick glance toward Warwick. He was still running in slow motion, his hair spun out behind him. His eyes blazing, his mouth slowly opening, moving. Perhaps he was talking to the rest of the guys, or trying to tell me something. I wasn't sure.

"I realized that I was beside a full-length mirror. It'd fogged over, so I started to doodle in the steam. I hadn't painted or created anything in so long. Even drawing on a steamy mirror was a relief. I drew Vanta on the glass. The way her tail flipped up when she was happy. I'd recognize that image anywhere, even just a few quick lines. I honestly expected you to see it and wipe it away, but you didn't. You got out of the shower. Wiped my memory like you always did. Then left me to clean myself up, safe in the knowledge that all the horrible things you'd just done to me were forgotten."

Crying softly, Vivi hugged me close. "You got out of the shower and saw her on the mirror."

I nodded. "Vanta. Right there staring at me. A sick, horrible feeling clutched like a giant fist in my stomach. I didn't know for sure what had happened, but it was bad. So bad that I had to go. I didn't stop to think. I just threw on some clothes and climbed out the window."

"Well done, honeybun." Jonathan clapped slowly, mockingly. "That was an incredible tale. Yet I must admit that your plan to distract me from your would-be saviors is in vain. They can't help you. Especially the leprechaun."

He gave a careless wave of his hand, and Warwick shot up beside me, stumbling at his change in momentum. He whirled so hard and fast that his hair slung back into my face, enveloping me for just a moment in the warm scent of summertime flowers. "Riann. I can't. Please don't."

I searched his face, trying to make sense of his words. His eyes were wide and panicked, guilty and heart-wrenchingly apologetic. "I know."

"You don't. You have no idea."

Jonathan's smile widened and he waved to my other men. Frozen between dimensions, they barely moved. Doran's teeth were bared, his eyes blazing with rage. Aidan's neck corded, his chest and shoulders wide, reared back on a deep bellow that I could feel in my bones, even if he didn't make any sound. Cold blue ice, his eyes locked with mine. He could hear me, see me, but was unable to move. For him, for them all, it was the worst kind of torture.

Exactly why Jonathan wanted them to see.

Ivarr's light boiled like a solar flare in slow motion, unable to break free. Keane had one hand near his mouth, the tip of one black gloved finger gripped in his teeth. Even filled with rage and desperation, his eyes were sultry, locked on me. Silently trying to tell me something.

No one would ever walk away from him unsatisfied. Then why did his eyes burn with never-ending hunger even now?

"Three wishes for a single gold coin. What did I ask for, leprechaun?"

Warwick's face twisted into a miserable grimace of shame. "I could not lift a hand or weapon, magical or mundane, against you. I was forbidden from searching for the treasurekeeper. I could not say your true name or any identifying information to anyone, on this plane of existence or beyond."

Jonathan clapped his hands again, this time with a giddy, excited happiness that twisted in my stomach like a rusty knife. "Oh yes. So much fun. I enjoyed watching you stew and fret around the city, almost as much as I enjoyed watching the Slaughterer drink himself into a coma. Knowing that he refused to even lift a finger to help you only made it sweeter."

He'd been watching me this whole time, even though I'd left him. My nape prickled with unease, imagining him trailing me on the dark, abandoned street to the diner. Or watching me stumble into *Sham-*

rocked that first night. Aidan had been there. He'd known who I was and had ignored me.

Jonathan knew that he'd refused to help me.

I'd thought I was free of him. Especially after the divorce finally went through. I'd thought I would have a new beginning. A new life where I'd never spend another moment thinking about my ex-husband. I'd never even see him again.

Meanwhile, he'd been listening and spying on me this whole time. Waiting for me to fall into his trap.

I couldn't even kill the bastard because he was immortal.

I inched my hand down into my pocket and wrapped my fingers around Warwick's coin.

"Ah." Jonathan licked his lips, making me shudder with revulsion. "So many emotions just flickered across your face, honeybun. Rage, despair, hatred, and now, resignation. You'll never be free of me. All of this magic and power at your fingertips, yet the treasures are helpless to save you. They're not the saving kind, darling girl. They're meant for war and killing, death and destruction. Come with me and escape the brutal death that awaits you if you remain as their treasurekeeper. You might think my techniques are cruel and unjust, but I assure you that I'm kind compared to what Evil Eye will do to you. I'll have no need to feed on you to sustain myself in Faerie. I'll be much gentler than he will ever be."

Lies. I could see the hunger lurking in his eyes. Not for my body, though yes, I would suffer pain and humiliation and degradation again. He wanted my pain. No, it was more than that. He wanted to experience the complete range of human emotions, playing me like a delicate instrument that he could enjoy at his leisure. Pain was just the appetizer.

"Be nice," he warned softly. "And I'll reward you by not taking your friend too."

Vivi stiffened against me. He must have done something to her because it wasn't like her to remain silent. He must have really hated that salt, or her words. Or both. Which gave me hope that my plan would actually work.

Dropping my gaze to the ground, I let my shoulders sag and I gave him a faint nod. "I'll do what you want. Just don't hurt her. She's not a part of this."

A deep, rumbling roar rolled up through the soles of my feet, vibrating through my body.

"Noooooooooo." Doran's howl of agony echoed like he was a million miles away.

I gently untangled myself from Vivi's arms, turning to see her face. Her eyes rolled frantically, her mouth working, though no sounds came out of her throat. "Everything's going to be okay."

Her throat strained, her lips tight and pale as she tried to speak. I touched her cheek lightly and turned to Warwick. His jaw flexed, muscles flinching across his cheek. His eyes were dark pits of desperate rage. The eyes of a wounded animal unable to escape.

I leaned up to brush my lips against his. "I have only one regret."

"Only one?" His voice broke but his mouth softened beneath mine, his lips trembling.

"You were supposed to leave green sparkles on me."

A choked laugh escaped his throat, and he pressed his forehead to mine. "The sparkles be on the inside, love."

"Remember your oath, Greenshanks," Jonathan warned.

Warwick jerked his head up, his mouth twisted into a snarl. "A leprechaun's oath on his gold is unbreakable."

"Good." His eyes flared at my words, and he jerked his gaze back to mine. I shoved the gold coin into his hand. "I want my three wishes."

29

I sensed movement behind me, as if he only now had realized that I, too, had a piece of Warwick's gold on my person.

"Eochu Bres!" I shouted. "High King of Maige Tuired, Pillars on the Plain. Names have power, changeling, and I know your name. You cannot hurt me."

"Well done, *mo stór.*" Warwick drawled out in a sinister voice that made me shiver. "She's invoked me gold. I'm powerless to object."

The ground rumbled and rocked so hard that I was afraid the roof was caving in. Stone engulfed me. Hands gripping my face, holding me tight.

Deadly silent, my other three treasures surrounded the changeling. Weapons at the ready.

"You've no such promises from me." Aidan slowly circled the fae, both swords twirling casually in his hands. "I'm only deciding which body part to hack off first."

Jonathan drew himself up and gave him a sneer that dripped with disdain. "Not even the mighty Spear of Lug can kill me. I'll return when you least expect it and drag your pretty little treasurekeeper to the bottom of my tallest pillar. Or Evil Eye will eliminate you for me. Then who'll stop me from sampling that fine flesh again, hmmm?

She's quite tasty. My hunger is almost as immense as yours, Cauldron."

Keane's breath hissed out. "I'll kill you with pleasure, changeling. There won't be enough for the Slaughterer to chop up once I'm done."

"I already know what my first wish is," I said.

"Be careful, love," Doran said. "Fae be wily creatures who'll wriggle their way out of most anything."

I focused on Jonathan, making sure to look him in the eyes. The man who'd trapped me. Hurt me. Crippled my artist, broken my spirit, and wounded my soul. "It's only fair to give him what he wanted to give to me."

His eyes narrowed and he reached up to smooth his hair, running his hands over his neck. Even now, he enjoyed the sensation of his skin, as if touching his stolen body soothed him. I'd seen him do that small gesture before, never understanding its significance. He enjoyed having a human body, just as he'd enjoyed torturing me to feed himself.

"I want Eochu Bres and the human body he inhabits trapped in Fhroig's stomach forever."

His eyes flared wide, his lips peeling back from too-sharp teeth that clanged with each word. "Impossible. Greenshanks swore to never harm me."

Warwick winked at me. "Oh, but it's not I who'll be hurting you." He reached out to take my hand and bowed low, pressing his lips to my knuckles. "Your first wish is granted, my lady."

"You bloody bit—" Jonathan disappeared.

"What's a fhroig?" Vivi asked faintly.

"A giant immortal frog who'll slowly digest him for all eternity."

"The perfect comeuppance for such a monster." Then she threw her arms around me and burst into tears.

30

"How bad is this going to hurt?"

Hammer spun around on his stool with an ink gun in his hand. "It's different for everybody. It really depends on your tolerance for short, sharp bursts."

"Don't be a baby," Vivi teased, admiring the delicate petals of her freshly tattooed rose on the side of her arm. "If I can do it, the badass treasurekeeper can do it."

"I don't really like needles, though."

Sprawled on a ratty-looking couch, Aidan huffed out a heavy sigh. "Don't think of it as needles but as art. You'd gladly suffer for your art and drag us all along for the ride too."

I rolled my eyes, fighting the urge to flip him off. He'd been especially grumpy since the cave incident. I thought that after a few hours, a day at most, that he'd get over being mad at me for showing up, but we were going on forty-eight hours of him barely speaking to me.

I got it. He'd been trying to protect me by sending me away, and then I'd fucked up his plan by coming straight into the danger zone. I'd disregarded his wishes in the matter. I'd put myself at risk. It didn't matter that we'd won. That *I'd* won. I'd stood up to the monster who'd tormented me for years.

I fucking won.

I stewed silently while Hammer worked. I'd taken the four-leaf clover from *Shamrocked's* logo, but I'd added, *"Get lucked,"* instead of the bar's name to the design. I thought it was hilarious, but we'd see what the guys thought of it once it was finished.

The pain wasn't bad at all. It stung, but I'd do it again. Maybe one of Vanta on my other arm.

"Huh." Hammer swiped a rag over my arm. "That's the weirdest shit I've ever seen."

"What?" I twisted my arm, trying to see the outer side of my biceps. Black ink smeared everywhere, but I didn't really see a design. Just streaks from where he'd wiped it. "Is it supposed to look like that?"

"No, not at all. It's like I didn't put the needle in. You felt it, though, right?"

"Yeah. It wasn't horrible but I definitely felt the needle. Did it leak?"

Aidan shoved up off the couch and came closer. He dragged his finger across my arm, smearing through the ink to reveal untouched skin beneath. The grooves between his eyes deepened in a furious scowl. "What did Warwick say when you asked him why he didn't have any tattoos?"

"He said that fae skin doesn't take to ink," I replied slowly, unsure what that had to do with anything.

"Exactly." Aidan leaned down into my space, nose to nose with me. His eyes searched mine, looking for something. Looking for...

My eyes widened. The tattoo hadn't stuck. The ink. Spilled. Like it wasn't going into my arm at all. But...

"Impossible," I whispered. "I'm not... I didn't even know about all this magical shit until I found Doran's statue in the bar. I'm just a regular, average woman. I'm mortal. Even Warwick said so when I asked, and he swore not to lie to me. I'm not—"

Aidan shook his head slowly, his voice gruff. "You're no more mortal than Pointy Ears, Riann. You be fucking fae."

THANK YOU SO MUCH FOR READING *LEPRECHAUNED*! THE FINALE OF Riann's story is Evil Eyed.

EVIL EYED

EVIL EYED

HER IRISH TREASURES

Three wishes for my leprechaun's gold coin. One down, two to go...

I won. I defeated the changeling who'd been feeding on me. My treasures escaped the trap set by Balor's dark fae. But now I don't even know what I am.

Am I fae? Like the monster who trapped me in marriage and fed on me for five years? Or like my leprechaun, Warwick Greenshanks, who plays a delicate game of neutrality between dark and light fae? He swore to never lie to me, but he didn't make that promise on his gold. Only his heart.

Balor of the Evil Eye is closer than ever to destroying the veil between the mortal realm and Faerie. The secret to defeating him is written in my very soul, but I have no idea what to do.

I don't even know who—or what—I am, and each battle the four Irish treasures wage may be their last.

For my Beloved Sis.

Thank you to Sherri Meyer
for all your help and late night edits!

1

You be fucking fae.

Aidan's words reverberated on an endless loop in my head. I fisted my hands in the front of his T-shirt. "How?" I asked hoarsely. "What do you see?"

I heard running footsteps and shouts as the other three men came at a run. The door to the makeshift tattoo parlor that Hammer had set up in an unused detached garage crashed open so hard it splintered off its hinges. Vivi ducked flying wood and flinched back against him as he swept her behind him.

Doran filled the doorway, a big, mountainous shadow of fury. "What be wrong, love?"

I couldn't answer. I didn't know what to say. My throat squeezed shut, my mind still reeling. Could Aidan be right? If so, everything I'd known about myself was a lie.

I was a lie.

Everybody had lied to me. Even Warwick. Could he have not known? But how?

It wasn't possible. It couldn't be. I'd lost so many memories during the captivity of my marriage to a changeling fae, but surely I would've known if I was fae myself. Or Vivi would've noticed something strange about me. We'd been friends since grade school. She knew me better than anyone.

I caught her wide-eyed gaze, but she looked as confused and shocked as me.

I had no idea that Faerie was more than a fairytale until I'd accidentally found my way into *Shamrocked*. I was a regular, average woman who'd worked at a diner part-time while trying to get back on my feet after a devastating divorce. Not... fae, a magical creature with unknown powers.

When I failed to answer quickly enough, Doran wrapped his massive palm around Aidan's throat and lifted him up off the ground, jerking him away from me. "You'd best be telling me that you're not the cause of her upset, Slaughterer, or you'll be feeling the wrath of Stoneheart." He squeezed harder, making Aidan's face turn red. "Mark my words, I'll send you back to Tír na nÓg in wee pieces."

The sight of Aidan—a large, fully grown man who'd made it his goal to be the most intimidating and formidable biker of the Demon Hunters motorcycle gang—dangling like a kitten in Doran's meaty fist shook me to my core. Worse, though, was the look of resignation, no acceptance, on Aidan's face. He didn't protest his innocence. He didn't look to me for a quick explanation. He didn't even try to peel the big man's fingers off his throat or reach for a weapon.

He'd been waiting for Doran to find a reason to kill him for centuries. I think in some way he'd expected it. Wanted it. A final absolution for his betrayal.

"Doran." I finally managed to say, though the breathy tone and shell-shocked look on my face certainly didn't help proclaim Aidan's innocence. "Is it true?"

"What, love? What has he told you?"

"Am I... fae?"

Doran slowly set the other man down on his feet and released him. "What now? Say again?"

Keane and Ivarr crowded in behind Doran. The four Irish treasures, reunited after I'd managed to break the curse holding Doran imprisoned in his stone gargoyle. The garage had felt roomy until all four of them stood before me.

Ivarr laughed and slapped Aidan on the shoulder despite the red fingermarks on his throat. "Sure now, you had me worried the Ellén Trechend had come to lose its other two heads."

"What's that?" Vivi and I both said at the same time.

"The three-headed creature in the cave," Ivarr replied. "Doran tore off one of its heads so hopefully it'll retire back to Faerie until it can regenerate."

Two days ago—though it already seemed like a year—the four of them plus Warwick had gone to clear out a nest of dark fae, fully expecting to die. They'd known it was a trap and they'd gone anyway. They'd refused to use their magic to drive back supernatural creatures because they were worried my ex-husband, a changeling fae, might be able to trace it back to me.

Heroes of legend. Yet blockheads just the same. As if I would want to live alone the rest of my life knowing they'd died horrible deaths to keep me safe.

"The tattoo didn't take," Aidan said, his voice gruff—though that was the norm for him. Not because he'd been half throttled by his friend. "Look at her arm and tell me she's mortal."

Doran leaned down and looked at the smears of ink that were supposed to be my tattoo. Fresh ink welled on my skin, as if my body completely rejected the foreign substance.

"This'll tell us what's up for sure." Hammer pumped some foamy soap into his hand and lathered my upper biceps. "I've seen people have a bad reaction to ink before. Their skin gets red and inflamed. It'll swell up or break out into a rash with heat. But there's still ink in the skin. You can see the design where the gun laid the ink." He dragged a clean cloth over the lathered spot, and the ink just wiped away. "But I've never seen anything like this."

My arm wasn't even red. I couldn't see a scratch or tiny puncture wound. Nothing indicated anything had gone into my skin at all, though I'd felt the raspy sting. Other than a few smeared traces of ink, nothing of the four-leaf clover that I'd asked for remained.

Meanwhile, three of the treasures had tattoos all over their bodies, even though they were reincarnated weapons of legend. They had human, mortal bodies with magical gifts. They weren't fae. The only reason Doran wasn't covered in tats was because he'd been imprisoned for hundreds of years.

My hands trembled, resting on my thighs. *What am I?*

"Call the leprechaun," Doran suggested. "He be our best resource in the matter."

Warwick had gone back to the Summer Isle to make sure my painting that he'd stashed away in a dark cellar for safekeeping was still undisturbed. Closing my eyes, I hesitated, dread churning my stomach. I didn't want to find out that he'd lied to me. That would break something in me that even my ex-husband hadn't been able to accomplish, even while destroying years of my memories.

I didn't even know what to say. I just sent a tumultuous tug toward him, hoping he would hear.

I smelled him before I opened my eyes. Flowers and fresh, green growing things. My heart clenched and I squeezed my hands into fists on my legs. Bracing myself.

Opening my eyes, I couldn't breathe a moment at his beauty. Long ebony hair swept around his shoulders, shinier than the finest silk. He wore loose, flowing pants with a matching tunic in emerald silk with heavy gold embroidery. His eyes spun with golden fireworks against the deep green of his eyes, spiraling with his magic. Sucking me under. Promising me the world—in all dimensions, mortal and beyond.

He knelt before me, heedless of the grimy floor, and wrapped both of his hands around one of my tightly-clenched fists. "Alas, *mo stór*, I never would have left your side if I had known you would receive troubling news. What has happened?"

"You said you'd never lie to me," I whispered. "You promised."

He nodded slowly, his eyes darkening to a deep forest green. "I did indeed, and I need no gold to hold me to that oath."

"In the warehouse." I swallowed, trying to get the words out. "Before we freed Doran. I asked you if I was mortal."

Warwick's brow furrowed. "Aye, the treasurekeeper is always a mortal woman. So it has been from the beginning to my knowledge, though the treasures were incarnated before my time." His head cocked, his gaze flickering over to Doran's glower and back to me. "You have treasurekeeper magic for sure. Indomitable courage, the heart of a lion, and a fine artist's eye, but I've seen naught to make me suspicious that you be anything other than a lovely mortal woman. Has something happened to make you think otherwise?"

"I asked Hammer to give me a tattoo. I wanted a shamrock on my arm with 'get lucked' beneath it." I forced out a laugh, shaking my head. "But it just wiped off."

Warwick's eyes widened. "Tattoos don't take to fae skin."

I opened my hand in his, twisting our hands so I could squeeze his fiercely. "I need to know the truth. What am I?"

～

WARWICK

COULD IT BE POSSIBLE?

If Riann wasn't mortal…

Ramifications fired through my mind in rapid succession. The treasures always died in their brutal war with Evil Eye, which meant her death as well. Without them to protect her, she would be no more. But if she wasn't mortal…

Regardless of what Evil Eye managed to do, she would regenerate in Faerie independently of the treasures. When they were spun back into the mortal world…

She would be alone. With me. At least until they returned to Tír na nÓg. To her.

Guilt tightened my throat. I wouldn't wish her to suffer such unimaginable grief and loss, even to have her to myself for eternity.

Her eyes swam with tears, shining like large, secret wells in an ancient, mossy forest. Bright and yet dark at the same time, change-able with her mood. Sometimes more brown than green, or even more gray-blue. Humans would say she had hazel eyes. Such a rudimentary word for the kaleidoscope of swirling colors. Unusual perhaps, but fae? Had I overlooked the possibility simply because of the many treasurekeepers who'd come before her?

"Let's think this through carefully," I said, fighting to keep my voice neutral despite the hope surging in my heart. While her treasures might be suspicious of all things fae, learning she might be immortal was a boon I hadn't dared even dream. "Her Majesty gave no indication that you were anything more than a mortal treasurekeeper."

"But would she have said otherwise?" Doran asked. "Fae don't volunteer facts or information unless it suits them."

I arched a brow at him. "Are you doubting my helpfulness now, Stoneheart? Or my sincerity and eagerness to aid *mo stór* down to the slightest task?"

"Nay, not you." Doran shook his head. "But I'd trust the queen's word about as much as I'd trust Aidan to have nary a cross word all day."

Aidan huffed out a disgusted laugh. "Same."

The big man squeezed Aidan's shoulder. "I regret leaping to assumptions earlier. My apologies."

Aidan knocked the man's arm away casually. "Don't spare a moment's thought on the matter."

Ignoring his rebuttal, Doran wrapped his massive arm around the man and hauled him in for a hug. "Ye bleedin' idjit. I know you'd never hurt *mo stór*. My blood still be high after the close call at the cave."

I wasn't sure what had transpired between them earlier, but I'd seen Aidan stare glumly at the gargoyle statue on my shelf and drink himself into oblivion too many times to count. Not just in this incarnation, either.

Her voice quivered with dread. "Am I a changeling? Oh god. What if... Am I like *him*?"

The man who'd tortured her for five long years, a changeling fae who'd used me own gold to bind me from lifting a finger to help her.

I pulled her into my arms and all four treasures crowded around us. "Never," I said firmly. "You're light and love, Riann. Not darkness and hunger."

She clutched fists of my hair, hiding her face against me. "But I am hungry. All the time."

I wasn't sure what she meant until an image filled my mind. All of us loving her. Keane shattering her with his orgasmic hands and mouth. Her ass bright red from Aidan's spanking. She stared up at me as I fucked her mouth, while Ivarr and Doran each took a turn fucking her. Again and again and again.

Ivarr let out a low groan. "Fucking hell, Riann. Take pity on a man and give a little notice before you broadcast something like that. I almost nutted on Aidan. He'd take my head for sure."

"Nah," Aidan growled. "Not as long as I get a turn too. Though I think she'd enjoy it much more than me."

"See what I mean?" She whispered. "That's not normal."

I tipped her face up so she could see the truth dancing in my eyes. "I assure you that's entirely normal for us."

Her gaze flickered over to her friend, her cheeks reddening.

"*Especially* for us," Doran added. "We're bound by magic, aye, and I've loved other treasurekeepers, sure. But nothing like how I feel for you, Riann. This is unlike anything I've ever known."

"Which only makes me feel worse!" She leaned away from me, burying her face in her hands. "What if I've trapped you, like I was trapped by Jonathan? If I've been feeding on you this whole time? Aidan..." She jerked her head up, her eyes desperate and dark. "You never wanted to be a part of this. You avoided me as long as possible until I reeled you in. I tricked you. I coerced you."

Aidan snorted. Chuckled. Which deepened into full-belly amusement the likes of which I hadn't even known the man was capable. I'd have wagered half of all me gold on the Summer Isle before I'd ever guess the man could laugh like that.

Her eyes narrowed and she pushed up out of the chair, brushing past me to stand before Aidan. Glaring at him with arms crossed over her chest, she waited silently for his mirth to quiet. "I'm serious. You never wanted to be with me."

He reached out and ever so tenderly tucked a loose strand of her hair back behind her ear. "You couldn't be more wrong, Riann. I always wanted to be with you, and if you had to coerce me to get me here, then so be it. Coerce me all the way to death and beyond."

2

This was a nightmare. How Aidan could laugh at the possibility that I'd forced him into some kind of changeling exchange...

"You're no changeling." Doran's voice rumbled like boulders tumbling down a mountainside. "I'm sure of it."

"You were sure that I was mortal until the tattoo wiped off my arm," I threw back. "How can we know for sure? Cut my head off and see if I get up again?"

Vivi let out a pained gasp that made my heart squeeze painfully. She'd been my only friend my whole life. If I lost her...

"Don't even joke about such a thing," she retorted. "We already almost lost you to the changeling."

I stepped closer, holding out my hands to her. She slipped her hands into mine, squeezing firmly. "Did you ever see anything in me that made you think that I wasn't... right?"

Her head tipped slightly as she thought about the many years of our friendship. I appreciated that she didn't give me an immediate knee-jerk *"of course not,"* answer. I wanted the truth. Even if it hurt.

"Other than when you were married to Jonathan, the only thing that comes to mind is how your parents treated you. I never could understand it."

"Were you adopted?" Doran asked.

I shook my head. "Not to my knowledge. I'm pretty sure they would have told me, too. We weren't ever close. They divorced while I was in high school and went their separate ways."

Not close was an understatement. I'd never felt like I belonged anywhere. Like I was wanted. Loved. I didn't have a home. My family had been Vivi, not the parents who were supposed to raise me. I hadn't even known that parents did things like kiss your forehead at night and tuck you in until I'd seen Vivi's mom do that one night at a sleepover.

"I couldn't understand how they could just move off and leave you."

I shrugged. "It was a relief, honestly."

"But you hadn't even graduated yet," Vivi insisted. "They didn't come back to see you receive your diploma, or celebrate when you got into the institute. They never visited you, sent you money, called. Nothing. It was like you didn't exist."

Old unhappy memories flickered through my mind. Coming home from school excited about a blue ribbon I'd won in the local art show, barging into our trailer. The shocked look on Mom's face as she jerked up from her chair at the table. A brief look of abject terror, as if she didn't recognize me at first, then the look on her face slowly faded to resignation. Very like the look that had passed over Aidan's face earlier.

As if even the sight of me had resigned her to an unhappy fate.

Jonathan had taken so many memories from me during our marriage when he fed on me. Why couldn't he have taken that one? I knew why, though it only made me angry all over again.

He liked my misery too much to take the *bad* memories.

Warwick mused, shaking his head. "Perhaps some kind of glamor was shielding you until you came of age. If so, it was gone when you came to Kansas City, or at least when I found the painting. Then the changeling hid you too well for me to feel any trace of your magic."

"But I don't..." My words trailed off before I could complete the sentence.

I don't have magic.

But I did. I'd seen the proof myself. I'd painted a picture of the cave and then willed us to travel there, *through* the picture. I'd painted something that was so powerful and magical that Warwick hid it in complete darkness on the Summer Isle, afraid it would draw unwanted attention to our new home.

"If I'm... *fae*..." I still choked on the word. "And I'm not a changeling, then what am I? How did I live a mortal life all this time with no clues to some otherworldly existence?"

"But there were clues," Vivi insisted. "We just didn't understand them. We were kids. All the stories we made up, climbing hills and trees looking for the lost prince. Vanta finding you and meowing like she was so happy to see you again, even though we'd never seen her before."

My poor, sweet black kitty who'd been trying to wake me up from the nightmare my life had become with Jonathan. He'd killed her every time she came back to warn me, torturing us both. If she was some kind of fae creature too, then hopefully I would find her again. Fae were nearly impossible to kill on the mortal plane.

Stunned, I met Warwick's sparkling emerald eyes. :*Am I immortal then? Like you?*:

Outwardly, he seemed as cool and calm as always. Our internal magical bond was an entirely different story. He shimmered with emerald and golden starbursts. :*Aye, it's very possible. A boon for sure.*:

A boon for him. For me, perhaps, though I couldn't wrap my mind around what it meant to not be human. But for my treasures...

In many ways, they were caught between the mortal and immortal worlds. They were spun back out into this world for a very short time, over and over, with only one purpose—to send as many dark fae back to Faerie as possible. Maybe even to defeat Balor of the Evil Eye himself, though it was a hopeless, endless battle. Balor was a powerful High Court fae, and while my treasures had magical gifts, they still had mortal bodies. When they died, they returned to Tír na nÓg, but I wasn't clear what they actually did in Faerie until they were sent back to the mortal plane again. Their original lands were gone, faded over time as their power waned.

Chills rippled down my spine. What if their power waned so much that... they faded too? If they just ceased to be?

No. I refused to even consider the possibility.

Jonathan had told me that the answer to defeating Balor once and for all was written in my soul. I would help them defeat Evil Eye, and somehow, we'd break the cycle once and for all.

3

"I smell snow," Keane said as I stepped outside the garage. He gave me a concerned look, assessing my hoodie and jeans with a worried eye. "The temperature dropped again. Doran can fly up to the house and get you a warmer coat."

I tucked my arm around his and stepped closer to him, soaking in his body heat. "I'm fine, really. It's not far to the house."

Ivarr slid up on my other side, ducking around Doran's bulk to cut him off. "You can warm her up when we get up to the house—like you did at the lake."

My cheeks blazed. Before we'd found Doran's prison and freed him, I'd been dragged into Lake Taneycomo by a kelpie. Soaked in frigid water, I'd been shivering and miserable without a change of clothes. But Keane had kissed me, using his gift to send pulse after pulse of molten heat through my body until even my clothes were dry.

The explosive climax was a delicious bonus.

Doran let out a low rumbling hum. "From *mo stór's* very pretty blush, this is a tale that I need to hear more about."

Ivarr opened his mouth but before he could gleefully regale his friend with the gory details, I called over to Warwick. "Was the painting still alright in the cellar?"

"Aye, still undisturbed and as glorious as ever," he replied.

"I'd like to study it in full light to see if I left myself any clues. Now that Jonathan's gone, do you think it's safe to bring it back here?"

"Possibly, though twasn't solely the changeling that I be worried about."

"If I did paint it, either before I came to Kansas City or before I left the institute, then it was here unguarded for months or even longer. I didn't know about any of this treasurekeeper business then, but the imps were already here, right? They didn't attack or destroy it."

Warwick shook his head. "I don't know what triggered the magic, but I felt it like a lightning bolt from miles away. Even humans were milling around the display, drawn to your magic embedded in the canvas. I can't imagine a single fae being able to resist the pull to investigate, whether dark or light."

I gnawed on my lip, trying to decide if my curiosity was worth the risk of bringing the painting to light. My only other alternative to study it would be to go with Warwick back to the Summer Isle. Would my guys be as nervous about me going to Faerie now that we suspected I might be fae? Or would their worry be even worse?

"It be broad daylight," Doran said. "If we treasures can't handle whatever shows up, then we deserve to end our time on the mortal plane before we even have a chance to locate Evil Eye."

"Are you sure?" I searched his craggy face for any concern or hesitation. "If we get attacked, and one of you is hurt…"

"Fucking hell," Aidan muttered, shaking his head. "Remember what we are, Riann. Let us do our fucking job. If the motherfucking fae show up to cause you or yours any harm or concern, then your treasures will send them back to Faerie to stew in their own magic until they can regenerate. By then, we'll all be dead and gone."

Ivarr took my hand and gave it a squeeze. "I've got something to show you while the leprechaun fetches the painting."

With a wink and a flourishing bow, Warwick disappeared in a puff of green sparkles.

Holding hands, Vivi and Hammer walked along with us. "I want to see this fabulous painting too," she said. "Maybe I'll be able to tell you when you painted it."

Gravel crunched as we headed toward the house. I was already shivering, but we were almost there. I could almost taste the ice crystals in the air. "Good idea. I don't remember anything about it, though it's definitely my work."

I still couldn't believe they'd managed to buy such a large house, let alone so quickly. I'd looked around the main floor a little but there was another story and several outbuildings that I hadn't had time to investigate. One larger steel barn with garage doors had been commandeered by the motorcycle gang that rode with Hammer. One burly man worked on a bike, while others were unloading crates and totes from the back of a truck. Probably Aidan's weapons stash.

Rather than walking up to the front porch with a beautiful view of a large lake, Ivarr led us around to the side door and then up a rear staircase that wasn't as wide or grand as the main stairs. "I think this must have been a studio at one time. The only entrance is up these back stairs, and you can't get to the rest of the house from here."

He pushed open another door at the top of the stairs and gestured for me to go inside ahead of him. Sunlight bathed the entire space from large windows along two walls and a set of skylights in the ceiling. Built-in shelving along the rear wall held my supplies from the warehouse that I'd been using.

My paintings of the men leaned against the walls. A quick glance assured me that he'd put the spicier ones behind the tamer paintings that I didn't mind for others to see. I loved Vivi like a sister, but that didn't mean I wanted her to see Doran or Ivarr in all their naked glory.

Tears burned my eyes. I had no idea when he'd had the time to bring all these supplies from the warehouse, let alone get them up here without me noticing. Though honestly, I had slept heavily the last two days. All the stress of the last week had finally caught up to me.

Fuck. Had I really only known them a little over a week? It seemed impossible, though I had almost died three times in those days.

I turned to Ivarr and wrapped my arms around his neck. "Thank you. It's incredible."

His golden eyes shone with liquid sunlight, brightening the room even more. The Sword of Light, nothing could stand against the light of his truth. "My pleasure, *mo stór*."

"I helped," Aidan practically snarled. "Where's my hug?"

I lay my head on Ivarr's chest, turning my head so I could at least see Aidan. "You haven't even spoken to me for two days. Now you want a hug?"

Scowling, he strode close and pressed against my back, smashing me up against Ivarr. "That's better. Forgive me, *mo stór*. I needed time to quell the overwhelming terror that strangled me at the thought of losing you to the changeling. I wasn't angry with you."

Tension slowly bled out of my muscles as their heat soaked into me. Their strength and comfort surrounded me. Wrapped in their arms, I wanted to believe that everything would be okay. I needed to know they'd be okay. They wouldn't die. My throat constricted.

"We won," I whispered. "Didn't we?"

"Aye, but the battle has barely begun," Doran replied. "Evil Eye will have hundreds of traps lying in wait for us. He's had thousands of years to devise his plans. Even if he only moves one of his minions per year to the mortal plane, we're severely outnumbered. Now he must only watch his masterful plans unfold, while we try to hack our way out and stay alive another day."

I lifted my head with a scowl to rival Aidan's. "It's so unfair. I don't understand what the point of this war is any more."

"All things must come to an end." Ivarr's gentle voice wrecked my heart, shredding it to ribbons. "The time of magic—and the Irish treasures—is no more. We've decided that this is the last time we'll be reborn. We refuse to return to the mortal plane again if you're not here."

Aidan breathed in my ear. "And that was *before* your tattoo trick today."

Doran dropped a big hand onto Aidan's shoulder. "I swore to find you again, whether this side of the veil or beyond. If you're truly fae, then we shall walk the rolling green hills of Tír na nÓg hand in hand for eternity."

"You'd best not be fooling us, Riann." Aidan's eyes glittered like chips of blue diamonds and his jaw clenched. "I'd given up hope of ever having anything but death and war and more death. The thought of having a life with you for eternity..." His voice broke, but his eyes blazed and his nostrils flared like he was furious. Doran squeezed his shoulder. Keane pressed in on his other side. And Ivarr enfolded me tighter against them all.

Aidan forced out a harsh laugh. "Hope's a brutal bitch, especially when you've all but given up."

I cupped his cheek, smoothing my fingers over his stubbled jawline. "Die a mortal death and give up all this? You've got to be kidding me. You're not getting rid of me that easily."

4

―――――――

"Not to burst your bubble..." Warwick drawled, returning to catch the last of our conversation.

Aidan bared his teeth in a growl as our group hug loosened, the moment of connection broken.

Unbothered, Warwick set an easel down on the floor, the painting covered with a gold velvet cloth. "If Evil Eye manages to take over the mortal plane, then we won't have eternity with *mo stór* in Tír na nÓg, because the Land Beneath the Waves will be his next target. None of the realms, Faerie or otherwise, will be able to withstand his darkness."

"Are humans that important to the magical realms?" Vivi asked.

Warwick grimaced. "Not exactly. Important, yes, but not to the magical realms."

Confused, she looked at me and then back at the leprechaun. "I don't understand."

Aidan snorted. "Humans are fodder. Evil Eye wants to take the mortal realm as an infinite food source for his minions. The more they eat, the stronger they get."

She paled and huddled against Hammer, who shot a dark look at

Aidan. "Don't you worry one pretty little hair on your head, sugar. Nobody's getting eaten on my watch."

Ignoring him, Aidan said, "Let's see this masterpiece."

We all moved closer to the easel, standing in a loose arc before it. With an innate sense of showmanship, Warwick gripped the edge of the cloth but didn't lift it to reveal the painting, drawing out the suspense. "Everyone have a weapon handy, just in case?"

Ivarr reached beneath his long trench coat and pulled out a sawed-off shotgun that he passed to Aidan, and then unsheathed his long, heavy sword. Keane unsheathed a curved wicked-looking knife that I hadn't noticed on his hip. Doran didn't pull out a weapon, but his broad shoulders rippled. I could feel his gargoyle surging inside him, ready to explode into wings and claws at a moment's notice.

Slowly, Warwick pulled the velvet cover off the painting. For a moment, I couldn't see. It was too bright. I thought that Ivarr's light must have blasted out of his chest like a massive sun, but this light shimmered like a prism. Dazzling rainbows spun around the room, glinting off the windows and walls.

Blinking rapidly, I focused on the people around me rather than the painting. I wanted to see their reactions to gauge whether Warwick's amazement was justified. Despite being practically blinded myself by the rainbows dancing in the air, I couldn't wrap my mind around the idea that something I'd painted years ago was actually magical and otherworldly.

Vivi's eyes widened and she breathed out, "Oh, Ri. My god. You painted this and you don't remember?"

"Not at all," I whispered. "You don't recognize it? I thought that maybe I'd painted it years ago in high school."

She shook her head. "I'd never be able to forget seeing this. The longer I look at it..."

"Tell me what you see."

"There's so much light in the colors, even the dark ones. It's almost like you painted with glitter or embedded crystals and glass in the paint. Glitters that seem to move and shift, shadows that writhe and twist along the edges. If I turn my head or let my eyes move across the canvas, I'd swear it's moving. The illusion is unbelievable. Even her wings seem to move and flutter behind her."

"They are moving," Doran rumbled, leaning closer to the canvas. "She looks so familiar, but I can't think of her name. Greenshanks?"

Warwick didn't answer. He'd gone down to one knee before the painting and stared at it intently, enraptured or just studying it, I wasn't sure.

"Dark fae all around," Aidan said. "Kelpie tentacles. Heads in the upper right-hand corner, the Ellén Trechend. Imps crawling everywhere. Pookas in the trees. You were warning us all along, Riann."

"Aye," Keane replied, pointing at a shape in the lower center. "I guess we can look forward to an oilliphéist soon."

I had no idea what that was, but it sounded bad.

"Where's Evil Eye, though?" Ivarr asked. "Or the changeling?"

Bracing myself, I finally let myself look at the painting. The girl, me, lifted her paintbrush up to a wall or huge canvas, painting a shining doorway. Vanta, her green-gold eyes shining with love, stared out of the doorway. The lingering resonance of her purr vibrated through me. My throat tightened and I bit my lip, holding back a sob. I wanted to see her again. Stroke her head and feel the heavy weight of her in my arms.

I needed to thank her for trying to help me, even though she'd suffered terribly. Why hadn't she come back after I finally escaped Jonathan? Was she gone for good? Maybe Jonathan had wearied of torturing her and found a way to keep her dead.

No. I refused to even consider such a thing.

The woman in the doorway shone with a pearly white light that cut through the swirling darkness. Her long robes fluttered about her, blending with her gossamer wings. Her face was delicate and beautiful, her eyes gleaming like huge moonstones. Soft lavender hair flowed around her shoulders and down to flow behind her like a billowing cape.

"The necklace," Warwick whispered hoarsely.

I leaned closer, focusing on the tiny circlet that hung from her neck. A red oval looked like a ruby stone, but up close, I could see four delicate wings etched against her shining skin. "Is that important?"

"Aye," Doran replied. "It explains much."

"Étain," Warwick continued. "The Shining One. The Fairest One."

"She was beautiful beyond words," Keane whispered reverently. "So lovely that Midir was obsessed with her, earning his first wife's jealousy. Fuamnach transformed her into a dragonfly and then blew her out to sea. She was lost for hundreds of years but fell into a cup and was swallowed by a human woman, who birthed a mortal Étain, still as lovely as ever. A thousand years after he first lost her, Midir came and took her back home to the Land Beneath the Waves."

I didn't understand why Warwick dragged his gaze from the painting and looked at me with such raw... emotion. Admiration, even adoration. As if... I forced out an uneasy laugh. "Don't look at me like that. I must have read a book on Irish folklore in school to come up with such a painting."

"You don't believe it," he said slowly, shaking his head. "When you painted the truth yourself."

"Believe what? What are you saying?" I looked from one man to another, increasingly bewildered. They looked at me like I'd sprouted angel's wings complete with halo. Even Vivi looked at me like she didn't recognize me. Her mouth opened slightly, her eyes round with awe.

"I'm not her, if that's what you're implying. I can't be." I forced out another laugh and held my arms out, turning from side to side. "In case you missed it, I'm just a bit shorter and rounder than the lovely fairy princess in the painting. Who has wings, by the way, and gorgeous purple hair and huge glowing crystals where her eyes should be. I'd be more inclined to believe Vivi was a reincarnated fairy princess than me. She's tall, willowy, and drop-dead gorgeous. All she needs is pointy ears."

Eyes narrowed and lips tightly pursed, that drop-dead gorgeous friend stomped over to me, planted her hands on her hips, and glared. "You've always been magic, whether you believe it or not. I've told you over and over that you're beautiful and crazy talented. You just never believed me. Now we have proof."

I rolled my eyes, more embarrassed than anything. "Proof? A painting I don't even remember doing?"

Doran cupped my chin in his big palm, tipping my face way back, turning my face side to side, as if looking for even some faint resemblance to the shining woman in the painting. "It's as clear as the dragonfly on her throat now that I know what to look for." He dropped down on one knee before me and bowed his head. "My lady. We're honored to protect you on the mortal plane until you can return to Tír na nÓg."

Cheeks burning, I pushed at his shoulder, trying to make him stop. "Get up. Don't be ridiculous. Nothing has changed. I'm not her. I'm me! Riann Newkirk. I'm a dork. Too quiet and shy and…." Human.

Not if I'm fae.

One by one, the other four men came closer and knelt in an arc around me. Shoulder to shoulder, they pressed together, a wall of broad shoulders and muscle.

Frustrated tears burned my eyes, unease and shame twisting my stomach. I wasn't her. I couldn't be. The idea that I was some legendary beauty was laughable and humiliating. I didn't want them to hold me to that kind of impossible standard, because I knew exactly how short I would come against that mark.

I would lose them when the truth came out. I didn't want them to think I was a fraud. A failure. I could paint, sure, but I wasn't even a famous artist.

Just me. An undiscovered, divorced, broke, awkward, wanna-be artist living in Kansas City, Missouri.

"I don't look anything like her," I repeated, my voice cracking. "There's nothing remarkable about my dark brown hair or muddy eyes. Let alone being so short that my feet dangle from most chairs. By the time I find jeans to fit my hips, they're ten feet too long for me. I know nothing about your legends and stories. I can't possibly be her. It doesn't make sense at all."

Vivi stepped around Keane and looped her arm around my shoulders. "Honey, shut your mouth and listen to me. You've always been beautiful. It's more than just surface beauty, though you have that too. When you're happy, you have a light that shines out of you that is so beautiful that I recognized it immediately as something magical long before we knew anything about the treasures or leprechauns. That light drew me to you when we were kids, and I'm sure it drew Jonathan's attention too. Just a glimpse is enough to make you want to see more.

"That's why I hated him so much, because your light started to die. You weren't safe, you weren't happy, and your light dimmed until I was afraid it was gone forever. You don't have to have purple hair and wings for me to place my hand on a Bible and swear that you're too magical for this world."

Warwick took my hand and kissed my knuckles. "You may not be Étain herself, but she shines in you. The essence of a fae princess swallowed by a mortal woman and born a mortal child, still shining with the purest light. I told you before that I fell in love with you as soon as I saw the painting, charmed by the beauty and light it radiated. Only someone carrying shining magic could create something so beautiful, and I was right. You're just as beautiful as the painting you created."

5

DORAN

A slow yet hot flame of fury kindled in my gut, building in intensity until I wanted to rage and tear this house down to the ground. I surged to my feet and seized Riann's hand, dragging her quickly to stand before her masterpiece.

"Give me a mirror," I growled, holding my hand back behind me.

I expected the leprechaun to slap a hand-held mirror into my palm but Warwick did one better. A full-length mirror shimmered into place beside the painting. I stepped behind her, planting my hands firmly on her shoulders, holding her in place. Watching her gaze in the mirror.

She immediately flinched away from looking at herself.

My rage shimmered hotter. "Who made you feel as though you weren't beautiful? Who told you such lies? The changeling? Your parents? Who dared commit such an outrage?"

She shook her head, a practiced move to make her hair tumble down over her face, hiding her eyes. "I don't know."

"If you won't look at yourself, at least look at your painting. Look at the girl with the paintbrush. Can you deny that's you?"

I watched her reflection in the mirror as she turned her attention to the painting. "I don't know when I painted it, but I think the girl is supposed to be me, or at least the girl I wished that I was."

My jaws ached with the need to roar and curse with fury. I knew nothing of her life before she'd freed me from the stone prison. But it wasn't right. At all. She'd been wronged so severely, abused and trapped by the changeling, and now I learned that she had been miserable as a child as well. When she could have grown up in the most lavish courts in Faerie.

Her friend came to stand beside us. "You were and are my very best friend in the whole world. I wouldn't be half the woman I am today without you."

Riann groaned, rolling her eyes. "Don't even start, Vivi. You were my only friend. Ever. I wouldn't have been able to get away from Jonathan without your help. I wouldn't have moved to Kansas City in the first place. You had the brains and the drive. All I wanted to do was paint."

"That's not true. You had the imagination. Remember how we used to lie awake for hours at night, looking up at the stars? You told such wonderful stories. You could look at a heap of tumbled down rocks and call it a castle. An old tree became a sentinel guardian. A wreath of daffodils, the most beautiful royal crown. We pretended we were princesses, playing dress up with cheap Halloween costumes. I think deep down you always knew you were secretly a fairy princess, but you had to hide to stay alive."

I nodded. "I'm sure that was why Vanta came to you, love. To protect you. Cats are formidable guardians, especially black cats."

"You had to hide," Vivi whispered, nodding to herself. "You knew it, even as a child. So did Étain, or whoever sent you here. You had to look and be mortal, hidden in plain sight. So hidden that even the changeling didn't know, did he? Because if Jonathan had known you were fae, I don't think he would have given you the chance to ever escape him. He would have taken you to the frog-hell immediately."

Riann shivered at the memory of Fhroig's lair. I smoothed my palms up and down her arms, trying to warm those chills away.

Vivi's lips curled in a soft smile, her finger tracing over the outstretched sleeve of the girl in the painting. "You loved that coat. It had red and gold embroidery on the lapels, remember? With large, chunky gold buttons."

Smiling, Riann nodded at the memory. "It was gaudy as hell. I had terrible fashion taste even as a kid."

"You wore it for years, even after it was too small. You loved that thing. Whatever happened to it?"

Riann's smile fell, her eyes darkening with shadows. I pulled her back against me, encouraging her to lean on me. Allow me to support her with my strength and heat and protection. "I came back from your place one day and couldn't find it. Frantic, I looked and looked, under the bed, outside by the rope swing, the picnic table, everywhere. I even begged Mom to drive me up to school so I could see if I'd forgotten it on the bus. She said there was no need." She swallowed hard, her voice gruff. "She'd burned it while I was over at your trailer."

Vivi's eyes flared with shock, her fingers shaking as she traced the painting. "Oh, honey, I had no idea! Why on earth would she do that?"

"She said it was an old rag, tattered and threadbare and too small anyway. My elbows had poked through, and I'd lost all but one of the buttons. I broke down and sobbed, completely hysterical. I couldn't believe she'd thrown my coat out. She ended up slapping me to get me to be quiet." Her hand fluttered up to her cheek in memory. "I ran outside to the fire pit to see. Sure enough, I found a little scrap of green and the last button, a bit charred and melted. I kept them anyway."

Rage boiled and simmered hotter. Normally I was the stoic treasure, steady and slow like my stone gargoyle. Aidan had the quick trigger, though he was oddly silent. So quiet that I turned my head to see if he was still in the room.

He must have dashed downstairs and back because he had his twin swords. He sat cross-legged on the floor, sharpening one of the blades in his lap. His eyes burned like cold blue flame and he flashed an unholy grin of sheer evil glee up at me.

If this woman who Riann called Mom still lived, she would soon make the Slaughterer's acquaintance.

"In that little tin box, right? Your treasure box. We used to find all sorts of trinkets and special things in the woods."

Riann's eyes widened, some of the tension easing in her shoulders. "I remember! Yes, my treasures." She laughed, rubbing her head gently against my chest. "I had no idea that I would someday meet the four Irish treasures. I wonder what happened to that box?"

"I still have it, I think." Vivi frowned, tapping her finger lightly on the canvas. "When you moved in with Jonathan, I'm pretty sure you left a box of keepsakes and memorabilia with me. I'll look for it when I go home, and if I do have it, I'll bring it over tomorrow."

"Yeah. I'd like that. Maybe I left myself some clues before Jonathan got a hold of me."

Something niggled in the back of my mind. "Where did you get the green coat, love? Perhaps we can do some shopping and find you a replacement."

She was silent for so long that I tuned in to her thoughts. Shadowed turmoil churned in her mind. The sadness and grief of a broken heart. The furious hurt of a child who knew she'd been denied the most basic support and love from her parents. Neglect and disappointment and loneliness clung to her like the muck from Fhroig's lair.

"I don't remember," she whispered, shaking her head. "It might have been a birthday present? Though I can't picture Mom buying something like that, even at a thrift store. She was much too prim and proper to buy such a bold color, even without all the embroidery. Do you remember, Vivi?"

"Nothing specific. You were five or six, I think. You wore it a couple of years, only putting it away for the summer."

Riann pulled away, bending closer to the painting. Completely unaware of the way light danced across her skin, rainbows and prisms of color flaring in the air all around her. "I look like I'm quite a bit older than that here. Maybe even twelve or thirteen. The coat was long gone by then." Sighing, she straightened and turned to us, a wan smile on her face. "Like I said, a wishful vision of the girl I wish I could have been. Is it safe to keep it here, or should you take it back to the Summer Isle?"

Warwick covered the painting. "I think it best that we keep it hidden, but whenever you want to look at it, I'll gladly fetch it for you, my lady."

With a snap of his fingers, the painting and easel disappeared. I watched as she hugged her friend and walked them back downstairs to leave. She didn't notice Aidan's swords or the grimness on Ivarr's face. The fire burning in Keane's eyes had nothing to do with desire. Only a thirst for retribution.

As their leader, I felt all that and more. A floodgate strained to the breaking point. A powder keg waiting to explode. Though I didn't burn for retribution. I had but one thought only. One determination.

I would help Riann see that she was more than the girl she'd wished she could be. She was the woman who'd been strong enough to survive all the girl had endured.

And I would ensure she received all the love and affection that she had long been denied.

6

With Vivi and Hammer gone, the house descended into eerie silence. On one hand, the quiet was a good thing. It let me think about all the things I'd just learned about my childhood and possible heritage.

On the other hand, it let me think.

Everything felt off-balance, as if an angry god had kicked the axis of the globe and knocked the poles an inch or two out of alignment. I'd never fit in with anyone but Vivi my whole life, so finding out that I might be fae made at least a little sense, though I still couldn't bring myself to believe it. Not completely.

To me, fae were beautiful creatures like Warwick and Queen Morgan. Wispy, delicate fairies of light with wings and flowing hair and robes.

Or worse, dark, nasty things like pookas and imps that fed on people.

I wasn't either of those things. So what was I? Really?

I still didn't fit in. I still didn't belong.

A hard hand clamped on my nape and dragged me up against a granite wall. Aidan lowered his face, glaring down into my eyes. "You fucking belong everywhere. And if anyone dares say otherwise, I'll have their fucking head."

I rolled my eyes but didn't pull away from him. "You can't chop off everyone's head."

"Watch me."

I tipped my head slightly, searching the harsh lines of his face. The deep grooves in his forehead from his perpetual scowl. The formidable lines of his grimly set jaws. The harsh slant of his mouth, lips hard and tight. "You don't even like fae, so why do you care?"

"I care because it's you," he growled. "Besides, I never said I don't like fae."

Ivarr laughed, shaking his head. "Oh, sure now. Seems as though I remember you trying your best to separate the leprechaun's head from his shoulders just days ago."

"A minor disagreement," Warwick replied, winking at me. "Nothing more."

I looked from one man to another, trying not to blubber like a baby. They'd start cursing and swinging swords, determined to end whatever had upset me. But I wasn't sad. Not exactly. Just... overwhelmed. By everything. But especially by how much I loved them.

I'd only known them for days, but it seemed like years. An eternity. I could barely remember life before Doran had barged into my dreams and started demanding that I find his prison. Though to be fair, my memory had been damaged for years by the changeling. Maybe all that trauma had made it too easy for me to fall head over heels for them. Or maybe I'd fallen in love with them in spite of that trauma because it was all meant to be. We were threads of the same tapestry, finally woven together as we were always supposed to be.

They just felt... right. Granted, I had a lot of holes in my memory, but they brought pieces of myself to life. It was more than treasure-keeper magic and Faerie gifts. It was Doran's steady, unfailing support. Aidan's formidable temper—turned on anyone who even thought of hurting me. Ivarr's glowing warmth and gentle spirit. Keane's passion, not just for sex but in beauty around us in the world.

Warwick's teasing and trickster personality that brought spontaneity and laughter.

They believed in *me*. In my gift of painting. My heart. My imagination. They didn't make me feel foolish or less in any way. They certainly never hurt me. Yes, that was my trauma talking, but the idea that five men could be so overwhelmingly dedicated to my happiness and wellbeing after the unending hell of my marriage...

I swallowed hard, willing my eyes not to fill up with tears.

"What ails you, love?" Doran asked.

Giving him a wobbly smile, I shook my head. "Nothing. I'm just a bit shaken by everything I guess."

"What you need is a fine homemade meal," Keane declared. "We've been eating carryout and junk food for days. It's time we sit down to a real feast. You had the kitchen stocked, right?"

"Aye," Ivarr replied. "Delivered and ready for you to work your magic."

"Perfect. Wash up, everyone. We have a feast to prepare."

~

KEANE

As the Cauldron of Dagda, I ensured no one ever went away unsatisfied. While I'd prefer to showcase my gift in the bedroom, I was more commonly known for my bountiful feasts. The saying about gaining a man's heart through his stomach? My cooking worked for men and women alike, and there was one woman I very much wanted to watch indulge.

Plus, it simply made me feel good to watch my friends eat well. To know I gave them sustenance, but also the opportunity to gather and laugh, cry, tell stories, even fight and drink and curse as needed. And yes, fuck, of course. The perfect dessert.

Once we lost Doran, all our gifts weakened with each incarnation. I hadn't been able to prepare a true feast at all—though the bikers loved it when I cooked even a simple meal in the tiny, dingy kitchen above the tattoo parlor.

This new house's kitchen was made for preparing feasts. The former owner had renovated the kitchen recently, including new commercial gas stoves and double ovens. Between the walk-in refrigerator and massive pantry, we were well enough stocked to open a restaurant. The agent who'd helped Aidan purchase the house had hired a top-notch service to supply all the cookware and dishes that a million-dollar house would ever need.

While I looked at the shelves of raw product waiting to be turned into a delicious dinner, my fingers began to tingle. Ah, the magic was happy to be used again. Too happy, perhaps. Visions of roasted meats and complicated layer cakes flickered rapid-fire through my mind, but all those things would take hours of preparation.

I didn't want us to be sweating over a hot stove in the kitchen for hours. Not when we could be sweating over a hot Riann in bed.

"What's your favorite food?" I asked her.

She shrugged. "I'm pretty easygoing when it comes to food. I eat anything."

I narrowed my eyes, giving her a firm stare. "That's not what I asked. What do you *like* to eat? Other than chocolate croissants."

Aidan smirked, making her blush. "Vivi makes a great sandwich."

"That's not *cooking*. I want to make you a real meal. What's your best memory involving food?" Though as soon as the words left my mouth, I wanted to kick myself. Her memories had been damaged by the changeling, and we'd only just begun to understand how lonely and miserable her childhood had been. "Any foods at all that you have fond feelings about?"

Her lips curved in a wry smile that broke my heart. "I don't remember family meals—and not because the changeling destroyed those memories. They never existed. We didn't do big sit-down meals at the table, not even for holidays. We did get drive-thru sometimes that we ate in the car, but usually I ate at school or fended for myself with quick foods a kid likes. A box of mac and cheese or canned spaghetti. PopTarts. Cereal. Sometimes I ate with Vivi's family. I thought her mom was an excellent cook, but she made what she called poor-man dishes. You're going to laugh but my favorite thing she made was meatloaf."

"I'm not familiar with that dish. Do you know how it was made?"

"Ground meat with lots of crackers and an egg. She said the crackers helped the meat go further and still taste good. She formed it into a log and put ketchup on top. Oh! The potatoes! She always opened up cans of green beans and potatoes and cooked them together with a little bit of bacon."

It took all my thousands of years of mortal experience not to shudder with revulsion. Though I did blink several times, trying to picture the dish despite the muttered growls coming from both Aidan and Doran.

Fury. That *mo stór* had endured such a lack of even the most basic of necessities like decently prepared food. Let alone the kind of emotional connections that people made while sharing a meal together. Her parents hadn't formed any kind of emotional attachment to her. She'd never belonged anywhere or been safe or cared for, other than her friendship with Viviana.

"Well, I'll do my best at creating something equally tasty," I said gruffly.

Doran grabbed her hand and pulled her closer to his bulk. "We're your family now, *mo stór*, and this is your home. We start a new life in this place. A new life of happiness and love."

"Can I ask something that might seem... offensive?" She rushed to add, "I don't mean to be, but I'm curious."

"Of course, love," Doran replied. "Your questions are always safe with us."

"It's something that I've always wondered," she began, looking at me hesitantly. "They're weapons, but you're associated with food and hunger. Has it ever made you feel less... dangerous, I guess? I mean, we all need food, I get that, but they're deadly weapons."

I smiled back confidently. "So am I, though agreed, my power is less obviously a weapon. Let me tell you a story, aye? Are you familiar with Cúchulainn?"

"No, I don't think so."

"He was a legendary Irish warrior—"

With a devilish wink, Ivarr leaned over my shoulder to add, "Not as legendary as us, of course."

"Who took a vow to never eat dog meat."

Riann grimaced. "Ugh. I love dogs."

"Exactly. I'm sure he thought that he would never have cause to violate this geas, for it would be easy enough to avoid and dog wasn't a commonly used meat in our country. By chance, he came across an old woman in the woods. She had very few possessions and lived in a rough hut with a leaky roof, yet she offered him, a wandering guest who just happened to stop by her door, a bowl of stew."

"Oh no."

"Of course, he realized what manner of meat the old woman had used in her stew as he held the bowl. If he ate the dog meat stew, he would break his oath. For a man like him, that would be like our leprechaun forgetting to give his three wishes."

Warwick added a dramatic gasp.

"Yet he took that bowl and ate."

Her eyes widened. "Why would he do that?"

"Hospitality. She offered food that she could barely spare, simply because he was a guest. He decided it would be a greater dishonor to refuse her gift than to break his geas, even though it later led to his death. Now consider the duty of hospitality for chieftains and leaders of our people. If the poor woman offered her last food to a guest, how much more were kings expected to share with not just their own people, but also any travelers who passed through our lands?"

"In our time, wealth wasn't something to hoard," Doran added. "Being wealthy meant that you could give away more to others. Kings even set up buildings dedicated to providing food and drink to travelers, showing their wealth through hospitality. The better the food and care provided to the traveler, the better the king. One of Eochu Bres' greatest failures as king was his distinct lack of care in providing hospitality, which was why the Tuatha de Danaan sent him packing."

She nodded, bringing her gaze back to me. "And so a cauldron from which no one ever left unsatisfied was the greatest hospitality anyone could offer."

Grinning, I bowed low, keeping my gaze locked to hers. "The Cauldron of Dagda is at your service, *mo stór,* making you the wealthiest person in the mortal plane."

She smiled back but shook her head. "I wouldn't use you like that."

"Ah, that's where you're wrong, *mo stór.* This cauldron enjoys being used a great deal." I put enough heat in my eyes to scorch her drawers into ash. "And in that regard, I am the deadliest treasure of all."

7

I wanted to help—even though I was hopeless in the kitchen—but Doran hefted me up on top of the large island and insisted I watch while Keane worked his magic. The mouthwatering smells wafting from the large oven were certainly magical. But more incredible was the seamless way the five men worked together.

Aidan wasn't the kind of man who took orders. Doran was their leader. Warwick wasn't even human. Yet they all deferred to whatever Keane told them to do, whether it was chopping up lettuce or washing dirtied dishes. I'd never seen so many fresh ingredients pulled out for a single meal. The giant fridge was better stocked than the local grocery I'd sometimes shopped at on the way home from the diner.

They took turns bringing me bites to sample. A sprig of a fancy burgundy colored leaf with a vinaigrette that Keane whipped up in a matter of minutes. Fluffy, creamy potatoes, rich with butter and cream, to see if they were salted enough. He had to know they were perfectly seasoned, but he asked me to sample anyway. Fresh green beans that Ivarr cleaned and snapped, lightly toasted in a pan with garlic and slivers of almonds. To die for.

Every bite made my stomach grumble a bit louder with anticipation. Keane winked at me over his shoulder. "That's the second-best sound in the world. Almost ready, *mo stór*. Warwick, could you set the table?"

Warwick snapped his fingers. "With pleasure."

I didn't see cabinets open or anything floating past my line of vision, but when I turned my head, the large dining room table was loaded down with beautiful dishes. Keane pulled a huge casserole dish out of the oven and carried it toward the table, while Aidan and Ivarr grabbed other serving bowls. Doran helped me hop down off the island and it was all I could do not to rush toward the table, jostling the men out of the way to get to my seat. I was that hungry.

Warwick pulled out a chair for me, bowing with a flourish. I sat at the head of the table with Warwick on my left and Keane on my right. Aidan and Ivarr sat beside them, with Doran at the opposite head. Nobody argued over where they were going to sit. Not with such a feast spread out before us.

Everything smelled so good I had to swallow saliva, or I'd be drooling like a rabid dog. The smells wafting up off the table were indescribable, almost like I was in a drug-induced haze. So good, promising to stroke and tantalize all my senses. Low rumbles around the table told me I wasn't the only one starving to death, but no one reached for one of the bowls yet, as if waiting for some signal. I didn't take them as the praying sort...

"Let no one leave this table unsatisfied," Keane said.

All hell broke loose.

Aidan surged across the table to snag a large cloth-covered basket, but as he was dragging it closer to him, Ivarr managed to slip his hand beneath the cloth and came out with a fresh roll. Doran picked up a glistening pitcher of brown liquid—somehow I didn't think it was iced tea—and instead of pouring some into his glass, he just tipped the entire pitcher up to his mouth. Even Warwick joined in on the craze, cradling the bowl of green beans in the crook of his arm like it was a newborn baby.

Chuckling, Keane picked up the casserole dish. "May I ladle some shepherd's pie for you, *mo stór*?"

"Yes, please."

He scooped some of the food onto my plate and his, and then passed the heavy dish to Aidan.

"May I share some of these delightful green beans with you, *mo stór?*" Warwick asked.

"Are you sure? It looks like they're your favorite."

He laughed sheepishly as he spooned some green beans onto my plate. "Well, I do indeed find all things green highly appealing, and I could surely eat the entire bowl myself, but I'll share with you."

"He jests," Keane said. "Nothing that I've prepared tonight will run out until my guests are well and truly satisfied. After all, I'm the Dagda's Cauldron."

I stabbed some of the green beans on my fork. "Who—or what—is that?"

"The Dagda is one of the original High Court Tuatha de Danaan, known as a father-god to the people of Ireland." He paused, lifting a brow expectantly at me, waiting for me to take a bite.

I liked green beans well enough, and I'd tasted the components of his dish earlier. They were great. But something about the final dish transcended the humble everyday vegetable to something heavenly. The freshness exploded on my tongue, sweetened and deepened by roasting. I could almost taste the individual crystals of salt as they danced along the legume's length. Garlic, mellowed by the oven and balanced perfectly with the rich nuttiness of toasted almonds.

The simple dish was a symphony that crashed through my senses.

"Try the shepherd's pie." Keane gave me a smug nod. "I'll get you a roll from Aidan to sop up the gravy."

Again, I'd tasted the delicious mashed potatoes earlier, but combined with the rich, meaty gravy and perfectly diced vegetables... Unbelievable. I'd never tasted anything so good. The mashed potatoes were like a creamy cloud of even more deliciousness on top. Adding fresh, hot bread made me whimper.

"Ah, yes, there it is." Keane chuckled, his eyes warm and sultry. "Would you like some salad too?"

I shook my head, embarrassed by the huge mouthful of shepherd's pie that I'd already shoveled into my mouth.

"Please," he crooned, picking up the wooden salad bowl, though he didn't spoon any onto my plate without my consent. "All the components work together to elevate the experience."

"Be careful," Aidan said around a mouthful of food. "If you climax at the table, you'll soon find yourself spread out among the dishes."

If he truly meant to caution me, his words had the opposite effect. "Then by all means, I should try some of the salad too."

Leaning closer, Keane spooned some of the salad onto my plate. Eyes heavy and dark, he watched intently as I filled my fork and lifted it toward my mouth. I hesitated, glancing quickly from him to the other men.

Despite the incredible feast laid out before them, they all stared at me as intently as Keane, even as they shoveled more food into their mouths. Like they couldn't get enough. They'd never be satisfied—despite Keane's cauldron magic.

Not until they had a taste of me.

8

How delicious could a bowlful of leafy greens be?

Evidently, orgasmically delicious—if the salad was made by the Cauldron.

I closed my lips around the tines of the fork. The sharpness of vinegar hit my tongue, mingled with honey and other herbs I couldn't identify. The simple shredded lettuce seemed to still be alive and growing, sparking with life and sunlight. I could taste the gentle shower of sparkling dew and glistening water. Minerals from the earth that had fed it nutrients. Olives ripening beneath a perfect, golden Tuscan sun. So warm and bright and alive.

As if waking from a dream, I blinked slowly and focused on Keane's smoldering chocolate eyes. His full lips just inches away. His breath warm on my cheek as he leaned closer. "If you think that's good, you should try all three at once."

"Fucking hell," Aidan muttered. "First decent meal we've had in years, and we won't even get seconds."

His words penetrated the sensual food haze clouding my brain. Embarrassed, I sat back in my chair, laid my fork down on the table, and reached for my glass.

I heard a thud and Aidan growled out, "What the fuck was that for?"

Evidently, Ivarr or Doran had kicked him under the table. Good. Though he was right. Surely I could get through a delicious meal without thinking about sex.

The glass was cool though there wasn't any ice in it. Since the liquid was clear, I assumed it was water—but the first sip made my eyes flare with surprise. It tasted a little like the healing elixir that Warwick had given me in the Summer Isle. "What is this drink called?"

"Drúchta," Warwick replied. "Or dew, though that simple English word doesn't capture the full meaning. Fae drúchta is made from the first drops of dew that gather in the delicate cups of morning glories in the pale light of dawn."

"Whoa," I whispered, at the same time that Aidan said, "Bullshit. It's mead flavored with flower nectar and honey."

I held the glass up to the light, looking for any bits of flower petals or sediment but the liquid was pure and clear. I glanced back at Warwick and he winked at me, lifting his chin in a silent encourage-ment to drink more. If it was alcohol, I hoped it didn't go straight to my head. I took several more sips—resisting the urge to down the whole glass.

Though as soon as I set the glass down and picked up my fork, I had to fight down the urge to shovel food into my mouth as quickly as possible. I wasn't normally such a glutton. I was hungry, sure, and we'd been eating junk food the last few days. I'd never really had large sit-down meals like this. Add in Keane's magical food and no wonder I was starving.

Though I couldn't completely suppress the niggling suspicion that this hunger might be a side effect of my supposed fae side. I'd never found eating to be erotic, though rolling around in all of this delicious food on top of the table with five sets of hands and lips on me sounded pretty damned good right now.

Had Jonathan felt like this when he was feeding on me? What if this kind of hunger had nothing to do with being a changeling—but was simply the reality of being fae?

I risked a quick look over at Warwick, afraid to ask him, at least with words, even in his head.

:Cauldron magic is immensely powerful, as powerful as the Sword of Light or Spear of Lug. You'd feel his pull even if you were mortal through and through.:

I breathed a little easier and gave him a smile. *:Thanks. I'm just so confused about what all of this means.:*

:With your permission, I can ask Queen Morgan for a consultation. She may be able to answer some of your questions.:

I read hesitation in his words. As if she might not be willing to answer all of the things I could ask. Or be unable to answer? Could Balor—or some other High Court fae—have put a geas on the queen of Faerie that would prevent her from telling me what she knew?

Warwick gave me a subtle nod. *:All of that and more.:*

I blew out a sigh. Ancient fae courts were a convoluted mess that I really didn't want to explore. Though if I wanted answers…

"You're not full already, are you?" Keane asked.

I'd never seen a grown man pout and still look so undeniably sexy. Quirking my lips, I picked up my fork, bracing myself for another food-gasm. "Not even close. Just needed a breather."

WE ATE AND LAUGHED AND ATE SOME MORE FOR WHAT SEEMED LIKE hours. I'd never eaten so much in my life, but I didn't feel stuffed or bloated or miserable. Every time I lifted the fork to my mouth, there was still room in my stomach. I had a feeling the drúchta might be helping Keane's cauldron magic somehow, making it easier for us to eat endlessly.

It was nice. Very nice.

They told so many stories and jokes that made my sides hurt from laughing. I didn't talk much but I still felt as though I belonged, because everything they did was for my entertainment and benefit.

I'm not sure when the light, sweet mead turned into amber whiskey but the pleasant, boisterous story time quickly turned into a rowdy pub vibe that took a distinctly raunchy turn when they started bragging about scars. Showing off their war wounds meant tugging shirts over their heads and soon unbuttoning pants too. I wasn't drinking the hard liquor, but it took me an embarrassingly long time to realize they weren't just showing off old scars for kicks and giggles.

Elbow braced on the table with his chin resting on his hand, Keane stroked the tip of his finger around the rim of his glass. No gloves. I wasn't sure when he'd removed them. "Doran said you healed one of his old scars."

I couldn't help but look down to the opposite end of the table where the biggest treasure sat. Formidable shoulders and chest, massive arms, a mountain of a man, Doran was covered from head to toe in battle scars. They'd all died over and over, countless times in their futile war against the dark fae invading the world. I'd kissed an old scar on his shoulder and the mark had faded back into his skin, smoothing away as if he'd never been wounded.

Keane let out a low, toe-curling chuckle that brought my attention back to him. "I've got a wicked foot-long scar in my groin that killed me over two thousand years ago."

I couldn't help but wince, thinking about how much that must have hurt him. "A spear?"

"Fuck, no." Aidan shook his head. "He got a little too close to Donn Cúailnge."

"Who's that?" I asked.

"Not a who—a what," Aidan replied. "A very large, very amorous bull."

My eyes widened. "You were gored by a bull?"

Keane rolled his eyes. "He's lucky he killed me before I could turn him into the largest feast we ever had."

"Would have saved everyone a whole lot of trouble," Aidan added. "That bull lay at the heart of war between Ulster and Connacht."

Of all my men, Keane was the only one who hadn't been inside me yet. He'd been involved, certainly. His magical hands and mouth had given me several climaxes. But he'd promised to be inside me the next time he kissed me.

I wasn't hungry for food any longer, though I wasn't satisfied yet. "I'd like to see that scar and see if I can heal it too."

I hadn't thought his sultry eyes could burn any hotter, but I was wrong. He picked up the black leather gloves and slowly pulled them on, flexing and splaying his fingers until the leather was just so on his hands.

Then he offered his gloved hand to me.

My heart thudded heavily as I slipped my fingers into his and pushed back from the table.

"Would you like anyone else to join us?"

I met Aidan's stormy gaze. He didn't ask. He didn't remind me of what I'd agreed to when they'd come to the bedroom dressed for war. I nodded. "A deal is a deal."

He shoved up out of his chair so hard it thumped against the wall. "The leprechaun made a promise too."

I didn't try to mask my surprise. Aidan had tried to cut Warwick's head off days ago. Now he was reminding me of something I'd asked for what seemed like ages ago. Inviting the leprechaun to join us in bed—a huge feat for a man like him.

Quirking my lips, I looked across the table to Warwick. "How do you feel about giving me some green sparkles this time?"

A wicked light danced in his eyes. He pushed to his feet and bowed low. His black hair slid down over his shoulder, spilling like black silk to the floor. "It will be my pleasure to give you anything you want, *mo stór.*"

9

Taking three men to bed at the same time was something that I had never even dreamed about, let alone put much thought into coordinating who did what, when, and where. I wouldn't have even guessed that I could possess that level of desire. That I could have one or two men inside me at once, let alone more. That I would relish their hot stares as I undressed.

I'd never felt attractive or sensually beautiful. Viviana was the lovely, desirable one. Not me. I'd never considered myself sexy, someone a man would stare after with hungry eyes and lustful thoughts. But they did stare at me, eyes heavy-lidded and dark. Licking their lips. Jaws and hands clenching and unclenching, holding themselves back. Dicks hard, the outlines of their erections straining against their pants.

I didn't consider myself a temptress by any means, but by the time I started to wriggle out of my jeans, there was a lot of heavy breathing in the room.

Aidan was the first one to crack. "Put me out of fucking misery and let me take over."

Partially bent over, my hands gripping the waistband, I looked up at him through my mess of hair. "I don't remember them being so tight."

"Motherfucker." A rough sound somewhere between a growl and a whimper escaped his throat. "Please."

I straightened, blowing my hair off my face. "Okay."

He seized my nape, tangling his fingers in my hair. But to my shock, he didn't lay a finger on those jeans he was so anxious to get down. Instead, he whirled me around to face the bed. "Warwick, you first. If we let Keane start the show we'll be done too quickly."

"Agreed," Keane said. "I should go last."

Aidan jerked his head at the bed. "Add to her torment though."

I wasn't sure what that meant... until Keane flopped down on the mattress completely naked except for the gloves. Warwick stretched out beside him, his clothes gone with a snap of his fingers.

Two gorgeous men, casually leaning back against the stack of pillows. Waiting for me.

Warwick's hair gleamed against the bedding, a thick sheen of silk that I wanted to wallow on. Feel those strands dragging over my back, down into my face, smothering me. Long and lean, his body gleamed like he lay in a pool of pearly moonlight. Tight muscle, long legs, his elegant fingers lying on his thighs. His dick arched back in a hard, sinuous curve against his stomach.

I dragged my gaze to Keane. Shorter than the other man, he was curvier too, though that wasn't the usual description for a man. Thick thighs bulged like thick columns of granite, golden skin stretched taut. His pecs were rounder, his abs more defined and ridged. A long, thick white scar ran across his groin and down the crease of his thigh.

Voluptuous muscles. Round and hard, begging for my teeth.

His eyes smoked hotter. "Be my guest."

Sometimes I forgot that they could hear my thoughts. Part of me— the part that had been raised believing I was human—thought I should be embarrassed. But I was way past any kind of shame or hesitation. When I touched them, it was absolutely magical. If they were inside my head listening, then we could get down to business faster.

Right?

So of course I couldn't help but picture Aidan shoving my head and shoulders down toward the mattress. While I sucked Warwick's dick and he pounded my ass.

"Minx," Aidan growled against my ear, his breath hot. "I thought I was going to get to spank that ass first."

"Be my guest."

AIDAN

This woman was going to be the death of me.

But what a fucking way to go.

I tightened my fingers on her nape, deliberately pulling her hair tangled around my fingers. "Walk."

She took a step closer to the bed, though I made it hard for her. I kept her head tipped back and made her walk on her toes. Keeping her off balance with just a little pain to sweeten the deal. Plus her jeans were still midway down her thighs, restricting her movements.

At the bedside, I twisted my wrist to change the angle of her head. She could see the leprechaun—but not touch. I kept her lifted on her toes until she made the sweetest fucking sound that always did me in. Part whimper, part groan that made my dick throb with anticipation.

"Time to wear some green sparkles, *mo stór.*"

Twisting in my grip, she moaned again, her hands stretching out toward the bed, though I kept her upright.

"How many swats am I going to give you before you make him come?"

"Not fair," she panted. "Warwick's magical. He has way too much stamina."

"Very true," Warwick replied. "You'll need to set some rules for this game if you want her to be able to sit down tomorrow."

Not to mention my arm would tire out eventually, though if I had my way, I could spank her for hours. Soft, gentle pats to wake up her skin. A sharp slap and then a stroke. A tease. I could make her come half a dozen times before her ass bruised. Though yeah, I wanted to really light up her skin. Cherry ass cheeks. Hard, deep swats that would make her gasp. Maybe cry.

A twinge of guilt crawled through my lust, dulling its edge. I wished that I could dull that side of me as easily. The dismal, hard bastard who relished being cruel and selfish.

"Make me forget," she whispered, breaking through the haze of self-recrimination clouding my head.

I snaked my other arm around her waist, pulling her back against me, sheltering her from whatever caused her pain. "Forget what?"

"That my entire life has either been a lie or a miserable mistake."

My jaws clenched on that gut-wrenching wound. "You're not a lie or a mistake. Period."

She jerked against my grip as if she would have stomped out of the room if I didn't have a handful of her hair. Her thoughts raged like a hurricane, an out-of-control tumult that boiled inside her, seeking release. She wanted me to hurt her enough to help get that rage out. To release all the hurt and confusion and doubts in tears and climaxes both. To tiptoe along the line of too much. Even while keeping her safe.

It dawned on me that she had never felt safe as a child, or as an adult. She'd never had a nurturing home or a loving family, other than her friend. While Red had done her best to be a good friend, she hadn't been able to protect Riann from her own parents or husband. She'd never had someone fight for her. Let alone take care of her, no matter how raw or ugly that need might be. She'd only been alone, out of place, or worse, fed on by the motherfucker who'd trapped her in marriage and then damaged her mind and memories for years.

She wanted to hurt enough to cry—but still be safe and loved and cared for. She needed to be a little scared. A little dangerous. Harsh and rough and raw—but safe.

In short, she needed *me*.

I locked my arm around her abdomen, making it harder for her to breathe. "I didn't say you could move a muscle." Panting, she froze, her body quivering against mine. I lowered my tone to the harshest, meanest snarl. "You're going to suck the leprechaun's dick until he's ready to explode but you're not allowed to come. I don't care how long it takes. Do you understand?"

Tension bled out of her. Acceptance. Relief. Unconscious, perhaps, but her body recognized that I understood what it needed, even if she hadn't wrapped her mind around what she wanted yet.

"Don't move." I released my fierce grip on her so I could shove her jeans down her mouthwatering hips to her knees. She started to lift her foot up to kick out of the pants, so I gave her a sharp slap on her thigh. "Don't move a single motherfucking muscle unless I allow it. Do you understand?"

She nodded her head, but that wasn't good enough. I gave her thigh another hard swat, making her flinch with surprise. "Say it out loud."

"I understand."

"What do you say if you need me to stop for any reason?"

Her shoulders shuddered softly as she drew in a deep breath. "Doran."

"Exactly. Reach for him or say his name and everything stops. Even if Keane doesn't get to strip off a single finger of his glove. Got it?"

"Yeah."

I picked her up and tossed her down in a heap on top of Warwick's legs. She started to reach for him, leaning forward slightly, but caught herself before I could correct her. Breathing hard, she fisted her hands on top of her thighs, waiting for the next order.

"I want to see you suck him dry, babygirl."

Her eyes flared wide at the endearment, and she jerked her head around to stare at me. I snagged her chin, squeezing hard so my fingers dug into her cheeks, and leaned down to glare into her eyes. "You got a problem with that?"

"N—no. Aidan," she said hesitantly, as if unsure what she should call me.

I didn't give a fuck what she called me. As long as she looked at me like that. Eyes wide and dark and dazed. Lips soft and lush. Her cheeks pink. But not as pink as her ass was going to be before I was finished.

"Then get busy."

10

I wasn't sure what had triggered Aidan's dark side to come out.
But I liked it.

I liked it a lot.

I didn't want to have to think. Or remember. I didn't want to be sad. I didn't want to worry about when the dark fae might attack us again. Or what my painting might mean. Or how we could possibly defeat an invincible immortal High Court fae. Or how I could keep my treasures alive. Or what it might mean if I really was fae.

All I wanted was right here. Warwick's emerald eyes glittering like green fire, staring up at me as I leaned down over his erection. The feel of hard satin in my hand as I dared to squeeze my fingers around his cock. Aidan hadn't said no hands, though I didn't want to push my luck too far.

I wrapped my lips around the head of Warwick's dick and swirled my tongue over his slit. I could taste him already. Not salty or bitter at all, but more like freshly crushed herbs.

He shifted beneath me, sitting up so he could cradle my head in his hands. Supporting my chin in his palm as I started to take him deeper into my mouth.

Aidan's big palm stroked down my back, making me arch and rub up against him like a horny cat. "Lift that ass, babygirl. Give me an easy target and make Keane drool with anticipation."

My cheeks burned, imagining what I must look like. My head in Warwick's lap, his dick gliding in and out of my mouth. My generous backside up in the air, bare to them. My breasts dangling and swinging as I bobbed my head. From the corner of my eye, I saw that Keane had rolled onto his side, moving closer so he could watch everything without interfering.

Aidan squeezed my ass, kneading his fingers down the curve of my buttock to my hamstring. His fingers were so strong, harsh and heavy without actually hurting me. Though the threat was there. He could leave fingerprints in my flesh if he wanted. He could bruise me.

Part of me wanted to see what that would feel like. What it would look like tomorrow if I looked in a mirror and saw his handprint on my ass. A kind of mark in my flesh. A brand. Though it wouldn't be permanent.

He'd already left a permanent mark on my heart. They all had.

His skin was rough against mine. The calloused hand of a warrior, well used to wielding a sword in battle. He stroked his thumb up my slit, the rough pad rasping my tender flesh even though his touch was gentle.

"So fucking wet, and I haven't even started yet."

My cheeks burned hotter, but it wasn't embarrassment this time. Heat and desire coiled through me, winching my entire body as tight as a drum. Warwick thrust deeper into my mouth, pushing my lips open wider. Making me feel the strain in my jaw. The burn in the back of my throat.

The first swat on my ass made me jump with surprise. My breath rushed out on a muffled oomph. So hard it took my breath away for a moment, much harder than he'd spanked me before. That had been playtime compared to this. I shouldn't have been surprised, though. I'd asked him to spank me harder next time.

Warmth bloomed on my skin. I jolted again when another swat burned my other cheek. Back and forth, heating my ass into a flaming bonfire. If he'd thought I was wet before, I was absolutely soaked now, even though my eyes watered. Every strike of his hand made another wave flood me. My pussy clenched and throbbed, a deep, empty ache of need that made me wriggle around on Warwick's thighs. I groaned around his dick. Louder. A wordless plea for more. Relief. Anything.

Aidan slapped the lower curve of my buttock, the edge of his hand striking along the hollow where my ass met my upper thigh. The sweet, sweet sting drew another ragged, higher pitched squeal from my throat.

"Ah," Aidan ground out. "There's that sweet spot. Let go now, babygirl. We've got you."

His words pounded through my head. *Let go. Let go.*

Something flipped inside me. A light switch toggle that made all my bones dissolve. All the thoughts in my head cleared away, leaving behind a faint buzz of static or white noise. A place where I didn't have to think or act or plan or react.

All I had to do was exist.

Distantly, I was still aware of them, though my head felt like a hot-air balloon drifting away from my body. Warwick supported me, controlling the speed and depth of his thrusts. Going deeper. His face tight with control, even though his eyes burned like twin pits of lust. His fingers tightened on my face. In my hair. Pulling me closer. Shoving his dick deeper into my throat.

Aidan changed the angle of his swats into a lifting motion that rocked my entire body. I couldn't feel the distinct strokes of his hand any longer. Only the continual blaze of heat through my core. It took my mind a moment to realize he'd stopped spanking me. That his hands were in my hair, pulling my head back. Lifting me backwards.

I blinked, trying to focus through tears. To understand. My lips were numb. My chin, wet with drool and slobbers but not cum. Warwick hadn't—

Slowly, in a daze, I watched him grip his cock, tipping it down slightly. His thighs shook beneath me, his breathing loud. My name on his lips. As thick liquid shot from his dick. A soft, pearly green that gleamed in the overhead light like the prisms of a cut emerald. Droplets splattered my breasts and throat.

Chest heaving, he gave me a wicked grin as he dropped back to lie against the pillows. "There be your sparkles, love."

I looked down at myself, ridiculously pleased to see that as the fluid absorbed into my skin, it left behind opalescent green glitter. I stroked a finger over the shining mark, and it didn't wipe away. "How long will the marks stay?"

"As long as you want them."

Not a tattoo like I'd planned, but this was way better. "Then I guess they're going to be there forever."

11

___

KEANE

Long before we lost Doran, I'd learned that hope was a cruel mistress. Hope brought expectations of better things. Instead, everything I'd ever hoped for had been damaged, lost, and destroyed for all eternity. It was so much better—safer—to not have a single expectation of what a new day would bring.

No expectation that in this life we would finally be victorious and allowed to rest. That our duty to drive back the dark fae would end any time soon. An end to this endless existence of war and death and loss. When we lost Doran, our existence became even grimmer.

Unexpectedly, after hundreds of years of failing, we finally managed to free him from his long imprisonment. Thanks to this woman, this treasurekeeper, who brought us all together, even Aidan and a leprechaun. She made this possible.

Where I could lie back and watch her shine with passion, basking in her pleasure until she was well and truly satisfied. Even if I never touched her myself.

The great irony of my gift as the Cauldron of Dagda was that I could satisfy everyone who came to me—but it was impossible to satisfy myself. My hunger was immense, a never-ending pang of need that could never be satisfied. Not completely.

How could I be fully satisfied when my touch alone was orgasmic? When my kiss could bring earth shattering climaxes? I could feast on a woman's pleasure and never tire—though she would be finished in minutes, unconscious and limp from the force of her pleasure. A thousand years ago and more, I had been known to pleasure any woman who came to me. The lines had been long on feast days. So much pleasure. So much feasting. Yet I remained empty, well-used but unsatisfied.

Thankfully, I barely remembered those days. Over the many lives we'd returned to the mortal realm, I'd adjusted to the other treasures and the best way to work together for our treasurekeeper's pleasure. We all benefited from my gift. I made us all fall into bliss like dominoes.

As long as I denied myself as long as possible.

Riann reached for me, my name a moan on her lips. "Keane."

I rolled onto my back, pulling her astride my abdomen. As she settled on me, she winced. I could feel the heat of her backside on my stomach. Red and swollen and sore. I clenched my jaws and took a deep, slow breath to steady myself. I'd never seen Aidan let loose like that, let alone guessed that it would shatter my resolve as well.

Not the violence or pain of it, though Aidan had controlled himself well. It was her trust that undid me. The open, raw, vulnerability that gave each of us space to be real. To remember who we truly were, or had been, or could be again. To hope…

Fuck me. Just watching her come on top of me would be more than enough.

But Aidan didn't join us on the bed. In fact, he walked toward the door.

"I thought I was going last," I called after him.

He paused at the door. Knowing Aidan, I expected to see a scowl on his face. A harsh snarl on his lips, blue eyes glittering like ice. He freely admitted that he was a jealous asshole. He'd wanted his first time with her to be alone, and we'd gladly given him that space.

But for him to walk away now unsatisfied after he'd just spanked her so hard…

Instead, when he glanced back at us, he fucking *grinned*. "You are. I primed her for you. I got to spank that sweet ass just like we agreed. Besides, no one's going to be complaining about you having a turn when you make us all come again anyway."

She turned toward him, and I braced myself. No expectation. Whatever I got would be enough. Plenty. A bounty that I didn't deserve. I'd seen the vision in her head earlier and it hadn't involved me. I could wait. I would be fine.

"Aidan?"

"Babygirl?"

"Thank you. That was exactly what I needed."

"Always, *mo stór.*"

Warwick sat up and leaned in to kiss her shoulder. "I can wipe those sparkles away with a snap of my fingers."

"Don't you dare."

With a wink and a nod, he sent his hair cascading down over her bare skin. She shivered, which made her moan again, her sore ass grinding on me. "As you will, my lady."

Then he disappeared. Leaving me alone with our precious treasurekeeper.

Her head lowered toward mine, and for a moment, sheer panic flashed through my mind. That she would kiss me—and my turn would be over in seconds. It took a few seconds for me to realize she gripped the ridge of my shoulder in her teeth. She bit hard enough that the muscle twinged and throbbed.

Releasing the bite, she ran her tongue over my skin. Up my throat. Biting kisses, not as hard as the first one, but teasing. Keeping me on edge, hoping she'd bite that hard again.

She nibbled on my ear. "Is that too hard?"

"Fuck no."

"Good. I'm so hungry for you that I want to eat you alive."

∼

LEATHER GHOSTED DOWN MY BACK. I LIFTED MY HEAD ENOUGH TO SEE Keane's eyes. My body screamed at me to hurry the fuck up. My pussy ached, so damned wet and needy that I could barely sit still, but every time I moved, my ass torched like a bonfire. Every muscle ached for release.

Aidan had primed me, alright. Like a nuclear bomb ready to detonate.

But that would be too easy.

Between Keane's magical mouth and hands, he'd given me incredible pleasure already, but I hadn't had him inside me yet. I didn't doubt my connection to him. His dedication to me was without question. But even when he was gloved, he kept himself apart, although he always offered an easy smile or a hug if I wanted it.

He rarely took any comfort for himself.

The man whose touch and kiss was orgasmic. Who touched him until *he* climaxed, not through his gift, but simply because it felt that good?

"No one," he whispered against my temple. "Or if they did, I don't remember that far back."

I'd thought Aidan was the most broken one. The man with the most baggage. Keane's pain was quieter, but so much more immense. A gnawing, infinite emptiness spread inside him, a vast wasteland of nothing. He'd given and given and given of himself until there was nothing left, and what he'd been given in exchange was but a drop in a bucket.

I'd enjoyed his gift several times. Which sent a wave of guilt flooding me.

"No, you should never feel a moment of guilt," he whispered fiercely. "It was my greatest pleasure to share my gifts with you, anytime and every time you wish."

I lifted my head, searching his face. My first instinct was to kiss the hurt away, but that would be just another way to use him, not make him feel loved. "I want you to feel as treasured as you make me feel."

His luscious mouth softened, one corner lifting up to reveal a dimple in his cheek. "I'm treasured every time you climax. I feel your love and pleasure spilling out through all our gifts. It's enough. More than enough. I'm honored to participate in any way that you wish."

Leaning down toward him, I let my breath whisper across his skin before I kissed his forehead. Dragging my mouth across his skin, down the bridge of his nose, skipping his mouth to kiss his chin. "My kiss isn't as powerful as yours."

He inhaled deeply and closed his eyes, a smile flickering on his lips. "I wouldn't say that at all, *mo stór*. Your lips bring my skin to life."

I scooted a bit further down his body, wincing at my tender butt. "Then I should kiss every inch."

"Do to me what you will, my lady. I'll love every moment of it."

12

Rubbing my lips over his skin heated my mouth. My lips felt puffy and tender, my tongue tingling against his skin. I'd joked earlier about wanting to eat him alive, but I started to wonder if there was something in his magic that truly did make me want to devour him. I could taste his skin on my tongue, a sweet, melting warmth like a dissolving truffle. Chocolate laced with caramel. With a kick— something spicy. A hint of smoky red pepper.

The more I rubbed my mouth on him... the spicier he tasted and the hotter my mouth burned. It was a good burn, though. My skin heated, slightly damp with a sheen of sweat. So sensitive that I could feel the delicate brush of air on my back. The whisper of his leg hairs against my inner thighs.

I opened my jaws wider and gripped his pectoral muscle in my teeth. Holding his flesh in my mouth. Dangerous, so dangerous. I bit a little harder, enjoying the feel of him. His smoky sweet taste. Saliva pooled in my mouth, as if I really was hungry. I swallowed and heat spread down my throat like a spicy hot cocoa.

My stomach even rumbled. Impossible after eating so much dinner. I couldn't possibly be hungry for food.

I was hungry for *him*.

I bit him harder, enjoying the pressure on my jaws. Licking the indentions of my teeth in his luscious muscles. Licked the ridges of abs running down his stomach. The heavy vee pointing to his groin. Wriggling lower on his body, I traced the thicker scar tissue where he'd been gored by the bull, feeling the texture difference of his unmarred skin.

Peeking up at him, I whispered, "Such a long, horrible scar. I can see why it killed you."

"Twas a stupid bet." He breathed heavily, his voice husky. "Even Donn Cúailnge wasn't immune from my gift. Thankfully I bled out in seconds and the bull lost interest in me."

Shuddering, I closed my eyes, trying not to imagine how much blood he must have lost. His pain. "I don't want to see you die. I can't bear it."

His fingers stroked over my head, the leather tugging slightly on my hair. "I'm sorry, love. Fighting until we die is what we do."

I let out a shaky breath, pushing that thought away. Not tonight. I wouldn't worry about when or how he would die. I refused to waste one moment fretting about things I couldn't change.

Can I change his fate? A still, small voice whispered in my head. *All of the treasures' fates? Can I find a way to save them? I must. Somehow.*

I'd been shocked to see Doran's scar fade away. I hadn't tried to heal it. But I wanted to erase this thick, wide scar on Keane. I wanted to wipe the evidence of that death away. As if maybe wiping away one of his deaths would eliminate them all.

What had I done before, other than kissing Doran's scar? Nothing in particular. At least not that I'd realized or understood.

My lips buzzed with energy, still warm and tingly. From his magic? Or mine? Did it matter as long as it healed him?

Closing my eyes, I didn't try to force or focus on anything in particular. I allowed sensations to flow over me. How good he tasted. The thick muscle flexing against my mouth as he opened his thighs wider, giving me full access to the tender crease. His sweet, melting taste intensified to thick caramel syrup laced with roasted peppers.

I opened my mouth against the scar and breathed on his skin. Flattening my tongue against the rough texture, I licked the full length of the scar. Again. His thighs trembled beneath me, a faint ripple that made my pussy tighten with anticipation. I cupped his balls in my hand, gently kneading my fingers over the sensitive flesh. Dancing fingertips up the length of his shaft, tracing the veins. Circling my fingertip around his cock head, teasing the slit and underneath the hood.

Turning my head, I lay my cheek on his thigh and let my breath become another whisper-soft caress. I dragged my fingers down his opposite leg, keeping my touch as light as a feather. Down to his knee and back up his inner thigh, spreading my fingers wider. My palm tingled, heating as if I was dragging my fingers through warm water.

I pressed the softest, lightest kiss on his scrotum, and a long breath shuddered through his body. Rising up on my elbows, I leaned down over his groin, letting my hair tickle his stomach, adding to the sweet torment. I wanted to drag out his pleasure as long as possible, to give him all the touch he could ever want, but I didn't want to actually torture him. He'd already endured watching me with the other guys.

"Fuck me."

The hoarse, desperate ache in his voice made my pussy throb. A groan caught in my throat, need surging through me with a vengeance. Fighting down the urge to scramble up and take him deep inside me, I let out a ragged laugh. "I was going to give you the same that I gave Warwick."

Keane shuddered beneath me. "I can't. I won't make it. I want to be inside you when I come."

Me too. Urgency hammered in my veins. I risked a quick lick across the tip of his dick just so I could taste him. Then I crawled up his body. His hands gripped my waist, lifting me astride him. I took him deep, one long, hard thrust to the hilt. My fingers dug into his stomach, my head falling back on a groan of bliss. He sat up, hauling me closer, rocking his hips beneath me.

Eyes dark and wild, he panted out my name. Not *mo stór*, my lady, love, or even babygirl. Just my name. Me. And it was perfect.

His mouth brushed my cheek, tightening every muscle in my body. Magic shimmered inside him. Inside me. So close.

"Gloves," I gasped.

With a vicious growl, he lifted one hand to his mouth and used his teeth to drag the leather off his hand. Then the other, the sound of a ripped seam making our breathing even faster. More desperate.

He cupped my face in his palms and locked his mouth over mine. He inhaled me, drinking me down like a man dying of thirst. A starving man. As if he needed to taste my climax on his tongue, the sustenance of my pleasure to feed himself. A long, deep pull on my psyche, my essence, as if he would devour me.

I felt the dip in my inner reserves, as if a tap had opened up inside me. It poured out of me, an endless fountain. A deep underground river that surged higher with every clench of my pussy. Another surge as I cried out into his mouth. Fireworks exploded behind my eyes, sparkling through the surge of energy that flowed into him. Not Warwick's green and gold magic, or Ivarr's golden light.

Rainbows, a prism of all colors shimmering with iridescent brilliance. Wave after wave crashed through me into him.

Distantly, I was aware of the conduit wheel spinning inside me. I felt the other treasures climaxing with us. Aidan's deep, heavy grunt of relief. Doran's head thrown back, arms outstretched, shoulders wide, as if any moment his gargoyle would leap into the sky. Ivarr's golden light shining like a noonday sun.

Warwick's lush green magic, sprinkled with flower petals. Even in the Summer Isle he basked in my pleasure. I hadn't realized that he'd left this realm. He lay on his back in a bed of rose petals, his hair spread out like a black cloak around him. For a moment, I could smell the heavy perfume of roses. The glide of his silken hair against my cheek.

Then I was tumbling. Falling, spinning out of control into a boneless heap of sweaty skin and shaking muscles.

"Goddess," Keane whispered shakily. "You filled me."

I wasn't sure what he meant but my head still floated somewhere between roses and leather and spinning rainbows.

His bare hand touched my cheek. My breath caught on a groan, my body bracing for another wave of climax to roar through me. But all I felt was the tender touch of his fingers on my skin.

"You satisfied the hunger that has never been satisfied. For the first time in my never-ending existence, I can touch another person without forcing pleasure to pour through their body. I didn't even know that such a thing was possible."

Rubbing my cheek against his chest, I made a soft, pleased sound. "I just wanted you to feel as much as you make me feel."

The mattress dipped. Exhausted, I managed to pry my eyes open enough to look up at Doran as he joined us. His big palm settled on my lower back, a heavy, comforting weight. "You healed his scar too."

Keane's head jerked up, his shoulders lifting so he could see down the length of our bodies. "Ha, take that, Donn Cúailnge! Now I won't have to remember the feel of his horns tearing me apart every time I take a piss."

I grumbled sleepily under my breath and he lay back down, wrapping his arms around me. "Thank you, *mo stór*. You're truly a treasure beyond compare. How can I repay you for removing that nasty scar? Breakfast in bed for all eternity? French toast, eggs, bacon, biscuits… You name it."

I yawned, sinking deeper into sleep. "There's only one thing I can think of."

"Aye? Anything you wish, it's yours."

I couldn't believe I was going to say it out loud. But I couldn't get it out of my mind. "Next time I get to sink my teeth into your ass."

13

Opening my eyes, I stared up at a dark room and tried not to cry. My throat ached and my heart hurt so much that I couldn't take a deep breath without letting out a sob, and I didn't want to wake the guys.

"Too late," Aidan whispered against my ear. "What's wrong?"

"Besides, we never really sleep," Warwick said on my other side. "Not when we have the chance to be with you."

I wasn't sure how many hours—or even days—had passed since the feast. The guys had taken turns cycling in and out of bed with me a few times, but I had no idea what day it was or even what time, other than night.

"Just a bad dream," I finally replied.

"Do you want to talk about it, or just go back to sleep?" Warwick asked.

I let out a long, soft breath that turned into a sigh. "It's already fuzzy in my head. I just remember holding Vanta and being so glad that she was okay. In the dream, I was thrilled that losing her had just been a bad dream, but the real nightmare was waking up and knowing that she's gone. Really gone. I haven't seen her since I left Jonathan that night."

I rolled over on my side to face Warwick. "Do you know what kind of fae she might have been to be able to come back despite the horrible things that Jonathan did to her?"

"It's sorry I am, love, but I don't know. She could be a High Court fae sent to act as your guardian, or just a friendly brownie masquerading as a cat."

"Do you think she's dead? Like dead dead?"

"Not if she be fucking fae," Aidan replied.

I craned my neck to look back at him over my shoulder. "Then why hasn't she come back?"

He scowled. "The fuck if I know. Maybe she's simply waiting for you to ask her."

My eyes widened. I hadn't even remembered that she existed until Jonathan used that memory to try and bring me to my knees in the cave. I sat up enough to fluff up my pillow so I could lean back against it, propped against the headboard. "I'd love to see you again, Vanta."

I waited, my heart pounding, straining my ears to hear her purr again. But as the minutes went by, my shoulders drooped. Maybe Jonathan had finally managed to kill her after all. Or he'd sent her to some kind of horrible prison like Fhroig's lair. Though if sweet, loyal Vanta was suffering like that for all eternity...

Wait. I'd used one of my wishes to send the changeling to that lair.

I still have two wishes.

"I wish—"

Warwick quickly lay his finger against my lips. "None of that, now, love. There's no need to waste one of your wishes on bringing back your beloved cat. The power to bring her back is yours. It's been yours all along."

My gift had always been art, even before I knew about the treasures. I'd even painted us to the cave when the guys had tried to send me away to safety. "I guess I should start carrying around some of my art supplies, or at least keep some in here for emergencies."

Warwick winked at me. "Now why would you need to carry around supplies when you have a leprechaun delivery service at your disposal? What kind of medium does my lady wish to use?"

"Um, does it matter? I used watercolors to get to the cave but my normal medium is oil."

"Art is art," Aidan said. "You could probably draw the fucking cat on the pavement with a piece of chalk and bring her to life."

Though that would involve going outside too and I didn't want to get dressed. "How about a sketchbook and charcoal pencils?"

Warwick snapped his fingers and the supplies appeared in my lap. The pad of thick paper was new, but I recognized the tin box of pencils as some of my favorites from the Art Institute days. Using the medium pencil, I started a rough sketch. The perk of her ears, her large oval eyes, the cute flip of her tail. Her fur was fairly long, almost Persian fluffy, especially her tail.

I filled in most of her body, using my fingers to smudge and soften the lines. While I drew, I ran through the few things I could remember about her, trying to hold that love in my heart.

"She loved to watch the birds and people outside. We placed the sofa in front of the living room window in our apartment so she could lay on the back cushions. She'd stare out there all day, sometimes making the sweetest little noises. Kind of like she was chatting with us, you know? We'd take turns making up things she was saying as people walked by. Like 'Oh my god, can you believe he went out dressed like that?' Or daring the big dogs to come closer so she could take a swipe at them. She always slept with me, right on the pillow by my head. I'd wake up and her tail would be curled around my neck or tickling my nose."

"Oh good," Aidan drawled. "What we really need is another hot furry body in this tiny bed."

"It's not tiny," I said with a laugh. "You're just big, and beds really aren't made for three or more people. Not unless you get those giant whole-room beds. Or maybe push two together?"

"Leprechaun delivery service," Warwick repeated. "Though I'd rather not have two beds pushed together. I've heard stories about people falling through the crack in the middle. I certainly wouldn't want to end up at the bottom of that pile."

Staring at my drawing, I couldn't find it in me to laugh. Not even at Aidan's disgusted grunt of agreement. With trembling fingers, I laid the pencil down.

Even in simple charcoal, her eyes gleamed with intelligence and knowledge. As if she could see me through the paper, pulling me deeper into her gaze. I didn't fight it, hoping she could pull me to wherever she was.

Something whispered, a soft, distant sound that I could almost understand. *Where are you? Can I see you?*

The sound deepened and clarified into gentle rumbles that vibrated from inside of me, rolling outward from my thoughts. Until I could feel the rhythmic sensation in my body, as if she were lying on my chest. Her heavy weight and heat, her comforting purr. The fluffy down of her fur beneath my hands.

"How can you see me if you don't open your eyes?"

I didn't remember closing them. Her voice didn't sound familiar at all—until I heard it. Then she sounded exactly right. As if she'd whispered to me many times, even though I couldn't remember it. Holding my breath, I opened my eyes. Her face hovered over mine, large green-gold eyes shining back at me. She dipped to lightly bump her head against my forehead, and I promptly burst into tears.

Her purr rumbled like thunder, drowning out the guys' words, though I felt them both press closer to hold me.

Trying to pull myself together, I asked, "You can talk? Did you talk to me... before?"

"Of course I can talk." Vanta sat on her haunches on top of my thighs. She was bigger than the vague images that survived the changeling's memory feast. Even sitting, she was nearly three feet tall. "I couldn't speak aloud to you before, but we were able to communicate very well." Her head cocked, her tail twitching restlessly. "You still don't remember?"

I swallowed hard. "No. Jonathan destroyed most of my memories, especially anything with you. He only returned a few to hurt me."

Tail snapping faster, she narrowed her eyes into slits and turned to glare at Warwick and then Aidan. "I hope the slimy rat received appropriate recompense for the harm he brought her."

Warwick huffed out a laugh. "Absolutely. She wished him to Fhroig."

Vanta let out a surprisingly melodious laugh that didn't sound feline at all. "Oh, dear. That's absolutely the perfect place for him. Well done indeed, Riann."

Even the way she said my name was beautifully strange—but exactly right once I heard it. I'd always answered to "Ryan," but she said my name like "Reeeen."

"You have questions."

She said it with a light lilt of expectation at the end, which made me suspect she was under some kind of geas like Warwick had been. Unable to help me unless I specifically asked.

"Are you fae?"

Her whiskers twitched upward, curving in the air like a wide smile. "But of course."

"Am I fae?" I asked breathlessly.

Her whiskers bounced harder. "Think you a human could have survived the changeling's appetites for so long? He suspected much, trying endlessly to force you to betray yourself. But you couldn't betray what you did not know."

"Am I like him?" I swallowed. "A changeling?"

She snarled a low, vicious hiss. "You're a creature of love, not self-ishness and hatred." Her tail flicked up and brushed my cheek. "You would never harm an innocent, even to save yourself."

The last bit of dread uncoiled in the pit of my stomach and dissolved. Not that I didn't believe the guys. I did. But it was nice to have someone who knew me from before Jonathan got his claws in me confirm it. "Why did you stay away for so long?"

Her head tipped to the side. "Why did it take you so long to call me? There be limits, especially upon the likes of me."

"What are you? Who are you?"

Her whiskers drooped and her pupils thinned to razor slits. "You don't know?"

Slowly, I shook my head.

"I'm Étain. Your mother."

14

I could only stare at her, stunned beyond words. My mother. My *fae* mother.

"There were so many restrictions placed upon me," she whispered. "Upon you. It was so risky. So dangerous. I didn't want to send you to the mortal plane to live as a human child, but there was no other way to end the cycle."

"That's the first we be hearing of this." Doran's deep rumble drew my gaze to the door as he strode into the bedroom, with Ivarr and Keane right behind him.

"There is much that I'm not at liberty to say," she began.

Aidan snorted and rolled his eyes. "Typical fae bullshit."

"And I can't speak for Her Majesty or her court," she continued undeterred. "I can say confidently that we have seen the never-ending struggle the treasures and their conduit have endured, and we wished to put an end to that brutal cycle. The legendary weapons of Éire long ago earned their rest. We did not foresee the extent of Evil Eye's dark influence, nor how he would tarnish and destroy your legend. We certainly never intended that your love should be used against you and bring such needless suffering to you all."

"How, lady?" Warwick asked, his voice hushed with awe. "How did you accomplish such a feat without anyone knowing?"

"I had a dream." She blinked at me slowly, and even though she wasn't purring, I felt an immense wave of love wash over me. "A dream from Danu Herself. She showed me a lovely, gifted child, lifting a single candle against the raging darkness. It shouldn't have been enough light to stand against Evil Eye's minions, but the candle kept shining, brighter and brighter, a spinning halo that cast out rainbows of magic to drive out the darkness entirely. She would be surrounded by love. I saw the cauldron, stone, sword, and spear clearly, though I admit that you, my lord leprechaun, were a complete and delightful surprise."

She laughed softly, a rumbly feline chuckle, though her whispers drooped again. "Every sword from the goddess be double-sided. You would be surrounded by love... but not *my* love. You live a mortal life without magical protection. You must find a way to bring the treasures to you on your own, which was no easy feat after the Stone of Destiny was lost to Evil Eye. I feared greatly for you, especially when the foulness that be Eochu Bres found you unprotected and alone."

Unshed tears thickened my voice. "You were there, though. You tried to warn me. You died over and over, suffering all the horrible things he did..."

She pressed her face against my neck, rubbing her cheek against mine. "Such a small price to pay, my dearest child. As fae are wont to do, I stretched the limits of every restriction placed upon me to help you as much as possible. I couldn't come to you in my true form. I couldn't give you my magic. But I could be with you as your beloved cat, and my heart whispered secrets to you."

I threw my arms around her, my tears dampening her fur. "I can't believe it. I always wondered why I didn't feel any kind of connection with my parents. Wait!" I jerked my head up, searching her gleaming eyes. "If you're my mother, who's my father? Was he really Dad, I mean, Samuel? How was I even born?"

"La, that's a whole other story. Are you sure you're up to more earth-shattering tales?"

I nodded and leaned back against Warwick, scooting over to make room for the other guys to at least sit on the bed if they wanted. Though now that I thought about it… It was extremely weird to think about all of us being in bed—me naked, no less—and my mother—as a cat—telling me how I was conceived and born.

I laughed out loud, shaking my head, even as I wiped away tears. Too many emotions swirled inside me. Giddiness, that I finally knew where I'd come from, even if it didn't all make sense and sounded like a wild fairytale. Literally. Love for Vanta, even before I'd learned she was my mother. Terror, because yeah, this shit was overwhelming to say the least. That I'd been born for the sole purpose of defeating Evil Eye, when days ago, I didn't even know any of this existed. "This really is crazy. I don't know that I'd even believe a fraction of this if I hadn't seen the painting earlier."

"Which painting would that be?"

"It was me as a girl, holding up a paintbrush to open a door of light. It reminded me of your dream about the candle."

"I would dearly love to see it."

"Warwick has it stashed away for safekeeping, but I'd like to study it more too." It dawned on me that she was stalling. "I'm sure we can look at it tomorrow."

I waited, watching her reaction. The tip of her tail tapped along my thigh, and she didn't meet my gaze. Softly, I breathed out, "Is my father so very bad?"

Her head jerked up, her eyes flaring wide. "Not at all. I'm just not sure how much to tell you. What will help—or hinder—your goal. The last thing I wish to do is put you at even more risk, or confuse you with details of a long and ancient mythology that you may not understand." She heaved a very human-sounding sigh. "Your father is Cromm Crúaich."

No one said anything. I wasn't even sure that Warwick breathed, he was so completely still against me. "Who's that?"

Her whiskers twitched. "An ancient fertility god.

My mouth sagged open. "Waaaaaait. A god? Like for real?"

Preening, she lifted a delicate paw and groomed herself. "I would have the very best sire for my child, and who better than a fertility god to do the deed?"

Stunned, I turned to look at the guys one by one. Doran's features were locked down like grim granite but that wasn't necessarily a bad thing. Though Aidan's perpetual scowl was wiped away. Even his eyes were wide, his mouth tight. Ivarr's golden eyes usually gleamed like burnished coins but his light was completely banked. Even Keane's luscious lips were clamped shut, as if he was afraid to say anything aloud. Usually Warwick's dimples and glittering eyes made me smile but he was just as somber as the treasures.

:*What's wrong?*: I asked in my head, hoping one of them would explain their alarm.

:*It's not everyday that one learns his lover's father is a god.*: Even Doran's deep rumbling voice was hushed.

"Um." I cleared my throat. "Is he still... alive? Like... around?"

Her tail flipped from side to side. "He's a god. Of course he's still around. Once you deal with Evil Eye, I'll take you to see him."

"About that... How exactly do I deal with Evil Eye?"

She made a low humming purr. "You'll know when it's time."

I sighed. So not helpful. "So what you're saying is we have to go in blind."

She bumped her forehead against me again, still purring. "No, child. What I'm saying is that you'll know when it's time. Everything you need is within you. That's all I'm at liberty to say."

"Jonathan said the secret to defeating Evil Eye is written in my soul."

She sniffed, her tail twitching faster. "For once, the slimy bastard is correct."

"Which makes no sense." I fought the urge to wail, cry, or bury my face in her fur. "I don't know what I'm doing. I don't even know where Evil Eye is. What can we do to prepare? I can't watch them die. I can't. I won't. I have to figure out what to do before it's too late."

She leaned closer, rubbing her cheek against mine, but then she whispered in my ear so softly I strained to hear. "He's already here. He's close. Someone you know. Beware."

In a blink, she was gone.

IVARR

A SERIES OF RESONATING BOMBSHELLS FIRED IN RIANN'S MIND LIKE dominos. Combined with the revelation of her parentage, we'd all be reeling for days. Especially her.

Our treasurekeeper wasn't only fae. She was also descended from one of the oldest and most feared Irish gods. Cromm Crúaich had been ancient even in my day. Very little information remained about him, and the precious few stories had been Christianized over the centuries. Though in one thing they all agreed.

He had been the kind of god who needed to be *appeased*.

Riann blew out a long breath. "Okay, now that she's gone, what has you so worried about him? My, uh, father. Cromm… whatever."

"Crúaich." Doran's usually deep and rumbled voice as hushed as if he were treading holy ground. "Some knew him as Crom Dubh, the Crooked or Bent One."

"Also Crouching Darkness," Keane added. "Or Cenncroithí, head of all the gods."

"Darkness?" Riann's voice quivered. "So he's a dark god? Dark fae?"

"Dark, aye, but not fae," Doran replied. "Some say he was worshipped by the Fomorians and brought to Éire thousands of years ago."

A few moments passed without anyone saying anything. Silence weighed heavier. She looked from Doran to Keane and then me. "What are you not saying?"

I was the Sword of Light, the truth that cut through all darkness. Though I hated to bare this truth. The last thing I wanted to do was dim the spark of light that had started to shine in her eyes as she learned about her true parentage. "We don't know much about him, but the few stories that remain all say that people worshipped him

through human sacrifice. Some even say he required the sacrifice of
the first-born child to guarantee good crops for the coming year."

She paled, her lips trembling, though she let out a harsh laugh.
"And I was worried about being a changeling, or a dark fae. Only to
find out..." Shuddering, she closed her eyes and drew her knees up to
her chest, hugging herself. "A god who revels in death and murder
fathered me."

Warwick leaned closer, letting his hair hang like a silky curtain
down her back.

Aidan wasn't usually a warm and cuddly type but he wrapped her
in a bear hug from the side. "It's not as bad as all that."

"No?" She kept her forehead pressed to her knees. "So I'm
supposed to feel better about people dying of their own free will to
appease a dark god blasting their crops with disease or drought?"

Doran dropped down on the mattress, making the bed frame
groan beneath his bulk. Lying across the foot of the bed, he pulled her
down onto his gigantic chest. "Have we ever lied to you, love?"

"No," she mumbled against him.

"Ivarr, come shine some truth for her. Keane, you too."

I moved around the bed and dropped down on my knees by
Doran's head. "How can I help?"

Keane sat on the opposite side of the bed, sliding in behind
Warwick.

"Look at us, love. See what magic and love surrounds you."

With a sigh, she lifted her head, bracing her arm on his mighty
chest. "I know *you* are love and magic. Even Aidan."

"Hey," he grouched. "How dare you call me love and magic."

Her lips quirked because she saw right through him even without
my piercing gift of truth. She always had. That was why she'd been
comfortable enough to walk right up to him in the tattoo joint and
grab his junk in front of the rest of the gang.

"Ivarr, call your light," Doran ordered.

I didn't have to call my light forth. It always shone inside me. I
simply had to open and let it pour out. Soft golden light spilled over

our little group, easing the harsh lines on Aidan's forehead. Even Doran's mighty stone softened in my light.

"What happens when this light touches something of darkness?" Doran asked.

"It hurts," she whispered.

"Damned straight," I replied, nodding. "Imps and pookas alike screech in pain and are forced back into their foul tunnels and holes. Even the Ellén Trechend in the cave would have drawn back to shield itself from my light, if I'd dared called my power without worrying about leading the changeling straight to you."

Doran cupped her hand in his meaty palm, gently unclenching her fist so her fingers lay spread against his much larger hand. "See how the light dances on your skin. Does that hurt you, love?"

"You know it doesn't." She tried to pull her hand back, but he tightened his grip on her fingers, keeping her hand fully in my light.

"Why is that?"

"I know what you're trying to say, but it's hard to believe when I don't even know who I am. Not really. Look at all the shit that's gone down in the past fucking week. I find out that leprechauns are real. A stone gargoyle starts talking to me in my dreams. I find out about the four treasures and dark fae for the first time. All of that makes for a crazy, exciting story, right? And then oh, by the way, the man you were married to for five fucking years was actually a fae changeling who was feeding on your memories and killed your cat every night to torture you. But oh, yeah, that cat wasn't really a cat, it was your mother in disguise. Finding out that my father was a dark god who reveled in human sacrifice is just the cherry on top of Shit Mountain."

She panted a little, out of breath from her rant. I waited a moment to make sure she was finished, but when she remained silent, I said, "Look closer."

Her gaze flickered up to mine, unsure what I meant.

Doran tipped her arm back and forth in the spill of my light. "His light doesn't hurt you. Far from it. His light dances on your skin."

Her forearm gleamed like someone had dusted her skin with

crushed opals and diamond dust, refracting into shining rainbows and pearly orbs around her.

She gasped softly, holding her breath. "Oh. But that's Warwick's magic."

"You know that to be untrue," Warwick replied, his voice a light, soft lilt of awe. "My magic is emerald green, sometimes sparked with gold. The rainbows are you."

I opened more, letting golden light spill across the bed. "You've always glowed like this. You just didn't see the magic because you didn't know to look for it."

She lifted her gaze to mine, her eyes shimmering in the magic flowing all around her. "The treasurekeeper magic, then. It's from you."

I shook my head slowly. "No treasurekeeper has ever cast rippling rainbows and diamonds just from seeing my light. But even more importantly..." I shuttered my gift, closing the golden glow back inside me. "You shine even when my light is banked. You shine with love. You shine with happiness."

"You shine with hunger," Keane added, his voice deep and husky. "You shine with pleasure."

Aidan huffed out a laugh. "You even shine while I'm spanking your ass, and not just because your butt is fire-engine red, either."

Torn between doubt, blushing, and laughing, she looked at each of us, dazed and a little confused. "You've always seen the rainbows? And it's *me*? Not you?"

"Always," Doran said firmly. "From the moment you walked into *Shamrocked*, I couldn't look away."

"Aye," Warwick added. "Spellbound I was from the very first moment. Your painting that I found was the same way."

"So, love, are you believing us yet?" Doran cupped her cheek and she turned her face into his palm, gently rubbing against him. "Nothing that shines with such magic could ever be evil. You're magic through and through."

15

"*He's already here. He's close. Someone you know. Beware.*"
As the days went by, we slowly settled into a routine. Our new normal. Though I couldn't forget Vanta's final warning before she left.

No one set an alarm clock. No one had anyplace we had to be. I slept as long as I wanted. Between Aidan's chocolate croissants and Keane's masterful skills in the kitchen, I'd probably gained ten pounds already, but I couldn't bring myself to care. Sometimes I didn't even get out of bed during the day.

Having a hot bodyguard with me twenty-four-seven made for some long, lazy, sex-filled days and nights.

When I did get up, I usually painted for an hour or two. Short creative spurts were a surprise after those long brutal shifts that had driven me to paint for hours at a time to find the clues to Doran's prison. I wasn't sure what I was supposed to paint now. My muse felt... quiet. Not blocked in any way, just... waiting.

We were all waiting for that other shoe to drop. For another dark fae attack. Something.

Though after years of grueling, soul-sucking office work or waiting tables at a diner, this new schedule was pure heaven.

Aidan interrogated every single one of his men and swore they were all trustworthy. I'd been especially worried about Hammer despite how much Vivi loved him. I'd never forgive myself if something happened to her.

But Aidan pointed out one very crucial fact. All his men had tattoos. Hammer had done most of them, and Aidan had seen Hammer get his from another artist. They couldn't be fae—let alone Evil Eye in disguise. Not that it prevented my guys from always making sure at least one of them was with me at all times, even hanging out right outside the bathroom door. All of them carried weapons too, ready at any moment to defend me to the death.

The thought made me sick to my stomach. Something dark rumbled in the distance like a black cloud on the horizon. Balor of the Evil Eye was closing in. War and death and destruction were imminent. I needed a plan. I needed to do something. Anything.

Yet I couldn't help but enjoy every single moment I had with them. Just in case…

No. I couldn't bring myself to think it.

With her usual innate sense of being needed at the perfect time, Viviana stopped by with a rusty box under her arm. "I finally found it! I stuck it behind my heaviest winter coat, and I didn't think to look back there until I took the coat to the dry cleaners."

Staring at the small box that she set on the island, I felt a wave of emotion and nostalgia flood over me. I recognized the little tin box immediately, even through chipped paint and rust. "My treasure box!"

I hopped up on the barstool and traced a finger lightly over the lid. I'd added several layers of paint over the years, especially as my talent developed. When I'd gone to kindergarten, I'd carried my lunch to school every day in my *Dark Crystal* lunch box that Mom had picked up at a yard sale. When the original design started to chip and scratch off from daily use, I painted the whole box red with some leftover paint I'd found in the garden shed. It faded quickly, so I painted the box green and started doodling on it. Flowers and leaves and badly drawn animals. Hearts. My name. Other girly stuff I was into for a while.

I got more serious in high school. I had better tools at my disposal and my art had grown into landscapes. I couldn't bring myself to sand off all the old layers, so I just painted over the top, incorporating the uneven textures and brush marks into my design. Then I'd sealed the whole thing in a couple of layers of polyurethane to preserve it.

I pried up the rusty latch. The hinges were tight and rusty too, so I had to grip the top and bottom with each hand and wriggle it back and forth until it popped open with a screech. Luckily I didn't spill everything out onto the counter.

Chin in hand, Keane braced an elbow opposite me. "Let's see all this treasure."

I huffed out a laugh. "You're going to be pretty disappointed by my favorite rock, a scrap of my old green coat, one tarnished golden button, and some string." I set the items out one by one. "Plus some dried up broken leaves. Or maybe these crumbs used to be wild-flowers."

Keane picked up the rock. "Don't tell me you didn't know what you were doing even as a child."

"Why's that?"

"See the hole? You found a hag stone. They could be used as wards for protection, and there were often tales about catching glimpses of Faerie by looking through the hole."

"Through a looking glass." Vivi leaned closer and touched the scrap of green cloth. "Oh, honey. You can see the burn marks. I'm so sorry."

"Do you remember what the design was on the buttons? It melted too much for me to tell."

She frowned, tapping her fingers on the counter. "Not exactly. I want to say fleur-de-lis but that's not right."

"I vaguely remember wings, like an insect. A butterfly. No, a drag-onfly! I wish—"

A hand clamped over my lips from behind. "Are you sure about that, love?" Warwick whispered in my ear.

I leaned back against him, shaking my head as he lifted his fingers.

"Oops. Thanks for catching me before I wasted one of my wishes on something stupid."

"No wish you ever have is stupid, but your wishes carry great power." He touched the crumbled plant matter and it reformed into a green leaf. "That's not wildflowers, either."

"A shamrock," I breathed out. "What about the string?"

"You used to wear the rock like a necklace on the string," Vivi replied. "And I think you're right about the dragonfly. Do you think the coat was a gift from your real mother?"

I'd told her about Étain-slash-Vanta being my mother, though neither of us could quite wrap our heads around how that was possible. "Maybe. I don't know if I found it somewhere, or if it was a gift. I'll ask her next time I see her."

:*Heads up,*: Aidan bit off sharply in my head. :*A cop car just pulled up in front of the house.*:

My eyes flared with surprise. :*A cop? Why?*:

"What's wrong?" Vivi asked.

"Aidan said there's a cop car outside. Shit. All those weapons the guys have been loading into the garage…"

"What weapons?" Warwick said smugly as he snapped his fingers. "I have no idea what you're talking about, officer."

Keane huffed out a laugh. "Sure way to piss off Aidan."

Indeed, usually Doran sounded like the deep rumble of thunder but this time it was Aidan's fury rolling through my mind. Evidently the Slaughterer didn't like it when his swords disappeared.

:*They want to talk to you,*: Doran said. :*They're asking for you by name.*:

"Me?" I squeaked. "What'd I do?"

:*We can make them disappear,*: Aidan growled. :*That lake isn't just picturesque.*:

I shook my head. :*Two cops can't disappear after they've been here. There'll be logs of their visit. Records. It'd cause more problems than anything.*:

Warwick coughed politely. "Did I neglect to mention that in addition to a leprechaun delivery service, I'm fully capable of handling clean-up jobs? Even messy ones involving human police."

I had to admit, it was tempting. If he could snap his fingers and make these guys go away... But my curiosity was piqued. What did they want with me? I was the most boring person I knew. "Can we at least hear them out? I wouldn't want to hurt anyone who's innocent."

:So says the woman who's been banging five guys including a leprechaun and a gargoyle.: Aidan snorted in disbelief. *:I guarantee they're far from innocent but you're right. We should at least find out what their angle is. It might help us pinpoint where Evil Eye is holed up.:*

Confused, I asked him, *:What does Balor have to do with the police?:*

:Evil Eye has a finger in everything. Government, banking, businesses, military. Of course he's got plenty of contacts in the police, especially here. They may even be changelings for all we know.:

A little shaky, I started to climb down off the barstool. Warwick took my arm, supporting me until I got my feet under me. *:How will we know if they're changelings?:*

Grimly, Aidan remained silent, but I caught an image from him. Two men lying on the ground bleeding. Their heads chopped off. Shuddering, I leaned against Warwick for a moment. My legs didn't want to work.

Aidan's growl softened to a silky whisper of menace. *:If they get back up, they be fae. If not, well, too late.:*

16

K eane went ahead of us toward the front door. Vivi grabbed my hand and gave it a squeeze. "Don't worry, Ri. I've got Boss Man on speed dial. Even the chief of police would hesitate before taking him on."

I'd never in a million years thought I'd need to hire Vivi's boss, the defense attorney she swore was the best in the state. What on earth could cops want with me?

Warwick stayed close on my left, ready to whisk me away at a moment's notice. I heard the deep rumble of Doran's voice through the door and felt Aidan and Ivarr with him. Keane opened the front door and they all stepped inside.

The two cops were dressed in suits, not uniforms. I didn't recognize either of them, and they both looked like normal men—humans —to me. One was slightly heavier and closer to forty. The other guy was younger than me. He immediately gave Vivi a wide smile of appreciation. "Mrs. Blake?"

My stomach rolled. I hadn't been called that since I'd filed for divorce. "I'm Riann Blake, used to be, at least. I changed my name back to Newkirk after the divorce."

The detective glanced my way, a sheepish look on his face, but Vivi flipped her long, red hair back over her shoulder. She tipped her head slightly and gave him the barest hint of a smile, and the poor guy was done for. He couldn't tear his gaze away.

The older detective wasn't so easy to distract. He held his hand out to me. "Sorry about that, Ms. Newkirk. I'm Detective Beasley, and this is my partner, Detective Short."

Nobody moved but in my head, I heard guns cocking and swords drawn at the thought of me touching one of these men. Not that I needed any kind of warning. If Jonathan had managed to bespell me with a touch, then the last thing I wanted to do was shake this cop's hand. Instead, I gave him a polite nod. "What do you want?"

His cheeks flushed and he pulled his hand back, covering up the gesture by reaching inside his suit coat to pull out a small notebook. "We just have a few questions for you. Speaking of your ex-husband, have you seen Mr. Blake recently?"

Uh... yeah. After he threatened to take me away from everything I loved, I'd sent him to die a miserable death in a frog swamp where he'd be slowly digested for millennia. Not that I could say that.

"Not recently," I replied.

"You were married for..." The cop scanned his notebook. "Five years? And you worked for him."

"I worked at Solobrex until our separation." Such a polite way to say that I'd fled the house in the middle of the night with nothing but the clothes on my back.

"Yeah, that's what I said." Detective Beasley looked up from his notes, his eyes hard and piercing. "Solobrex was his company."

I hadn't known that Jonathan owned it at the time. I hadn't known anything about our finances. Though I didn't know if the cop would believe me or not. He kept staring at me, his eyebrows raised slightly with expectation, but I didn't say anything else. Listening to Vivi rant about some of their clients, I knew the best thing I could do was keep my mouth shut as much as possible.

"Mr. Danielson at Solobrex reported your ex-husband as missing last Monday. Mr. Blake hasn't been seen since."

"Oh?"

"Do you know Mr. Danielson?"

The years I worked at Solobrex were thankfully gray and hazy. A miserable little cubicle. Soul-sucking monotony—though I couldn't remember exactly what I'd done every day. "I don't think so."

"He wasn't your former boss?"

I resisted the urge to look over at Vivi for help. I shrugged and gave the officer a hopefully sheepish smile. "I hated the place. I don't really remember much. I guess I blocked it from my mind."

"Hmm. That's strange. If you hated the place so much, why did Mr. Blake leave Solobrex to you?"

My eyes flared. "What? That's not right. He kept all of the property in our divorce. I didn't want any of it, not even a percentage."

Detective Beasley gave the younger cop a sharp poke with his elbow and the man finally dragged his gaze away from Vivi. "Show Ms. Newkirk the paperwork."

He held out a manilla folder toward me, but Vivi quickly snatched it from him. She gave him a smile and started to flip through the papers, moving away from the older detective when he tried to take it back.

"It's Jonathan's will," Vivi said. "He lists you as his sole beneficiary."

I couldn't help but shudder. "I don't want his money. I don't want any of it, especially that horrible place."

"You didn't know about any of this?" Detective Beasley asked. "And you have no idea where he might be or what has happened to him?"

"She already said she didn't," Aidan barked out.

"But you're not surprised that Mr. Blake is missing, are you?"

"Get out." Doran didn't raise his voice but the deep timber rattled the cops. Detective Short even dropped a hand to his gun.

"I don't want any of it," I said again, firmly and loudly to try and diffuse the situation. "I don't want anything from my ex-husband except my freedom. That's what I told the judge, even when he said I was owed fifty percent of everything. I don't want a dime from Jonathan Blake."

"We'd like you to come down to the station for some additional questions, Ms. Newkirk," Detective Beasley said.

:*Like I said, that lake is a damned fine place for nosy cops,*: Aidan growled.

Doran's gargoyle wings flapped in my head. :*I'll crack their heads together like two rotten melons.*:

Even Ivarr's soft glowing light blazed like a piercing shard of jagged glass.

Out of all the things I thought we might face, I hadn't put "get arrested for my ex-husband's murder" on my Bingo card. I certainly didn't want to leave this beautiful house and go on the run because the guys had disappeared a few cops.

I met Vivi's gaze. "I think it's time to call Boss Man."

"Already on it, honey." Phone to her ear, she stepped toward the other room. "Don't say another word."

17

I'd never met Boss Man. I didn't even know his real name. All I knew were Vivi's stories about all the cases he'd won. She'd always said he'd be the first person she'd call if she ever needed legal help, and though he didn't practice family law, they'd gotten me set up with an excellent divorce attorney that I'd never have been able to afford on my own.

He paid Vivi extremely well, and she adored her job. If she said he was the best defense attorney in the state, then I believed her wholeheartedly. Especially when Detective Beasley's phone rang a few minutes after Vivi called her boss.

He and the other detective stepped outside, though we kept the front door open. Glowering with his arms crossed over his chest, Aidan stood like a sentinel at the door.

After a minute or two, the detectives came back toward the door but didn't enter the house again. Red faced, Beasley didn't say anything and stood slightly behind the younger cop, letting him take control.

"Would it be convenient for you to come to the station at two this afternoon, Ms. Newkirk?"

I glanced at Vivi to be sure, since I hadn't talked to Boss Man, and she gave me a subtle nod. "Yes."

"Ma'am," Detective Short nodded at me and then at Vivi, though he gave her a big, winning smile. "Ma'am. It was a pleasure to meet you."

She was too busy flipping through the folder to acknowledge him.

Aidan slammed the door shut in the man's face. "Why the hell did you agree to meet them again?"

"Because we have enough to worry about with dark fae attacking at any moment. We don't need to worry about pissing off the police too." I stepped closer to Vivi to see what she was reading. "How bad is it?"

"It's not bad at all. In fact, if you weren't the treasurekeeper with a leprechaun at your beck and call, I'd be thrilled for you because you just came into a shit ton of money. You'd be set for life."

"But I don't want his money! I never wanted anything from him, even before I knew that he was a changeling."

Keane handed me a cup of tea. "Money's not a bad thing to have in this world. When—"

"If," Doran broke in. "If something happens to us, it'd be a relief on my mind, at least, if you have plenty of resources at your fingertips. Human laws can be tricky things for us to maneuver around."

"This house is in your name," Aidan added. "The bank accounts are handled by the club, but we've added you to all the documentation. The Demon Hunters will take care of you as long as any of them are still alive."

My throat ached and my hands trembled enough that I sloshed tea onto my jeans. "I don't want to talk about this."

Doran dropped down in front of me, sitting back on his knees. His big palms gently cradled my hands, steadying me. "You know what we are, love. We'll stay by your side until forced to part by death, but we all know how this battle ends."

"No," I whispered fiercely, staring into his eyes. "We don't know how this ends. I refuse to let you go."

He sighed, his wide, massive shoulders falling. "I don't want to see your heart shattered, love. It's a horrible thing to endure any lover's death, let alone four."

Perversely, his sadness and acceptance only made my defiance more determined. I lifted the teacup to my mouth but I didn't take a sip immediately. I breathed in the perfume, closing my eyes so I could concentrate on its soothing warmth and aroma. I smelled the darker, earthy scent of tea leaves but also lighter floral scents. Almost like the faerie mead.

:Just a splash of drúchta,: Keane whispered in my mind. *:I thought you could use a little extra kick.:*

:Definitely.: Opening my eyes, I took a sip of the hot, lightly sweet tea. Another. Letting the soothing warmth flow down my throat and through my body. *:Perfect. Thank you.:*

"We should talk about this visit," Aidan said. "We have to assume that Evil Eye's minions will be nearby. You'll be at great risk."

Vivi sat down in the chair beside me, her brow creased with worry. "You mean changelings, like Jonathan? How will we know?"

"You won't," Aidan replied grimly, shaking his head. "Some fae won't be out and about in broad daylight, but the sun won't affect stronger fae, even if they be dark. High Court fae won't be affected by anything but salt and iron. Even then, they'll just return to Tír na nÓg and regroup. Water will usually break a glamor and reveal the true creature beneath the human-looking disguise, but you can't go about throwing water on everyone."

"Especially in a police station." Vivi heaved out a sigh. "Can we tell Boss Man about—"

Five vehement "noes," echoed around the room.

"We don't tell humans anything," Doran added. "I'm not in favor of the men Aidan already brought into the group. The only reason you're involved at all is because you're Riann's friend."

"You were gone," Aidan replied, his voice flat and hard. "We had to survive. The three of us couldn't hold off shit without some backup."

"I know, but I'm still not a fan of involving humans in our warfare. They're mere appetizers for the likes of foe we face."

"Don't forget what Étain said," Ivarr added.

"He's someone I know." I took another sip of the tea, hoping it would calm my churning stomach. "He's close."

"Exactly," Aidan bit off. "So you expose yourself needlessly by agreeing to speak to the police. They will likely try to separate you from us for questioning."

"Do any of you have ids?" Vivi asked. "Like if the cops ran your fingerprints, what would they find?"

"The fuck if I know," Aidan replied. "We try not to leave any evidence behind when we clean out a nest, but I'm sure we've left fingerprints. Think about that fucking cave. We got out fast but there was at least one human witness."

"So it's best if I go in without you." Five furious, pissed off sets of eyes glared at me. "The cops don't have your names. They didn't ask about you. They're asking about me. I don't want to give them any reason to come snooping around here again, or trying to figure out who you are. Why there's no birth certificate or driver's license in your names."

"Exactly," Aidan retorted, pacing back and forth. "A human cop would have asked all of us for identification, or at least our names. Those two bozos acted like we didn't even exist, which smells like a trap. What the fuck kind of idiots ignore a man the size of Doran without even checking if we had any weapons? They want you, Riann. If you go in by yourself..." Whirling toward me, he leaned down over the side of the chair. His voice crackled with ice. "We may never see you again."

AIDAN

I'd been royally pissed off plenty of times, but never like this. Breathing hard, I fought to contain my rage. To keep from seizing her shoulders and shaking some sense into her. Or better yet, sweeping her up against my chest and running for safety as fast as I could go.

Safety. Straightening to get out of her space, I barked out a harsh laugh and ran a hand over my head. There was no safety. Not for her. Not for us.

I flinched at her touch. She'd stood up and came closer, wrapping her arms around me from behind. Tension sang through my body, vibrating my muscles, urging me to fight. Pick up a sword. A gun. Anything.

Demand that she stay hidden and safe and alive.

"I can't fucking lose you," I ground out.

She lay her cheek against my quivering back. "I know. I can't lose you either."

Doran lay a hand on my shoulder, a heavy, steady squeeze that kept me from exploding into a thousand pieces. "None of us can bear it, love. So we must think this through carefully."

"Let's assume it is a trap," she said, not lifting her head. "For what purpose?"

"To get you away from us." Usually the softest and gentlest of the bunch, Ivarr's voice rang with the same rage as me. "Anytime we're separated, we're vulnerable."

"What if Warwick goes in with me?"

To the casual onlooker, the leprechaun lounged gracefully on a chaise in the corner. I knew him well enough now to read the fine crinkles in the outer corners of his eyes. Fae didn't age. They certainly didn't wrinkle. Plus his eyes flashed like electric emeralds. "That would be the equivalent of showing your ace in the hole before you can get your opponents to fold. If it is a trap, we don't want them to know that you have a High Court fae directly helping you."

"Wouldn't Jonathan—as Eochu Bres—have told someone about you? Maybe as a warning?"

Warwick shrugged. "Possibly, but I doubt it. Bres assumed that he had neutralized me with the oath. If anything, he may have bragged about it to others, but I don't think Evil Eye would know. I can mask what I be, but if they know you're the treasurekeeper, they'll expect me to be one of them. And if I'm not..." He shrugged again, though his eyes flashed. "They'll know you've got an ally before we know what we're up against."

"Are you saying those cops weren't actually human?" Riann asked. "Or are they human allies to Evil Eye? Or something else entirely?"

"They didn't act like human police," Keane said, shaking his head. "Aidan's right. No regular human cop would have completely ignored five able-bodied men. Let alone scruffy motorcycle gang members like us."

"They could be human but on Evil Eye's payroll," Doran added. "He has plenty of humans in service to a multitude of companies and organizations. But even corrupt cops would have shown some kind of alarm at being outnumbered by the likes of us, unless they were ordered otherwise."

"So they're changelings?" Riann asked. "Like Jonathan?"

"That's a possibility," Doran replied. "Or they could be dark fae casting a glamor to disguise their true nature, though that's less likely in broad daylight. An imp can wander the streets at night and look like a stray animal, but it wouldn't be able to hold such a glamor in sunlight."

"So what I'm hearing is we need to be in and out before dark," Vivi said.

I whipped my head around to glare at her, though I didn't say anything. Riann held a soft spot in her heart for the woman, so I didn't want to upset her by bellowing at her friend.

"It's not safe," Doran rumbled deeper and louder than ever. "Day or night. I don't want her out of my sight."

"If she doesn't show up voluntarily, they'll be back out here with an arrest warrant. Boss Man bought us time by agreeing that we'd be there."

"Let the motherfuckers come," I growled, clenching my fingers into fists.

Riann curled her arm around my waist, pulling me closer. "What if that's exactly what they want? What if they want a reason to bring a swat team out here and gun you down?"

"They're welcome to try. They'll find me a mite harder to kill than the average human on the street."

"Every cop in the city would be out here," she whispered, her voice shaking. "They'd come with tanks and shields, automatic weapons, K-9 units, tear gas, bombs. Can your magic withstand that kind of firepower?"

I twisted in her grip and turned to face her, clamping my arms around her. "You fucking know we can."

She stared up at me, dark eyes shimmering with so much emotion. Love, yes, but also heartrending terror. The same fear that must be raging in my eyes. "And then the feds will come. Maybe the Army. Cannons and tanks and airstrikes. Missiles. It'll just keep escalating into full-blown war. You can't win that war."

My rage crystalized into grim ice. "Exactly. We never do."

"But don't you see?" Her voice broke, tears spilling from her eyes. "That's what he wants. He wants the war. He wants the escalation and chaos that ensues. We can't give him what he wants."

Gripping her chin to tilt her face up to mine, I leaned down and pressed my forehead to hers. "I'll die. Gladly. Over and over and over. But don't you dare ask me to give you to him, love. I won't allow it."

Doran stepped closer, wrapping us both in his mighty arms. Ivarr and Keane joined us. Then Warwick. All the men who loved her, pressing around her, shielding her with our bodies. We would die like this if we could. But what would that solve, if she died too?

"Do you trust me?" Soft and gentle, her voice flowed around us, laced with glittering rainbows. Hope and magic, light and love. All the things we'd given up long ago.

Gods. How could I ever bear to leave her?

"Aye," Doran answered for us all. "With our lives and hearts, *mo stór.*"

18

Sitting in the back seat of the swanky car that Boss Man had sent for us, I gripped Vivi's hand and tried not to fidget with nerves.

It certainly didn't help that I could feel the guys' worry hammering inside my head.

I didn't know anything about criminal cases, but this was Vivi and Boss Man's territory. She'd been able to prep me about how the police station would be set up. Who would be there. What would happen. I'd hashed out a plan given those details.

:*Plan, my ass,*: Aidan growled. :*Show up and don't die isn't a plan.*:

:*I need to know what they have on me. Then we'll go from there.*:

Vivi assured me that while the police certainly suspected me of murdering my ex-husband to inherit his business, they didn't have any evidence against me, or they'd already have arrested me. Having me come down to the station for questioning was part formality and part fishing expedition. They were hoping I'd slip up and give them some information to use to prosecute me for Jonathan's murder.

Ironically, I was guilty. I had sent him to his very slow, very painful death.

Not that they'd believe any of those details. If I tried to explain about the fae creature who lived in a swampy portal on the other end of the fountain outside our old townhome, I'd end up in a different kind of cell entirely.

"What's the worst that could happen?" I whispered softly, not sure we could trust the driver of the car.

"They arrest you, and we immediately bail you out. It might take a few hours to get before a judge, but Boss Man should be able to get you out today. It could take months or even years before you'd ever go to trial. Plenty of time for new evidence to materialize, or for us to get some kind of plea deal worked out. Absolute worst case, you could always go to...uh...with Warwick."

True. Worst case, I'd go to the Summer Isle for a while. But what about the guys?

:*We've faced worse than some shitty human cops,*: Aidan retorted. :*Give us a little credit.*:

:*Chill, dude,*: Ivarr replied. :*You're only making her more nervous.*: In my mind, he glowed brighter, sending saves of warm, molten honey flowing through me. :*D and I are already here.*:

Knowing they were going to be close helped settle my nerves. As long as they didn't try to storm the police station to get me out. Aidan and Keane followed this car, and Hammer and company had spread out up and down the freeway both ahead and behind us, casually make sure the road was clear of anything unexpected.

Vivi said we'd have to go through security at the door, which included metal detectors and manual bag checks. I didn't think it'd be a good idea to have pockets or baggies full of suspicious white powder —even if it was just salt. Certainly no crowbar or spike would pass through security. So from a *"facing the fae"* perspective, we were going in completely unarmed.

Aidan was practically frothing at the mouth just thinking about it.

I did carry a simple leather sachet with a sketch book and supplies. I was an artist after all—that certainly wasn't suspicious. I'd already painted a couple of landscapes in the sketchbook, including the cave where we'd faced off with Jonathan. I'd used that painting to travel to that location without moving, and though I didn't necessarily want to go back there, the cave was better than the police station if things went south. I'd also added a rough sketch of the gazebo on the shore-line of the lake that bordered our new property. Hopefully I'd be able to concentrate enough to travel to either location in an emergency, and then we could regroup with the guys.

:Don't forget about me.: Warwick cast a sparkling curtain of emer-alds through my mind. *:I'll be hovering nearby and ready to pull you to the Summer Isle at a moment's notice.:*

The car pulled over and parked outside a modern-looking three-story building with a circular atrium tower in the center. Sheets of glass reflected the sky and sunlight so brightly that it was impossible to see what the interior of the building looked like.

"Here we go," Vivi said brightly as she pushed open the door. "Thanks, Lars."

"Anytime, Ms. Rourke."

I scooted across the seat after her. "Where's Boss Man?"

She linked arms with me and confidently walked toward the rounded glass doors. "He's waiting inside. He came over as soon as he got out of court this morning. From now on out, don't say anything out loud that you don't want cops to hear. Even if they say we're in a private interview room. The less you say, the better."

I took a deep breath. "Got it."

I felt a subtle tug or heaviness to my left. Glancing out toward the parking lot, I saw Doran's bulk leaned up against a big black SUV. The reinforcements were here, armed and ready. *I can do this.*

Four decorative black columns lined the circular entryway. As we neared them, the hairs on my nape prickled.

:Stop,: Warwick said quickly.

I jerked to a halt, resisting the urge to whirl around and race toward Doran. *:What's wrong?:*

:This building is warded.:

:Oh fuck no.: Aidan's bond pulsed and swelled in my mind, a grim thunderstorm threatening to obliterate everything in his path. *:What kind of ward? Will we be able to pass if we need to get her out?:*

:It's impossible to know for sure until she's inside,: Warwick replied. *:It's very subtle, which makes me think it's keyed to ward against fae.:*

Vivi gave me a worried look, one eyebrow arched to silently ask what was going on. I gave her a smile. "Just a second. I'm admiring the architecture."

:Does that mean you won't be able to get me out in an emergency?: I asked Warwick.

:No ward will be able to keep a leprechaun from fulfilling a wish on his gold.:

So I still had two wishes, and he'd be able to get me out. Relieved, I started walking again, despite the bone-rattling roar inside my head.

That was Doran. *:I can't bear it, love. I can't bear to know you're in danger and alone and there's nothing I can do to help you.:*

:I'm okay.: I tried to soothe him but his gargoyle paced and thrashed inside my mind, wings straining, claws rending with fury. *:Warwick can still get me out, just like he did from Fhroig's lair.:*

Someone brushed past me, making me do a double take. Ivarr? But—

He pulled the door open for us. "The least I can do for such beautiful ladies is open the door."

"So kind!" Vivi pretended like she didn't know him. "Thank you, sir."

"My pleasure." He inclined his head and winked at me. "And to think that I was mad when I got that parking ticket. It was worth it just to see you today." In our bond, he added, *:I don't feel any ward. It's not like the one at the fountain. We four should still be able to pass through without any issue.:*

That settled Doran down a little. As I passed the pillars, goosebumps flared down my arms, almost like I stepped through a sheet of cooler air. But it didn't keep me out. Hopefully I hadn't set off some kind of fae alarm with my presence. I still wasn't sure I understood how I could be human but not exactly, let alone fae, but not exactly.

I reached for Warwick. *:Can you still hear me?:*

My step faltered as we entered the building. Silence echoed in my head.

Warwick was gone.

19

I plastered on a fake, stiff smile, trying to pretend that everything was okay as Vivi spoke to the female officer at the desk. Ivarr waited a polite distance behind us. A female officer gestured to us and led us down the hallway. Vaguely, I heard Ivarr speaking to the same person, asking about where to pay parking tickets. I wiped clammy palms on my jeans and willed my stomach to settle down.

This isn't like that nasty swamp. I'm not trapped. I'm not alone. All the guys are close. Warwick heard me in the swamp. He'll hear me now when I make the wish.

I tried to block out the doubts and what ifs. I didn't have his gold coin in my pocket this time. I'd given it back to him already. Hopefully that wouldn't make a difference in his ability to come to my aid if I needed him.

The officer opened a door and stepped aside. "The detectives will be with you in a moment."

"Thank you," Vivi said. "Riann, let me introduce you to my boss, Sloan Archer. Mr. Archer, this is my best friend, Riann Newkirk."

The man stood and held out his hand. "A pleasure, Ms. Newkirk."

I didn't need Aidan's vicious growl in my head to remember not to touch him. I gave the man as wide a smile as I could muster under the circumstances and said, "Thank you so much, Mr. Archer. Vivi says you're the absolute best attorney around."

He wore a slick, tasteful gray suit that managed to look conservative and yet extremely expensive at the same time. In her heels, Vivi was a bit taller than him. "High praise indeed coming from the best paralegal I've ever had. I've certainly heard a great deal about you."

Pulling out the seat beside him, he gestured for me to sit down, while Vivi walked around the table to sit on his opposite side. The only other chair in the room had its back to the door. He didn't seem upset that I didn't shake his hand, but I didn't like being separated from my friend. Granted, we were all on the same side, and I didn't want my back to the door when the cops came in, but I didn't know this guy.

:*Do you sense anything off about him?*: Doran asked.

I watched Mr. Archer as he sat back down and pushed a thick blue folder over to Vivi. She immediately flipped open the folder and scanned the papers, already slipping into work mode.

:*Nothing specific.*: I finally said. :*Maybe I just don't like lawyers.*:

:*Or maybe he's working a glamor,*: Aidan replied. :*He's someone you know.*:

:*I don't really know him, though. Only through Vivi. I haven't even met him until today.*:

:*But he knows all about you through her. No fault of hers, but beware. He knows you were in an unhappy marriage. She very likely told him plenty of details about your life without even realizing it.*:

"Keep your answers to yes and no if at all possible," Mr. Archer said. "I'm assuming that Viviana gave you a quick background about how these kinds of interviews usually go?"

"Yeah," I replied.

"If you don't want to answer something, just shake your head. I'll tell them to move on. You're not legally obligated to answer their questions. Don't incriminate yourself. 'I don't recall' is one of the best answers you can give."

"Okay," I whispered, clutching my hands together in my lap.

The door opened and the same two detectives who'd come to the house entered. Beasley sat in the chair across from us, but the younger cop stayed standing by the door.

"Thank you for coming in today, Ms. Newkirk," Detective Beasley said.

I nodded but didn't say anything. He slapped a folder down on the table in front of him and started shuffling through papers. I couldn't help but notice a greasy spot on his shirt to the right of his tie. It'd only been a couple of hours since he'd come to the house, but he looked more rumpled. His tie was lopsided, his shirt stained, and his hair looked unkempt, as if he'd passed through a wind tunnel.

I checked the younger cop—I couldn't remember his name—and he was grinning at Vivi. Maybe that was why he looked more put together than the older detective. He'd slicked his hair back and straightened his tie so he could make eyes at my friend.

"When was the last time you saw your ex-husband?"

"I don't recall."

Detective Beasley looked down at the papers in front of him and then back up at me with a creepy, knowing smile on his face. "Really? That's odd. You were seen at your former home where Mr. Blake resides just a few weeks ago."

The way he worded it was strange. I hadn't been "seen." As soon as my feet touched the ground, I'd been sucked into the fountain and transported to Fhroig's lair. If I'd been seen on some kind of neighborhood surveillance camera, they'd also have seen a gargoyle trying to fly me up out of the trap. It would have been all over the news.

:He knows,: Doran said grimly. :He's definitely on Evil Eye's payroll.:

Instead of being worried or scared, I was oddly relieved. Even better, it pissed me off. I didn't need this cop yanking my chain, trying to get me to slip up and reveal something that we both knew no human would believe.

I gave the detective a small smile. "I didn't see my ex-husband at the townhome."

"Oh? Why were you there?"

"I wanted to celebrate my freedom."

"But you didn't see Mr. Blake?"

"No."

"Why not? Was he not there?"

"I didn't go up to the door."

"What did you do?"

"I ended up going to a bar with my friends to celebrate instead."

The cop gave me a slimy smile. "So you chickened out."

I resisted the urge to mouth off something snarky, or defend myself from snide comments like that. I didn't commit a crime that night.

He flipped a page over in the folder, studied the paper a moment, and then pushed it across to me without saying anything.

It was upside down so I couldn't make out much other than it was a picture. Until I turned it over and saw me, Vivi, and Hammer walking into the cave where we'd all almost died.

When I raised my gaze back up to his, the detective asked, "Do you recognize the location?"

"Yes."

Boss Man slid the paper over in front of himself to look at it and then quietly passed it to Vivi. I heard her sharp inhale but I didn't look at her.

"Can you state for the record where this picture was taken?"

"A cave in Roanoke Park."

"And who's in the picture with you?"

"My friends, Viviana Rourke and Hammer. I don't know his legal name."

"What were you doing there?"

Thinking quickly, I pulled my satchel up on top of the table and pulled out my notebook. "I'm an artist. I like to paint interesting scenery. Here's one I did of the cave that day."

I didn't really want him to touch my watercolor painting, but I lifted it up so he could see it. His eyes narrowed, a muscle ticking in his jaw. "There was a cave-in that day."

"Oh?"

"An officer was guarding the cave to keep bystanders out. He took a blow to the head. I don't suppose you know anything about that?"

"No."

"Did you see the officer?"

"I don't recall."

"Were there other people there too?"

"Yes."

"These men, correct?" He offered another picture. It must have been taken before we'd arrived. Several of the Demon Hunters motorcycle gang stood around the cave, sawed off shotguns and other weapons in hand. A man stood in the mouth of the cave, but he was blurred. I couldn't see his face. But the way he stood, defiant and somehow angry even without seeing his eyes or mouth, reminded me of Aidan.

"Do you know these men?"

"No." Truth. I didn't know any of the other motorcycle guys by name other than Hammer, and I couldn't be sure that the man entering the cave was Aidan.

"Did one of them injure the officer?"

"I have no idea."

He shuffled through the papers, spreading them out and crumpling the edges a little. His face reddened and sweat trailed down his forehead. "Short?"

The younger detective jerked his attention from Vivi. "Yeah?"

"Do you have any questions for Ms. Newkirk?"

"Oh. Yeah. Why'd you kill him?"

"Don't answer that," Boss Man retorted. "Just because you're incompetent doesn't mean that you can bully my client with baseless claims."

Ignoring him, Detective Short stepped closer to the table and leaned down to brace both palms on the table. He gave me the same knowing, smarmy grin that he'd flashed at Vivi before and licked his lips.

Ice trickled down my spine. I'd never had a man look at me like that. Like I was nothing more than a piece of meat. Something to claim, use, and then discard in the nearest Dumpster. I suddenly felt bad for being jealous of all the looks Vivi always got when we went out. I hadn't realized how disgusting it felt when men acted like this.

"Come on now, Ms. Newark. We know you did it."

I held myself very still, keeping my hands clasped in front of me. I didn't answer. I was afraid my voice would betray my repugnance.

:Definitely dark fae,: Doran warned. *:Trust your instincts, love. Ivarr is only a minute away from you. He'll rip off that bastard's head before he can touch you.:*

:I'm okay.: I said it for myself as much as them. *:He hasn't tried to hurt me. Yet.:*

"Did one of your *friends* kill Mr. Blake for you?" Detective Short continued, leaning out further over the table toward me. "Or did you do it yourself?"

"What evidence do you have that Mr. Blake is even dead?" Boss Man asked. "There's no body. There's certainly no motive for my client to commit such a crime. She didn't know that he left Solobrex to her in his will. Until you produce anything beyond circumstantial evidence against my client, she has nothing else to say to you."

Dread weighed heavier in the pit of my stomach. I hadn't had the chance to tell Mr. Archer anything about Jonathan's will, let alone the company he'd supposedly left to me. It was possible that Vivi had told Boss Man over the phone, but I couldn't be sure.

Though his words gave me an idea.

The police would have a difficult time charging me with murder without a body. But if Jonathan was seen alive... Or someone who *appeared* to be him...

I pictured Warwick in my mind: the long, silken fall of black hair, the sparkle of his emerald eyes, his playful wink and the graceful way he moved. *:I wish that Warwick Greenshanks could walk into this police station using a glamor to look exactly like my ex-husband, Jonathan Blake, right before I sent him to the swamp.:*

The door slammed open making everyone jump. Detective Short whirled, his hand dropping down to the gun on his hip.

Jonathan Blake stood in the doorway. Basic, boring businessman with brown hair and eyes, receding hairline, nice suit, shiny black shoes, and a heavy gold watch. "Why hello there, honeybun. Did you miss me?"

20

WARWICK

The instant revulsion that flickered over Riann's face at my appearance distracted me just enough that I almost dropped the glamor. Worse, I felt a surge of abject terror from her, as if she feared she'd made a terrible mistake and accidentally freed the real man from Fhroig's lair.

Keeping my face smooth, I tightened my mental focus, willing the repugnant face of her abuser to remain in place. Though I couldn't resist sending her a quick mental hug. :*It's still me,* mo stór.:

:*Whew.:* She laughed shakily. :*I wasn't sure for a moment. What's wrong?:*

Leprechauns didn't sweat, but it was all I could do to hold on to the hated glamor. Magic was an innate part of my nature, even on the human plane, but I was breaking enough magical rules right now that my power didn't want to respond. It was too complicated to explain and maintain the image at the same time, so I simply said, :*We need to hurry.:*

"They said you were dead." Riann's voice raised, higher than normal like a stressed, anxious woman. "You bastard! They thought I killed you!"

Splaying my fingers, I opened up my arms slightly. "Here I am. I was out of town on business, and I lost my phone."

The two cops spluttered a bit, staring at each other and then Riann. They knew we were lying, but they couldn't prove it. Not without revealing that they knew all about fae both light and dark. They'd chosen to attack Riann on the human plane, and so must play by human rules.

"But—" Viviana started to rise from her chair, face pale and eyes huge with terror. "Riann, run!"

"It's okay." Riann forced out a harsh laugh. "He can't do anything to me here with witnesses. Are we done here, detectives?"

The older human ran a finger around his collar. By his alarming puce complexion, he was either extremely upset or having an aneurysm. The younger man gripped the gun on his hip, as if weighing his options. Not that I'd allow a regular bullet to harm me.

Though this place... A crushing weight settled on my chest. I gritted my teeth, hoping the expression would still manage to look offended or angry rather than desperate.

"I want to speak to you outside." Riann gave me a shove toward the door. "You have to take me out of your stupid will. I want no part of your company, do you hear me? Who's your attorney? Outside, now!"

I made some harsh, wordless sounds and allowed her to shove and push me out the door and down the hallway. Ivarr stepped out of the shadows and followed us, protecting her back. Though the cops didn't follow. A few people looked up as we passed the front desk, but no one tried to stop us.

As soon as I stepped out of the ward made by the front pillars, the sense of impending doom eased. I kept the glamor in place, though I lifted a hand to my forehead, surprised to see the tremble in my fingers.

"Are you alright?" She whispered fiercely.

"Aye, love, I'll be right as rain soon enough."

We kept up the charade until we rounded the SUV. My knees

quivered and my heart pounded a slow, heavy throb of agony. I barely made it to the opened passenger door. I didn't try to climb up into the seat, but simply dropped down to sit on the carpeted floor. Panting, I braced my elbows on my knees and let the glamor drop away.

"You're glistening like someone threw a glitter bomb at you." She draped an arm around my shoulders, pressing against my side and knee. "I'm so sorry. I had no idea making that wish would be so hard on you. What happened?"

"The wards." I grimaced, shaking my head. "That place be warded as heavily as Stonehenge."

"Evil Eye's headquarters, then?" Doran suggested.

"Makes sense," Aidan said. "He loves places of power, and in the mortal realm, there's few places with more power than a police station."

"Was he one of the cops?" Her voice quivered and she leaned harder against me.

I shook my head. "I don't think so, though they be tainted by him. Everybody in that building is touched by his magic. The air was thick with it."

Gnawing on her lip, she straightened. "But I don't know anyone who's associated with the police."

"We need to get the hell out of this fucking place," Aidan said. "I have the distinct, unpleasant feeling that you met Evil Eye already."

Her eyes flared. "What? Who?"

"Archer," the four treasures said in unison.

She stared at them one by one and then her gaze fell on me. "Boss Man? But I never met him until today. I don't know him."

"Fae speak in riddles," I reminded her with a wry smile. "Vanta was trying to be helpful but couldn't be specific. You might not know him, but I guarantee that he knows just about anything he could want to know about you."

Staring at me, she paled. "Vivi. I can't leave her." Whirling back toward the police station, she rushed a step before Doran caught her up against him. "I have to go help her!"

"Our first priority is you, love. We have to get you to safety. Then the lads and I will come up with a plan to help your friend."

"He's been her boss for years, right?" Keane added. "She's been safe that whole time."

But we were all thinking the same thing. She'd been safe because none of us knew her boss's true identity. If he suspected we knew...

Riann's phone started ringing from inside her bag. Luckily she hadn't left it inside the police station because Stoneheart would sooner break his gargoyle into a thousand pieces than let her anywhere near that place of darkness again.

She pulled the phone out. "It's Vivi."

"Stay calm," Doran replied. "She's safe as long as she doesn't know. Tell her to meet us back at the house."

Nodding, Riann hit the button. "Hey. I'm okay. He's gone."

"I'm so glad to hear that," a man drawled in a voice dripping with amusement. "You left so quickly that we didn't have a chance to talk about my retainer. There's a lot of paperwork to be done if you're going to be my client."

"Oh." She laughed awkwardly. "I didn't know you had my number."

"I don't. This is Viviana's phone. She's regretfully unavailable at the moment."

A wave of emotion flooded me through her bond. Terror, mixed with a churning, turbulent storm of rage.

"I want to talk to her." Riann's voice rang with the clang of swords.

"Is the leprechaun part of your little treasure harem now?"

Her eyes locked with mine, dark with desperation and dread. The treasures pressed closer, laying a steadying hand on her. Lending her their power as the wheel in her mind began to spin. She held her free hand out to me.

I pushed to my feet, still wavering with exhaustion, but I slipped my hand into hers. *:My magic is yours, drained though it be at the moment.:*

"Yes," she said evenly. "What do you want?"

"I thought that was painfully obvious, my dear. I want you, of course."

VIVI!

I gripped the phone fiercely, biting my bottom lip to keep from screaming. I'd gone off and left her without a single thought that she might be in danger. She never would have left me.

I stifled a sob.

"Don't hurt her."

"I wouldn't dream of it," Boss Man replied in a kind, gentle voice that made my stomach heave. "She's the best assistant I've ever had, and that's saying quite a lot. But then you're the most gifted treasure-keeper who's ever brought the four treasures together. Am I not right, Stoneheart?"

I looked up at Doran, his jaws grinding before he finally bit off, "Aye."

"So it's only fitting that your friend and confidante be so talented. She's told me so much about her beloved friend that I feel as if I know you as intimately as she does, Riann."

I hated the way he said my name, drawing out the vowels like Vanta had done into one long syllable. *Reeeen.*

Aidan snagged the phone away from me. "If you be wanting a trade, then I'm your man this time. Set the woman free and you can do whatever you want to me."

Boss Man laughed, a genuine, light sound of amusement. "Ah, the sound of the Slaughterer in love is such a delight. I think not, mighty spear."

"Take me, then," Keane retorted. "Take us all. We're dead anyway. Give Riann back her friend. Let them live a life of peace, and you can have this crumbling world for all eternity. We're done fighting this useless war. It's all shite anyway."

"No," I whispered, choked with tears. "No! I won't let you die! I can't bear it!"

"Exactly," Boss Man replied, ignoring me entirely. "This war is over. It's been over for centuries. You treasures were only too honorable to finally lay down your magical weapons and walk away."

"Is that what you want?" Doran retorted. "If so, we surrender now. This is over. We're done."

"Excellent. Return to the Land Beneath the Waves or whatever dimension you wish. It doesn't matter in the end. All the worlds and realms be mine."

I took the phone back from Aidan and took it off speaker. "Why? Why now? If you've been so close this whole time? The whole cop thing and charging me with murder was a complete waste of time. If you wanted me to meet you, all you had to do was tell Vivi to set it up. I would have agreed in a heartbeat, and she'd be safe."

My voice broke and I sucked in a shaking breath.

"If you must know, I've quite enjoyed watching you from afar. It's amusing to see how each treasurekeeper's fate will play out. How she will pull the treasures to her side. How long it will take her to bend them to her will. After Stoneheart's capture, I doubted even you could pull the Slaughterer out of his abysmal funk. But the greatest challenge of all is to see if the treasurekeeper will succumb to me or not."

"Never," I whispered, shaking my head vehemently.

"Many have," he replied nonchalantly. "Some came to me almost at the very beginning of their war. I must admit that I find those treasurekeepers the least interesting. It's so much more entertaining if I must lure them to their downfall. That slow, agonizing journey to their breaking point is the sweetest reward. Though it's almost as amusing to watch the treasures crumple when they realize the truth. They are such honorable fools after all."

"So that's it? You just want to break me?"

He laughed, a high, sweet trill that should have been magical and beautiful. "Oh, sweet one, no, not at all. You're more than the treasurekeeper, Riann. You're the key."

Throbbing pain shot through my skull as if someone was hammering a spike into my temple. I flinched, absently rubbing at the spot with my free hand. Doran squeezed my shoulder, his big hand turning me toward him, trying to comfort me. But there was no comfort. Not while Vivi was in danger. Not when my men were talking about surrendering to their enemy to save me. *There must be a way out of this.*

Key. Again with the key. Jonathan had said the key to defeating Balor was written on my very soul.

"Come to Dún Bhalair and I will explain everything to you. I will not kill you. I will not kill your treasures. Not if you come to me willingly."

"And Vivi?" I rasped out.

"My lovely assistant remains unharmed and eager to see her best friend once more. You know the value of a fae's word. Unlike your leprechaun, I need no gold to hold me to my oaths."

Fae didn't lie. But that didn't mean he spoke the truth either.

He wouldn't kill us. Not directly. But maybe his minions would, or some other dark fae creature at his bidding. Vivi was unharmed—for now. But she might be scared out of her mind, mentally tortured or worse.

I couldn't take any fae at his word except one.

Silently, I held out my hand behind me without turning to look. Warwick's fingers clasped mine. "I'd take a leprechaun's oath over yours any day."

21

We started the drive back home, all of us crammed into the SUV. The silence weighed heavily in the vehicle, thick with fury and worry. They worried for me.

I worried for them and Vivi.

I still couldn't believe that I'd blindly gone off and left her in the jaws of danger without a clue. I'd been so focused on getting out of the legal tangle that I hadn't even considered how being accused of murder gave Boss Man the perfect opportunity to bring us together. He even positioned me so that I needed to call him for help.

Stupid.

"You couldn't have known," Doran said. "None of us did, and we've been fighting Evil Eye for centuries."

"Standing in the same room as him, I couldn't identify him as fae," Warwick added. "You certainly couldn't have known."

"It just blows my mind that he's been sitting back watching me for years. Just waiting. Through Vivi, he would have known that I was miserable in my marriage. Did he know that Jonathan was a changeling? Did he realize his true identity? For that matter, does he know who my true mother is? Or my father?"

"I'm sure that he suspects quite a lot of things," Warwick replied.

"You managed to survive what no mortal would have been able to endure. He may not have known exactly who the changeling was, but I guarantee that he knew everything there was to know about the human Jonathan Blake, and he would have found the man's history as suspicious as we did. Evil Eye is a master at manipulation and court intrigue, and he's older than you can even imagine. The longer you stayed alive, the more he would have begun to suspect that you were no ordinary mortal treasurekeeper."

At least Warwick looked more like himself. His voice sounded firmer, and he wasn't quite as shiny, though his usually vibrant, flowing hair seemed duller than usual and hung flat to his body. "Do you need to revive your power in the Summer Isle?"

He blew out a sigh. "I do, at least for a short time, or I'm afraid that I'll be completely worthless."

"I've never seen a leprechaun sweat like that," Aidan drawled, looking back at us in the rearview mirror from the driver's seat. "You still look like shit."

"That wasn't sweat." Warwick huffed out, tossing his head slightly to stir his lifeless hair about his shoulders. "I merely glistened."

Keane laughed, shaking his head. "And I'm only ever going to take a single bite."

"Those wards were formidable. If *mo stór* hadn't invoked me gold oath, I couldn't have penetrated the building at all."

That didn't make me feel better. At all. "That should have been the first clue, then. We should have stayed far away."

"Fuck the police," all four treasures said in unison.

Aidan couldn't help but mutter, "I told you so," under his breath.

I blew out a frustrated sigh. "You were right."

"Don't be so hard on yourself," Warwick said. "There be many institutions in the mortal realm as heavily warded."

"The Church," Doran said grimly. "Your White House and Supreme Court. Buckingham Palace. Mecca. Shanghai Tower."

"But also Stonehenge, Newgrange, and other stone circles," Keane added. "The pyramids at Giza. Machu Picchu. Not all are warded for ill."

I frowned, trying to follow along. "If Evil Eye's headquarters, so to speak, was the police station we just left, then why are all those other human places warded? I could get maybe the wonders of the world, but government offices?"

"The mortal realm falls further into darkness with each passing moment," Doran replied. "Most of those places were long ago lost to darkness or corrupted to be used for ill."

I shook my head in disbelief. "You mean the entire United States government is ran by dark fae? Under Evil Eye?"

"Not precisely," Doran began, though Aidan said, "Exactly," at the same time.

"Evil Eye is just one reflection of darkness in this world." Ivarr's voice echoed with sorrow. "He's *our* battle, the legendary Irish treasures, but there are other battles to be won."

"And we're all fucking losing," Aidan growled. "Even if we somehow manage to force Evil Eye back to Faerie, there'll be more darkness to take his place. It's a losing battle we wage."

"Yet we fight, and hope, and live another day," Doran said.

"It all just seems so... so..."

"Useless? Sheer folly and stupidity?" Aidan barked out a harsh laugh as he turned off the freeway. "Aye, all the above, and yet there's the barest glimmer of hope that brings the warriors back, again and again, hoping that this time we may yet make a difference." He looked up in the mirror again, capturing my gaze with his fierce intensity. "For us, that difference is you. I would come back again a million times if that meant I would see you again."

Given Keane's gift in the kitchen, I supposed it was only natural for his domain to become our war room. Aidan, Doran, and I sat at the island while Keane and Ivarr worked some magic to restore my spirits. Though I couldn't imagine any confection or dish they produced could ever make me feel better.

Not while Vivi was in danger.

Warwick had poofed back to the Summer Isle to soak in some magic and regain his strength. He promised to speak to Queen Morgan and see if she had any advice or help that she could provide. I wanted to talk to Vanta again, but I couldn't muster up the focus or strength yet. My mind was too frantic and disjointed, flitting from one thought to another. Random things that didn't even make sense.

I remembered lying in Vivi's little twin bed and giggling under the blankets, telling stories and reading books by flashlight. My dread at showing anyone my first "serious" artwork, terribly afraid that it was horrible. Unable to voice the tiny speck of hope that burned inside me to become an artist. To live wild and free on a canvas—so unlike our boring, average lives.

She'd always believed in me. Encouraging my shyly whispered dream, no matter how fantastical.

And I'd left her.

My throat ached with unshed tears. She never would have left me.

The rusted tin box she'd saved all these years seemed to stare back at me with reproach. Absently, I pried the lid open, remembering the heartbroken look in her eyes when I'd told her about finding my favorite coat burned. Had she looked at my back the same way when I pushed Warwick out of the interrogation room?

"Stop it," Aidan growled, bumping his shoulder against mine. "You didn't do anything wrong. You had no reason to think her boss was up to no good."

Ivarr set a steaming cup in front of me. "He's right. Vivi's heart is too full of love for you to think she'd be angry with you."

I ran my finger over the melted lump of a button from my childhood coat. "I know. She'd tell me the same thing you're telling me. But she still wouldn't have left me behind."

"But she did leave you to deal with the changeling alone," Doran said.

"No, not at all. She was always there for me."

"Was she, now. So she knew the changeling tortured you every night, and she did nothing to help you escape?"

"No, of course not. She didn't know how bad it was because I didn't tell her."

"She knew enough to feel badly about it once you were free of him. She took herself to task for not acting sooner and becoming so involved in her job. I don't say this to upset you, or to try and make you think ill of your friend, but only to point out that she left you to your own devices. To live your life and deal with the choices and decisions you made. She chose to work for Evil Eye himself for years. In some ways, that taint has affected her whether you or she could tell. That taint dulled her concern for you and delayed any kind of action she might take to set you free."

I hadn't thought of it that way. I couldn't imagine her working so closely with a dark fae for so long... Almost as long as I'd been with Jonathan. That relationship had changed me forever. I had to assume that Vivi had also been changed and damaged by being so close to dark fae.

Lightly, I rubbed the charred scrap of green cloth between my thumb and finger. "Things were so much easier when we were kids. When we played in the woods, it was just me and her against..." My brain slipped into neutral, my words falling off into nothing.

Doran laid his big hand over my forearm. "Are you well, love?"

A memory played out in my mind, fogged by time and age and damage, like a delicate wisp of cloth with moth holes and frayed strands. Playing in the forest with Vivi. Just children. Dancing and laughing, whirling without a care in the world. I held something up against my face, my eye, like a lady with opera glasses.

Then we collapsed in a heap beneath our favorite old tree, roots arching up out of the ground. Massive low branches sweeping out, inviting us to climb into a leafy treehouse. We lay there in the shade beneath that tree, and I told her stories.

Of all the things I'd seen with my special glass. Imagination? Or...

Snapping back to the present, I reached out and picked up the stone with the hole in it. "What did you say this was again?"

"A hag stone," Keane replied. "It's a stone of protection."

"And you can glimpse Faerie through the hole," I whispered, lifting my gaze up to his face. "Right?"

"Aye, supposedly, though I can't say that I've ever taken the time to try it out."

Holding my breath, I slowly lifted the stone up toward my eye. I didn't know what I hoped to see. Why my fingers trembled. I'd just been a kid with a vivid imagination.

A fae child trapped in a mortal body. Could I have been seeing...

The stone passed up my cheek until I could see through the hole.

I sucked in a harsh breath. Keane stared back at me, but he looked completely different. His skin glowed so brightly that I could barely make out the color of his eyes. Glowing golden tendrils flowed all around him, stretching out toward the pots on the stove. The mixing bowls on the counter. The fridge.

Cauldron magic at work.

Heart pounding, I turned toward Doran, keeping the hag stone pressed to my eye. His gargoyle stared back at me with glittering ruby eyes. Red ribbons of light danced around him, swirling around his wings and wrapping around his glistening claws.

Ivarr shone like the noonday sun, making my eyes tear up at his brightness. Molten honey dripped from his fingers, golden droplets of warmth and truth and love that lingered on everything he touched.

Slowly, I turned my head to my right, braced to see the Slaughterer in all his gory detail. Blood streaked his face like the red paint I'd painted on Keane's forehead. Where light dropped from Ivarr's fingertips, Aidan left fingerprints of blood. He gleamed like a silver, vicious blade, so sharp that it hurt to look at him. His eyes glistened like chips of ice and jagged shards of glass.

I pulled my gaze away, dropping my head slightly. Opal light filled my vision, softening the blood and cutting edge seared into my eyes. Confused, I turned my head, trying to see where the light came from.

Me. It came from me.

Aidan huffed out a harsh breath. "Fucking told you so."

"Whoa." I lifted my hand up before my face. Rainbows spun from my fingertips, brilliant arcs of multi-colored light that danced like prisms in the air. "If I'd thought to take this to the police station, what do you think Evil Eye would look like?"

"Thick shadows dripping like crude oil on everything he touches," Doran replied. "Tainting the very air, staining everything he comes in contact with. When you realize you've picked up a shadow, it's too late. It's already spread too deeply."

I shuddered, my heart squeezing with dread for Vivi. Did I want to look at her through the hag stone and fully understand the toll that working for Boss Man had claimed from her? I lowered the stone from my eye, but I kept it in my palm, rolling it over with my fingers. Maybe that was why I'd gravitated toward gothic, weird paintings even in high school. I'd been seeing the creatures of fae all around me.

"Oh shit." I jerked my head up. "The painting that Warwick has. If it spins out magic in sunlight, what will we be able to see through the stone?"

"Only one way to find out," Aidan replied.

I glanced at the window to gauge how much sunlight we had left. Thirty minutes or so, an hour at most before dusk. I decided to risk it.

:Warwick?:

Emerald green flashed through my mind. *:Aye, love?:*

:Are you feeling well enough to bring the painting to me for a few minutes? I want to test out a new theory.:

I'd barely finished the thought and he stood on the other side of the island, canvas and easel in tow. He'd changed into what looked to be emerald silk pajamas and a long, flowy tunic. His hair gleamed once more, softly swishing down his body as he moved.

"At your service, *mo stór.* I'm quite refreshed, thank you for asking. What have you discovered?"

Rather than answering him, I put the hag stone back to my eye. Rivers of velvet magic flowed around him, glinting like crushed emeralds and diamonds. His eyes were huge sparkling jewels, dominating his face. Even his bone structure looked different. His face slender, his shoulders slim, extremely long, elegant legs and delicate fingers.

"Um, wow. Do I look like that?"

He snapped his fingers and a full-length mirror shimmered in front of him, reflecting my image back at me. My hair looked like gleaming, sable-black fur, flowing all around me. I didn't recognize my face at all. My eyes were huge, like his, shining like a black oil slick. It would have scared me to see such dark eyes—but the black was iridescent like an oil slick. Opals, mother of pearl, and diamond swirls danced all around me, fluttering like tiny, delicate wings.

Dragonflies. My heart ached, my throat tight. My mother's sign. Even my hair looked like Vanta's fur.

Warwick snapped his fingers and the mirror disappeared. Then he began to drag the cover off my painting.

Eyes tight, I braced for the flash of light to be magnified through the hag stone. But the brilliant rainbows I'd seen before were gone. Everything was gone. It looked nothing like before.

I slid off the barstool, stumbling a little in shock. Doran caught my elbow, steadying me before I fell. I staggered around the island, keeping a hand on the granite top for balance.

"I don't understand," I whispered, shaking. "It looks completely different."

"What do you see?" Warwick asked softly.

"The doorway... it's shut. There's a hint of light shining through the cracks around the doorjamb, but it's dim and thin. Weak. The woman in the doorway is gone. So's the girl. Even the trees and tentacles, the monsters hiding in the shadows. It's all gone."

I leaned closer, adjusting the hag stone back and forth in front of my eye to see if I could bring it into focus better. "Bones. The trees look like skeletons. There are bones scattered on the ground in front of the door. Old, shattered, like they've been there so long they're fossils. Nothing's alive. No leaves. No plants. Just... darkness."

"I think you're seeing what Evil Eye will turn this world into," Doran said. "Everything's dead and gone. Nothing living remains. No magic. No light. It's all gone."

I ran my finger over the surface of the canvas. I could feel the brush strokes where the younger version of me stood, but those details were invisible through the hag stone. Slowly, I lowered the stone, watching the light flow from the painting once more. The gentle movement of the woman's wings in the doorway. Vanta's soft rumbling purr. The magic was still there, though not as brilliant as when it'd been bathed in sunlight.

I stepped back, trying to think. I had too many ideas swirling around in my head. Frantic birds swooping and spiraling out of control with no sense of order. There was something I needed to understand. A clue hiding right before my nose. But what? "Would looking at it in the dark with the hag stone change anything?"

Ivarr reached out, his hand hovering over the light switch. "There's only one way to find out."

Aidan and Doran both stood and went to the windows in the living and dining area, shutting blinds and drawing curtains. Keane did the same over the kitchen sink.

A gloomy hush fell over the house. The guys gathered around me and the painting. Aidan had even snagged his swords from some-where—I was sure he hadn't been wearing them across his back earlier.

"Ready?" Ivarr asked.

I took in a deep breath and let it out. "What do you think will happen? Are pookas going to tear a hole in the side of the house or something?"

Aidan shrugged. "You never know. Remember what lurked in that Branson lake. Dark fae for miles around have already sensed the magic flowing out of the painting. Without daylight to stop them, they're guaranteed to come investigate."

I met Ivarr's gaze and he nodded. "If anything dares show its scaly hide, I'll blast it with light. We'll have crispy imps in no time."

"Okay," I whispered, lifting the hag stone to my eye.

He turned off the light.

And I was no longer in the kitchen.

23

I stood on a hill that I didn't recognize. Night wrapped the hill in silent darkness. No insect noise. No wind.

For a moment, blinding panic filled me. I didn't want to be trapped again, separated from the guys, stuck in a nasty swamp or worse.

Doran's deep, rumbling voice came from miles and miles away, though I could still hear him. "What do you see?"

My head fell forward with relief, my shoulders drooping. Panting, I concentrated on them in my mind. I could still feel them. The magical wheel shimmered in my head, ready to spin out power to the treasures to defeat our enemies. I wasn't trapped or powerless.

Part of me was still there on the hill in the silent night, but the other part of me could sense the kitchen and men around me.

"There's a hill," I said aloud, my voice echoing strangely. "It's nighttime."

"What else do you see?" Warwick asked.

I turned my head, scanning the top of the hill. As my eyes adjusted to the darkness, I could make out dark shapes circling me. Not trees or poles—they were too thick. "Stones, I think? Standing stones."

"How many?"

I wasn't sure why it mattered, but I started to count them, whispering out loud. "One, two..." As my gaze fell over each stone, it lightened from dark black to granite gray. Chills crept down my spine, hairs rising on my arms and nape. The air thickened as I counted. The night weighed heavier. My ears ached as pressure built.

"Eleven. Twelve."

Twelve stones lightened to gray in a circle around me, but the oppressive weight grew. My bones ached. My ears rang even though I didn't hear anything. The air felt close and stifled. Maybe it was my imagination, but the stones seemed bigger and closer, looming over me. Surrounding me.

I blinked, trying to break the illusion, but towering stone encircled me, leaning ever closer.

"Magh Slécht," Warwick said, his voice hushed and reverent. "There should be another stone in the center, covered in gold."

I turned a full three-hundred-and-sixty degrees. "I only see the twelve stones. Nothing else."

"Look on the ground, in the center of the stone circle. It could be covered."

I was in the center, as far as I could tell. I scanned the ground, but in the dark, it was hard to see much. Knee-high grass rippled around my feet. My ears throbbed and I couldn't stop looking up at the stones, back over my shoulder, sure that they closing in on me. I kicked through the grass, looking for anything that could be hidden.

"Do you have the hag stone there?" Doran asked.

Duh. I tightened my fingers on the forgotten stone and lifted it up toward my face. Had I stopped looking through the stone when I stepped onto the hill? But surely I was still holding it in the kitchen, or I wouldn't still be seeing the stones leaning in like grim sentinels.

Looking through the hole, I froze. Another stone lay flat on the ground just a foot away from me. The grass had been trampled down all around it, but I'd never seen or sensed it until I looked through the stone. It wasn't nearly as big as the others, maybe a foot or so long and a few inches thick. It looked like a toppled gravestone.

Lightning arced across the sky. I looked up as another bolt tore through boiling black storm clouds. A gust of wind blew my hair whipping behind me like a flag, trying to steal my breath. No wonder the air felt so heavy and charged with power.

I dropped to my knees and touched the tip of my finger to the stone, braced for a lightning bolt to blast me. The edges were carved into some kind of design, though even with the hag stone, I couldn't make out exactly what it was supposed to be. The flat edge on top seemed to be the back, mostly smooth except for pocked marks from age and weather. I pried my left hand underneath the edge, but it was too heavy for me to lift one-handed.

Slowly, I lowered the hag stone from my eye. Now that I was touching the toppled stone, I could still see it, so I put the other stone into my pocket. With both hands freed, I heaved the stone up and flipped it over backwards. In the dark, I couldn't see anything written on its surface. I ran my hands over the rough stone, trying to tell if there were any carvings.

Lightning boomed overhead, making me jump, but in the brief light, I saw a face carved into the stone. The carvings on the edges resembled arms and legs, turning the stone into a boxy representation of a person.

"I found it, but it's not gold. It looks like a person."

"It's an idol representing Cromm Crúaich," Warwick replied. "You're in a place of great power." He hesitated a moment before adding, "And darkness."

I swallowed, shivering a little even though the air still pressed in like a heavy, suffocating blanket. My father, a dark god who'd supposedly been worshipped—or appeased—with human sacrifice. Lightning crackled again, illuminating the face of the stone idol. The arched top resembled a head, the edges thick shoulders. The stone was stained darker than the rest.

Dirt and moss from where it'd lain for centuries? Or something worse?

"Why am I here?" I said aloud, tipping my head back to look at the night sky. "What do you want?"

Another gust of wind pushed against me, carrying my words away into the storm. Lightning cut across the darkness and the sky opened like it'd been cut with Aidan's sword, emptying cold, pounding sheets of rain. Wind tugged at my hair, my shirt, buffeting me harder. Swirling around inside the stone circle, building with intensity like a mini tornado.

Urgency rose inside me. I needed to do... something. Cold rain pounded against my back as I hunched over the stone. I ran my fingers over it, searching for a clue. The ground. Digging through grassy roots and gnarled earth, I found it. A notch carved into the ground, a stone footing or foundation.

Lightning pounded through the night, giving me plenty of light. I ran my fingers over the bottom of the tumbled stone and felt a matching tab on its base. The wind spiraled harder through the stone circle, whipping my hair into my face. Driving rain sliced like sheets of ice over my skin, chilling me to the bone. Hurrying, I pulled the stone upright, wriggling it back and forth to get the tab closer to the slot. Almost there...

With a heavy thunk, it slid into place.

The wind died. Rain ceased. Heart pounding, I scrambled to my feet, not sure if I'd done a good thing or not.

"What..." Warwick's voice came from even further away, a thin, stretched out warble that went on and on through space and time. "Happened?"

An explosion burst up from the ground, slinging earth and mud and roots in all directions. It picked me up like a giant's hand and slung me up into the air. I didn't have time to be scared—even though it seemed to happen in slow motion. I could see it all. The upright carving now gleamed gold. Power rippled through the air, a shock wave that slammed the standing stones outward, knocking them flat to the ground.

I hovered in the air, looking down at the blasted circle. Huge, heavy slabs of granite knocked down like a child's set of building blocks. The short golden stone burned brighter like a beacon. Then the power caught me, slamming me backward through darkness.

24

I opened my eyes.

Stone engulfed me. For a moment, I thought the giant stones must have fallen on top of me, but I felt a heavy, steady thump against my cheek. Warmth wrapped around me. I lifted my head, and the deep grooves etched around Doran's eyes eased.

"Gods, I thought we'd lost you, love."

My head wobbled, as if my neck was too weak to hold it up. "What happened?"

"You tell us." Ivarr spoke behind me. The warmth of his light soaked into my chilled back. It felt incredibly good, as if I'd been lying on a beach drinking in the sunlight for hours. "You fell backward, drenched, muddy, and unconscious."

"Drenched?" I looked down at myself, surprised to see my shirt was indeed wet enough that I'd also dampened Doran's T-shirt. "Oh. Yeah. There was a huge storm."

Doran shifted me around in his arms so I could sit back against his chest while he supported me. We were on the floor in the kitchen. He leaned back against the island. Swords drawn, Aidan had his back to us, braced for battle. Ivarr and Warwick both hovered nearby. From the dance of magic on my skin, they'd both been sending me their power, trying to revive me, or at least warm me. My back was dry, though I was still damp from where I'd been pressed against Doran.

Keane squatted down and pressed a teacup into my hand. "This will help warm you up too."

I wrapped my hands around the cup, soaking in its warmth as I sipped the drink. Tea spiked with drúchta. I closed my eyes, letting the warmth and love all around soak into me, though I couldn't help the twinge of worry niggling in my stomach. "I hope I didn't fuck things up."

"What happened?" Warwick asked again, his voice echoing faintly, as if still reverberating through multiple dimensions of time and space to reach me.

"I found the stone in the center. It looked kind of like a person, though it was only about the size of a tombstone." Saying that last word made me shiver, my teeth chattering a bit. "It wasn't gold at first, but it did have a head, arms, and legs. After I put it into the slot, it turned gold."

He frowned slightly. "What slot?"

"There was a hole in the ground that fit the stone perfectly. I felt like I needed to do something. Urgently. Everything kept tearing at me, urging me to hurry. When I set the stone into the hole, the storm stopped suddenly, like a switch had been flipped. I thought that was what it wanted me to do, but then there was an explosion that knocked all the stones down."

His eyes widened. "All twelve stones?"

I nodded, gnawing my lip. "They fell like they were just toys, but the small stone was still standing in the center. Then it was gold, shining like Ivarr. That's all I remember. Was I not supposed to fix the stone?"

"Most of our knowledge of Cromm Crúaich was lost long ago," Warwick said. "The only tale I know is fragmented at best, but he was supposedly brought to Éire by the Fomorians."

"Balor's a Fomorian, right?"

Warwick nodded. "There is little that Evil Eye fears but I would hazard a guess that he knows all too well the power of Crouching

Darkness. He was the head of the gods, lost long ago on the seas of time, yet his power still lingers."

"The only tale I've heard is Tigernmas," Doran said. "Keane, do you know it?"

"When Tigernmas was king, a Fomorian ship arrived," Keane replied in a soft, sing-song voice. "They demanded a share of Éire's wealth, but when Tigernmas refused to pay tribute, they sent dark druids ashore carrying an idol of Cromm Crúaich. Some say there were twelve bronze idols of other gods as well, which is why Cromm was known as the head of the gods. To appease them, Tigernmas built a temple. When the people refused to bow before the foreign gods, the priests demanded the sacrifice of every firstborn child, or the crops would fail and the animals would wither. Some say the skulls of the sacrifices were dashed against the idol on Samhain to appease the god for the rest of the year."

My stomach heaved and I swallowed hard, remembering the dark stain I'd seen.

"Furious and afraid, the people fought back, some flinging themselves against the idols and rocks, trying to break their power. Three fourths of all the men of Éire died that night, including Tigernmas."

"Holy fuck," I whispered, my voice shaking.

"The Fomorians left but they didn't take their dark god with them. He continued to be revered—and feared—for centuries, until he was supposedly driven out by St. Patrick. He destroyed Cromm's idol and the other twelve stones sank into the earth."

Aidan snorted. "Of fucking course. Let me guess—they built a church there too to sanctify the demons."

Keane chuckled. "Supposedly, though mysterious dark figures are still seen on the hill, especially around Samhain."

"And I put him back into place." I curled against Doran, hugging myself, my teeth chattering again, though I wasn't cold any longer. "Is there still a stone circle in Ireland for him?"

"I know of the plain where Magh Slécht supposedly was, but there be no stone circle in the mortal world," Warwick replied. "A nearby village has a stone that the locals claim to be part of

Cromm's original statue, but it's quite large and round, like a giant's head."

I shook my head. "The thing I saw was smaller and flat. I thought it was some kind of tombstone at first. It was heavy enough that I could barely lift it."

Doran rested his chin on top of my head. "I know you're afraid of what you saw, love, but you must remember that *you* painted it. You saw something at the height of your magic before the changeling affected you. It was a message you left for yourself, not some trap you should fear."

"But what does it all mean?" I winced at the hint of a wail in my voice. "I don't understand what Cromm has to do with Evil Eye. Am I supposed to use that power somehow? But how can I if the twelve stones fell down? How do I help Vivi if the circle was destroyed? Boss Man said to come to Dún Bhalair, but I don't know where that is or how to get there."

Warwick snapped his fingers and a scroll appeared in his other hand. He spread it open on top of the island. Ivarr gave me a hand up and we all gathered around.

The scroll was an ancient-looking map of an island—Ireland, I assumed, though I sucked at geography.

"Today, it's known as Tory Island." Warwick pointed at a tiny dot off the north-western coast of Ireland. "Various groups fought over the island until Evil Eye rose in prominence and took control of it. Dún Bhalair means Balor's Castle. There are jagged cliffs on three sides, making it nearly impenetrable. The jagged stones are still called Saighdiúirí Bhalair, or Balor's Soldiers."

"Is the island inhabited?" I asked.

"Aye, to my knowledge. Pirates used the island for centuries. Today, the island isn't known as Dún Bhalair, so that's not where he wants us to go."

I pulled my phone out and Googled for pictures of the island. "He wants us to go to the Faerie equivalent."

"Fuck that shit," Aidan retorted. "He's damned near invincible on the mortal plane. Even if we can get into his realm in Faerie—which there's no guarantee even you or the leprechaun can pierce the veil to Dún Bhalair—there's no hope that we can defeat him in his own place of power."

"He's right," Warwick replied, shaking his head. "Think how hard it was for me to enter his warded place of power here. I fear even me gold oath wouldn't be strong enough for me to come to your aid in Faerie."

"I don't have a choice." I flipped through several pictures, getting a feel for what I needed to draw. "I'm going to get Vivi out, one way or the other."

Aidan closed his fingers over mine and forced the phone down to the island, trapping my hand beneath his. "Listen to me."

He didn't yell. He didn't curse. In fact, his voice was flat and devoid of emotion, making it all the more terrifying.

"If we go to Dún Bhalair, the best-case scenario is we all die in minutes of our arrival, including your friend. Worst case..." His jaws worked, his eyes flashing like slivers of glass. "We're prevented from entering with you. We die on this side of the veil, knowing that you need our assistance. Feeling what you feel. Hearing you scream. Feeling your pain. What the changeling did to you is nothing compared to what Evil Eye can do. Not even Warwick will be able to help you."

My vision swam with tears, my throat aching. "What choice do we have? Give me another option. A plan B, C, or D that we can try."

His fingers trembled on mine and his shoulders sagged with defeat. "At least slit my throat before you paint your way to Dún Bhalair."

"No," I whispered, shaking my head violently. "Never."

"Someone has to put me out of my misery before you die. I can't bear it, Riann. I won't."

25

AIDAN

I turned to the only hope that remained. "Doran, if you have any love and friendship left in your heart after all these lifetimes, I ask that you do me this one last favor. Kill me. Please."

Eyes sealed shut, I waited for steel to enter my body. I welcomed it. I needed it.

"Lad, you know that I love you like me own brother, and so I cannot kill you." Doran gripped my shoulder, squeezing hard enough my bones creaked and the muscle throbbed beneath his fingers. "You said yourself that she be fucking fae, and right you are. *Mo stór* will not die on us like the treasurekeepers who came before."

I gritted my teeth, quivering beneath his fierce grip. "So what you're saying is that Evil Eye will fucking torture her for all eternity rather than kill her outright. That's fucking great. I feel so much better."

Riann ducked beneath Doran's arm and wrapped her arms around my waist. "Look at me."

Sighing, I opened my eyes, not surprised to find her glaring up at me like a little fireball.

"No one's going to be tortured for eternity."

I feigned surprise, arching my eyebrows. "Oh? How's that? Pray tell me of this fucking brilliant plan you've concocted."

"He swore he wouldn't kill us."

"My fucking point exactly. It would be a blessing to be killed cleanly and quickly. He has something much worse planned for us."

"How have you defeated him before?" She turned to Doran. "You said you remembered chopping his head off before."

"Sacrifice," Doran replied.

She shook her head slowly. "I don't understand."

"Flip a fucking coin," I drawled. "Winner sacrifices himself first, creating a distraction for any of the dark fae that Evil Eye keeps nearby. Though I believe that time it took all three of us to buy you enough time to take his head."

"I went last." Ivarr nodded. "I was the reserve. Aidan and Keane waded through a wall of oilliphéists, hacking on all sides, bellowing and screaming a war cry to cover up the sound of Doran's wings. He swooped down at Evil Eye's head but one of the largest oilliphéists caught him in its jaws. I let loose my light to free him."

Doran chuckled. "If by 'let loose your light' you mean you fucking roasted yourself to a cinder, than aye, you freed me."

Face pale, she looked at Ivarr. "You... burned yourself? With your own light?"

Grinning, he shrugged. "If I pull too much power, I incinerate from the inside out. It was a hell of a way to go. I've never killed so many dark fae at once."

Doran slapped him on the back. "You even singed my wings off with the massive fireball. That's why I had to take Evil Eye's head—I couldn't hold the gargoyle form. Aidan tossed me his sword so I could finish the deed."

"I was already dead anyway." I regretted the words when she turned back to me, her eyes shimmering with unshed tears. "We always die, mo stór. Perhaps we should have been telling you all of these stories all along rather than spare you the gore so you know what to expect."

"But..." Her voice quivered, making me feel like dog shit. Especially when tears trickled down her lovely face. "Doesn't it hurt? Aren't you afraid to die like that? It sounds so horrible. Awful. It makes me want to scream and throw up and wail at the top of my lungs. I want to spare you that kind of agony."

Ever so gently, I wiped her tears away with the backs of my knuckles. "The only agony I care about is yours. I've died a million different ways already, and I'll do it all again a million times over, if only to save you. Dying is nothing."

"Not to me," she whispered raggedly.

I snagged her neck in the crook of my elbow and hauled her against my chest. "As long as I open my eyes to your face on the other side of the veil, then Evil Eye can do anything he wants to me. But I need to know you're safe or I'll go mad, Riann. You've not seen me fully out of my head, insane with rage and fear."

"She can always make a wish," Warwick said.

Jealousy and relief battled inside me, a swift, vicious war of emotion. I hated the leprechaun in that moment. He wouldn't die at Evil Eye's hands. He hadn't been doomed to return over and over to the mortal plane to die brutal deaths for humans who didn't even care. Immortal fae, he was powerful enough to walk into Evil Eye's wards and pluck Riann out from beneath his very nose.

Which wiped away the wave of jealousy. Gratitude welled up inside me, inside us all. We treasures couldn't guarantee her safety. Treasure magic was for war and killing, not penetrating Faerie. We hadn't been able to get her out of Fhroig's swamp. We wouldn't be able to get her out of Dún Bhalair either.

But the leprechaun had... and would again.

"Can you keep even Evil Eye out of the Summer Isle?" Doran asked.

Warwick tossed his head slightly, making the long fall of hair ripple about his shoulders. "I can indeed—unless me magic fails entirely. Queen Morgan herself restored me to full health and has promised that all the might of the High Court stands at my back. Though if we fail, and the Summer Isle joins the Windswept Moors at the bottom of the Land Beneath the Waves, at least Riann won't be at his mercy."

If all the powers of Faerie fell... I didn't know what the mortal plane would look like. Very likely the empty skeletons of her painting. Without us to keep the dark fae in check, they'd feast and ruin and destroy until there wasn't anything left. Best case, if we were killed and forced to return and continue this never-ending war, at least she'd be safe.

Silently, I held my hand out to him. Warwick closed his fingers around mine with a firm, unwavering grip. I didn't have to ask him to swear it on his gold. I could see the promise gleaming in his eyes.

She still had one wish remaining from his golden coin.

He was Riann's ticket to safety, and for that, I owed him my life. I would pay that debt gladly.

26

I still didn't have a fucking clue what we were going to do once we got there, but I was confident that I could get us to Tory Island. How we'd gain entrance into Dún Bhalair... well, we'd have to figure that out once we got there.

Warwick whisked my painting back to the Summer Isle for safe-keeping. Vivi said I used to wear the hag stone like a necklace, but it took us a while to find it. I must have dropped it when I fell backwards. Keane and Ivarr spent a good five minutes crawling around on the kitchen floor with me until we found it under the refrigerator on the other side of the room. Luckily it wasn't broken.

"Do you have a string I can thread through the hole?"

Warwick snorted and rolled his eyes. "The leprechaun delivery service can do far better than a string. Turn around and give me the stone, please."

I placed it in his palm and turned around, lifting up my hair.

He settled the stone around my neck—on a beautifully delicate gold chain. "I would have given you a thicker one coated in diamonds and emeralds, but I thought you might want to hide its existence from Evil Eye."

"It's perfect." I whirled around and laced my fingers behind his neck. "Thank you."

He leaned down and lightly rubbed his lips against mine in a soft, gentle kiss. "You might wish to wear a different shirt."

I glanced down at my front, not sure why he might care about my clothing. He'd never commented about what I wore, other than putting me in that sexy corset top I'd first worn to *Shamrocked*. The nicer sweater I'd worn to the police station had been streaked with mud, and I didn't want to wear something nice to battle. Especially if...

I forced that thought away. "What's wrong with it? This is my favorite shirt. Vivi got it for me as a graduation present."

It was just a slightly faded white T-shirt from the Hard Rock Cafe.

His lips quirked. "Absolutely nothing is wrong with it, though again, I thought you might wish to conceal your magic from Evil Eye."

"What magic? I'm not..."

A soft green light glowed beneath the thin white cotton T-shirt. I pried the neck away from me and looked down my shirt.

The green glittery splatters that Warwick had gifted on my breasts were glowing with magic, easily visible through the thin cotton. Blushing, I bit my lip. I hoped my nipples weren't prominent too but the more I thought about it, the harder they felt. "Um, maybe a hoodie instead. I'll go change."

Lightly, he dragged a finger down the side of my throat and the swell of my breast. "No need." His finger brushed over my nipple, making me gasp. "Your wish is my command."

I blinked and the scandalous T-shirt was replaced with a heavy green hoodie. A large dark-green shamrock covered the front with "Get lucked" in glittering gold letters. My tattoo—that I hadn't been able to get.

Warwick's lips quirked and he winked at me. "A message for Evil Eye, and also free advertising for *Shamrocked*. Can't beat a two-for-one deal. Plus it hides your hag stone quite well."

"Maybe I want to get lucked," Aidan said.

"Me too," Keane and Ivarr said at the same time.

"We all want to get lucked," Doran rumbled. "But first, we must end Evil Eye's reign of terror."

Ivarr elbowed Aidan. "What he means is we have to get Evil Eyed first."

Aidan rolled his eyes. "You idjit. That means he's Evil Eying *us*. Not the other way around."

"I've been meaning to ask about that," I started to say, raising my voice over their banter. "He's supposed to have a terrifying eye, right? Was that hidden beneath the Boss Man glamor?"

"Aye, the great eye was so massive that it took half a dozen men to hold the lid open," Keane said, immediately going into story-time mode. "His eye blasted whatever it saw, killing men and animals, withering the ground, sometimes bringing fire or poison, depending on the tale. But I can't say that I've ever seen this horrible eye of his."

"Even when I chopped off his head, I saw no terrible eye," Doran added. "I always assumed it was just a metaphor for his evil personality."

"Where did all the stories come from, then? There must be some truth behind it."

"Fomorians were sometimes associated with chaos and natural disasters," Warwick said. "As such, Balor's terrible eye could have been the sun. Burning out of control, it would certainly blight the land and kill through drought."

"I always thought he was more like a giant Cyclops with one horrible eye blasting from his forehead." I laughed self-consciously, shaking my head. "I guess I took 'Evil Eye' too literally."

"He's High Court fae," Warwick replied. "Like me—only even higher, older, and much more powerful. In my experience, the higher the fae, the more terrifyingly beautiful they be. Fae beauty be a dangerous thing indeed. I've never seen Evil Eye in his natural form, but I wouldn't expect him to have a giant head with a baleful glaring eye."

"Queen Morgan was beautiful, but not overwhelmingly so. Was she still wearing a glamor when I met her in the Summer Isle?"

"Of course. A High Court fae rarely exposes their true form."

Thinking, I absently touched the hag stone hidden beneath my clothes. Maybe if I looked at Evil Eye through the stone I would see his infamous eye. But would he even allow me to pull it out and look at him? Especially if High Court fae didn't like to expose their true forms. I blew out a sigh. "I guess in my head I always imagined that defeating Evil Eye would somehow involve putting out his horrible eye, or at least blinding it somehow. But if he's never revealed it, how do I trick him into showing us?"

Aidan's head whipped around to glare through the wall as if he could see outside the house. "Times up. If you want to take us to Tory Island, you'd best do some art shit now."

"What? Why?"

Something thudded against the covered sliding glass door. "They're here." Aidan positioned himself between me and the glass. "Time to go, *mo stór*, before the battle ends here and now."

Glowing softly, Ivarr closed his eyes a moment. A pulse of golden light radiated from him, and his face tightened. "They used the lake as a portal. They've got a whole host of creatures outside."

Something squeaked across the glass, making me think of the kelpie tentacles and suction cups. Thuds continued against the side of the house and now the roof. Yikes. Nothing like painting under pressure.

Already shifted to his gargoyle, Doran snagged my bag from the other room and sent it skidding across the floor to me. I whipped out the sketchbook and charcoal pencils. I didn't have time for watercolors. Hopefully a rough sketch would be good enough.

The jagged line of black rocks rose in my mind, looking like an old skeleton key. Angry waves dashed against the base of the peninsula stretching out into the ocean. I wasn't sure where the original castle was supposed to have stood, so I created my own smooth, flat landing spot that looked across a deep channel at the jagged rocks.

I looked up at Warwick, who'd already attached himself to my hip without a single word from one of the treasures. "Is that good enough to get us there?"

He glanced at my sketch but quickly pulled his attention back to the pounding overhead. "I recognize it as An Eochair Mhor, but it's more about your intention than anything else. Not to sound like a broken record but we must hurry. They've penetrated the house."

I scrambled to my feet and the guys backed up against me, forming a living shield. Staring down at the sketch, I tried to calm my breathing, but something roared, an awful cross between a Jurassic Park dinosaur and fingernails on a chalkboard. The shrieking roar made me flinch, a continuous sound of terror that made me want to cover my ears and find a place to hide.

"He released the Bocánaigh," Doran bellowed. "Work your magic, Riann!"

I had no idea what that was—and I sure as fuck didn't want to stick around and find out. I clutched the paper against my chest and closed my eyes. Intention. I wanted us away from here. Standing on a green hill, looking across the chasm at Balor's domain. I could see the dark, jagged stones rising up like teeth from the crashing waves below. Seagulls called overhead, not the sound of nightmares on the roof. I could smell the salty, fresh air, feel the cool breeze off the ocean—

A frigid blast of damp air slapped me across the cheeks, shaking me out of the vision. Wind whistled around us, tugging at my legs, though Doran's wide bulk protected me from the brunt of the gale. Rain pelted the top of my head and my cheeks.

Aidan raised his voice over the howling wind. "Of fucking course it be raining."

"It be Éire after all," Doran called back. "I don't suppose the leprechaun delivery service could rustle up a giant umbrella?"

"Working on it," Warwick said. "Or something better, I dare say. There."

A glittering net rose above us like a delicate lacy web, managing to block both the wind and rain and give us a moment to breathe and think.

I stepped up between Doran and Warwick to look at the distinctive spires jutting up out of the ocean. It didn't look like people could have ever lived there, though it would certainly be impenetrable.

Keane pointed to the rocks at the end of the line furthest out into the water. "Supposedly that's where Evil Eye locked his daughter, Eithne, in a tower to prevent the fulfillment of the prophecy that one of her children who'd grow up to kill him."

"Tor Mór," Warwick replied. "The High Tower."

"She had triplets, and Balor threw them into the sea. Only one survived."

"Lug of the Longarm," Aidan said.

"You're the Spear of Lug," I mused, trying to put the pieces of mythology together. Though perhaps in the end it didn't matter. In the stories, Balor may have been killed by Lug on the plain where Bres' pillars once stood—but Bres went on to be the changeling who'd tormented me, and Balor had been killing my treasures for thousands of years. "How did Lug kill him?"

"The stories vary." Aidan shrugged. "Some say Lug overheard Balor bragging about killing his father, and he simply pulled out a red-hot poker and shoved it through his horrible eye. Others say that Lug used a slingshot to kill him. The evil eye burned a crater into the ground and eventually turned into Lough na Súil, the Lake of the Eye."

"Like David and Goliath."

He shrugged again. "That's the problem with mythical stories. They usually share commonalities because they came from the same place or bore the same message, just told slightly differently by the people in that region."

We fell silent a moment, staring out at the remains of what might have been Balor's ancient fort. I could almost see the foundations of walls rising up from the cliffs. Hear the shout of soldiers on guard around the towers. A woman, leaning out over the treacherous seas below, sobbing for her babies and her lost lover.

"How do we get to Dún Bhalair from here?"

A man's chuckle echoed from everywhere and then Boss Man appeared, striding across the grassy hill toward us. "You're already here. Welcome to my home, treasurekeeper."

27

I barely got a look at him before Doran slid over in front of me. The four Irish treasures formed a solid wall around me. Doran bristled, his tail snapping side to side along the ground, his claws raking the earth. Aidan deliberately clashed his swords together. Keane flipped a switch on his flamethrower, ready to bathe the hill in fire. Already shining with pure, golden light, Ivarr slowly drew the massive broadsword that hung down his back over his shoulder in a long metallic rasp of warning.

Warwick's palm settled in the small of my back, ready to sweep me away to the Summer Isle.

Leaving my men to die.

:Don't you dare,: I whispered harshly.

He didn't answer me. I'd seen the way he and Aidan had shaken hands earlier. They expected to get me out at all costs, no matter what happened. *We'll see about that.*

"Now, now, Stoneheart, why the threats? I gave my word that I would not kill any of you."

"Aye, so you did, Evil Eye, though you gave no such promise for anyone else at your command."

I ducked beneath Doran's wing and stepped up beside him so I could see. Appearing as a very human-looking man, Sloan Archer stood before us as Boss Man, not the formidable Cyclops fae of legend. He wore an expensive-looking blue-gray suit and a deeper sapphire tie that brought out the brilliant blue of his eyes. His sandy brown hair was expertly styled in a modern wave across his forehead. Unlike Jonathan—who'd always seemed so desperate to make sure people realized how wealthy and successful he was—Boss Man didn't wear a gaudy watch or any jewelry.

"Where's Vivi?" My voice rang a little too shrilly, betraying my nerves.

"She's waiting for us inside."

My gaze flickered over toward the rocky strip where his castle had supposedly been, but it still looked the same to me. Inhabitable, rough cliffs and stone.

"Come now, my friends." He smiled, spreading his hands out, palm up, before him. "I know it's been a very long time, even for me, but I haven't forgotten the rules of hospitality. I welcome you to break your fast at my table."

:Wait, is this a trap?: I asked through our bonds. :Like Persephone getting trapped in the Underworld because she ate some pomegranate seeds?:

:I don't believe so,: Doran replied. :The rules of hospitality be clear. What do you think, Keane?:

:I'd be worried for regular humans consuming food or drink in Faerie, but not the treasurekeeper, let alone one who's fae herself.:

Despite his assurance, none of us moved.

Aidan growled through our bond. :Something smells fucking rotten and it's not a fucking fish.:

Yeah. Balor wanted something from us. From me. But what?

Giving a mental shrug, I decided to fuck around and find out. "I have a question first."

Boss Man gave me a wide smile. "Of course, lady, it would be my great pleasure to help in any way that I may, especially if it assuages your reluctance to enjoy Dún Bhalair's hospitality."

Giving him an equally wide—fake—smile, I pulled my hag stone out from beneath my shirt. I watched his face carefully, hoping he might betray himself somehow.

"Ah! A hag stone." He clapped his hands like a delighted child. "Now Dún Bhalair's full magnificence may be revealed to you. That makes my objective much easier."

"You don't mind if I look at you or your castle?" I asked suspiciously.

Boss Man ducked in an elegant, sweeping bow, though his eyes never left mine. "Be my guest, lady."

28

Staring at Boss Man, I lifted the hag stone to my eye. Staggering backward, I would have fallen without the guys around me.

Brilliance assaulted my senses. Blinded, tears streamed from my eyes. My ears rang like a massive gong hammered inside my head. My skin shredded beneath that majesty, zinging with a million tiny needles. Everything burned inside me, as if I'd swallowed the sun and burned from the inside out.

He wasn't an ugly one-eyed giant. He was the most brutally beautiful creature in all the worlds that had ever existed.

So fucking dangerous.

Beauty that wounded with a glance. Brilliance that punished and burned. I could only imagine what it would be like to touch him, or be touched by him. One innocent stroke of his finger would rock the foundations of the world and destroy time itself.

I cried in agony just looking at him. It hurt. So much. I couldn't even think, my mind blanked and broken beneath the onslaught of his gods-level power.

We had no hope of defeating him. None whatsoever.

He stepped aside, removing himself from my line of vision. I sobbed with relief, sagging against Doran and blubbering like a baby.

"What is it, love?" Doran rumbled, tucking me under his wing. "What has he done to you?"

"Absolutely nothing, Stoneheart," Boss Man replied. "I have only allowed her to see my true form."

Warwick's fingers dug into my back. Aidan growled a string of intelligible words in a language I didn't recognize, undoubtedly cursing to blue blazes. My fingers ached with cold but I kept the hag stone to my eye. I had to see. I had to know. There had to be a weakness. Somehow.

Without his brilliance destroying my senses, I could see a shimmering curtain similar to the net that Warwick had thrown up over us to keep out the rain and wind. However, this curtain had no end—it stretched upward as far as my human eyes could see.

Through that glittering veil, I saw Dún Bhalair in all its glory. Rather than rough, jagged stone, elegant towers and thick walls formed a massive castle that rose from the ocean like a jeweled crown. Massive sea monsters and kelpies the size of ocean liners swam in the waters around the castle. Winged dragons made slow, lazy circles over the grounds. Soldiers lined the walls, shining High Court fae and green hairy pookas and other creatures I couldn't identify.

Hundreds. Thousands. Weapons, teeth, and claws at the ready. Magic shimmered all around them, ready to fling at us if we so much as twitched. Tentacles curled up out of the ocean, thicker than sequoia trunks. It'd take the Slaughterer hours to hack through something that thick.

All the might of Dún Bhalair... against the *six* of us.

:*Do you see them?*: I asked Warwick, my mental voice small and shaking like a child waking from a nightmare.

:*In your mind, aye*,: he replied back just as softly. :*But to my eyes, it's still the rocky key. Remember the magic in your painting, love. The hag stone reveals magic—but that doesn't mean it's the truth.*:

I'd known this battle was hopeless. Even these mighty, legendary warriors with magical weapons hadn't been able to end the war against Evil Eye. I'd been so damned foolish and arrogant to think that I could do anything to change our fate. To save them.

To end this war once and for all.

My throat ached as I lowered the hag stone. I buried my face against Doran's side, unable to bear the sight of Balor's might.

"So now you see," Boss Man said in a kind, gentle voice. "Don't despair, lady. Come now, and see your dear friend. She's waiting for you."

I swallowed down the sobs threatening to tear out of my chest.

"Touch one hair on her head and your head is mine," Aidan growled.

Boss Man laughed, shaking his head. "I wouldn't dare, Slaughterer."

There was a sinister thread to his joviality. A snide edge, as if he was laughing at us. And why not? He'd already defeated them countless times through the ages. Why should this time be any different?

Eyes closed, surrounded by more love than I'd ever thought possible, magic rippled through me. The brilliant, spinning wheel waited in my mind, ready to serve as the conduit for treasure and leprechaun magic.

Plus my magic. I'd painted us here. I'd left clues from my parents—before I'd even known them as such—in my painting. Warwick brought the full might of Queen Morgan's court. Vanta's purr thundered in my head. The mightiest heart pounded beneath my ear, a steady, formidable drum of honor and love.

I sank deeper into those comforting sounds, and just let go.

All my fears and doubts. My dread and desperate agony at the thought of losing even one of my men. My dismal childhood. My worry for Vivi. Sinking deeper within myself, my breathing steadied and slowed. Deeper into the quiet darkness of my innermost mind, something gleamed. A hint of gold against the darkness.

For a moment, I stood on the dark plain again, only this time I stared into shining fiery gold eyes. The tombstone-sized stone was now as tall as me, and the carving a better representation of a man with distinct features. He didn't smile or speak but his eyes burned with a steady promise that sparked inside me.

Rage.

All the times I'd been silenced, hurt, and manipulated by Jonathan's abuse and lies. The horrible ways Vanta and the treasures had died, sacrificing themselves over and over. Burning themselves up. Losing their heads. Loving and dying, over and over and over, for a world that didn't even care.

So much pain and death and for what? No fucking reason whatsoever. Darkness still won. Balor always regrouped and came away stronger than ever. More monsters roamed the world, feasting and ravaging with no consequences.

No more. The god had awoken, and he wanted justice. He wanted blood.

If it meant Balor died—and my men lived—then I would find a way to give him exactly what he wanted.

Blinking away the vision, I lifted my head from Doran's side. My chin came up. My shoulders straightened. The wheel inside me began to spin, weaving all our gifts together, though this time, I had something new to add to the magic flowing through me.

Black velvety shadows, a parting gift of death from my father.

I'm the motherfucking treasurekeeper of the Irish treasures. Daughter of Étain, the Shining One, and Crouching Darkness, Cromm Crúaich, head of the gods.

I will have justice. Justice for the world, for my men, and for me.

29

A t the edge of the cliff, a shimmering bridge arched across to Dún Bhalair. Even without the hag stone, it looked like a giant, clear bubble, transparent but also reflecting pearly light. Without hesitation, Boss Man stepped out onto the fragile-looking bridge and then paused, looking back at us expectantly with a challenging glint in his eyes.

I tried not to think about the fall down a jagged, rocky cliff into angry waves and tentacles if he changed his mind and let the bridge disintegrate into thin air. My stomach quivered and I gripped Doran's arm in a white-knuckled hold as we started across. *Don't look down.*

Something thwacked against the bottom of the bridge, rocking the entire delicate structure. An embarrassingly high-pitched squeal escaped my lips. Oh shit. Tentacles that could reach up that high…

What was it, forty feet? Further? I sucked at estimating distances. But the motherfucker had to be some kind of mythical kraken to grow so big.

"Forgive my guardians." Boss Man laughed. "They're overly enthusiastic at the prospect of having guests. It's been so long."

:*Guests my ass,*: Aidan growled. :*He means they're starving to death because he hasn't thrown anyone into the sea in the past couple of hundred years.:*

:*We'll be but a wee snack for them,:* Ivarr replied. :*Even Doran.:*

:*They'll find me a tough, grisly bone that sticks in their craw,:* Aidan fired back.

As we neared the opposite side, I could see a faint shimmer in the air. Without the hag stone, it looked like tiny, glistening dewdrops. My brain chittered nervously with a thousand questions. What would happen to us once we passed through? Would it prevent us from getting out? What would it feel like? Why didn't *Shamrocked* have that kind of curtain protecting it from the mortals who might stumble inside?

:*That I can answer,:* Warwick replied. :*Me pub sits half in the mortal realm, and half in Faerie. Thus there's no visible veil to pierce. I wanted you to be able to walk inside if you were so drawn, but I had to change the wards once the changeling found me. Evil Eye created this boundary himself, likely as a show of his power. He melded Dún Bhalair with the physical site on the mortal plane rather than transporting us to Faerie. There's no fae boundary to cross.:*

:*But I saw it through the hag stone. Was it still just some kind of glamor?:*

:*Aye, a glamor of a glamor, fae magic at work. You saw the magic—as he wanted you to see it. It's not actually in Faerie, though he might wish you to think so. What you saw was nothing more than a glamored copy of the real Dún Bhalair.:*

:*That doesn't make a bleedin' lick of sense,:* Doran replied. :*He must know you'd tell us it be naught but glamor. The danger is less if we're not actually stepping into Faerie, and his power be limited here. Why would he do that?:*

It dawned on me that Doran could actually hear Warwick's answers in my head. I didn't think that had ever happened before. Evidently I was becoming the conduit for more than just magical workings, which I guess made a ton of sense after all the sex we'd shared.

:*I don't think he expected me at all,:* Warwick answered. :*A leprechaun was never part of his plans. Why else would he go to such an elaborate ploy to get Riann into a position to need his assistance with the human police? He meant to lure her in before she knew what he was. Having a fae walk into his headquarters changed everything. He may appear to be as confident as ever, but you've already shaken him, love. Keep him reeling and off balance as much as you can.:*

Boss Man swept his arm to the side, carrying the shimmering veil aside. "Welcome to Dún Bhalair."

:He didn't want you to touch it since it's not the actual veil,: Warwick said.

:If I think it's real, then I'll believe that we can't get out,: I said. *:Like Fhroig's lair.:*

:Exactly.:

I dug in my heels, giving Boss Man a wary look. "What do you always say about Faerie, Aidan?"

"Faerie be a fucking dangerous place." He spat over the side of the bridge. "Naught but trickery and illusion."

Boss Man nodded. "Aye, so it is, but aren't you weary of fae trickery and illusion? How can we come to an agreement if we don't even talk through our options?"

Aidan snorted. "Sure now, are you planning on dismembering us first or merely tossing us into the sea for your creatures' enjoyment? Or did you have some other option on the table? I'm all ears."

"Ah, Slaughterer, we would make better friends than enemies, don't you agree?"

"So it's hospitality you offer us," Keane drawled, patting his stomach. "I could definitely eat and drink."

Boss Man inclined his head. "My table is yours, Cauldron, though I'm sure my feast is nowhere near as great as yours be."

"You heard the man." Doran slapped Ivarr on the back and grinned down at me. "Time to eat, love."

More than a little bewildered, I nodded and allowed him to lead me through the parted veil into Dún Bhalair. I glanced back at Boss Man, not surprised that I couldn't see him through Aidan, Warwick, and Keane, who'd formed a wall at my back. On this side, the veil appeared to be a milky opal, blocking the view outside.

:*A sure sign that we're not in Faerie,*: Warwick said. :*If we'd truly stepped into Dún Bhalair, you wouldn't see the veil, just as you didn't see it in Fhroig's lair. It's an alternate dimension, a place that you can only reach through magic or clear intention.*:

Without the hag stone, I couldn't see the shining magic that made up the glamor—only the illusion that Boss Man wanted us to see. Fine white marble covered every surface of the castle walls and floor, giving the place a luxurious yet sterile feeling. Unlike Warwick's home, there were no flowers or magical plants. Colors and sounds didn't assault my senses. Though if I'd never been to the Summer Isle, I might have been convinced that this place was in Faerie.

Everything was too perfect and ostentatious, I decided as we neared a long table set with gold place settings. A whole roasted pig dominated the center of the table, but the entire surface was laden with food. Dishes I couldn't recognize. Pitchers of ales, bottles of wine, loaves of bread, fruits from all over the world. A feast, right?

But my mouth didn't water. Nothing smelled as delicious as what Keane had made for me in our kitchen at home. Even shepherd's pie, which he'd insisted was a simple dish, had been orgasmically good. On the surface, everything on the table looked fine, though it didn't tantalize my senses. The more I looked at the dishes, though, the less appetizing they were. The fruit was too ripe, approaching squishy or even rotten. I couldn't tell what kind of meat or vegetables were in the biggest pot of stew. Which unfortunately made me remember Keane's tale about Cúchulainn.

My stomach quivered. I didn't know that I could eat a single bite, even if my life depended on it.

Glamor, again. A fake feast.

I could only hope it wasn't our last.

KEANE

I SHOOK MY HEAD IN DISBELIEF AT THE SO-CALLED FEAST HE'D LAID OUT for us. This was insultingly bad, even for Evil Eye.

"The food isn't to your liking?" Chuckling, he sat down at the head of the table. "I know it's not a cauldron-level feast but I freely offer food and drink to my guests. Be welcome at my table."

To keep Riann as far away from him as possible, Doran sat her at the opposite end of the table. Warwick and Doran sat on either side of her, the first line of defense, while Aidan and Ivarr took the next seats. Leaving me to choose whether to sit on Evil Eye's left or right hand. Both seats would leave me looking at one of the suckling pig's bulging eyes, which seemed alarmingly alive and aware.

:This feast be a trap,: I warned the others in case they hadn't seen through the glamor.

:It doesn't even smell good,: Riann replied. :What is it?:

:You don't want to know.: Aidan replied grimly.

Evil Eye smiled down the table at her, by all appearances just a successful businessman making a deal. "Once you're finished, I'll ask my lovely assistant to join us."

"What do you want with Vivi?"

"Why, nothing, lady. She's free to go now that you're here."

"Great. Send her home, then."

"Have your treasures told you about the importance of hospitality?"

She nodded. "Keane has told me some very interesting stories."

"I'm sure." He smiled at me, making my skin crawl. "The might of a king is told through his hospitality, true. But also, if guests refuse to partake of their host's offerings, it's considered a grave offense."

She met my gaze and grimaced. "I understand now."

"What have you come to understand, lady?" Evil Eye asked.

"As you said, the importance of hospitality. This, I'm afraid, is not a feast. In fact, it's not even close."

Aidan pushed his chair back, kicked his legs up, and planted his boots carelessly on top of his place setting. The crystal glass shattered and silverware toppled to the floor. "This is going to be good."

Evil Eye's face darkened. "This is beyond insulting, even for you, Slaughterer."

Throwing his head back, Aidan bellowed out a laugh that rang through the fake hallway. "You haven't seen anything yet."

Riann made a big show of picking up the nearest pitcher and sniffing the ale. Her lips curled with distaste, and she set it aside. "And I thought dining with Bres was bad."

Evil Eye leaned forward. "Who was that you said?"

"Oh. You didn't know? My ex-husband, Jonathan Blake, was actually Eochu Bres. He could have learned a thing or two about hospitality from Keane as well."

"So he was indeed a changeling. How interesting. And you, lady, I find you quite... intriguing. How did you stay alive for so long? Five years, if I remember correctly. That's a long time to be at the mercy of someone like Bres. His appetite must have been..." He paused, his lips curling in a cruel smile. "Painful."

She didn't try to hide her reaction. Her eyes tightened and her cheeks paled. Even after experiencing love at our hands, she drew inward on herself at the slightest memory of her former husband. A silent flinch that spoke of unspeakable trauma and hurt that would never completely go away.

Fury crawled through my veins, marching fire ants blazing with poison. I wanted to punish him for those words. For making her remember such unpleasantness and misery.

"He destroyed everything," she said, her voice quivering faintly. "But I'm stronger now than ever. As foul as he was, even he wouldn't have expected me to eat such revolting food."

Indeed, the longer we sat here, the viler the food became. Maggots squirmed in the fruit. The trussed pig twitched and made a faint cry that chilled my blood. That didn't sound like an animal's sound. :That's not a pig, and it's alive.:

Riann stiffened in her seat, her eyes flashing like crystalline daggers. :Is it Vivi? Oh god.:

I searched the pig's eye, trying to tell if it was her friend. Evil Eye's goal was to allow the glamor to slowly reveal its true horror to us, though I wasn't sure what his game was yet. *:I can't be sure. He wants something from you, and she's his only bargaining chip. I don't know that he would put her on display so close, let alone in such a distressing way.:*

:He fucking loves it,: Aidan retorted. *:He loves to watch the suffering unfold. The agony of trying to save someone you love, and knowing...:*

His mental voice broke, and quite honestly, I feared his mind as well.

:That there's no hope,: he finished hoarsely. *:None whatsoever. The agony never ends.:*

I'd known that he suffered intense guilt all these centuries after Doran had been captured. But I hadn't realized exactly how personal Evil Eye had made that defeat for him. To lose our beloved leader was one thing, but to also lose the treasurekeeper they'd both loved at the time... To pit one love against another, and fucking relish the unfolding agony and despair as Aidan tried to save them both and failed. Utterly.

"It's so much better when love is involved." Evil Eye sat back in his chair with a glass of wine, grinning around the table at us. "Don't you agree, Slaughterer?"

"What do you want?" Riann asked, cutting off whatever Aidan might have said.

"I want my guests to enjoy my hospitality. Otherwise, well, lady, dire things happen when the rules of hospitality are violated. Honestly, I hoped to see who would win the curadmír."

"What's that?"

He gave her a slow, sly smile that confirmed my worst fear. "The best cut of meat from the table. I've prepared such a lovely suckling pig for my guests. Who'll take the haunch?"

Riann pushed to her feet. Rainbows began to spin around her, though I wasn't sure that she was consciously drawing her magic. "I will."

30

K eane rose to his feet so quickly that his chair tumbled
backward. "No, Riann. You can't do this."

If there was any chance at all that Vivi lay trapped in that pig, I was
going to get her out. Whatever it took.

"Be my guest." Boss Man practically oozed with smug glee. As if he
thought I was too stupid to understand what he'd done to my best
friend. Or maybe he thought I wouldn't challenge him. I wouldn't try
to save her. Or, more likely, he *wanted* me to try and save her—so he
could watch me fail.

But I wasn't going to fail. Not this time.

Rage simmered hotter, fueling the gleaming wheel of magic that
spun in my mind. Golden treasure magic hummed to a fevered pitch,
desperate to be used. Emerald green sparked through the golden
strands, taking our power to a whole new level. Nothing that
compared to Evil Eye's power, but more than the treasures had ever
pulled before.

Not to mention *my* magic. I could see it now, the dark velvet
ribbons winding through the wheel. My love of all things gothic and
strange, shadows with faces and tentacles closing in. I wasn't scared of
that darkness, because there were also strands of rainbow light

dancing across the canvas. Brushstrokes of hope and love, as delicate as a dragonfly's wings.

A painting without darkness and shading was flat and one-dimensional. I needed the shadow for distance and depth. To make the highlights shine all the brighter and bring the image into perfect focus.

I poured all my heartache and loss into the power streaming through the wheel. My frustration and anger at myself for falling for Jonathan in the beginning. For staying in a horrible marriage, unable to break out of his trap for five fucking years. My inner child, aching loneliness, suffering that horrible feeling of never fitting in or belonging. Never accepted because I was too weird and strange.

The child who'd lain awake at night and wondered why the people who were supposed to love her didn't care about her at all. Vivi had been my dragonfly then, my only ray of light in this dark, miserable world. I would do anything to save her.

I walked over to stand between Keane and Warwick. A giant butcher knife lay on the table, waiting for whoever claimed the prized cut of meat.

Aidan dragged his boots off the table, thumping his feet down so hard the entire table rattled. "You offer hospitality. Fine. I'll eat every last motherfucking crumb on this table as long as you let Riann take her friend and leave."

"Ah, now that's very tempting, Slaughterer. Very tempting indeed. Perhaps you haven't taken a long enough look at the delicacies I've prepared for you."

Aidan flicked a wriggling maggot off the tablecloth. "I've looked. It's all shite and I'll eat it anyway. Just let them go."

"Now why would I consider letting the most powerful treasure-keeper you've ever called to your side go free, when she could do so much more for me?"

I picked up the butcher knife, surprised at how heavy it was. It felt more like one of Aidan's swords. "We had a deal, Evil Eye. I came to you willingly. I even brought the treasures with me. All I ask is that you allow Vivi to return to her home unharmed."

"I say again, lady, all will be granted once the rules of hospitality are fulfilled."

"Remember what I said about Warwick before we came to an agreement?" Aidan asked casually.

I nodded, a wry smile quirking my lips. "You said that I'd been lepre*conned*."

He gave me a startling wide smile, his blue eyes shining like brilliant sapphires. "I refuse to let you be Evil Eyed. Not on my watch."

Boss Man clapped slowly, a mockery of amusement. "Good show, Slaughterer. So sweet and touching. Yet again, I must express my doubts about your sincerity to uphold the rules of hospitality. None of you have even taken a bite of the feast I've prepared for you."

"Well, then, I should get busy carving that pig." At my words, the poor thing quivered, increasing the sinking weight of dread and horror in my stomach. Whether it was Vivi or not, the animal was still alive, even though it looked like a crispy, roasted pig down to the rosy apple in its mouth.

My men all stood, thickening the tension in the air. Deadly weapons at the ready, they hovered in my mind, one whisper away from drawing blade and fighting to the death. Warwick pressed against my back, though he didn't wrap his arms around me. One slight misstep and he'd whisk me away to the Summer Isle. The treasures would die fighting around this table of nightmares, and I would never see Vivi again.

:*I need to see through the glamor but I don't want Boss Man to know what I'm doing before it's too late,:* I whispered to Warwick.

: *I'll bring the hag stone to your right eye at your word.*:

To the treasures, I said, :*Create a diversion.*:

"Ye bleedin' idjits!" Doran roared, slinging his chair aside so hard it exploded into a pile of kindling. "I'm the greatest warrior at this table. The curadmír is mine!"

"I don't need to draw the Sword of Light to cut through that lie," Ivarr yelled back.

Keane hopped up on top of the table, flamethrower on his hip. "I'll roast you all back to Tír na nÓg."

:Now.:

Warwick pressed the hag stone to my eye. Magic billowed all around me, cascading translucent rivers that showered us with brilliant sparks. I avoided looking at anything except the table directly in front of me, though I had to blink several times to focus my eyes. There was so much magic involved in this so-called feast. I had to pull back thick layers one by one like an onion, each layer tougher. Nastier. Like trying to wipe away sludge that blended to feces to something even worse.

Crispy pig skin flickered to red hair. I leaned closer, running my hand over her, helping to break the illusion. Vivi lay on her stomach, appropriately hogtied, with an apple gagging her. Her makeup had smeared and run all over her face from her tears, but as far as I could tell, she was unharmed, at least physically. I slipped the tip of the heavy blade beneath the ropes binding her wrists to her ankles. As soon as I got one hand free, she reached up and yanked the apple out of her mouth.

Sobbing, she scrambled up toward me. Dropping the hag stone back against my chest, Warwick helped me get her down off the table. I pressed her behind me, holding the knife up before me.

Keane kicked the strange floppy meat sack that had disguised Vivi off the table. "No one has left your table satisfied, Evil Eye. Thus there has been no hospitality. You failed."

Lounging in his chair at the head of the table, Boss Man somehow still managed to look amused. "Such a shame, Cauldron. I could have accomplished much with your magic. And you, mighty Sword of Light. Even the darkest fae can make use of the gift of truth."

"Only when it serves you, twisted and corrupted to your cause," Ivarr replied. "You can't face my truth. That's why you always make sure I die before I get too close."

"Indeed, you all die so easily. It's become rather boring. I had such high hopes this time around. After all, you have a treasurekeeper finally worthy of the magic that first brought you together. Do you even know what you are yet, sweet Riann?"

I grimaced at the fake sugary sweetness in his voice. It was almost as bad as when Jonathan had called me honeybun. "I do."

He shook his head. "I think not, or you wouldn't be standing here debating the life of one pitiful human, four washed-up warriors who've lost every battle they've faced in thousands of years, and one greedy leprechaun who can't see beyond the glint of his gold."

"I beg your pardon." Warwick sniffed loudly and tossed his head, making his hair flutter about us. "Aidan could definitely use a bath, but I think about quite a lot of things other than gold."

Aidan grunted. "Like how good it was to treasure *mo stór* on top of your bar."

"Exactly," Warwick replied in unison with the other treasures.

I laughed, keeping my voice light as I backed Vivi further away from the table. "Well, you are pure gold in your pants."

"I weary of this game," Boss Man said with a sharper edge to his voice.

"So do I," I shot back. "It's time for you to keep your word."

He chuckled, but it wasn't a sound of amusement. The harsh tone jangled my nerves, making me wince deep inside. As if I'd accidentally bitten down on a piece of metal on a raw nerve. Chills raced down my arms and my hands trembled.

"My word? You want me to keep my word? Are you quite sure, treasurekeeper?"

The edge of his laughter cut sharper, deeper, increasing that sense of wrongness and raw twinges of nerve pain through my body. "Yes, I want you to keep your word. You said if I came to Dún Bhalair that you would explain everything. You wouldn't kill us, and you would let Vivi go."

"I never said that she would be free to go. I promised that Viviana would remain unharmed."

"Do you call being bound on the table like a roasted pig waiting for someone to cut you open unharmed?" I retorted.

He huffed out another vicious laugh that stole my breath like a slap of icy wind. "*I* would not have been the one to harm her, so I am absolved of any harm that may befall her. You disappoint me, trea-surekeeper. I thought you would be more intellectually challenging."

"Same, actually."

His laughter cut off and his eyes narrowed. "Perhaps I was wrong. Perhaps you're as big a fool as Slaughterer."

I nodded, inclining my head toward Aidan. "I count that as a compliment, but you're the fool, Evil Eye. Did you think we wouldn't see through your thinly-veiled hospitality ruse? How about that so-called *veil* you so carefully parted for us? Or the giant, tacky, very fake replica castle you call home?"

He shrugged and flashed a magnanimous smile of too-sharp teeth. "So you've passed a few of my tests. I assure you that there are many more ahead."

"Enough." Doran's voice thundered. "You've taunted us long enough. Allow the women to leave and let the battle begin."

"There won't be a battle this time, Stoneheart. You're free to go."

Doran dropped his hand on my shoulder, his claws digging into my skin through the sweatshirt. "I don't go anywhere without her."

"Fine with me." Boss Man stood and gave a tug on his suit jacket to smooth it. "You're welcome to attend, all of you. I don't mind whatso-ever. In fact, that makes everything so much easier."

I didn't like the way Boss Man looked at me and then Vivi. A kind of greasy, oily stare that made me feel ill.

"I worked for you for years," she cried, whimpering and hiccup-ping with choked sobs. "I poured myself into the job, helping you win. Building the business. 'Burn that midnight oil,' you'd tell me, and I did. At the cost of my friendship and my life. The cost—"

Her voice caught on an aching inhale as she finally understood. "You betrayed me. You used me. All along."

His head tipped slightly to the side. "I did. I am. Be glad that I had a use for you that didn't involve tossing you into the darkest pits beneath Dún Bhalair."

Her shoulders quivered, her arms wrapping around my waist in a fierce hug. "I'm so sorry, Ri."

I patted her hand. "I'm sorry that I left you behind. Go home and live the happiest of lives with Hammer, okay?"

She squeezed me harder. "What about you?"

:I wish—:

"Don't you fucking dare!" Aidan roared, swinging around toward me with both swords over his head.

:That Viviana is safe in the Summer Isle until she can return home to her happy life.:

Warwick sucked in a harsh breath and then whispered, "Granted."

And Vivi disappeared.

31

AIDAN

Red. Everything dripped blood, painted and coated and burned. I slammed my blades against the table with all my force, cracking it in half. Broken cutlery and disgusting dishes of moldy, rotten food slid onto the floor. I hacked at the table again and again, breaking it into smaller pieces. Then the chairs. The walls. I slammed my fists into the stone, tearing them apart. Heaved giant blocks over my shoulder. Off the rocky cliff. It didn't matter.

Nothing mattered.

Hands jerked at me, but they couldn't stop me. *Once I'm revealed, there's no escape. Even from myself.*

I had enough sense remaining not to turn the weapons on the ones who loved me, but not enough will to stop fighting and destroying everything in my path. I burned to kill and rage out of control. I ran toward the edge of the cliff, determined to throw myself into the sea so I could attack the water guardians of Dún Bhalair.

Talons tore into my skin, a massive mountain crushing me to the ground. Refusing to let me leap out over the cliff.

"Don't hurt him," Riann cried.

Oh, but I wanted to be hurt. I needed to be hurt. I needed to die. Now.

Before I had to watch what Evil Eye would do to her.

"Be still, lad," Doran growled in my ear. "You're scaring her."

I couldn't. Wouldn't. Blades sliced in my mind. I roared and bellowed out my rage. Slammed my head down into the ground, tasting blood. Wishing he would twist a little harder and yank my head clean off.

"Aidan." Her voice was close. Too close.

I didn't want to hurt her, but I couldn't stop flailing. Fighting. I had to find something that could kill me. Now. :*Please.*:

Teeth sank into my shoulder, locking me against solid granite and concrete. I couldn't breathe. I couldn't move. Something held my arms down. My legs. Blackness threatened because I couldn't draw breath. Good. I welcomed it. I flung myself headfirst toward infinity.

Her hand on my cheek. Her fingers stroking over my jaw. Droplets fell on my face like gentle rain, though they tasted salty.

"I'm sorry," she pleaded, her voice quivering with anguish. "Please forgive me."

Forgive her? For what? For existing? For loving me when no one else would or could? For becoming my whole world, my entire existence? My own personal hell?

Because to lose her would be the ultimate punishment. I could bear anything. Anything but that.

"Let. Me. Die."

"Never," she whispered, pressing her lips to my forehead.

I was broken apart, a wrecked, damaged heap of worthless bits of flesh and bone. Nothing could hold me together any longer. Not without her. She was the sinew and muscle that connected me into a functional, rational man. She connected us all, the conduit that brought selfish, violent, heartless men with a thirst and unlimited capacity for killing—to our fucking knees so we could worship her.

"I need you too much."

Her words found one small, solid bit that had managed to hold together, and broke it too. A sound tore out of me. Wordless. Hopeless. Agony.

She smoothed her hands over me, kissing my face, her tears wet on my skin. "I know. I'm so sorry. I love you, Aidan. Come back to me, just for a little while. I need you. I need the asshole back. The grumpy, take-no-shit, leave-no-prisoners badass motorcycle guy. Tell me to go luck myself. Threaten to beat my ass with your belt. Growl and stomp and curse and kiss me senseless again. Please. I need you."

The melody of her soft voice. The stroke of her fingers like butterfly wings. The gentle shower of her tears. Rough rock against my other cheek, abrading my skin. A knee in my back. Teeth in my shoulder, gripping the muscle hard enough it convulsed and quivered. The red haze slowly parted, dissipating like morning fog beneath the force of her shining love.

"I'm here," she crooned. "I love you."

I blinked, shaking my head a little to clear the vicious mire clogging the rational side of my brain. The side that knew there was nothing we could do. No escape. We were going to die. Fine. Great. But...

She would die too.

My brain stuttered, flinching away. I didn't mind dying—but I couldn't bear to watch her suffer.

:I'm not going to die,: she retorted sharply in my mind. *:Neither are you. None of us are dying today. Do you hear me?:*

:My fucking skull feels like a motherfucking shattered eggshell but aye, I hear you just fine.:

Her joy swept through my mind, relief like rapid hummingbird wings, love shining like Ivarr's light of truth. *:I have a plan.:*

I made a sound again, trying for my trademark grunt, but it came out rather anemic. Truth be told, it sounded more like a whimper, not that any of them dared tell me so.

:My thoughts exactly,: Doran replied. *:Sorry for the bite. It was the only way I could get you under control.:*

The mountain lifted off me. Keane and Ivarr each took an arm and heaved me up to my feet. I wavered like a drunk between them, too dazed to even worry about Evil Eye.

She tucked herself up against me, squeezing her arms around me fiercely, glaring up at me even though her eyes shimmered with tears. "I thought I lost you."

"I would die for you," I answered automatically. No hesitation or question in my heart.

"I know," she whispered against my lips, brushing her mouth back and forth. "But I don't want you to die. I want you to live."

I heaved out a sigh. "It would have been fucking easier to die."

HEART SHREDDED INTO RIBBONS, I WATCHED AS AIDAN PUT HIMSELF back together. Stack by stack, brick by brick, he rebuilt the thick concrete walls around his heart. He'd given me the key to reach him, so I wasn't worried that he would lock me out. He needed the wall, even if there was a heavy iron door he'd built just for me. It was as much a part of him as the leather jacket and the dual set of swords.

Holding both blades, Warwick stepped closer and offered them to him.

Grim, Aidan stared back at him, his face drawn and hollowed as if he'd been suffering a long illness. Accusation and fury flickered through his eyes like fleeting thunderstorms. He'd never liked the leprechaun much, and certainly hadn't trusted him in the beginning. He'd been counting on Warwick to be my ticket to safety with my last wish. I knew what they'd planned, but they had to know my heart as well.

Never in a million years would I have been able to leave them behind to die.

Gruffly, Aidan reached out and took his swords. "I guess we're all fucked then."

"I guess so," Warwick replied lightly. "Though I think *mo stór* has more to say on the matter."

"*Mo stór?*" Boss Man threw his head back and laughed. "That's what you call her? How original, Prince of the Summer Isle. Did you honestly think they'd allow you to make her your princess?"

"I have no such designs on the treasurekeeper. I am but a hapless bartender who kept a gargoyle statue on the shelf in his pub until his treasurekeeper could find and free him."

"And you just happened to find his gold, *mo stór?*" Boss Man turned their endearment into a sneer. A joke. His lips curled with distaste.

Maybe some of Aidan's rage still burned in my veins because it was all I could do not to charge over and stab my finger into Boss Man's chest. "Don't you dare call me that."

His contempt shifted toward mocking delight, as if he was relieved that I would be providing him a little more entertainment after all. "What did your dear husband call you, Mrs. Blake?"

My stomach churned. "None of your fucking business."

"What happened to him, if you don't mind me asking?"

"I'll answer your question if you answer one of mine."

He thought a moment and then nodded. "Agreed. One question each will be answered by us both."

"No delays, no funny business."

Still amused, he nodded, trying to give me a disarming, human grin. "Of course, lady."

"I wished him to Fhroig's lair."

Boss Man's eyes widened. "Fhroig? How did you even know such a place existed?"

I batted my eyes and gave him back a fake, sugary smile. "That's a second question. Do you want to bargain for another?"

Perhaps he was still pretending to have human mannerisms, but he huffed out an annoyed breath and shook his head. "No, no, just curiosity. Very well, lady. What's your question for me?"

"They call you Balor of the Evil Eye."

One eyebrow raised quizzically, he tipped his head to the side. Pretending disinterest, I fiddled with Aidan's jacket, brushing at the scuff marks in the leather. Rubbing my finger lightly over the punctures where Doran had bitten him. I slipped my hand beneath the coat and found Aidan's shoulder sticky with blood, though he didn't react in pain when I touched it.

"They say it was such a terrible eye that it would destroy everything it looked at. It was so huge it took several men to hold the eyelid open. Yet strangely enough, my treasures can't recall seeing this massive eye. Only the fairytales and ridiculous folktales."

"And?" He prodded. "What is your question, lady, if you will?"

I turned to face him, watching his reaction. "What is the Evil Eye of your name?"

I thought he'd be annoyed or shaken or surprised. At least insulted that none of us even knew what this supposedly terrible eye actually was.

Instead, his shoulders relaxed and he nodded. "I thought you'd never ask."

32

"Right you are." Boss Man swept his arm out to indicate the castle around us. "This is only a replica of Dún Bhalair, a shadow of its full glory in Faerie."

The air shifted. My ears rang with a heavy gong that went on and on, the sound stretching out over an endless distance. The white marble halls disappeared, leaving us standing on a rocky hilltop. Wind tore around the hill, whistling through the towering spires of jagged rock, tugging on my clothes so hard that I staggered back against Doran.

Thick, cold, and wet, the air smelled like salt and something else. A musky, fishy smell that ruffled the hairs on the back of my neck. Something my lizard brain recognized as a predator, or at least dangerous.

:Now we be in Faerie,: Warwick said.

Indeed, the opaque barrier that had surrounded the white marble castle was gone. Endless gray skies arched overhead, meeting storm-gray angry seas. Waves thundered against the cliffs, adding bass to the steady roar of wind. The same dark, rocky spines rose like jagged teeth, An Eochair Mhor, the key. There was a raw, wild, natural elemental beauty to this place, untouched by any mortals. What Tory Island might have been like at the time of its creation.

Balor snapped his fingers and the winds and waves died, leaving behind an unnatural silence that throbbed in my ears. "This be the eye for which I am named."

Confused, I looked at him first, though his appearance hadn't changed. I turned in a slow circle, looking up at the sky, the rocks, down at the ground. Nothing resembled an eye, let alone a giant, destructive orb of legend and myth. "I don't understand."

"You thought my eye would be a huge red orb flaming atop the spire?" He laughed, shaking his head. "Only in movies, lady. Even your hag stone cannot reveal my eye unless I allow it."

Not sure that I wanted to look, I wrapped my fingers around the hag stone. He mentioned it for a reason, so I distrusted what I would see. He'd already proven that he could lay glamor on top of glamor to hide the truth.

Truth.

Of course. I turned my gaze toward Ivarr. Eyes shining like burnished golden coins, he nodded and stepped closer, offering me his hand. His truth would always shine.

I lifted the hag stone to my eye. Thick, milky fog billowed around us, concealing the ground and the ocean below, softening the brutal rocky edges with puffy clouds. Wisps stretched up from the billowing layer, crawling up our legs like ghostly vines. Shivering, I resisted the urge to shake my foot free of the clinging mist. I couldn't feel it touching me, so I wasn't sure that it was real.

A rich, golden glow brightened beside me, a halo that burned brighter, surrounding both me and Ivarr. In that light, the fog still flowed and swirled around us.

It was real, then. Not just a glamor.

The brighter light seemed to call to the wisps. The fog deepened around my legs, rising above my knees. Tendrils snaked around my arms. Heart pounding, I checked each of the guys to see their reaction. Aidan was still as pale as the swirling fog, but he didn't seem to notice it. He stood facing Boss Man, swords in hand, his lips curled back in a harsh grimace.

Doran braced behind me, down on one knee, talons unsheathed, wings cocked, ready to snag me up against him and leap into the air. Though now that we were actually in Faerie, I didn't think we'd be able to escape so easily.

Keane stood at Aidan's back, his flamethrower dripping molten flames into the fog. The fire didn't dissipate the mists at all. In fact, they swirled faster around him as if eager for more.

Gleaming emeralds flashed around Warwick, though each spark of magic was quickly swallowed by the fog.

The mists flowed around my waist now. Definitely deeper, and my teeth chattered with the sense of ghostly chill spreading through my body.

:It's feeding on us,: I whispered. *:Our magic.:*

Deeper now, the flowing billows swirled like a slow whirlpool or hurricane, sweeping in a circular pattern that became more defined as I watched.

A circle.

And I stood at its center.

Lowering the hag stone, I jerked my head up to meet Boss Man's knowing gaze.

He nodded. "You're a natural conduit. Treasure magic flows through you, magnifying their gifts exponentially. You've seen how it works. You snared Greenshanks into your whirlpool, sucking him deeper into the swirling magic around you. You draw them all closer, even the Slaughterer, a man broken by jealousy and betrayal. You found and freed Stoneheart when no others could. You even pulled the changeling into your proximity, much to your detriment. He tried to break you, did he not? He tried to use you. Unlock you. But he couldn't."

His words twisted in my stomach like a rusty blade. "Way to victim blame, asshole. I didn't pull Jonathan to me. I didn't ask him to hurt me."

"You didn't have to ask—it's your nature. This ability to pull and transform magic through yourself is innate. Every treasurekeeper was born to pull the treasures together through the mists of time. No matter how many centuries passed, no matter how many times they died in a million awful ways, they still return to the treasurekeeper's call. Not for you, dear lady. Not for this so-called love they profess. They return to you because you're the conduit. The only way their magic flows is through you. Otherwise, they're just tired, old stories that humanity forgot long ago."

He paused, letting his words soak into me. I felt ill, my stomach queasy as if I'd accidentally eaten some of the wormy, rotten food. Chilled, I wrapped my arms around myself, briskly rubbing my arms. The fog wasn't feeding on us, not exactly. It felt like something had snagged deep inside my intestines and was trying to drag me down. It didn't hurt exactly. It just felt...heavy. Like I'd swallowed a bowling ball that was still falling.

"Lies," Doran retorted, tucking me back against him. "Take the magic away, destroy our gifts, break my wings, steal Ivarr's light, break the cauldron and the sword, and still we will return to her call. Not because she's the conduit, but because she's the light of our hearts."

Cold seeped into me like a poison. Automatically, I pulled Ivarr's golden warmth into me, trying to ease the chills. His arm looped around my waist. Warwick on the other side. Doran behind me. Keane and Aidan backed closer to me, still facing the threat but walling me in. Trying to keep me safe.

The wheel spun in my mind, making me dizzy. Spinning, like the whirlpool. The same direction. The same speed. Sucking us all under. Draining the magic away.

Into... *what? Where?*

Wrapped in their protection, I let my consciousness glide down into the foggy mist. My stomach dropped and I rocked back on my heels. The men wavered slightly, bumping against me. I opened my eyes and everything had changed. My mind staggered, confused and unable to make sense of what I saw.

Upside down. Streams of glittering, multi-colored light shot *up*

into the sky where a roiling black storm spun overhead. A massive
hurricane spun in the sky, and we stood below the eye. Lightning
flashed, thunder a distant boom. The rocky teeth of the key were
gone. The sea had become the sky, rolling waves instead of clouds.
Lightning flashed again, revealing huge, dark shadows swimming in
the whirlpool like sharks.

Land Beneath the Waves.

My stomach pitched again. My teeth jarred together at an abrupt
stop. The guys gripped me harder, pressing in on me. I couldn't see
anything. Couldn't think. My head throbbed, dozens of icepicks stabbing through my temples and eyes.

:*We've fallen through another dimension,*: Warwick yelled in my head.
:*Take us to the next layer before your eardrums explode.*:

I wasn't sure if it was me doing it or just the eye sucking us under.
Dry, hot air blasted my face. I tried to open my eyes, but it was so
fucking bright. Light everywhere, a punishing burning ceaseless sun
that made my skin burn.

:*Riannnnnnn!*: Warwick's voice seemed to come from eons away,
even though I felt him right beside me. :*Again!*:

I staggered, bones aching. Crushing weight closed in, smashing us
together. It moved around us, coiling tighter.

"We've got to shut the eye!" Doran rasped, his voice strained as if
he heaved against an impossible weight, trying to lift the crushing coil
off of me so I could breathe.

Again. Blistering cold, blowing snow, blue and white everywhere I
looked.

Again. Darkness so black that I couldn't see anything at all, but
something like rough bark dug into my cheek.

Again.

"Close the eye!" Doran roared louder. "Riann, love, you've got to
close it!"

:*All the dimensions of space and time are yours to command,*: Boss
Man's voice echoed in my head.

That had to be a lie. I wasn't doing anything to flicker through
these dimensions other than struggle to breathe and keep my feet. I

certainly wasn't commanding anything.

:All worlds, all magic, flow through the eye,: Boss Man said. *:My eye.:*

Lights flashed and flickered, worlds coming and disappearing in rapid succession. Distant planets and stars. Places of mythology and folklore. Pyramids and towers, massive world trees and secret pools, deep seas and barren wasteland.

:They all fall to me eventually.:

The flickering images finally stopped. Panting, I tried to calm my pounding heart. My bones hurt and I tasted blood. I couldn't feel the guys around me. I couldn't feel anything outside of my body at all. No injury. No wounds. Nothing.

Am I dead?

:Don't even fucking think such a thing.: Aidan's voice cut through the fog around me. But why did he sound so far away? *:You're not dead. I forbid it. Do you fucking understand me?:*

"See my eye in all its terrible glory," Boss Man said, this time aloud. The words echoed as if we were in a deep chamber or cave. Light slowly grew around me, illuminating a silvery floor that stretched in all directions. I couldn't see any walls or ceiling above, but it felt deep like a well. An endless well that went on forever at the lowest foundations of the earth.

I stood alone on a round, flat medallion set in the silvery floor. I turned, frantic, looking for the guys. A way out. But there was nothing to see. No walls to climb. No doors to break open. No locks.

My heart tried to burst through my ribcage. *:I can't get out. I'm trapped. Doran!:*

:You're not alone,: Doran rumbled through me, settling some of my panic. *:We still hold you in Dún Bhalair.:*

I couldn't feel them, though. I couldn't feel their arms around me, their bodies against me.

:Come back to us.: Keane's voice curled through me, stirring my hunger. Reminding me of his gift.

:We shine for you alone,: Ivarr added.

:What does it look like?: Warwick asked. *:Is Evil Eye with you?:*

:Yes and no.: I wasn't cold, but my teeth wouldn't stop chattering. *:I hear him but I don't see him.:*

:It's an illusion,: Warwick replied. *:It's one of his tricks. You still stand with us in Dún Bhalair. Do you still have the hag stone?:*

I didn't turn my head to look, but now that I remembered I'd been holding the stone, I could feel it against my palm. My hand curled around the stone, holding it over my heart. *:Yes.:*

"What is this place?" My voice echoed off the silvery floor. Ripples formed in its surface, flowing outward like gentle waves. Stepping closer to the edge of the medallion, I bent down and touched the silver with my left hand. Not water—it was thicker. The substance coated my finger, but when I tried to shake it off, it rolled into a ball and danced across the back of my knuckles like mercury.

"See, lady? Magic clings to you even here."

"This is magic?" I raised my hand closer, watching the way the tiny ball moved and flowed. It didn't feel like the ribbons and swirls of magic when the wheel spun in my head. This tiny ball had substance, and it didn't glow or spark.

Glittering emeralds. Soft, warm gold. Sparkling rainbows. My kind of magic. My kind of love. Where was that in this dismal, silent place?

"Pure source, from which all magic flows. It feels amazing, does it not?"

I wasn't sure what he meant—until the blob sank into my skin. One second it rolled like a tiny ball, and the next, it felt like I'd taken a shot of heroin. My eyes flared. Every hair on my body stood at attention, vibrating with sudden energy and awareness. I could feel the individual cells in my body, sparking and flowing, pulses of electricity communicating with each other. Nerves like complex highways and rivers, flowing with data and power. Thoughts rippled through my mind laser fast.

:I'm standing in a pool of magic. It's endless, like an ocean. It goes on forever. He said it's the source of magic.:

"So much power," Boss Man crooned.

:No walls,: I continued passing along information rapid fire to the

guys. *:No doors. No way out. I don't know where it's coming from or why it's here.:*

"Soon, all the worlds will belong to me. They fall, one by one, descending just as you did to reach my eye. Only by the time those worlds reach this level, they're distilled into their purest forms."

A larger silver ball slowly slid down from the darkness above, approximately the size of a grapefruit. It slipped into the silver lake without a single sound, though ripples rolled from where it'd disappeared.

"Some worlds garner more magic than others."

"That was an entire *world?*"

"Only what was left of their magic," Boss Man replied, his tone remaining casual and matter-of-fact. "Most of the magic is gone now through all the dimensions. Very little remains."

My brain grappled with the implications. An entire world reduced to a grapefruit. Destroyed for its magic. All this magic, pooling in the eye.

His eye.

Very little magic remained.

I didn't need to reach for my treasures and leprechaun to know that was a lie. Magic flowed all around us. I'd seen the wonders of Warwick's Summer Isle with my own eyes. I'd been painting magic for years before the changeling damaged me.

If Evil Eye took the painting that Warwick had stashed away and distilled it into silver essence, how big a splash would it make in this never-ending lake? Let alone all of Faerie.

"What do you want?" I asked. "Why am I here?"

"You're the conduit. You pull magic through you effortlessly and naturally, which would make all of this easier."

All of this... Did he mean destroying worlds and dimensions so he could distill their magic into his eye? "I don't want to destroy anything."

He laughed, a deep belly chuckle that echoed and bounced over the silvery surface. "Ah, lady, you are a pure delight. Of course you want to destroy things. Look at how you destroyed the Slaughterer just a few moments ago. Look at what you've done to Greenshanks, shackling him into a harem of other men, none of which will ever own your heart."

My throat tightened, tears burning my eyes. "My heart is theirs. I love them. All of them."

"I'm sure you do. At least with what's left after the changeling ravaged you. Why, I'm shocked that you're still alive." A deliberate pause. "Let alone that you're able to love five men after what he must have done to you."

Pain choked me but worse was the shame. Shame that I had been trapped and hurt and unable to escape. Jonathan had damaged me. I'd never be the same. My capacity to love...

Is still whole.

He told me lies again, trying to make me doubt myself. My capacity to love had not been destroyed. I'd been damaged, but my men had shown me truth and love and light. I'd healed from those years in darkness. I didn't have a fragile hand-blown glass heart. No, my heart was made of stone and steel and blazed with all the power of the sun. It hungered for my men and their touch, reveled in their pleasure, and then showered them with love and power.

Pure gold burned in my heart, and a leprechaun's oath on his gold was unbreakable.

So is mine.

33

I was done with the bullshit.

"Let me get this straight," I said slowly, holding up my fingers. "All of the worlds fall to you eventually." I put down my thumb. "There's very little magic left." My index finger. "I'm too damaged to love anyone." My ring finger. "Yet I can make your crazy universe-domination easier?"

I put down my pinky finger. Leaving my middle finger up.

"Get lucked, Evil Eye. I'm not helping you do anything."

Boss Man's voice slithered around me. "Even to save your precious treasures?"

"You said it yourself." I shrugged, putting as much bravado into my voice as I could muster. "They always die. Why should this time be any different?"

"I'm surprised that you're so short-sighted. Surely you understand that there will be no paradise in the Land Beneath the Waves waiting for them. This is the end of their long, bitter battle. No one believes in magic any longer. No one needs them to keep fighting."

I do. I need them. My throat ached, holding back a sob at the thought of their deaths. *:I need you. Always.:*

This time, I received no answer.

:Doran?:

"Besides..." I couldn't see Boss Man's face, but I could hear the snide little sneer creeping into this voice. "It's too late to save them."

The silvery surface shimmered brighter and began playing images like a movie screen. Doran roaring and howling with rage while another, much larger creature ripped and tore at his wings. One wing already appeared to be broken, dragging limply at his side. Bellowing curses, Aidan stood surrounded by giants with red heads. Dozens of them. Yet he slashed and whirled with both swords, trying to clear a path to Keane and Ivarr. They stood back-to-back, blasting fire and laser-bright bursts into a horde of imps that rolled toward them like an endless wave. As I watched, a huge tentacle snaked around Keane and lifted him up. Another wrapped around his legs and yanked, tearing him apart.

"Nooooo!"

Frantic to help them, I reached for the spinning wheel of magic inside me. Treasure magic danced with leprechaun emerald, sparkling with rainbows, as strong as ever. Panting, I made myself pause. Think. The magic wouldn't be so strong if they were truly in danger. If Keane were dead. A sob escaped my lips at the thought.

But if any of them were actually dead, the wheel wouldn't evenly spin. It'd be dark and empty, not bright with sparks.

"You can save them," Boss Man whispered. "The power lies before you."

The wheel spun faster in my head, streaming all the colors of our magic. One drop of the silver source energy had lit me up like a Christmas tree. What would all of that pooled magic do to me? Even more importantly, *why* did he want me to try and use it?

Doran screamed, a horrible sound of pain that made my heart tremble. On his back, he kicked and struggled to get up, but the creature ripped open his midsection so deep that organs and intestines pushed up out of him in a tangle. "Help us, *mo stór!*"

"It's not real," I whispered softly, swiping tears off my cheeks.

"Are you sure?" Boss Man's voice slithered around me. I could almost feel the brush of his breath on my neck, which made all the tiny hairs on my nape shiver with alarm. "They're so pretty when they cry for you, Riann. It makes my black heart burn with vicious pride."

Doran wouldn't ever yell for help. Like in the cave—they'd refused to use their own magic to try and protect me. They'd faced what could be their final battle with stoic courage, determined to take as many with them as possible rather than escape death.

Plus, it suddenly occurred to me that I hadn't seen Warwick in trouble and dying. True, he was fae and wouldn't die like the treasures, but I suspected Evil Eye couldn't pull that kind of glamor on my leprechaun.

Tipping my chin up, I said firmly, "I'm sure."

The surface of the pool shimmered back to silver. "Very good. You passed the final test. No other treasurekeeper has ever made it so far. I knew you were the one."

"The one for what?" I asked sharply.

He didn't answer. I looked around the endless space again, looking for another trick. A way out. Something. Anything. If I could see a wall or...

See. I fumbled the hag stone back up to my eye.

Rather than molten silver, the distilled magic looked more like thick oil or even tar. The finger on my left hand that I'd dipped into the pool was stained with what looked to be black ink—that was slowly creeping up my finger. I tried to wipe it off on my pants, but the black only kept spreading, now up to my knuckle.

Rounded stone walls surrounded me like a wide, massive well. I tipped my head back but I couldn't see the top. Just darkness. Whether a night sky above or endless depths, I couldn't tell.

A wobble beneath my feet drew my attention back down to the medallion.

The *shrinking* medallion, because of fucking course it was getting smaller by the second.

"What do you want?" I yelled, trying to get Boss Man to expose his plan to me. Or at least delay whatever he had planned. If my finger was stained by the black stuff after a simple dip, what would sinking into that mess do to me? "What am I supposed to do?"

He didn't answer, so I needed to up my game. He might be a High Court fae but he was still a man with an inflated ego who'd had legends and stories told about him for thousands of years. He wanted to brag about how brilliant he was. I just needed to get him talking.

"Some fucking Evil Eye you have here. Wait until I tell Doran it's just a well full of shitty tar. Actually I'll just tell him now." I waited a minute, pretending that I could still hear him in my head. Then I laughed. "Yeah, I know. What a moron."

"So confident," Boss Man drawled, his voice echoing around me. "So naive. Do you think you'll see Stoneheart again?"

I opened my mouth to say, *"I see him now,"* but I couldn't get the words out.

"I..." I choked. Swallowed. Tried again. "I see..."

"Ahhhhhh," Boss Man drew out the sigh with light lilt of pleasure at the end. "So sad."

A fae can't lie.

Boss Man didn't know *which* lie, though. I absolutely would see Doran again. I had no doubt of that at all. I wanted to feel my men's arms squeezing the life out of me. I wanted Aidan to growl and grumble. I wanted the warmth of Ivarr's light, the sultry heat of Keane's smile, the sparkle of Warwick's grin, and the indomitable heart of stone thumping beneath my cheek.

Keeping up the illusion, I let a ragged cry escape my throat, but I didn't try to say anything else. Aidan had said that Evil Eye loved this kind of broken pain the most, so if I could draw out this moment, I might buy myself time to come up with another plan.

The wheel still spun arcs of sparkling magic in my head. I couldn't see the guys but I had to trust they were still alive. Still fighting. As long as the wheel was balanced, they were okay.

"Do you know why the treaurekeeper was always mortal?" Boss Man crooned in his sly, silky voice. "Even then, we were afraid a fae conduit would be too powerful."

"We?" I asked hoarsely. Shivering, I wrapped my arms around myself and kept a wary eye on the shrinking medallion. I still had plenty of room to stand. Maybe if I kept him talking... Though I didn't want to listen to this blowhard covering all the many ways he'd tortured my men through thousands of years.

"All High Court fae in my day and age agreed. Lug wanted to bring his weapons back time and time again, allowing them to re-live their —and his, of course—glory days. It was a fine and dandy idea until it became apparent that they were going to die in increasingly excruciatingly horrific ways."

"At your hands."

Boss Man chuckled, so close that it sounded like he hovered behind me. I whirled, scrunching my shoulders tight. I couldn't see him, but he had to be there, cloaked in glamor.

"They didn't know that each time a treasure died that he would release some of the fae magic that sustained them back into the mortal plane, making it easier each time for them to die."

"Magic that you stole."

"I prefer *distilled*. Look at all this power they helped me generate. Most of it was spawned in their early days of legend. They're weakening, now, so I've turned my attention to other realms and worlds. Treasure magic is thin and weak. Soon they won't be reborn at all. Lug of the Longarm can't have that, now, can he? I knew he would have to take the risk eventually and refill the well, so to speak. He couldn't leave his mighty treasures to wither forever."

Talk about playing the long game. "So you've been killing them for thousands of years, draining more of their magic each time, all so a fae conduit might *someday* be born? You're even crazier than I thought. Why do you..." My words fell off into silence, my brain tumbling faster with the spinning wheel.

Why did he want a *fae* conduit? Not a mortal one.

When he'd been distilling magic from the treasures on the mortal plane. Using their mortal conduit...

"You want me to help you drain Faerie magic," I whispered, shaken. "Tír na nÓg."

Something tightened around my throat and slithered down my body, a tight chokehold from neck to below my knees. "I knew you'd figure it out eventually."

34

At least I still had the hag stone pressed to my eye so I could see through the glamor, though seeing exactly what pinned me wasn't a blessing at all. A thick purplish-black snake wrapped around me, only it had spiky hairs instead of scales. Its tail snaked across the medallion and disappeared into the inky black pool.

More hairy worms arched up out of the lake. Reaching for me. Surrounding me. Bristle-like hairs rasped along my skin, digging through my clothing. My ears hurt. My throat burned. Only then did I realize that I was screaming.

Gulping for air, I fought to bring myself back under control. *:If you can still hear me... I love you. Always.:* Breathe. Again. *:Some snake worm things are wrapped around me. He's going to use me to drain all the magic out of Faerie.:*

Another breath. In. Out. I made myself laugh at least inside my head. *:Well, he's going to try, at least. I hope...:* Gritting my teeth, I forced out a growl that would have made Aidan beam with pride. *:Fuck that shit. I fucking know that you're alright. You're hearing me. You're fighting to reach me as hard as I'm fighting to get to you. And we're going to win this time, right? I will it to be so.:*

Closing my eyes, I repeated that mantra again. Magic was all about my intention. *I will it to be so.*

Magic spun through the wheel faster, brighter, a cascade of rainbows and velvet ribbons, sparkling emeralds and gleaming gold. My treasures. My leprechaun. Vanta, my black kitty, the mother I'd never known, trying so hard to protect me the only way left to her. Dragonfly wings, glittering like delicate stained-glass windows.

I thought of my painting that had called to Warwick so much that he'd immediately whisked it away to safekeeping. Everything I needed to know was there—if I could only put the pieces together.

The wide-open door with magic spilling out all around me—when I'd looked at the painting in full sunlight. A glimpse of Faerie. Only the door was shut when I looked at it through the hag stone. And in the darkness...

The somber plain of standing stones. The smaller idol stone representing Cromm Crúaich, that had turned into gold when I put it upright into its slot. Releasing so much power that the huge stones had fallen.

Not fallen—blasted. Into a circle. An eye.

This huge well holding all the magic that Evil Eye had stolen. Magic that needed to be returned to the mortal plane and the other worlds he'd drained.

Doran had shouted that I needed to close the eye but that wasn't right at all.

I needed to blast the motherfucker wide open.

The wheel spun brighter, faster, and I embraced it. I became the wheel, pulling energy from my men and magnifying it. Even though I couldn't see them, I felt them. Their gifts poured into me without hesitation, trusting me. Giving me everything they had, all their strength and will. I braided their magic with sparkling rainbows of my mother and the grim shadows of my father, just like my painting. The door wide open, magic spilling through me. Dark and light alike. Shadow and highlight, shade and accent. I needed all the layers to create the perfect masterpiece.

I stood at the center of the wheel, the hub for the spinning spokes.

"Magnificent." Boss Man's voice rose with a twisted glee. "Drop the veil, and Tír na nÓg is mine!"

Holding the wheel around me, I stood on the stormy plain. Twelve standing stones surrounded me, and I was the golden stone in the center. I allowed myself to drop into the waiting slot made for me.

Thunder rumbled. Lightning tore across a black, stormy sky. All the hairs on my body quivered and rose, electricity arcing all around me as power ramped up higher. The golden wheel whirled so fast it blazed into a fiery ring wrapped in emerald ribbons. My teeth ached, and pressure built, making my bones throb.

More. I needed more.

I tipped my head back, straining to hold on as the magic built even higher. My skin felt gossamer thin, dissolving in the steady stream of pure energy. As if my mortal body was burning away, torn apart beneath the force of such magic. Ivarr said he'd burned himself up before.

Cromm Crúaich required sacrifice.

So be it. If that's what it takes to set my treasures free.

"You fool!" Boss Man roared. "Not even fae can hold all the magic of Faerie at once!"

I'm the conduit. I can hold it all!

Something shook me, tearing at the creatures that bound me. A distant distraction that I ignored. Lightning cracked overhead, a blazing jolt of energy that tore open the night sky above Magh Slécht and exploded through me.

Power blasted in a rolling, vicious wave of devastation. The twelve standing stones didn't fall—they crumbled into oblivion. The black sky blazed with molten gold and the lonely plain crackled with wildfire. Everything burned, my clothes disappearing in wisps of ash and char. My hair. My skin. I screamed endlessly until no voice or throat remained.

Power swept through me, blasting through the stone walls of Balor's eye. I spilled into the black pool, a liquid, boneless thing of pure energy. I burned the sticky tar away, pulling the tainted magic back through me, cleansing it through the wheel of fiery gold. Up. Up the eye. Through the dimensions. The endless darkness. The brutal world of an eternal sun. Bark against my cheek, drinking in the flood of magic like a sweet, gentle rain ending a devastating drought. The upside-down world tilted in a dizzying flip into a rocky, windy cliff.

I pulled harder, draining the bottomless lake. Taking back all that had been stolen. Burning. Dissolving. All the bits of me that Jonathan had left behind.

The dark god required sacrifice. His own first-born child. So be it.

A door opened in my mind. Giggling, I ran forward into the shining light.

35

So much light. Colors I couldn't even describe. So much love. So beautiful. Beauty was dangerous. That much I remembered. But I couldn't think why.

Slowly, like a tight bud gently opening after a hundred years, light coalesced into my mother's embrace. Étain's wings fluttered around me and Vanta purred against my cheek. Another eon passed, and I smelled the lush flowers of the Summer Isle and heard the symphony of riotous color.

I remembered the dancing grin of a cute barkeeper and the sparkle in his emerald eyes. His ebony hair flowed around me like a cape, his arms pulling me close. Closing my eyes, I breathed in his fresh green scent and soaked in his love. I even remembered his name. Warwick Greenshanks.

"Did I do it?"

He carried me somewhere. I didn't care where as long as he was there. "Aye, love. You blasted the eye wide open and released the power Balor had been storing for thousands of years. All the worlds shine with magic now, even the mortal plane. Dún Bhalair sank beneath the waves and is no more. Only the rocky cliffs remain in the mortal plane."

I didn't have to ask him where my treasures were. I could feel the throbbing emptiness inside me. There wasn't a wheel to spin any longer. Nothing remained, not even a few broken spokes of the wheel. They were gone.

My chest ached so badly that I couldn't breathe.

I didn't need to breathe here. My body felt... different. Like I was made up of nothing but light.

"Aye," he whispered, laying me on the green cushions where I'd rested so long ago. "You shine like opals and rainbows and all the love in the world."

"Vivi?" I whispered.

I didn't realize that I wept until he gently wiped my cheeks. "She's back home safe just as you wished. You can see her any time that you wish. She'll be relieved to see you."

Time passed, though I wasn't sure how long I lay on the elegant velvet couch and breathed in the peace of the Summer Isle. Time was meaningless here. My body felt more like flesh and blood than light, though that meant I hurt even more. The constriction in my chest and throat made it difficult to talk, and I didn't want to ask.

I didn't want to know how they'd died. I only knew that they were gone.

"Are they gone forever this time?" I finally managed to whisper.

Warwick's lips quirked into a chiding, teasing smile that only confused me more. "Have you not learned anything at all, love?"

Confused, I shook my head. "I guess not."

"What did I tell you in *Shamrocked*? Before Aidan and I came to our agreement?"

That seemed so long ago. Before I knew the truth about the man I'd married. Before we learned who Boss Man really was. Before I even knew much about my treasures at all. How much I needed and loved them.

Which only hurt more.

"Why did we call you *mo stór*?"

"Treasure," I rasped out.

He shook his head slowly. "*Our* treasure. You be treasure for me too. A leprechaun's treasure is gold. What did you learn about a leprechaun's oath made on his gold?"

Bewildered, I fought the urge to wail. "Your oath is unbreakable. But—"

"You be treasure for me too," he repeated, stroking my hair back out of my face. "What do you wish for, love?"

Sighing, I closed my eyes. "I wish we could all be together like before. Only this time, we're here in your Summer Isle, but it's... it's... No offense, but it's better."

He chuckled softly, still stroking my hair. "How is it better?"

"It's still as beautiful as ever with your flowers and brilliant colors everywhere, but it's also Doran's Windswept Moors and Aidan's Fallen Dells."

"Are they still fallen?"

"Of course not," I grumbled. "That wouldn't be a very good wish, would it? A place where Ivarr's light shines forever, and Keane feeds us all with his incredible food, and none of us go away unsatisfied. And I can see Vanta—or rather, my mother—in her true form whenever I want. And I can see Vivi whenever I want. I paint you all the time, and we're all together. Forever."

"Is that all?"

I couldn't resist opening my eyes and glaring up at him. "How can you be so amused when I'm so miserable?"

"Is that all you wish for at this time?"

Rolling my eyes, I huffed out another sigh and nodded.

"Granted."

I swallowed the lump in my throat. "That's not funny, Warwick. I already had my three wishes."

"Don't make me call you a bleedin' idjit."

That voice. I pushed up off the cushions, my heart in my throat. Turning, I saw the four Irish treasures striding toward us.

Ivarr in his long black coat, his golden eyes blazing with light. Keane's lush mouth curved in a wicked, knowing smile that promised nothing but pleasure for hours. Aidan in his leather jacket, swords crossed over his shoulders, his face lined with a perpetual scowl, though this time, he grinned widely enough that I was pretty fucking sure I saw a dimple in his cheek. And Doran, mighty Stoneheart. Wide shouldered and tall, busted nose and heavy features hinting at his gargoyle. My noble warrior.

He swept me up into his arms and gave me a toss in the air that made me squawk. "You be fucking treasure, Riann. Treasure we died for."

"Treasure we *lived* for," Ivarr added.

They crowded around Doran, all of them. Holding me. Kissing me. Though thankfully Keane settled for kissing my neck so we didn't all fall down in orgasmic bliss immediately.

"I still don't understand how I have more than three wishes, but I don't care." I clutched Doran's neck with one arm and Warwick's with the other. "I'm just so happy to see you all. I thought you were gone forever."

Aidan seized my chin and twisted my head around to glare into my eyes. "What the fuck did I tell you from day one? Leprechauns love their fucking gold so much they'll give three wishes to any fool who manages to find even one coin. So how many fucking wishes do you think he'll give up for *you*?"

"Every last coin I possess," Warwick admitted, grinning sheepishly. "Did I neglect to mention that I'm from a long line of very wealthy—"

"Greedy," Aidan coughed.

"Leprechauns." Warwick continued. "I have a lot of gold. But none of that compares to you. Look around your new home, love, and tell me if I've met your wish."

The white marble floors with green and gold veins had been replaced by dark gray slate inlaid with strips of gold and chunks of emeralds. We stood in a square tower that looked out over a rocky cliff, just like Doran had remembered. But instead of waves crashing against the rocks, brilliant blue waters rolled in to dance along a shining white beach. Flowers tumbled over the castle walls, filling the air with perfume, though I smelled something that made my stomach rumble.

Keane waggled his eyebrows at me. "Wait until you taste chocolate croissants made by the Cauldron of Dagda."

My mouth watered so much I almost choked on my own spit. "I just have one thing to say to you. To all of you."

"Aye?" Doran asked. "What is it, love?"

"Get lucked."

Aidan barked out a laugh. "I thought you'd never ask."

AUTHOR'S NOTE

I hope you've enjoyed Her Irish Treasures – and that you were able to find a few Their Vampire Queen easter eggs throughout the trilogy. This series is set in the same supernatural world as Shara's, though obviously focusing on the fae aspect rather than vampire.

But all are children of the Mother.

What's next for me? I'll be finishing up the expansion of Monstrous Heat next.

My apologies for the delays the last few months. I can finally say that the court cases are done. He won't be taking me back to court again. Finally, I'm free.

I'm hopeful that means my pace will pick back up now that I don't have doom hanging over my head. 2022 has been really slow for me, and I'm itching to get back to Shara's world. I left Helayna at a crucial midpoint and will be returning to Queen Takes Darkness3 as soon as I can. I have so much planned for our vampire queens! Even a short Xochitl story that I wrote for the Literary Love Savannah Booklife conference. I'll share that as a freebie at some point for those who were unable to attend.

Long live House Isador!

Keep reading for a sneak peek of Monstrous Heat.

MONSTROUS HEAT

I'M LOST IN THE JUNGLE, AND SOMETHING IS STALKING ME.

Discovering a Mayan ruin in the Guatemalan jungle should have catapulted my archeology career, but I'm lost hours from camp. Worse, something is stalking me. It's not a jaguar. It's bigger than anything I've ever seen before and wicked fast. I can't outrun it. I don't have any weapons.

When it catches me...

I can't help but think I've fallen back through time to the Jurassic Period, because the creature looks like a T-rex and raptor had a very vicious baby. It's hungry, too. Very hungry. Though it doesn't hurt me. Yet.

Then a naked man comes to my rescue. Not sus at all.

Kroktl says his squad is on a top-secret mission to Earth, and his outrageous physique certainly fits the part of a lab-created super-soldier alien. Who coincidentally smells exactly like the dino-predator that chased me.

He claims that I can help him through the heat. By the burning way he looks at me, he doesn't mean air temperature. In fact, I suspect that I'm next on the menu. After he plays with his food. He's even calling his squad to come see what he caught.

I don't think I'm getting out of the jungle alive.

Grimly, I climbed to my feet and trudged ahead, scanning the ground constantly for pitfalls. The jungle howled and screeched like a living thing all on its own, adding to my jangled nerves. I'd never heard so many animal calls before. I tried to imagine what kind of animal would make those sounds but decided that I had too good of an imagination for that game.

A particularly loud screech made me jerk to a halt. *What the hell...?*

The jungle silenced around me, an eerie dearth of sound after the cacophony. A jaguar? It'd certainly sounded like a predator.

My hands started shaking. My legs tensed, prepared to run. Run where? I had no idea how far camp might be, and I didn't have any hope of outrunning a big cat. It'd probably just lie in wait on a limb and jump on me as soon as I ran right underneath it.

I jerked the flashlight up and scanned the branches overhead. No big glowing eyes reflected back. As quietly as possible, I crept down the path. At least it was a little wider now, a real dirt path rather than a few hacked-up branches to mark the way. But maybe that was a bad thing. Maybe this was a game trail and that big cat was hungry. Of course, it'd hang out near a game trail or a water source. *Shit.*

Everything in me screamed to run, but my brain held on to reason against the panic flailing inside me. Running was bad. I didn't know what was out there. I'd already fallen twice. If I got seriously injured while the guides were gone, I'd probably die waiting on them to find me.

Silence weighed heavier, a complete absence of sound that made my heart pound.

Something was out there. Following me. Or at least watching me. Something that scared all the other animals into silence.

The metallic screech roared through the night again, so loud and close that I couldn't suppress the terrified squeak that escaped my mouth. I clamped my hands over my ears, nearly fumbling the flashlight. Crouched against a thick tree, I flicked off the light and pressed against the rough bark, trying to disappear. Or at least be as small as possible.

Predators hunt by smell so it won't matter. It'll still find me.

I wanted to smack that know-it-all voice inside my head.

Leaves rustled. A low whuffing snort. Maybe it was a wild boar. Was that better than a jaguar?

Something moved in the shadows. A sharp click, like the tap of a hammer. *Tap, tap.*

What the fuck is that? I strained to see anything that would give me a clue. Stay? Run? Scream?

Though running away really wasn't my style.

I straightened from a crouch. My pulse thundered in my ears as I stepped out onto the trail. I squared my shoulders and lifted my head high. Better to appear as big as possible.

The *tap, tap, tap* came again, drawing my gaze to a thick, dark shadow about ten feet down the trail. Between me and camp. Of fucking course. Huge, too, and way too tall and wide to be a jaguar. Nothing moved, and it was too dark to be sure.

Maybe it's a bushy tree. I'll have a good laugh at myself for being so scared.

Firming my voice into the loudest, meanest *I'm-only-the-professor's-teaching-assistant-but-sit-your-ass-down-anyway* tone I could muster, I yelled, "Get! Get out of here! Leave me alone!"

The low whuffing came again, a deep, rough *huff, huff, huff.* Almost like a laugh. A dare.

Tipping my chin up, I marched down the path, refusing to look at the mysterious dark shape. It had to be a trick. An illusion that my terrified mind had created. No animal was that tall. The dark blob towered over my head. It had to be a tree all twisted up in vines. Or maybe some long-lost stelae, swallowed by the jungle. That was far more likely than a... giraffe.

Tap, tap, tap.

Despite my bravado, I jerked to a halt. So close. Stiffly, I held myself very still, straining all my senses. No other sound, but that smell. What was it? A kind of musky scent, not completely unpleasant but foreign and strange. It didn't belong. Hairs prickled on my nape and goosebumps raced down my arms. I hadn't smelled anything like that all day. A bear? No, it didn't smell like fur. Besides, there were certainly no bears—or giraffes for that matter—in Guatemala.

A slight movement caught my eye. Something glittered on the ground, catching the fragile moonlight filtering down through the canopy. Black and sparkly, almost like a crystal. The Maya had used obsidian for some of their blades and ornaments. Despite my fear, my heart leaped with excitement. That would be an extremely interesting find, especially if it was an intact blade. It was big enough to be a knife, at least six inches long.

I started to bend down to pick it up. Then I noticed another one. Just like it. No, three.

And then the longest one moved.

Tap, tap, tap.

Claws. Black. Long. Certainly big enough to gut me like a fish. Or lop off my head with one powerful swipe.

I bolted. Blind with terror, I ran, pushing through the trees. Off the path. It didn't matter where. I had to get away.

The jungle seemed to come alive, fighting to trap me for whatever that... *thing...* was. No way in hell that claw belonged on anything that was indigenous to Guatemala. Branches clutched at me, ripping at my hair and clothes. Roots snagged at my feet. I tripped and caught myself on my hands, scrambling like a crab over a huge fallen tree. I fell into the hollow behind it. Probably the hole left from its roots. I huddled there, hoping maybe I'd lost the...

Tomas's word played back to me. The symbol on the stone wall.

Monster.

Grab Monstrous Heat.

BOOKS BY JOELY SUE BURKHART

Their Vampire Queen
Shara Isador
QUEEN TAKES KNIGHTS
QUEEN TAKES KING
QUEEN TAKES QUEEN
QUEEN TAKES ROOK
QUEEN TAKES CHECKMATE
QUEEN TAKES TRIUNE
QUEEN TAKES MORE

HOUSE ISADOR BOXED SET
(Knights – Triune)

Gwen Camelot
QUEEN TAKES CAMELOT

Mayte Zaniyah
QUEEN TAKES JAGUARS

Helayna Ironheart
QUEEN TAKES DARKNESS 1
QUEEN TAKES DARKNESS 2
QUEEN TAKES DARKNESS 3

Karmen Sunna
QUEEN TAKES SUNFIRES 1
QUEEN TAKES SUNFIRES 2
QUEEN TAKES SUNFIRES 3

Xochitl Zaniyah
PRINCESS TAKES ACADEMY 1
PRINCESS TAKES ACADEMY 2
PRINCESS TAKES ACADEMY 3

Belladonna Titanes
QUEEN TAKES VENOM (prequel)
QUEEN TAKES VENOM 1
QUEEN TAKES VENOM 2
QUEEN TAKES VENOM 3

Their Vampire Queen Returns
COMING SOON

Her Irish Treasures Trilogy
SHAMROCKED
LEPRECHAUNED
EVIL EYED

Dynosauros

MONSTROUS HEAT
MONSTROUS HUNGER
MONSTROUS HUNT

Carnal Heat: A Dark Monster Reverse Harem Romance
CARNAL HEAT

The Shanhasson Trilogy
THE BROKEN QUEEN OF SHANHASSON (free prequel)
THE ROSE OF SHANHASSON
THE ROAD TO SHANHASSON
RETURN TO SHANHASSON

THE COMPLETE SHANHASSON TRILOGY

Dragon Cursed
FREE MY DRAGON
SAVE MY DRAGON

A Jane Austen Space Opera
LADY WYRE'S REGRET (free prequel)
LADY DOCTOR WYRE
LORD REGRET'S PRICE
LADY WYRE'S REBELS

HER GRACE'S STABLE

The Connaghers
LETTERS TO AN ENGLISH PROFESSOR (free prequel)

DEAR SIR, I'M YOURS
HURT ME SO GOOD
YOURS TO TAKE
NEVER LET YOU DOWN
MINE TO BREAK

THE CONNAGHERS BOXED SET

Billionaires in Bondage
THE BILLIONAIRE SUBMISSIVE
THE BILLIONAIRE'S INK MISTRESS
THE BILLIONAIRE'S CHRISTMAS BARGAIN

Zombie Category Romance
THE ZOMBIE BILLIONAIRE'S VIRGIN WITCH

The Wellspring Chronicles
NIGHTGAZER

Other Free Reads
THEIR TYGRESS
THE VICIOUS

Joely Sue Burkhart writing as Sharan Daire

My Over The Top Possessive Alpha Harem
BROKE DOWN
KNOCKED UP

FOUR MEN & A BABY

BROKE DOWN TRILOGY

BLIZZARD BOUND

Made in the USA
Middletown, DE
03 September 2022